Moose ~~~ blic Library
Box 277, 313 Elm
Moose Lake MN 55767

I, TOM HORN

Speeding in on the fallen girl, I yelled for her to "get up, get up!" The three mounted Apaches were fast closing in on us.

I do not remember pulling my Winchester .73 carbine from its saddle scabbard. But when my feet hit the sand of the Big Cibicu Wash, the rifle was in my hands and blasting.

I shot the foremost of the three Indian riders at forty feet—square in the face, with his mouth open, yelling.

I missed the second Indian at ten feet, but only because his horse hit a snake hole and collapsed, throwing him clear.

My third shot was into the back of the third Indian, as he raced past me. My bullet took him about five joints up his vertebrae from his saddle. It was a hit of the purest outhouse sort, but I took it.

Bantam Books by Will Henry

THE GATES OF THE MOUNTAINS
I, TOM HORN

I, Tom Horn

Will Henry

To Clark Kinnaird

I, TOM HORN

PRINTING HISTORY
J. B. Lippincott edition published January 1975
Bantam edition / December 1975
2nd printing ...... January 1979   3rd printing ...... January 1979
4th printing .... April 1980

All rights reserved.
Copyright © 1975 by Will Henry.
Cover art copyright © 1980 by Bantam Books, Inc.
This book may not be reproduced in whole or in part, by
mimeograph or any other means, without permission.
For information address: Bantam Books, Inc.

ISBN 0–553–14086–8

Published simultaneously in the United States and Canada

Bantam Books are published by Bantam Books, Inc. Its trade-
mark, consisting of the words "Bantam Books" and the por-
trayal of a bantam, is Registered in U.S. Patent and Trademark
Office and in other countries. Marca Registrada. Bantam
Books, Inc., 666 Fifth Avenue, New York, New York 10019.

PRINTED IN THE UNITED STATES OF AMERICA

13 12 11 10 9 8 7 6 5 4

Contents

BOOK THREE

Is there a warrior left who remembers me? A woman remaining who will weep to know that Talking Boy will bring his horse no more outside the jacal of her father? A single child, a sister, an old man to light one dark face with the candle of its smile thinking back to him the soldiers called Tom Horn?

Yo no sé, amigos. Montad en vuestros caballos. Ride on, ride on.

Tom Horn
in Cheyenne Jail

The Beginning

footnote to a flat tin box
found in a courthouse fire

In the summer just past, Allard Kroeger, the Los Angeles attorney, backpacking through his native Wyoming, became lost and sought direction at a remote ridgetop cabin. Midway in his ascent of a ridge, he was met by a gaunt and growling dog. Not having prepared a brief for this contingency, Kroeger rested his case in some alarm. The dog, however, gave way upon nearer approach and, when it turned to trot whiningly back up toward the cabin, the city man understood there was trouble in this lonely place, and he went forward quickly.

Inside the log shack, dirt-floored, sod-roofed, smelling rankly of its hundred years of human denning, he found an inhabitant as ancient as the outpost itself. The old fellow was plainly hard upon his time, the fear of that fact no less within him for his great age. He was pathetically thankful to know he would not be alone.

Kroeger quieted him, prepared a meal from some beef scraps, suet, and cornmeal, all that was available. As he fed the old man, the latter insisted his visitor understand it was his own beef they were eating. Kroeger appreciated the concern.

"I was born in this county, old-timer," he said. "I remember those times when it mattered to know whose beef you were eating. I'm Allie Kroeger."

"The hell!" the old man cried, the faded eyes alive with brief memory. "I knowed your paw and grandpa both. They was cattlemen, sure." He labored for breath. "I'm Charley Starrett," he said. "The one that testified for Tom

Horn. I'm ninety-three years old. I was twenty-three then."

He fell back. There was a disquiet in the smoky air. An unease in the wolfish dog whimpering by the fire. The other visitor was coming. "Mr. Starrett," Allard Kroeger said, "is there anything you would like done; do you have a will?"

The question reached the old man. He struggled up, a sudden urgency within him. "No," he said. "But I hold another man's testament that sore burdens my soul. God sent you here, lawyer, to do His justice. You wasn't lost."

"Old-timer, we never know. What is it you want?"

"Yonder. The flat tin box on the mantelpiece."

Kroeger brought the old box to the bedside, curious at its unexpected weight.

"There's a man's life in there," the old man said. "Dug out'n the ashes of a courthouse fire."

The attorney's eyes narrowed. "Tom Horn's life, Mr. Starrett?" he asked softly.

The old man moved his head in assent. "You're cattle people and law-trained, too," he whispered. "I deed you the trust of it." Then, barely audible. "That's Tom Horn's handwrote last testament."

Allard Kroeger, born of that lonely land, felt the violence of the shadowed past reach out and draw him in. He opened the old box, took from it the heavy document wrapped in oilskin. "Are you saying you *know* Tom Horn wrote this?" he asked.

The old man said that he was. Somewhere, he had kept a penny postal from Horn dated 1901 that would prove it. It was the exact same writing as the papers in the flat tin box.

Moreover, he would recognize Horn's hand anywhere. "He writ it," he said. "God's witness."

Kroeger drew breath. Could this be? Was he holding the legend's last holograph in his hands?

He angled the unopened packet toward the coal-oil lamp. Peering, he made out a date, *December 6, 1903,* and a place, *City of Cheyenne, County of Laramie, State of Wyoming.* Then, in starkly bolder script of the same hand, leaping at him through the yellowed oilskin, there it was:

FOR TOM HORN
AGAINST THE PEOPLE OF WYOMING
That Justice May Be Done Before God

In the stillness broken only by the pine chunks settling on the fire, Allard Kroeger read on:

> To brave men everywhere who, seeking justice uncringing to the cries of the beast people for popular vengeance, will bring this history before the courts of posterity where the law will not be the sicklied servant of the mob that it is here, and where an innocent man may finally know honored peace, to come before his God "not guilty" in the Last Great Judgment.
>
> *Received in trust by an atty of record for the defense who dares not enter his name in witness.*

Kroeger heard a small sound, put aside the ancient manuscript. "Old man, Mr. Starrett," he said anxiously, "you all right?"

There was no answer but the low crying of the dog. "Damn," said Allard Kroeger softly, and he pulled the frayed horse blanket over the shrunken small man who had been, seventy years before, the last, best friend of Tom Horn.

Next morning the attorney took the wolfish dog and the tin box with him on the long hike out to the pavement. At the county seat, he reported the death of Charley Starrett, arranged lifetime care for the old dog. The flat tin box with its presumptive last testament of Tom Horn he bore back to California, determined to publish the contents.

One problem of substance intervened.

An "official" Horn autobiography already existed (*Life of Tom Horn, Government Scout and Interpreter*, by himself, Louthan Book Company, Denver, 1904). To now publish a second true-life story, also allegedly by Horn's own hand, could be awkward.

Yet Kroeger was of the frontier by blood himself. He

loved the larger-than-life badmen heroes of the western
past. And shadowy Tom Horn above them all.

There had to be a way.

Now wait. How was it Horn had ended his story in
the Louthan book?

> I then came to Wyoming (1894) and went to
> work for the Swan Land & Cattle Company, since
> which time everybody else has been more familiar
> with my life and business than I have been myself.
>
> And I think that since my coming here the
> yellow journal reporters are better equipped to
> write my history than am I, myself!
>
> Respectfully,
>
> TOM HORN

That was it of course! Horn had deliberately stopped
short of the terrible Wyoming years in the Louthan volume.
Deeply hurt by the indifference and hostility shown him by
press and public alike, he had refused to tell the rest of
his story at that time. But the Starrett papers told another
story. He had changed his mind. They *were* the rest of
Tom Horn's life!

So it was decided, and so it was done.

What follows is the recreated autobiography of Tom
Horn taken from the text in the flat tin box. It is not history,
surely. It is only a fable, a Green River folklore stirred to
that larger life named legend. Except for one thing.

There is still that old, flat, black enameled box of tin.
And in it, smelling of must and age and the burned faint
stench of gun smoke, that strange dark story that begins,
I, TOM HORN. . . .

Book One

Out There

"I, TOM HORN, do solemnly swear—"

That's the way the lawyers would start it off, and so shall I. It will let those who are against me understand it is a man's testimony given here, and not the hassayampa trash seen in the yellow journals. As for the friends of Tom Horn who may read this, they will not need any oath to tell them who wrote it; they will know. And they will know it is the truth, the entire of it, and nothing tacked on, nor taken back.

I could have told the same thing at the trial, with my hand on the good book, and would have, but they didn't want to hear it. They just wouldn't let it be my way. If Jesus himself had of come down and swore for me, they'd have got it struck from the record and bought him a free ticket out of town on the next train.

But that's all washed down the river now. It can't be roped and towed back upstream again. Yet a man has to try. He has to set it right if he can. He has to say how the times were that ended him in Cheyenne Jail. What the laws were and what they wasn't. How justice failed. The way witnesses lied under vow. How judges turned deaf and juries went blind. And oh how different the rules read when twisted to convict the innocent. It has to be remembered, *always*, what happened to the law "out there." It was *not* the same.

Out there, a man took the law to be as good as his own word. Which he ever gave straight-out, with no tangles in the mane or tail of it. He neither whined nor tucked his croup when lies and libels rode him down. Nor did he burn over his brands once he put them onto the hide of

3

his testimony. Whatever he done, or said he done, he stuck by it. He depended on the law to do the same.

But sometimes a man wouldn't get his entire herd to railhead the first drive. Sometimes there was trail going on past where he believed he had all his cattle safe-loaded on the stock cars. He doesn't see it at the time. It's afterwards that it comes to him. Like when the drive crew's been paid off and the dust of their ponies has settled into the prairie twilight south toward Texas. That's when a man would look the other way, north, to Wyoming, and his eyes would slit down and he would say to himself, outloud soft, "Damn."

For what he saw up there, God help him, was the rest of his life's track, and it made him shiver hard in the gloom.

He knew then that he must tell the truth about that last dark part of the trail. The part his grand, good friend John C. Coble had not wanted to put into the book Coble had in mind they would write as a "vindication" of all that had gone wrong in Wyoming.

The first bright part of the trail, Coble had insisted, that was the true part. Tell it straight-out and fair, as you know it to be, he had advised. Your happy boyhood in Scotland County, Missouri. Working as a rawboned lad, not yet fifteen, out in Kansas on the Atchison, Topeka & the Santa Fe. Helping to lay the rails clean and shining-pure, from Kansas City to the Pacific's fartherest shore. How you became a famous stagecoach driver in New Mexico at just past fifteen years of age. How you rose, not yet quite eighteen, to be second only to legendary Al Sieber in the famed Apache Scout Corps of the United States Cavalry, in Arizona Territory. The way you captured the evil Geronimo single-handed—almost. The way you were made blood brother to the savage Apache. Why they honored you with the name of Talking Boy, because you spoke their tongue as no other white man had ever been able to do. The resolute and fearless manner in which, commended by the Pinkerton Detective Agency to the vast Swan Land & Cattle Company, you cleaned out the rustlers from all of southern Wyoming in but two seasons of lone-hand daring, 1894 and 1895. And thusly on and on.

Why! Coble had said, there was no end to the admirableness of such a life.

"Tell all those fine and upright things," John Coble had finished, "and you will go free. The people will know the law has the wrong man charged for the terrible Willie Nickell killing."

Well, maybe this would work for Mr. Coble; a man couldn't tie hard and fast to it for himself, though. It sounded wrong somewhere. It had an off ring to it. Like a horseshoe on a fouled anvil. Coble's story would run only up to the edge of the real hell that Tom Horn rode into in Wyoming. It would rear up short and shy off, where the dark part began.

A man had to know that—if he was me, Tom Horn, the one they were going to hang that coming sunrise, at Cheyenne Jail.

I never doubted John C. Coble and don't doubt him now. He was the best friend and whitest pal a man could find in this hard life.

But that was last year.

The trees have turned again since then. Mr. Coble sticks with me but doesn't come so much anymore. The other men I worked for, and saved their stock and ranges from the nesters, have all gone away from me. Sheriff Ed Smalley, a truer friend than most who said they were, tells me it is all over for me.

"It's ended, Tom," he says. "God knows, and you know, Tom, that I am sorry."

Well, it is not over yet for Tom Horn.

I have been where the bear turned back before. I have been run by the wolf and made him whimper. I have felt the bullet whisper at my ear and the arrow brush my eye. The knife has sought twixt my ribs, the lance struck my belly, the ax gone in me to the bone, and it doesn't matter. A man knows when his time is on him, and mine isn't yet.

My friends will get me out.

The word has come to me that they will, and they are true pals and I believe them. All is ready, they say,

and the hangman's trap will never spring for me in Cheyenne Jail. The plan can't fail. The men who are doing the
job know their game and won't blink to the light nor jump
sideways of the trail. They will break me out of here, that
is certain this time. No more mistakes.

Before they come and take me free, I must leave this
truth where it will be found. The story is all told, all
written down, waiting only to be passed to the one who
will get it from me tonight when he comes for the last
time. No one could have told this story but me. I rode
that trail in Wyoming alone. What happened at Iron Mountain, and beyond, wasn't kin at all to the days in Arizona
or New Mexico. Or even to the Denver times.

From the first day into the Wyoming country, It was
Tom Horn against the pack; and the pack run mean and
hot and relaying on me all the while, quartering me down.

There was no Al Sieber to show a man the way in
Wyoming. In Wyoming, there was nothing but me and
my horse and my rye bread and raw bacon and rat cheese,
and that smokeless powder .30-30 Winchester model '94,
riding to the far-off call of the old loafer wolf going home,
with me, from his kill in the murk of early dawn.

Not John Coble, not Marshal Joe LeFors, not Deputy
Snow nor Sheriff Smalley nor Prosecutor Stoll nor any man
alive knew where Tom Horn went or what Tom Horn did.
Only the ones found looking empty-eyed at next morning's sun, with the round, smooth trademark rock wedged
under the flyblown head, could say if they had seen Tom
Horn; and they never said.

This is my *other* story, then.

My enemies will deny it, my friends will hear it too
late. But no man follows that nightshade trail over the last
river but that he says his hasta la vistas straight.

One way or the other, this night will see it done.

Right up to first snow-fly it looked to all that I would
get off clean as a drawed shoat. They said Tom Horn
would not do thirty days in Cheyenne Jail, nor ever come
to trial. Nor, if he did, would ever get convicted. The
shameful charge against me would surely be dismissed for
simple lack of decent proof.

But now that first year has rolled away. The trees have

gone bare and the old grass clumped-up to wait for winter. It is November, getting late-on, and good Sheriff Smalley would not lie to me, or any man.

By God! what was that?

Out yonder in the alley back of jail? Down there in the early winter dusk where I can see it from the bars of my cell's lone window. The form of a man on foot skulking along. No, two, three forms. Drifting along past the trash barrels where the note had said they would drift if the break was still on.

There! O, Christ Jesus be praised.

The lead man is waving as though to warm his arms. Three times he gives me the signal, shucking the cuffs of his sheepskin coat, then blowing into his cupped hands. Jesus, Jesus, it *is* on.

Get away from the cell window. Quick, move back. A boot has scraped in the corridor. Somebody comes.

But God Amighty let them come.

In only hours I would be away. On this very last night, in the shadow of the scaffold being put up for me by the daft architect James Julian, the boys would gather and, swift as the strike of a Chiricahua knife, cut me out. There in the blackest pool of night they would have Old Pacer waiting under saddle, rifle in scabbard, bread and bacon and cheese tied on the horn. Up I would go aboard him and we would be gone, Old Pacer and me, like two bullbat shadows on the underbelly of the moon.

South! south! to Arizona and the territory. Why, within the hour of getting loose, the grand old gelding and me would be near into Lost Range, beckoning down there on the Colorado line where I could see its hump-ribs sticking up through the snow like old dry buffalo bones. An hour? *Wagh!* Me and Pacer would be shut of Cheyenne by sight in thirty minutes.

When the storm growling around outside the past few hours had rolled on and the sun come again to glisten on Granite Gap, Lone Tree River road, and the Buck Eye cutoff, long down into Colorado, Wyoming would see Tom Horn no more, nor ever know his trail again.

My Apache woman, Nopal, Old Pedro's dark-faced daughter, would be waiting yet for her Talking Boy down

there where the sun went winters. We would lay ourselves
together like when we were young. I would tell her why
it was that so many snows had melted since that last spring
when I went away from her. She would make it all the
same once more. The Apaches would be my people again.
It would be like the old times, sweet and wild and safe.

All a man had left to do in Cheyenne Jail was pass
his secret testament to the young defense attorney who
had promised to come for it this night. With the testament's
burden lifted, its untold wrongs set right, lawful and square
and written out by his own hand, Tom Horn had only to
wait for his friends to get him free.

Free and riding far, and far.

Free and away forever free to Arizona and the old
times.

Just him and the wind and the wolf, lone three.

Out there! out there!

Stump Hill

We came out of the woods, old Shed and me, and
clambered up on the little rise where the old hickory stump
was sentinel post to all I knew of the world at fourteen
years of age. Me and the old dog just hunkered up there
in the summer sun, soaking it all in. We were that kind
of friends, Shed and me. Never had much need for hauling
or tugging at one another. Nor talking neither.

He just wheeled twice around in the grass, spread
himself out belly to the warmth and likewise where I easy
could reach him to put my feet up on him, and was snoring full tilt in about the time it took me to get backed up
real good to the stump. I left him wheeze on whiles I made
myself a Scotland County cheroot—corn shuck, shredded
willow bark, dry tassel silk—and lit up. After I'd got over

the coughing, I reared back and grunted happy as a pig turned out in pink clover.

If this wasn't the life, it would answer meanwhile.

Down below, Wyaconda Creek threw a loop about Stump Hill, then wandered off across Scotland County to spill into the Mississippi somewheres below Keokuk. Our six hundred acres lay both sides of the creek and both sides of the Keokuk road. It was in corn where the plow would bite deep enough but mostly ran to wild pasture and brush-choke lands like me and Shed loved. We were hunters, the both of us, and that northeast Missouri hill and woodland, when laced with a stream twisty and thick of cover as Wyaconda Creek, well, it was grand game country, and me and the old dog was the masters of it. Or at least all of it that we could see from Stump Hill that summer of 1874.

Yonder, a good wagon ride, was Memphis, our county seat. A scad nearer we could make out Scotland School, where me and my seven brothers and sisters went for our learning. Well, they did. Most times that Shed and me set out for school, we would cut hot sign and away would go old Shed yapping and squalling and, well, naturally, he was my dog and I didn't want him lost.

My sister Nancy, the one I liked, and who led our line of little Horns down the old road to the schoolhouse every day of its term, would beseech and holler after me that I knew father would hide me again.

"Please, please, Tom!" she would call. "I cain't stand to see you whupt agin! Don't run off today." But it wasn't any good. She knew I would go.

And I knew father would be waiting for me when I got back. You could trust father. He would never fail you.

That's mainly the reason me and Shed would lay out in the brush three, four days at a stretch. Old Shed, he didn't relish seeing me shellacked with a harness strap any better than sister Nancy did. So when I would slip away to run wild for a spell, Shed he hung with me. It agonized him when I was lashed. He would actually yelp out like it was him taking the cuts.

Once, when I was little, and father came at me, Shed took into *him!*

That's the wherefor that Shed goes lame in the off forequarter; father liked to beat him to death, and would of I reckon. But mother came running up and prayered him off the dog. They were devout Campbellites both of them and when mother threw arms aloft and called on the Lord in Shed's behalf, my father left off kicking him and fell square down on his shinbones in the mud and manure of the barn lot and demanded in the name of Christ Jesus that God lead him to see the light fall on his son Tom and that damned traitorous old sheep dog, before he kilt them both.

Shed and me lit out that time!

It was the first trip I laid out overnight, and my mother wept in her apron for half an hour when we showed up scratching at the back door next night, after father had gone on to bed. She set and splinted Shed's leg but made me swear never to whisper who had done it. My father was a God-fearing man, but not foolishly much. You couldn't bank on him getting prayed out of something two times running.

I was thinking about that up there on Stump Hill. It kept me awake against the drowse of that late summer sun. That and keeping a weather eye out on the run of the Keokuk road, where it edged around the rise on the south, going on its way from the Mississippi River and Keokuk Landing, to Kansas City. Fact is, once past Memphis, it was called the Kansas City road. That was account of it carried a lot of travel out of Illinois, across the big river, going west to find new places out yonder. And, naturally, all of that kind of traffic was Kansas City bound. Kansas City was just plain *the* place to hit for, happen you were heading west. All the trails led out from there. Oregon. California. Santa Fe. Denver. Texas. Every one of them.

It was the stirringest thing, short of hunting and laying out in the wild of nights, that I knew about in those parts. Seeing those big Murphies and Studebakers, and even some old Conestogas, rumbling and creaking over Wyaconda Bridge down below, would whirl up the blood in a dead man. And I was a far rifle shot from dying and only a boy, though already bigger than a sizable cut of the men I'd seen. You can risk a prime coon pelt against three rotten rabbit skins that *my* blood like to boilt at the view of those covered wagons rolling west.

It made me wild to go with them.

That's why me and old Shed hung up there on Stump Hill that late afternoon, before going home to get thrashed. It was to watch those folks coming down *our* road on their ways to out where the Indians were, and the wild horses and the buffalo herds and the soldiers and all of that. You could see troops moving on the road too. Long dusty lines of horse soldiers on the march. There was trouble with the redskins out there. The big war was nine, ten years over, that summer of 1874 when I was dreaming of the West. But the Indians didn't know it. They just kept warring and helling the white folks out there like to run the cavalry ragged.

That was the greatest thing for me.

Those Indians out there.

Maybe it was true what my mother said, that I had "Injun ways" and was bound to see trouble because of it.

Well, that didn't bother me. I couldn't wait to catch up to my fair share of such grief. Not ever, I couldn't.

Matter of fact, another load of it was just then jouncing the bridge planks over Wyaconda Creek. Three big wagons under white canvas, lots of trailed and rear-tied livestock with them, and following up away behind, two kids about my own age dawdling along on an old bay mare that went spooky to her right and was certain to be moon-eyed on the offside or I would lose another coonskin.

"Shedrick," I said, punching the old dog in the belly with my big toe, "yonder comes a couple of little pecker heads lagging behind. They got to be looking for trouble. Specially the big one."

Old Shed tottered up and let out a half-livered "woof," as to say, well, if that's what they're looking for, they're looking for us, and away we went down Stump Hill to cut them off at Wyaconda Bridge.

"Howdy," I said, grinning like a jackass. "Welcome to Missouri."

The bigger boy stopped the old mare, still on Wya-

conda Bridge. She nervoused around on him, first at the
plank-rattle under her and second at me standing spraddled
out in the middle of the road, my rifle butt grounded in
the dirt like I'd seen a picture of Quantrill's Raiders stopping Kansas jayhawkers to rob them of their slaves they'd
made free niggers of.

But when the old bay swung about, she let me see
that the emigrant boy had a nice 16-gauge bird gun in
his hand that dangled down on the offside where I didn't
see it from up on the hill. He kind of gave this piece a
little shift of its two barrels to let their muzzles look me
over, and I stretched my grin another three teeth on each
side.

"Name's Tom Horn," I scrinched. "What's yourn?"

"Git your ass out'n the way," he answered. "Elst I'll
dust you with these quail-shot. You a robber?"

I could see right off he was big-talking now. I had
him scairt, bird gun or no bird gun. But scatter-guns are
mean close up. "Hell no," I said. "I'm just out hunting pot
meat. This here's our farm you're on. What you doing?"

He brought the mare on off the bridge and I gave
way as was proper. To make things decent, I leaned my
rifle up against a fence post. He handed over the bird gun
to his kid brother, who never said anything the entire time
of what happened. He then slid off the mare and came
over to me, where I had picked out a good grassy place
just off the shoulder of the road.

"Ain't doing nothing," he scowled at me. "And this
here ain't anybody's farm; it's public road."

"Where we're a-standing is Horn land."

The Illinois boy spit on the grass and evil-eyed me.
He was a big younker. Bigger even than me. And he looked
able. But us Indians had our tricks.

"Listen," I said, "you like land?"

He stared at me like my brains was smooth, then answered, sort of puzzled, "Sure, that's why we're heading
west. Land is all pa talks about."

"Why," I smiled, "no need to go all that ways. I can
give you a couple of acres of your own, right here and
now. You want 'em?"

He sobered over it a minute, as slow kids will, and said, "Well, I swan. Sure. Give 'em to me."

I did. Got him perfect, too. I was always quick as a buttered cat. He didn't know what happened to him. All he knew was that he was one minute going to get rich on giveaway land and the next was down in the dirt grabbing for his crotch and bawling like a just-cut bull calf.

"You needn't beller so," I told him, leaning over so's he could hear me good. "You got your two achers, didn't you? Hah! hah!"

I naturally knew he wasn't going to die, but didn't think to give myself the same guarantee.

Whiles I was still scrooched down crowing over him, I took a belt from the rear that like to spilt those smooth brains of mine down twixt my shoulder wings. It was the damn little kid down off the mare and hammering me with the buttstock of the shotgun. Only his short swing and poor grip of the barrels saved me. I managed to wobble up off my hunkers before he laid my head open. The minute he saw he hadn't killed me, he took off, squirting dust like a stomped-out cottontail.

But they had my dander up now.

I was aiming to gallop him down and kick the, well, whale the tar out of him, leastways. Then to naturally pry him loose of the damned shotgun before he kilt somebody with it. Howsomever, I didn't anymore than get gathered together for the first jump after him when the big kid left off groping his parts, picked up a stone the size of a Rocky Ford mushmelon, and caught me in the side of the neck with it, full fly.

I couldn't breathe for a minute, nor get my throatbone to go up or down. Then I got a whiff of my wind, and we went at it, mid-rut of the Keokuk road, ripping away at one another like two bear cubs caught inside the same beehive.

Pretty quick he saw that I was using him up faster than he was me. Right off, he give a yell for the kid with the 16-gauge. The little turd came a-racing back and set to thumping me with the gun butt again. Before long I was seeing things fuzzy, and the two of them were like to whumping me right on down into the horse apples of the

Keokuk road, when yonder came old Shed. He never could abide seeing me on the bottom, and I sure didn't auger it with him this time. "Hie on!" I yelled, the same as when we would chivvy the old sow and her pigs out of mother's collard greens. "Grab and holdt!"

Well, Shed he grabbed and held and shook and nipped and bit away so swift, those Illinois peckoes didn't know what had lit upon them. They peeled off of me like skin off a roast snake. I was laughing even though it hurt something fierce when I did it. They made so much dust digging out of there that me and old Shed didn't even know where they'd gone till way too late.

I was still yockering and yahooing after them when up out of the cloud they'd raised departing, here they came again up on that old bay mare. The big kid had the gun now, and he never said a word but just leveled it down and triggered it off and like to blowed out poor Shed's whole belly, with me still laughing.

They were gone, then, clumping the old mare on west to catch up to their wagons. I gathered up old Shed and bore him home. I had him still alive out in the stockbarn when dark came down and father come in from cultivating the south forty, where I'd been told to be with him the day long.

He didn't say anything about missing the work. Not then he didn't. That was for saving, and savoring.

He just said, "Who done that to your dog," and I answered him who had, and he went in the house and got his hat and coat and took the spring-bed wagon and the sorrel team and went on the jingle-trot for Memphis.

It was way late when he came back.

I snuck over from nursing Shed at the barn and peep-tommed into the kitchen window. Mother was washing the blood off father and patching him up with bed sheets and carbolated coongrease. He was a fearsome sight, but I knew he had won. After a bit, he said to mother, "They won't gutshoot no boy's dog no more." I don't think she ever got more than that about his going to the emigrant wagon grounds outside the county seat of Memphis, Scotland County, Missouri, and whipping five grown men with nothing but his bare knuckles and sodbuster boots. Or about his leaving all five either unconscious or flat down in the mule marbles puking up their blood. And only explaining to their poor wives and other weeping womenfolk that it was for "what was did to my boy's dog."

That's all he ever said to them, or to my mother, that anybody remembered.

I wish he had said something to me.

Or me to him.

Maybe a lot of things would have come different than they did. But my father was a strange man, and I was his own-son. Somehow, we never got it out.

I don't recollect when old Shed died. I had gone back to the barn and laid with him in the hay of the front stall. I dozed off, and when I came around again it was just tingeing gray daylight outside, and he had crope over to me and put his head on my flung-out arm and gone without a whimper to rouse or fret me.

There was still no light in the house. I took up the draggled body. Toted old Shed like that clean to the top of Stump Hill. There, I put him under where he could feel the sun and have the wind heldt off his back by the old hickory stub. And where he could peer down on Wyaconda Creek, the rattly plank bridge, Keokuk road, and all of it that used to be his and mine. But specially his. It was his favored place.

I knew he would want to wait up there for me.

One day I would come back for him, and me and Shed would go on over the far side of Stump Hill and see what lay yonder past the creek. We'd always said we would. Meanwhile, he would be safe and snug and not hurting anymore, nor fearful.

"Old Shed," I whispered. "Hie on—!"

And I took up the shovel and went on back down the hill. It was the prettiest morning of the summer. Old Shed had picked a good day.

Sam Griggs

With Shedrick gone, I was down to one friend; which was Sam Griggs.

Sam lived on the next farm up the road toward the county seat, and was a boy of my own age and of about a similar heft. We were like as pod-peas excepting that Sam was a trace fitter. I never could whip Sam Griggs.

It was not from failing to try.

I expect I tackled Sam on an average of two, three times a week, all summer long, every summer of all the years we both was heldt prisoner by the Scotland School. If I ever once put him down, it was in my slumbers. Sam had muscles made of mule-whang. He was raspy as a bobcat. That boy would fight a buzz saw with a willow-switch. He would give a bear the first chomp and outrip him three bites to one. There wasn't one good-sized, chesty farm kid in Scotland County that he hadn't tamed down into a regular teacher's pet, saving for a single, smoothbrain exception—me.

I just had it mortised-and-glued in my thick head that Tom Horn could lick Sam Griggs.

I was certain I could one day make him spit an eye-tooth or bleed a shirtfront from his own nose. My poor mother used to despair of it. "Tom," she would heave out with a big sigh. "Don't you never learn nothing? Ain't it in you to wisen-up just onct?"

Then she would box my ears, which had just come home still ringing from getting hammered on by old Sam Griggs. Naturally that would ire me into running off into the woods again. And that would get the butthide beat off of me by father, when I tried sneaking back home after dark.

Anyhow, Sam stayed my friend. So it seemed only sensible to me, trudging down Stump Hill and trying to cipher out in my mind where I might go to tell somebody about Old Shed, that I thought of Sam Griggs.

Matter of gospel, it wasn't Sam I thought of firstly.

It was his brute-dumb dog named Sandy.

That animal was the prize-poorest critter ever I see to use his head. The onliest way he could tell a skunk and a squirrel apart was that one of them couldn't climb a tree. And he never could get it straight which one. He would always come home upwind and full of wood pussy reek, no matter how hard Sam tried to learn him proper. I used to wonder how that dog had sense enough to lick his butt.

Shed could have given a tenth his brains to Sandy and still been smarter than him by forty rods. I used to put it to Sam Griggs that way, too. Fair is fair, I'd say. You got to grant what's so. But Sam was willful as a moonblind mule and would never admit it. We had some of our liveliest scrapes over it. Which they all wound up the same way, somehow: Sam was right.

And so was my mother.

This was Sunday morning, now, because it had been Saturday night that father had gone to the wagon camp, and I ought to have gone right home from burying Shed and got my feet washed, and everything, to go to church. Rather, I cut around the barnlot and kept going.

At the Griggs place they were up earlier than us. It wasn't the same church they went to. So I darn near missed Sam. But he was hanging back in the line of his folks going out to the wagon from the house, and I was able to give him our special crow squawk signal from out back of the corn-rick. He walked on behind the wagon and when it pulled out there wasn't anything to see but the softwater rainbarrels up against the kitchen wall. But directly old Sam slud out from twixt the barrels, whistled up Sandy, and away we went. "There ain't nuthin," Sam advised, hearing my sad report, "to take your mind off a good dog dying-up on you like going right back out on a coon hunt with another dog that's even better. Come on, Sandy. Cut fer coon!"

I was going to back water right there but, after all, Sam had called Shed a good dog, which was the best he had ever said of him, alive or departed. So I went along.

Well, that was the quickest coon hunt ever.

We hadn't more than struck the creekbrush and got into some good bottomland timber when Sandy commences to yell and we saw fresh sign and all three of us lit out to end up at the foot of a big slippery ellum growing orphan in a stand of beech and black walnut.

"Tree! Tree!'" Sam hollered at his dog, which the damn fool was yammering and fussing up the trunk of the wrong tree and not the ellum which he'd run the trackline to himself. Dumb? That dog was pathetic. I thought of Old Shed and near commenced weeping, but didn't.

I couldn't see a thing up that big ellum but Sam was certain he could. "He's a old buster!" he cried. "Big as a bearcub. Cripes, he's really suthin! Cain't you spy him out on that old under-rot limb yonder?"

I confessed my eyeballs weren't up to his, and I guessed he'd have to climb the ellum and knock his grand champion he-coon out of it, account he knew where he was. Sam wasn't a site too much quicker in his head than his dog was, and up the ellum he skinned, old Sandy finally coming over to bell at the right tree when he saw Sam clambering up it. He was still there squalling and slobbering when there came a split and cracking from up in the tree. Down out of the foliage, thrashing and crashing, came the old under-rot limb. It had broke off under Sam's weight crawling out on it, and if that was the he-coon we were after yet clinging to it, he was surely the granddaddy raccoon ever. Sam's dog Sandy thought so too.

With one screech he dove onto the poor critter.

This was his chance. Old Shed was gone and this was Sandy's time. He made a grand show of it. He was no more feared of that giant coon than of a fieldmouse in the shelled corn bin. He like to tore the poor thing limb from brisket. He must of bit it in the butt, the head, the spleen, the gizzard and the gullet, for you never heard such coon-yelling in your life.

Only trouble was, it wasn't the coon yelling. It was Sam Griggs. The old he-coon was still up the ellum laugh-

ing. Sam had fallen down on the limb and Sandy had like
to chewed him apart from every last stitch of his Sunday
clothes, fores I could get the damnfool loose of his own
master. Even then, when I'd pried him off and turnt him
loose, he went in again for the finish.

By this time, Sam had found his footing and he fetched
the idiot hound a couple of thumps with his new brogans
that caved in three ribs and sobered up old Sandy long
enough for me to pin him down again.

After that, is when I lost Sam Griggs.

I looked at my one other friend and saw that he was
bit in one ear, shoulder, arm, both hands, and his belly.

The seat of his trousers was down around his brogan-
tops and his galluses was wropped around his gullet and,
well, I ought to have said something else than I did.

But brains always work better later on.

"Sam," I said. "Too bad. But I reckon my dog Shed
would have had more sense than to jump on me if I'd
been tomfool enough to fall down on him out'n a coon tree."

The fight lasted about three minutes. It was the longest one we ever had. I spent all of it on the ground but
Sam wouldn't let up on me this time until he had had his
"full satisfy." When him and his dumb yellow hounddog
finally went off limping wounded soldier-wise through the
beech and walnut grove, nobody had to tell me Tom Horn
had managed it again. There wasn't anybody left to me
in Scotland County of kith, kin, dog, or other friend. Excepting maybe for my sister Nancy, which was a girl and
didn't count.

But I had a head like a millstone.

Round and hard and full of grit and flat on top.

I had one more whipping to go.

My Father

Lying in my loft bed up under the south gable that last night, I listened to the west wind drive in the sweet, soft rain from away out there where the wagon trains were going. Lordy! but that rain smelt exciting wild. I could taste the farness in it where little drops would seep and run under the sheathing boards and I could reach a finger and bring them to my tongue.

Buffalo grass! Wild horse manure! Cowboy saddle sweat! Longhorn dust! Tepee smoke! Grizzly sign! Gunpowder and rifle grease! Sagebrush in perfumery!

Lord God but I could imagine it all brought a thousand and more prairie miles just for me to whiff and feel from far out there. Out there where the feathered redskins rode. And the gaunt horse soldiers chased them down. And where the flash and clap of their guns was what I truly heard in the thundersplits and lightning rivens that rattled the warped shingles of that old Missouri farmhouse on the Keokuk road.

It was then I knew that I was going.

That I had to go.

And that all that remained was to tell mother and father of it in the morning.

It is said that only the just sleep sound. To that, add the simple of mind. I slept that night like a winter calf in a warm barn. I was counting coup on Cheyenne, Sioux, Pawnee, and Arapaho without fear or favor. I took more redskin hair and rescued more outnumbered pony soldiers that one night than the regular cavalry did in the ten years since the war. I could have won the whole West by myself except that, as always, daybreak came in the dark on the Horn farm.

With a start I came awake. The night was gone and the west rain with it, and down below in the kitchen of my mother I could hear the bear's growl of my father's early morning voice wanting to know where the hell at was young Tom. "Ain't he been told he's to finish in the south forty today? By God, you send him direct out to me, woman. I'll be in the barn hitching the mule."

I could hear mother moving to the loft stairs.

A little shiver trembled me.

My feet thumped the floor, my heart thumping right along with them. I knew something neither one of my folks knew. This was their final day of me. I had made up my mind during the night. Tom Horn was heading west.

My father was waiting for me. He had the mule hooked to the single-row cultivator just like it hadn't rained at all. And he was mean-eyeing me. I could smell the brimstone stink of trouble in that storm-cleared air and went careful as a cat the rest of the way toward him.

"Morning," I said, drawing up.

He only nodded and stood there looking me over, and I knew what he was up to. After a downpour such as we'd had in the night, it was daft of anybody to go into the corn with a cultivator; he was box-trapping me.

"Your mother tell you about the south forty?" he began.

"Yes," I said. "You ain't finished it yet."

He eyed me, then sort of let his glance wander on beyond where we were standing. In the stillness, the mule blew some wind, then spraddled and commenced to stale. I watched father's eyes. The mule splattered on.

My father was called the hardest man to whip in northeast Missouri. He would have things his way, or you would have to break his head open to halt him. Top of that, he was fevered of religion. His was the Lord's job. Everybody else worked for the devil. Specially his son Tom.

My father figured you had to *beat* that out of a boy.

Don't know why that was so, but it was.

Austin or Martin or Charley, my brothers, or Nancy, Hanna, Maude, or Alice, the four sisters, they, all of them, seemed better than me. Did better in school and never had trouble with anybody important. It never did come clear to me why I was the practice post, where not one of them ever took the hidings I did. But one thing I knew and had decided on last night; I had run out of hide: I wasn't taking no more whippings.

Somehow, father knew it; his eyes quit wandering.

He didn't say anything to me. I just looked at him.

We both knew where we were at then.

I could see his hands working on the singletrace harness leather he held in them.

"Mule's hitched," he said.

I nodded, still saying nothing.

Father shook his head. "Had you worked that field when I asked, boy, you would still have your dog."

He crouched a little, settling his grip on the trace.

"You got something to tell me?" he asked, saying it slow-quiet, maybe almost like he wanted I should have.

"I got something to tell you," I said. "It's good-bye."

It throwed him.

He turnt black in the face with insult blood, but he didn't know quite how to handle what I'd said. After a minute, he got aholdt of himself.

"Last chance, boy." He handed the lines of the mule toward me. I didn't reach to take them. "School's commencing," he went on, "corn's to be got in and shelled. Pigs to butcher and pickle down. It ain't no time to be left shorthanded, nor to talk of leaving."

"Ain't no time to be running a cultivator in a muddy field neither," I said, wagging my head stubborn as a bay steer. "Not unless you're aiming to do it. I ain't, that's for certain sure. Good-bye, father."

It was mean-eye time again. Both ways. With him watching me and me watching his hands and that heavy leather singletrace. He dropped the mule's lines but held onto the trace, and I could see him settle himself.

"That all you got to say to me, boy—good-bye?"

"Yes sir, father," I answered, letting it come out from fourteen years of holding it back. "Good-bye, and go to hell."

I was still watching that trace, but he got me with it

anyway. He was faster than a blue racer snake. It missed my face but cut the shirt right off my shoulder.

Then I grabbed the free end of it before he could recoil to hit me again, and the trace was torn loose from his grip and I had it in my own hands and, by God, I hit him with it like to take his head off his body.

It knocked him into the barn siding, but not down off his feet. He held up a minute bracing against the sunblister of the boards. His face was strange when he finally turned it to look at me. It was like he didn't know me. Like I was somebody else's boy Tom. Of a sudden I knew that I had already left home.

I pitched the singletrace to one side.

"All right, father," I said. "Just help yourself; this is your last time at me."

He didn't say a word, just came for me.

I looked up through the haze of sweat and blood in my eyes. The world was spinning around and I was sick to my gut, and the face of my father was leaning down through the wavy lines and cloudy streaks that hung heavy all about. Whirl as it would, there was one thing my blurred brains understood about that barn lot turning like it was. Father had beat me within a breath of killing me, and I might die yet.

"*Now, if you are set on leaving home,*" his mouth opened above me to say, "*go on and do it. Just remember that the last time the old man whipped you, he gave you a good one.*" The face misted away, then hove back down upon me for one brief time more. "*Ask your mother for a lunch to take with you. You will be back by night if you start this morning, and if you take something with you, you won't miss your noon dinner.*"

This time, when the face dimmed away, it didn't come again, nor did the ghosty voice of my father.

Stories would get spread about that fight.

Some would hold that father took me up out of the mud and lay me gentle in on the fresh hay of the dry barn. Or that mother came, with sister Nancy, and got me up into the haywagon standing half full in the lean-to shed,

so they could hide me there till father left. The straight of
it was that nobody picked me out of the mud. It came on
to storm again, and I was still laying there too weak to
move and I almost drowned from pooling water. But a
cold wind came back of the rain and it freshed me enough
so that I could crawl. Which I did, as far as the barn
door and then through it to hide myself back of the down-
fall pile from the loft.

I laid there the day and night through.

It wasn't till next morning, and father gone into Memphis to trade for a Justin Morgan mare, that mother and all
the girls came out to the barn, or dasted to. They got me
onto an old storm-shelter half door, toting me that way
into the house. I passed out from the jolting, I was that
sick, and don't know how they got me up to the gable room
by the loft stairs.

They never had any doctor for me, but they prayed
hard.

I lay up there under the shingles for ten days. I
couldn't even stand up for six of the ten. When I could
walk, I didn't tell anybody but waited for that night. Under
its cover, I stole out of the house. I took a lunch with me
out of the kitchen and just kept going. My way led up
Stump Hill and to old Shed's grave, where I said my only
good-bye—to that old dog of mine. After that, I straightened out and hit for Memphis.

There, next morning, I sold my rifle to Mr. Jessup at
the Memphis Mercantile, and it fetched me eleven dollars.
It was all the money I had to get me out west, but I
was on my way. That was the grand thing. I don't believe my feet touched solid gound for at least the first
mile.

Maybe I didn't know where the West was, exactly.

Which I didn't.

But I surely knew how to start on the way to it. You
just took the Keokuk road over to the county seat, hung
to the south, and hit out for Kansas City. Sure it was near
onto seventy-five miles to get there, but Tom Horn would
make it. He had to.

Kansas City was where the West commenced.

Kansas City

One thing has got to be set right about me and Kansas City. That's what year it was I got there. There's been argument over it. I said, and remain saying, 1874. And I was either fourteen, or "about fourteen," depending on how a person looks at it.

My older brother Charley, the level-headed one, always said that was precisely the trouble—the way I looked at how old I was. "You keep track like a damn horse," he would say, discouraged. "You don't count birthdays, you count years. Way you see it, you're born in 1860, November, why that's one year gone when 1860 goes. You're one year old come January 1, 1861. So, come 1874, you're fourteen that year. No matter you really ain't, until November. I got to tell you, Tom; you ain't real quick."

Well, Charley always saw things complicated.

I still say fourteen, and 1874, for Kansas City.

Leastways that's the way it's going to be with such dates for me; perhaps a body should bear it in mind.

Like maybe you would say I was thirteen years and eight months when I got into it with my father. I would say I was about fourteen. I sure wasn't about thirteen, was I? Shucks no. It was August of 1874 that I left the farm, and August of 1874 that I hove into view of Kansas City on my way to the West. But I will copy a final date here for them that holds such matters serious, just the way mother wrote it into the family Bible, along with the other seven she bore:

"Tom Horn, Jr. b. November 21st, 1860."

Past that, take your own trail. I was either thirteen or fourteen or fifteen, and I will graciously give everybody his pick of which. Of all the lies told of Tom Horn in his hard

25

life, to miss my age a year or so would be the kindest way possible to go wrong.

One thing for certain sure, though: I was a big one for any of those ages; big and likewise looking much older than most that was even sixteen, seventeen.

And I did have a useful store of farmer-boy wisdom as to sharpers, grifters, roughs, highwaymen, and all of the wandering kind, bad and good, which store I got from my years of hanging along the Keokuk road talking with the emigrants, horse soldiers, freed black men, foreigners, freighters, drovers, all the hundred breeds of folk heading for the new country, from the old parts.

So I got to Kansas City in one piece and with all of the eleven dollars I set out from home with.

I did have one squeak with the money, getting there.

It was in Clay County, where I took a wrong turn at Kearney late in the day. Come dark, I was way deep into hill country and somewhat fearful of what to do. But by and by I saw a fire off through the timber and smelt the aroma of roast meat. The pangs of my empty belly cramped me so fierce I set off nearly on a blind run for that fire's light. It was some damn-fool stunt. When I blundered in out of the timber and groping up to where the camp was, a couple of burly men jumped me from the back, fierce as bear dogs. They jammed pistols into my smallribs near up to the cylinders and snarled out, "Hoist 'em!"

I shrunk up like a cold leech on a hot stone and gulped, "Y-y-yes s-s-sir," sounding more like four years old than fourteen.

The two of them backed off of me like they had grabbed skunk. "Why Christ Jesus, Ding," the huge one of them said to their leader, over by the fire. "This here pilgrim ain't even legal size to keep. Ought we to throw him back, you reckon?"

Ding came over to where we were at. He was of medium heft, brown spade beard, and had bad eyes. He blinked all the time, and fast. But he wasn't in any way nervous. Just those watery, flick-winking eyes.

"Where you from, boy?"

"Memphis, mister."

"You're off the line for Tennessee."

"It's Memphis, in Missouri. Scotland County, sir, up toward Ioway."

The blinking man said he knew where it was, that there wasn't a decent bank within fifty miles of it, nor a railroad line anywhere short of six other counties, and that anybody born in Memphis, Missouri, ought to be shot, or at least have the courtesy to apologize for it. At which the four or five others of them had a good guffaw and the big fellow told me to pull up a stump and "dig in." This I did, taking a rare-big chunk of the roast. As the one with the bad eyes kept standing there looking at me, I said kind of awkwardlike, "Thanks, mister. My name is Tom Horn." At this, all the bearded hardcases about the fire grinned and chucked one another with elbows and the leader blinked and cocked his head at me and said in a high, tight-word voice, "One name's as good as the next; mine's Jesse James."

I close to choked on my mouthful of meat. One of them that had flanked me, the big one, hammered me on the back and knocked the roast loose from my throat.

"Chew more slower, younker," he advised me. "You don't want to die with but eleven dollars in your poke." He reached inside his shirt and pulled out my "roll," which he had plainly thieved from me while prodding me with his horse pistol. "Count it, kid," he said, tossing it back to me. "You cain't trust a passel of crooks like these here. Take it from old Cole, they're a desperate pack."

So that's the way I met Cole Younger and, in their grinning or scowling turns, the others of them: Charley Pitts, Marl Barker, Bevis Hill, Woodson Stode, Clell Miller, and Cole's brother, Bob Younger.

Never was told where at was Frank James and Jim Younger that there night in the Kearney woods. But when I got to Kansas City next day I heard the James gang had hit the Liberty National Bank, scant miles from where we camped. Counts was dead and Bevis Hill that bad shot he wouldn't last. It was only on account that Frank James and Jim Younger were hid out as "cover" for the raid, in Liberty, that the entire gang wasn't riddled and rode down. Or so I was told in Kansas City.

I don't truly know about the James gang. But I never

peeped that I et and slept with them, nor hinted at where
their camp was. Well, they didn't take my eleven dollars.
It would have been mean and small to inform on them. I
never would have done it.

I wasn't to alter my mind about that, nor about them.

Folks can say it wasn't really the Jameses and Youngers
I camped with. But let them. I saw those race-bred horses
all greyhound lean and groomed to the tailhairs. Yes, and
hooked on one long picket line just like the U.S. Cavalry,
full saddle, full bridle, ready to wheel and go at the snap
of one harness ring. Hell, and all those belted pistols and
each one with a rifle stacked handclose to his reach from
the fire? Oh, it was them right enough. But they still didn't
rob my eleven dollars.

Wish I might say as much for Kansas City.

Kansas City was big, built all out of bare-board lum-
ber, nothing painted but the churches, and had horse-
manure dirt roads like any other town. But that's where the
resemblance desisted. People! There were more of them
in two minutes than I'd seen my whole life previous. They
were hiving like bees. And the noise! You simply could not
believe it. And wagons? God Amighty, it was hub-and-hub
jammed with them. A body could scarcely wedge through
the streets. And when he got out of the roadway, he was
trapped in such a herd of folks on the woodwalks in front
of the stores that his watch could run down and need winding again before he made twenty rods.

Say, it was fearful full of people in Kansas City.

Which I figured made it fat and dandy for me.

It was so crowded no crook nor sneak could find the
pickpocket room to get at my eleven dollars. If somebody
in that pack had had to go to the bathroom, he couldn't
have raised his hand to save his bladder. I thought that
was right cute of me. It kind of tickled me that a farm boy
could come up with a sly notion like that. Fact is, I was still
smirking over the humor of it, when a nice old lady with
a pea-green parasol and a big wicker basket over her arm
tottered up to me and pleaded for aid.

She wanted to get over the main stem and was too
tuckered from the crowd to make it alone.

The poor thing.

She had a pitiful winceful game leg and was toting to a sick friend a fine hot lunch. The friend lived in yonder hovel, down the mud alley next the livery. She was desperate ill with the sweats and heaves and might never know another meal in this life. Could a fine young and Christian boy spare five minutes of his time and heart?

Well, you don't declare out of a duty like that.

Not brought up in Scotland County, you don't.

I gave her my arm and away we went twixt wheelhub and neath tailgate and over whiffletree safe to the far side. Whereat, partways down the dark alley, I gave her something else. It was my eleven dollars.

She persuaded me by opening up the wicker lunch basket and pulling out of it a Colt's pistol big as a Civil War artillery piece. She then asked me to turn about. Which I done spry enough. For by this time, poor light or otherwise, I was seeing a lot better. The old lady hadn't shaved for a week and had hair on her chest, where her dress popped open, thick as the wool on a black ram's belly, and, well, when her voice changed over low enough to sing bass at a bull fiddler's funeral, I *moved!*

Soon as I did, two hairy hands grabbed my hatbrim and shoved my round beaver hat square down over my two ears. Which took heft, for my ears were hooked on like jug handles and hard to bend as shoehorns. But it was done and I couldn't see a wink for staring straight into my own hatband. Then, before I could get my mouth open to bawl out for the police, or anybody, there was a terrible crackling of bright lights, and I knew I had been pistol-whupt over the back of my hat and had best just stay down there in the mud of the alley to think things over.

Well, after a bit I wobbled back out on the street and sought the law. When the deputy at the station heard I was flat busted, he recommended I find gainful employment or they would have to run me in for being a vagrant—which is a bum with no money, he explained—and the best course for me was to haste down to the Atchison, Topeka & Santa Fe railroad depot, where they were hiring section hands. At this, my sore ears perked upright.

"Mister," I said, "I don't reckon I ever heered of Acherson nor Topeeky, but did I understand you correct to add on Santy Fee?"

"You did," the policeman answered. "The line's a-building west, younker, fast as you could walk afoot. Three miles a day, and more. And paying a dollar a day, every mile of it. It's the only place I know you're going to get your eleven dollars back this year. But they don't wait, you hear? Train's leaving just about right now—" He pulled out a railroad turnip with stem winder and punch reset. "Yep, 11:47. Work train pulls out at noon. She's late to toot, right now."

He hadn't more than snapped the lid shut on his watch when there came from down at the trainyards the screech of a steamtrain whistle—three long toots followed by two shorts—and my heart like to cut off my air with its hammering. Santa Fe! Great God Amighty, I could ride the cars to Santa Fe and get paid a dollar a day whiles I was at it. Cripes! I lit out of that police station like they'd turpentined me. Santa Fe, my God. That was about as out west as a boy could get.

And a dollar a day to go there!

I guess I had old Kansas City wrong, after all.

It was some grand town.

Santa Fe

They were hiring all right down at the A.T.&S.F. I got my work ticket and stuck it in my hat, as I saw the men all about me doing. Over on the tracks, the steam engines were huffing and chuffing. Behind them, I saw the strings of chair-car coaches, each one bright painted and carrying a name on it. And some of those names! General Fremont. Jim Bridger. Kit Carson. Why, it was enough to fire the mind of any youngster. I could barely keep from shouting my joy to be aboard those wonderful coaches. Off to Santa Fe, first-class!

Well, not quite.

They marched us right on past the puffing passenger trains to track three where where was a string of brown old flatcars hooked back of a broke-down wreck of an engine. The engine didn't have a diamond-stack smoke-belch, nor any brass brightwork, nor not even a damned cowcatcher on the front of it! "Hobos, over here!" some railroad fellow yelled out, and we all skulked in that direction knowing he meant us. Hobos to the railroad people weren't bums or drifters but day-hired trackworkers. And that was surely Tom Horn and those two hundred other men now shoving to be first for the good places.

Aboard the five little flatcars we went, or tried to go. It was a coon fight right off. The cars were loaded already with crossties, wire, rail iron, spike barrels, flanges, bolt and nut crates. It was like a stampede, and those men were rough runners who did not mean to get a poor seat. Leastways not so as to give a good one to a farm boy from north Missouri. I came powerful close to getting muscled out, but was "rescued" at the last minute by an old one-eyed hobo. He was dug-in in a great spot right behind the coal car, which was a cordwood car on this dinky run. He saw me and give a rebel yell and a big wave. When I run up alongside the car, which was already moving, he reached me down a hand and I swung up and hunkered in alongside him.

Well, he had a rat-tangled beard to his belly button and was dirtier than a wallowed hog. The greasy black eye patch he wore didn't help any either. But away in under the jut of his brow burned that one good eye, and it gleamed like a pale-hot ember in there. I knew in the instant that he wasn't like the others, no more than was I. Quick as that, he read my thoughts.

"Name's Bronson," he said. "They call me Wolf-Eye."

"Who does?" I said stupidly.

"The Cut Arms," he answered. "The bastards."

"Who's the Cut Arms?"

"Why, the Cheyenne Injuns, young un. Don't you know nuthin' atall?"

My blood stirred at the name Cheyenne Indians. I didn't know much, but I knew enough to understand they weren't any of your tame Indians. Not hardly!

"They give you the name? The wild Cheyennes, I mean. Honest Injun, Mr. Bronson?"

The lone eye burned brighter still beneath its dark overhang of eyebrow brush and jut of skullbones. He looked out across the land, and I knew he wasn't seeing that Missouri River railroad bridge, or the stockyard pens, or the bottoms shacktown that I was looking at. He was seeing "out there." Out yonder and far away, the places I wanted to see. This terrible-looking and unscrubbed old man beside me was no section hand. He was the real article. He was inside wild, like me, only he had already been out there his whole lifetime, and he was out there again, right that minute, on that wheezy work train chuffing out of Kansas City for Santa Fe.

"Mr. Bronson," I said, "you was going to tell me how the Chey—, how the Cut Arm Injuns, give you that there name; I mean, if it was them really did it."

He came back with a little start, scowling like he resented being brought back, then easing.

"They not only give me the name," he nodded, "they likewise arranged for it in the first place."

"Huh?"

"They het up a rifle barrel in the fire and burnt out what's under this here patch," he said, touching the eye cover. It was the first I'd noticed that there was Indian beadwork on the filthy patch, a sign of some sort. "Afore that," he concluded, "I didn't have no Injun name. Most folks called me Staked Plains Bronson. Some sawed it off to just Llano Bronson. That was from my early years out yonder in Comanche country, when I had two eyes." He paused, and I knew he was making that long journey again in his memory. "But that don't mean nothing nowadays. Not to you, younker. It's been long forgot afore you was born. *Wagh!*"

But he was wrong. And my heart pumped fast.

Staked Plains Bronson? Why, I had read about him in the only book I ever read, at all; it was by a fellow named Ned Buntline, and he called it *The Comanche Killer,* and it was entire devoted to Staked Plains Bronson.

I wasn't apt to forget that book. It took me a month to read it, word for word, and my lips got aching tired just forming the letters for all those pages—there was over seventy-five of them—but I never quit till done.

I reached over and touched the old man's arm.

He looked around and he wasn't scowling this time.

"Mr. Bronson," I told him, "you got it plumb wrong about folks forgetting you. I know your whole life and heroed adventures. I can *read. Comanche Killers* was the onliest book I ever had. You won't never be forgot."

The old man just looked at me.

I started to look back at him but then turned away natural as I could when I seen it; there was a tear rolling out from under the beadwork eye patch.

His hand, big and knotted up as a burl-root, dashed at that tear and he grumbled out something like, "damn them firebox cinders," and then he handed me his heavy-barrel Sharps Big Fifty buffalo gun. "Here," he said, "you kin cradle this awhiles; I'm tire't of its cumber."

I thought that was all of it, and it was honor enough to get to hold that great old rifle, believe you me.

But there was a tidbit more.

"Younker," he said, when I had settled the Sharps and myself up against our windshelter of flange crates, "you will do." Then, soft-gruff, "Call me Wolf-Eye."

All day and night we rattled and banged and wood-smoked our way across country flat as a corn fritter. I kept waiting for distant view of the mountains—it was a day-bright full moon that night—that I knew humped up all about Santa Fe. But sunrise came and we took a water stop at a place called Newton, and damned if we weren't still in Kansas and it wasn't any water stop but the end of the line!

I looked and couldn't believe it. But I had to, because yonder to the west there wasn't anything but short curly grass and old buffalo chips and heaps of white bones. Not a crosstie, nor a rail pile, nor one single sign of a railroad ran on west.

I had been cheated bald.

It was three hundred and more miles on down to Santa Fe and the New Mexico country. And I didn't have a dime of money to get me there. I would have quit the A.T.&S.F. right smack in the middle of my first cussword at them duping me into going to Newton, Kansas. Except that you can't quit a job you haven't started to work on yet. So I got off the flatcars with the other two hundred hobos and we commenced to laying rails. I lasted twenty-six days. That meant twenty-six dollars. It was the amount Wolf-Eye Bronson calculated we would need to make it on down to Santa Fe in some style. For it turned out that the meat hunting he'd hired on to do ahead of the track-laying crews had petered out about as bad as my expectations of getting west had done when halted at Newton, Kansas. So old Wolf-Eye had consented to go with me. Only trouble was, the part of the money that was to come from him, he was never paid. The company maintained he brought in but three buffalo—two of them sick—and two ribby doe antelope, one of which was wolf-bit, and that this just did not fill the terms of its meat hunting contract with Mr. Clarence Wesley Bronson.

Fact was, Staked Plains Bronson owed the railroad $93.75 advanced him on his busted contract.

Which Wolf-Eye had drunk up in Taos Lightning whiskey the first ten days.

Still he was a bulldog and would not quit. He said that no matter the twenty-six dollars wasn't what he'd planned on, he would come along and share the hard doings with me anyway.

"I ain't never let down a blood brother yet," he vowed to me. "And me and you have took the Cut Arm oath."

I never did learn what that oath amounted to, but it scarcely mattered. Wolf-Eye knew the trail to Santa Fe, and more. He knew a teamster freighting out of Newton down into the Llano Estacado country. Fellow name of Blades, who needed two drivers and didn't give a hoot if one of them was fourteen years old and the other a hundred and forty.

"We're hired," Wolf-Eye said loftily. "Just go and draw our twenty-six dollars from the paymaster, and may the Great Bull Buffalo shit his scared pile square on the A.T.&S.F. railway."

Mr. Blades had good stock and good wagons. We didn't hit Indians, Comancheros, nor even any white horse thieves. There wasn't any high water at any of the rivers, excepting for the Cimarron which we hit so high up its course that the flooding wasn't but brisket-deep at worst. For the rest, it was just like the trailmaps said it was; not a mile off nor a half day's time wasted in the whole run.

And right here let me say something for all the brainy experts who can tell you more of where I went and what I done than Tom Horn ever could.

Depending on which of them you listen to, you can hear your choice of stretchers from A to Izzard. One claims I went all the way back to Kansas City to take the Santa Fe Trail! Now wouldn't that be brilliant? Way we did it was go right due west from Newton, little over one hundred miles, to hit the trail along the Arkansas River, between Pawnee Rock and Fort Dodge. It was the old Fort Larned wagon route Blades followed, and it was well traveled, had good grass and easy grades the entire way of it. Had we gone back to Kansas City, like that damn fool said, it would have taken us *four hundred miles* to get back to the same spot on the trail as the Fort Larned cutoff! Another of those natural-born geniuses had me hiring out to drive Texas cattle up from the Panhandle. That loony had me wintering in San Antone, learning Mexican in two months, killing some old lady in a outhouse crapper whiles riding home to the ranch drunk, and fleeing the law all the way back up into Kansas and the Flint Hills, where I was supposed to hide out on brother Charley's place. My God, I surely did cover a lot of territory! Trouble is, Tom Horn never took one step into Texas. I would like to have them try it in my place! The ninnies. Listen:

It was getting into October 1874 when me and Staked Plains Bronson hired out to Blades. Just short of Christmas Day, the selfsame year, 1874, we rolled Santa Fe in Blades's wagons. That's three months. There were many

stops on the way. Blades was a trader. We would load and
unload, deliver and pick up, and swing out of the way to
do either and in any part of the trail. There was also frequent outspannings and grass camps where the stock would
rest and fat up for more pulling. The trail was in deep sand
a lot of its way. Rocks like bear teeth studded up other
stretches. There was breakdowns. And blacksmithing, wagons and horses, all the while. Sometimes we'd miss our
water, or find a spring gone bad, or a rocktank alkalied
thick as flapjack batter. Hell, going down the Santa Fe
Trail in 1874 wasn't any light buggy ride. You did damned
good to cover it—and make a profit—in only three months.
Still those "experts" had me all those other places—you
know it wasn't just Texas, some of them threw in Denver
and Leadville, Colorado, for good measure—and they still
got me to Santa Fe in the same time that I made it my
ownself with the Blades train!

   Well, good luck to them, too, as old Staked Plains
says; may the Great Bull Buffalo bless them likewise as he
has others of our good friends along the way.

   Santa Fe for real?

   I will never forget the sight and feel and smell of it that
Christmas Eve of 1874 that I came into it from out of the
north on the high driver's box of a four-mule hitch freight
wagon, just ahead of a New Mexico snowstorm. I was just but
fourteen years old. I was six foot tall in my body and
muscled up like a snake from a man's ways and work. But
I was yet a far ride from being growed in my mind, or
turned hard of imagination. That legend town beyond the
Sangre de Cristo Mountains was like my whole life being
taken back and me born over again into a different world.
It was all one big blaze of yellow lamplight and soft
candleshine and wonderful smells of piñon and juniper
smoke and the beautiful haunt of the guitar music and
Mexican laughing and singing and, ah! it was wonderful
coming down into old Santa Fe that snowy winter's night
so long ago.

   And I was never the same again, after it.

Pajarita Morena

Christmas Eve in Santa Fe was one too many for Tom Horn, Jr.

When we had got the freight wagons parked and been paid out by Mr. Blades, friend Wolf-Eye says to me, "Come on, younker. I am well acquainted here and will introduce you to the right people. Bring your money."

Well I had always been a swift grower. By this time I was chewing my own tobacco and spitting it pretty far, too.

"Lead out!" I answered, full and clear; and me and Staked Plains Bronson woke up next morning, which was Christmas, in the local *juzgado*, sick as two poisoned coyotes and not a *peso* left betwixt us.

"What ever will we do now?" I asked him, dependfully.

He peered hard at me. "Who are you?" he said.

The town marshal turned out to be a white man, but we were hauled up in front of a Mexican judge for sentencing. Up to then, I had always figured New Mexico was U.S. of A. territory. And I sort of liked Mexicans. They struck me as happy-go-lazy folks who would rather sing and dance than sweat for hire. They loved horses and cattle and living out on the range, and, well, hell, I got along so great with them on my way to getting roostered Christmas Eve that I remember telling them I was a Missouri Mexican. But that judge set all that back about a year; in fact, exactly one year: "to be served in the Santa Fe Jail, in lieu of fifty dollars fine and five hundred dollars legal fees."

Old man Bronson, due to his age and busted-down condition, plus having a Mexican wife and eleven half-breed kids over in Taos—which he surely never mentioned to Tom Horn nor freighter Blades—was turned loose with a

37

fine which he paid by putting his Sharps rifle into soak down at the La Fonda Loan Office. I later learned that the old devil had been in and out of the Santa Fe hoosegow so many times they'd lost count. It worked out to be about every time he came back to town. And since each time he did that he got his Mexican old woman big-bellied again, the folks down there figured it would be eleven years that Staked Plains had been hocking his rifle in Santa Fe. Give or take one year, or one kid.

In any case, this time he must have decided to stay over in Taos, for I never saw him again in Santa Fe.

As for me, the marshal's deputy, likewise a white fellow, hauled me back to the jail and locked me up in solitary, "so's you won't contaminate the local prisoners." Which, naturally, were all Mexicans that had been my dear new friends just before the big fandango wherein I and Staked Plains had challenged "every brownskin son of a bitch in the house." Strong drink had done me in in three hours, where three months on the Santa Fe Trail had left me fit as a catgut fiddle. There was a lesson there which I was determined to learn. If I ever got out and was give the fair chance, that is. Which right then it surely didn't appear that I would be.

"Horn," the deputy said, clanging the big old bronze key in the celldoor lock. "Iffen you want anything, you had best learn to speak greaser. Me and the marshal are bound by tonight's stage over to Prescott, in the Arizona Territory, to pick up a prisoner. We'll be a week away. But don't you worry now, hear? Even if the Mex jail help don't savvy a word of English, you won't be starved nor harmed. These here *chollos* are a generous and butter-hearted sort. They'll treat you fine, unless you try something."

"I suppose should I try something, I'll get shot," I snapped, turning smart-ass with him.

"No," the deputy answered, politelike. "Knifed."

Which naturally ended that.

Praise be, that deputy was right; the Mexes were good people. Hadn't they been, I might yet be in that old adobe-mud and Spanish-iron birdcage down in Santa Fe.

Not that I then, or ever, learned to love a knife, or

came to admire knife fighters. To me, a man that uses a knife on another fellow human being is the lowest scum of the frontier. Knives are for cutting up meat. Damn a man that will use one otherwise. That's Mexican, white man, heathen Chinee, or red-ass Indian. It ain't right.

But I don't change my story on *good* Mexicans.

Pajarita Morena was her name. The *pajarita* part meant "the little bird," and she was just that. Tiny, soft, quick, beautiful, easy-hurt, wild to fly. Ah, Pajarita! Eyes luminous as a doe fawn. Voice trilling sweet as any songbird throat, yet low and husky, too, in a way to make a man's nape-hair rise up. Lord God, but she was a wicked-bodied little thing. And didn't even know it!

I didn't realize it right off, either, those first few days she brought me in my noon dinner at the jail. It was her job, she murmured, with those slanty-hot eyes cast down. Paying her what she needed to support her agey grandmother, the only kin she had in the world. The men in the jail near always respected her, prisoner and keeper alike, for they knew her want. She hoped the tall new Anglo prisoner from far Missouri would be as kind. It was very much in the heart of Pajarita Morena to have that hope come true. She had never seen a *vaquero* like the young Missouriano. So lean, so brown, so very brave. It was a thing of sorrow to contemplate his future. One year is as a lifetime to the young. *Ay de mí!* Were there but something that she, Pajarita Morena, might do. But, alas. *Qué tragedia.* There was nothing.

Now I heard this talk one day and the next. And was polite and grateful to her for it. But it didn't really sink in. Here I was not yet fifteen years old and in jail for a year in a foreign place. I didn't have a friend nor a penny of money nor any actual way to know I might not rot for a *hundred* years in that mud-wall Mexican *juzgado*.

I for sure as hell wasn't dreaming along about then of getting under the shimmy of Pajarita Morena.

But, come the first weekend after Christmas, things were changing swift and rough.

It was Saturday night, New Year's Eve.

The Mexican girl was plenty late with my supper and

the winter darkness was full down when she finally showed.

"It is for a reason, *hombre*," she told me in that soft low voice. "I have here more than your food to eat. *Mira!*" She pulled aside the cover-cloth of the shallow Indian basket she brought the meals in. There on my supper plate was the big bronze key. "Be sure it is the one, *caballero*," she nodded. "I know them all. It will fit the lock."

She stared at me the shakiest moment of my life; I felt it to the toes of my both feet and back up again.

"I will be waiting for you," she said. "You will find me in *numero tres*, the third doorway from the cantina where they took you and the old one. Hurry there, but stay to the dark places of the streets. Do not go by way of La Fonda."

"But the doorway," I protested. "I might count wrong!"

"There is a light over it," she smiled. "You will know it. *Cuidado* now, I must go."

"But the other prisoners, yonder," I said. "They will raise a ruckus when they see me getting free."

"No," she said. "They have all been freed for the New Year. It is our tradition, tall one."

"Sure," I said, foolish with bitterness. "You mean they was all Mexes but for me!"

She came very close up to me. I could feel the female of her, though she was yet a foot away from me. "*Hombre*," she whispered, "Pajarita brings you the same message of peace and love. The same gift of freedom. Take it!"

I started to bumble and stumble that love and peace was dandy things but you didn't buy freedom without you took it. And I had no gun and the guard was armed, maybe more than one guard. Also, I had no money to pay for *el morbito*, "the bite," the bribe, that I had heard was paid in Mexican jails. So how was I to win free, after all?

Again she moved into me to where the fragrance of her swirled about me to upset the senses. Her eyes shone wild. Of a sudden, I aged. It came to me with a jolt, like being thrown on hard ground by a mean horse. This "little bird" was full-feathered out. It seemed to me that I was plenty old to do anything, and the first thing I wanted to do *was* to get my hand under whatever it was Mexican girls wore for shimmies. But she backed away quick.

"I have given the jailer a bottle of wine. It is heavy with a drug my old grandmother knows of. In ten minutes he will not know a footstep from a shadow's whisper. Count those minutes when I am gone. Then call to him that you have finished your food. When he does not reply, you will know he cannot. *Hasta la vista.*"

She was gone before I might worry her more.

Out in the office of the jail, I heard her low and throaty laugh. And the Mex jailer growling back in Spanish. It plainly was something off-color that he said. There was more laughing and whispers and gruntings and soft cries of, "don't, don't!" all of it in Mexican but clear to me as mountain air. Afterwards there came a quiet spell. Then a thud as of something heavy falling to the whitewashed mud floor, and more silence, this time fit to pain the eardrums.

Directly, I tried a yell. Nobody hollered back at me. My breath came hard. Pajarita Morena had played it true to her word. Where the hell was that key?

The key made no sound in the lock, the celldoor swung as though fresh-greased, the empty cells watched me past their bars like ghost holes in the adobe wall. Christ, maybe I would make it yet. Maybe that little old smolder-eyed Mex meant it all. It was enough to make a stone shake. I eased open the outer door, trembling hard.

The jailer was floor-flopped, wine bottle in one hand, a rose-green garter in the other. I rolled him over with my boot. And was glad his pants weren't open-buttoned. I surely didn't want to owe that little sungrinner girl *everything*. I was in deep enough with her, just for the wine and the key. Not even counting the peace and love.

But the freedom, ah!

I took the jailer's pistol and stuck it in my pants-band. There was a short old .44 rimfire Henry rifle in the corner of the room back of the desk. I took that, along with my pockets full of ammunition for both guns. The Mex had a hideout knife, and I took that too. Next, I drug his body in behind the desk. As a last act, I pitched an old horse blanket over him, as it was freezing cold outside and the stove in the office smoked out.

After that, I just slipped to the street door, cracked it three inches, slid on out into the snowy dark. I was at the cantina in twenty shadow-clinging minutes, and the only living things saw me were two cats. I circled four or five dogs that never dreamt a six-foot Missouri boy had soft-walked square around them, not eight feet off, and gone on by with not a woof nor a whimper from them.

Giving the cantina a good big downwind detour, I drifted over the dirt wagon ruts of the street and started to counting doorwells on the far side. But I broke off the count at two. I didn't need three. For Pajarita had said it straight again. There was the little light over *numero tres,* and all the others dark, up and down Calle Cantina. "Damn," I said to the wind and the lonesome coldness of the night. "Ain't that suthin', now."

And went on, shadow-quick, into the archway recess of *numero tres,* square under the little red light.

The Hero

Pajarita got up from the bed. I watched her go and wash herself and come back. The shine of our one candle in the room made her body look unreal, it was that slim and beautiful, yet full where it should be full. She laid back down with me, and I loved her again and we rested a quiet spell, still holding on. She was wondrous to me.

But it grew so still, by and by, that she said to me, "*Hombre,* listen." And I did and heard the loud ticking of the old Spanish granddad clock over near the washbasin stand. "You hear it, Tomas?"

"Yes. *Qué hora es?*"

"Eleven," she said. "There is only one hour now."

She meant that the stage for Arizona pulled out at midnight. We had been talking of how I was to get away when I got there from the jail. She had told me a Mexican story. Some of it in English, which she spoke real good. A lot of it in Spanish, which I did not speak so great, but was getting the hang of it.

The idea of her little *fábula* was that, according to her sainted grandfather, *Dios* perpetuate his soul, the wise fox did not run from the dogs but with them. Senor Zorro would double around and trot behind the pack, making the pursuit endless. Or, better yet, would leap into the moving haycart or *carreta* of passing firewood and so remove himself from the countryside preceded by the pack as honor guard or, *qué tal!* even as *dueño primero*, as principal chaperone. The dogs never caught the fox because they never thought to look for him behind them, or in their very company.

Ending the example, Pajarita had smiled and said, "Do you understand that story, Tomasito?"

"No," I'd said. "You'd best lead it past me one more time. At a halter walk."

It was her turn to frown, but it didn't stop her.

"Tonight, Saldano, at the jail, told me Marshal Beck and Deputy Simms will come in on the eastbound stage with the prisoner from Prescott. Saldano had that word by *telégrafo* from Bernalillo early this day. The stage will come before the other one departs. An hour perhaps."

I'd jumped a foot at that.

And should have, for it was past ten o'clock—we had been loving and hugging around and the time had seeped away like campsmoke—when she first told me. Somehow, though I'd wanted to cut and run, right then, she had made it seem "foxier" to wait and "take the midnight stage," a thing no lawman, at least no white lawman, would ever look for an escaped prisoner to attempt.

It had seemed fair enough then, for she made it so by shrugging off her things, one by one, and letting me have what we'd been tussling and giggling over for those flown-by hours of the night. But now, God knew, with eleven o'clock striking and me as loved out as a stray dog, things were tightening like wet rawhide drying over fire.

That little whorehouse room in Santa Fe was like to be the last stop Tom Horn ever made.

The damned marshal and his wiseacre deputy might even now be swinging down off the Prescott stage. At this exact minute, they could be herding their manacled prisoner into the old adobe jail and finding that blockhead Saldano sprawled back of the desk. I had to figure it *could* be that way. And, right now, those white lawmen might be fanning out to cut off the great Missouri fistfighter and fandango-wrecker. The idea of that year in the Santa Fe Jail made me wilder than a mustang.

Of a sudden, the soft-yielding body of Pajarita Morena was *no más importa.* The low voice, the sweet scents of her, the hard, high breasts and appled buttocks, all of it was as if it wasn't there and never had been.

Tom Horn was being run for the first time in his life, and he didn't like the feel of it.

Pajarita had come up to me as I dressed in the smoky darkness of the candle's lowering flame. She was yet naked as the day God sent her seed into her mother, and she touched me with the little brown-pink fingers and said animal things to me, moaning soft and wanting me again; it was way, way late in the night for that.

"*Mujer,*" I said, "*basta!*"

I was reaching for the Henry rifle and the jailer's pistol, stomping into my boots. She shrunk back with a hurt cry, and I took her shoulders in my two hands.

"It ain't you," I said, "and it ain't me. It's only the way things are. I ain't going back to that jail."

I give her a hug and a kiss, and she was crying like a little girl and holding onto me, and I had to break hard-away from her. I could still hear her sobbing in the door-well behind me as I went out into the winter night and sliding along the adobe walls of Calle Cantina, in old Santa Fe, outwardbound for the sagebrush west of town, where the stage road turned south for Bernalillo.

And where, inside the hour, along would come the Prescott run of the Overland Stage Company, six-horse hitched and rolling hightail, long gone from Santa Fe.

There was a three-quarter moon and ragged scud of fairly low clouds, with gusty, dry winds blowing cross-quartering. I dogtrotted about an hour along the stage road. Passed only some Mex wood carts going into town and one man on muleback which looked white but I wasn't sure. None of them saw me. If I had learned one thing on Wyaconda Creek, it was to make myself scarce in just about any landscape. Especially by dark.

I always felt at home in the dark.

So I found the place I wanted, and no trouble. It was a top-out of a little rise that dropped off sharper on the far side. That is, going south toward Bernalillo. Here, the teams would have to move out at a brisk gait to keep the coach off their hind hocks. The coach would be swaying and running "light," and nobody in her, or atop her, would "feel" me go aboard of her from the back. When the teams steadied out and commenced to pull again down off the slope, they wouldn't know the 180-pound difference they had picked up cresting the rise.

It worked just that smooth way, too.

To a point it did anyway.

Which point was down on the flat beyond my rise, with me safe atop the baggage boot and with a fine handholdt on the straps of same, riding free and fancy as a dude.

I had seen this place from up above whiles I was waiting for the stage to get out from Santa Fe. I'd thought then, the way the outcrop of base rock rose in a jumble thirty foot high both sides of the road, what a hell of choice lay it made for a stickup by road agents. But it was 1874 and my imagination was getting the best of my good sense. What kind of a haul could robbers expect from that old Concord rattling through the night toward Bernalillo? Shucks, there wasn't anybody aboard it but some women I could hear talking inside, and a whiskey drummer I could *smell!* Them, and then the crew on the box. One man. An old bastard. The driver. No guard, nobody riding shotgun. Imagination, nothing more. Just hang on and watch for traffic that might spot you on the boot.

Well, Jesus, we were into the rocks now and the old driver was yelling at his leaders and hauling back on his wheelers; the coach skidded slanchwise of the road, and there was a crash of rifle or shotgun fire and the driver pitched off the box like a toy duck in a .22 rimfire gallery. Our skid had raised a big funnel of road dust. Through it I could see three mounted men milling and fighting their own horses. They were all masked and cursing ugly and yelling "get ahold of them headstalls, you dumb bastards!" at each other. But our teams spooked out straight all of a sudden and began to run. The coach stayed upright and I stayed with the coach and, by God, we were away from them and racing.

It was then I remembered we didn't have any driver. About the time I reared my head up to peer over the top-rack luggage to make sure of this, I saw the road ahead dip off to the right, down the face of a big arroyo. It was narrow and plastered to the drop-off cliff like a damn burro track, and there was no chance in the New Mexican world that any six horses would get down it safe with no driver and no brakes set.

In that instant I started to jump for the brush.

Then, atop the women inside beginning to cry out, I heard the voice of a little kid, a girl, sure. And who was going to high roll into a safe place in the sagebrush after that? "Goddamnit!" I yelled. "I don't never have no luck." And I went swarming over the top of that rickety Concord and got to the driver's box.

The lead-team lines and the swing-team lines were all trailing down among the horses in the roadway. The only set I could grab were the wheelers. I jammed on the brake, full-pull, and lay back with every ounce of my 180 pounds on the wheel team's lines. And, oh God, was it an act of His mercy that I was able to get those six horses veered off the roadway and the coach upright just ten foot short of the pitchdown into the cut.

For, just as I got the teams hauled up, out of the black pit of the arroyo comes another stage going against us. Had we gone down over the lip, even with me to drive and with all six lines in hand, we would have hit, head on, with both coaches winding up in the rock-jagged bottom of Big Tesuque Gulch, midway of Agua Fria and Cerrillos, out of Santa Fe.

But it was all right.

My folks piled out of my coach and the passengers in the other Concord got down and heard our story, and all of them was telling me what a hero I had been. I was about to let it go at that when I saw that two of the men in the other coach had a fellow between them that was walking funny. Next thing I noted was that anybody would walk that way with leg-irons cuffed over his pants and boots, and I went down the far side of my coach like a hot-greased cat and would have got away into the sage and piñon scrub clean, except that this balloon-busted woman grabbed aholdt of me and commenced bawling and slobbering on me in her gratitude for saving her and her little girl.

I was about to knee her and break for it, anways, when I felt the poke of a side-by-side shotgun's muzzles in my middle backbones. "Ease away, Horn," the marshal advised. "You been hero enough for one night. Besides, I need you in one piece to drive our rig on into Santa Fe. Our driver will take your run down to Bernalillo."

So that's how I never made it to Bernalillo that night, but got a free ride back to Santa Fe.

They were good about it, though.

They gave me back my old room at the jail and never charged me a thing extra, saving for one quart of wine for Saldano.

I didn't make any fuss over it.

Neither did Saldano.

Fair was fair.

Something Strange

It was something like noon next day when the fat lady who had grabbed me and blubbered about saving her fat little kid showed up at the jail with her husband. The idea was that no boy as clean-cut and valuable a Christian lad as young Tom Horn, Jr. ought to be made to languish in a territorial jail. Not when he hadn't done anything but whip up on a bunch of drunk Mexicans celebrating Christmas Eve.

It's funny how fate picks out certain ones to follow around. It sounds bogus, too, to say that "fate" decides this and dictates that. It's like a body couldn't come up with any better explanation. But fate did dog the trail of Tom Horn, for good and for bad. There was never any other way to figure it. I surely didn't arrange it the way it all came out. It was always that in the nick of down luck, or the last grasp of a good hand, *something strange* took ahold of Tom Horn's cards. Always.

Like in this very case.

It really wasn't the fat lady. Nor even her fat kid. It was her skinny stick of a husband turning out to be nobody but Mr. Murray, general super for the Overland Mail people. And the Overland Mail people having the contract for all the stageline business between Santa Fe and Prescott. So that anybody Mr. Murray wanted to put to work on the line, he could do it.

Yes sir. Mr. Murray drug the town marshal out of his snug bunk that January A.M. He got him to persuade the Mexican judge to open up court on New Year's Day and retry the case of the *Territory of New Mexico* v. *Tom Horn* and, well, ten minutes after that fat lady hit the Santa Fe Jail, I was a free man.

Nor was that the whole of it.

Mr. Murray then put me on as a straight-pay employee of Overland Mail. I wasn't hired to clean out no corrals nor to hitch up relay teams neither. Nor yet to muscle up luggage to top rack or into trunk boot. No sir. The fat lady wasn't going to let the line super put "that fine Christian boy" to such Mexican chores. Her hero wasn't born to shovel manure nor swamp baggage; he was a driver!

The super wasn't that convinced, but he understood who sat on the driver's box at his house. So that is how it went. I was hired on to handle the Santa Fe–Los Pinos run of the regular Overland Mail contract, as of the next morning, Monday, January 2, 1875. It was from that time that the "something strange" commenced in earnest to take over the life of Tom Horn.

For two months I drove the Los Pinos section. They paid me fifty dollars per month. As well, I was provided a rifle. This was supposed to be to be for "guarding the mail and protecting the passengers." Actually, it was to keep up appearances. That is, to remind folks they were "away out in the wild West," but of course safe as hickory nuts in a squirrel holler with good old Overland Mail Company.

It wasn't, however, "west nor wild enough" for me.

I asked for a transfer to the Los Pinos–Bacon Springs run, which was the same as the Crane Ranch run. I was given it and drove this section two more months and wasn't happy yet, so complained to Mr. Murray, who then called me back to Santa Fe. I thought I was fired but instead was given a helper and sent really on west with a special trust —the safe herding of a big bunch of replacement mules to the Beaver Head Creek station. You may think my heart didn't bound up at that news!

Beaver Head Creek was hard by Verde River. That was in Arizona. And in that part of Arizona that was the heart of the wild Apache Indian country. More. Those mules were to replace ones just run off by the Indians. The hostiles were off the reservation again out there. Tom Horn was at last going to get where he'd all along been bound. Out where the fierce red horsemen rode and the U.S. Cavalry bugles blared right behind them.

It was high time, I figured.

Two months short of a year after I had left home, I arrived with the herd of mules at Beaver Head Station. I had over a hundred dollars cash money on me. I had an as-new Winchester '73 rifle, a top saddle horse, a .44 Colt's revolver, and all my own outfit to ride range or work a way station or nighthawk against stock thieves, anything.

Behind me was two thousand miles of chancy trail, Scotland County, Missouri, to Yavapai County, Arizona Territory.

I ought to have had sense enough to lay over and fatten up on the Beaver Head job, but no, not me. Within a few weeks of getting there, I quit Overland Mail and struck out on my own. My course lay down river to Camp Verde, a government post as well as outpost, being the base camp for the Fifth Cavalry. I worked my way, as I always did, and weeks got confused into months—I never could remember time except by seasons or maybe holidays—and it was way late in the summer of '75 that I got to Camp Verde.

There, in the fall, I went to work for a wood contractor supplying the army and government civilians with fuel. My job was night boss, putting me in charge of all the Mexican teamsters and choppers, as well as guarding the work oxen from Indians raiding them. The pay was seventy-five dollars a month, half again what I'd been getting driving stage. The fellow I worked for was George Hansen. He was a foreigner Swede or Skowegian, but all right anyway. The

job lasted till the winter's supply of cordwood was in, three
months. By then, it was Christmas again. I had been away
nearly a year from Santa Fe and still wasn't to Prescott,
where I'd set out to go.

But I had learned a lifetime in that year.

A born Mexican could not separate his Spanish from
mine. I had picked up some Apache. I had grown to six foot
one inch. I was quick as a scrub bull, wily as a water-hole
mustang. I could disappear like a collared wild pig, live on
slime water and green mesquite beans, was a mean fighter
with my hands, expert with either pistol or rifle or sawed-
off shotgun, and getting wise enough not to boast of any of
it. I had passed a birthday that fall, November 20. By my
count, it would make me sixteen, soon as the year turned.
And I didn't believe there was any man I couldn't hold up
my hub of the wagon with. Youth equals ignorance, however. The boy wasn't yet born who could hold even with a
man in a man's game. I would never have made it without
help, but there was that strange force guiding me yet.

In Prescott, a man was waiting for me who would alter
my life forever. The Apache, some of them, called him
El Hombre Hierro, the Iron Man. Others of the hostile bands
called him Old Man Who Is Always Mad. Yet others, those
living on or nearby the army posts, called him Seebie. The
Arizonans, a good many of them, referred to him as that
g.d. son of a bitch. Or, with equal heat, that g.d. *German*
son of a bitch.

The U.S. Cavalry knew him by another name.

As did history and Tom Horn.

It was Al Sieber.

Hello Prescott

Prescott looked like home to Tom Horn.

I came to it over the Mingus Mountains by the pass

above the mines at Jerome. Then down the long sweeps of that high-country grass, which was as fine a cow and antelope pasture as God ever made, into the Granite Dells. Once past the dells, the town lay before you in its cup of gray rock and green pine.

Near on sat the unbelievable spreadout of buildings that was Whipple Barracks, the biggest army settlement west of Fort Leavenworth, Kansas. Whipple was where I was bound, only my luck or my chance or whatever you want to call it hadn't told me so yet. First, it sent me on into Prescott itself. And, once into that place, I saw what it was that made this main hub of Yavapai County rouse up my memories of old Missouri.

Prescott was built by middle westerners, not Mexicans. It looked more like Memphis, my hometown, than it did anything in New Mexico or what I had seen, so far, in Arizona. It had a town square and false-front Kansas City buildings all around it. The houses fanning away into the rocks back of the center of town could have been freighted in and reerected from Topeka, Saint Joe, Independence, Sedalia, Jeff City, why, just anyplace a body could name from back home. Hell, better even. The houses in Prescott were painted. And the hotels, like the Yavapai House, were full of brass spittoons and real-live palm trees planted in dirt, where you could stub out your cigar butts, handy as anything. It was a real town, Prescott.

The saloons began just beyond the stage office at Gurley Street and Mount Vernon Avenue and ran from there on. I had heard the rumor that there were other businesses than sour-mash mills in Prescott. But from what I could see, riding in at ten A.M. of the morning, it appeared from the sheer number of saloons that there would be more whiskey drunk in that one town than in all the rest of Arizona Territory. It was told about that Prescotters used whiskey to chase their water with. A man had to admit it was possible. There likely was more rotgut than good water available.

The only things natural that growed there was granite outcrops, rock dust, and red-bark bull pines. The creek that ran through town was said to be damp in certain years but mostly it ran to ragweed, rusty cans, chicken dusting puddles, and old bedsprings. It was therefore and desperately needful, the natives claimed, to drink bottled fluid so as not to dehydrate and die of thirst right spang in the middle of the big city. As far as I saw, even that early in the morning, a scant few of them were taking any chances on such a terrible end.

I decided it had been a long ride from Verde.

Besides, at the 5,600-foot altitude, the wind, just then on the rise, cut at a man like an Apache scalp ax. After a quick tour of the square and turn of the sights along Whiskey Row and Tomcat Alley, with detours to see the old log Governor's Mansion and the site where they were aiming to raise up the new all-stone courthouse, the damn wind got sharper still. I reckoned I had seen enough of the tourist attractions to hold me till noon dinner.

What I needed was a shot of that antidehydrater.

I shanked a spur into the flank of the rangy bay I was riding and swung him for the hitchrail outside the Red Geronimo Saloon & Theatre of the Performing Artes.

At the time, I thought nothing of that place's name. But the day in my life was fast running up on me when *Geronimo* would mean the difference of live or die for Tom Horn. And I would remember back to that morning in Prescott, and the Red Geronimo.

For now, I only wanted a drink before setting out to find lodgings less splendid than the potted palm trees of the Yavapai House, yet still more accommodating than my high-cantle Mex saddle for a pillow and the bay's trail-sour horse blanket for coverlet. The need was imperative. Or at least the choice of common brains.

In late December in old Arizona it can freeze a man's nose-drips twixt nostil and mustache. Cold? You can break off your horse's breath and melt it in your mess-kit can for coffee water. It gets so cold at five thousand feet in north central Arizona that the snow won't fall but freezes in the air. You have to build a fire to thaw out enough of a hole in the flakes to move about and breathe. In Verde, I heard of a man up in Holbrook that froze his stream solid in a rainbow arch from his front-fly to the hole in the crapper seat. He couldn't bust himself loose, either, for fear of snapping off his pecker. So he set fire to the cob box on the wall next the seat, figuring to free up his stream from the heat. But somebody had soaked the dry cobs in bear grease to soften the swipe of them against the winter chafe. The smoke from the oily cobs clotted up the outhouse air so thick and fast the poor feller strangled hisself and wasn't found till the spring melt thawed his body and let it fall out the door.

So I needed that one glass of rotgut rye I had promised myself at the bar of the Red Geronimo Saloon.

As it turned out, one glass wouldn't do it. I ordered up one more. Which called for a third to fortify with full safety against the storm that surely must be building up outside. Three good belts of course called for four. To which five is only one more. So I had that.

When I next looked around, I was laid out snug in the snow of an alley just off Gurley Street. From the mine-shaft blackness all about, it had to be way along in the night. Also, my pockets was all turned out, empty as a whore's hope chest, and I was right back where I started out in Kansas City in that other alley—flat-ass busted.

My bay horse was gone, my whole outfit with him, including my new 1873 model Winchester. My colt belt pistol was likewise lifted. Along with my money poke pinned inside my horsehide button-up vest, near some two hundred dollars saved up from the three months of wood camp bossing in Verde.

But it wasn't until I wiggled my toes to see if I was still working all of a piece that I discovered what I thought was the last straw; the sons of bitches, or some son of a bitch, had stolen my boots!

But it stayed for another, real son of a bitch, to apply the actual clincher, or drencher.

Down the alley came a mongrel stray dog. He was nosing into every trash barrel, sniffing out any crumpled paper or heap of horse dung that might give promise of something to eat, or at least carry off and bury. But when he got to me, he veered off. After a long stare and a spooky snort or two, he lifted his leg on my hat, wheeled about, scraped snow and grit in my face, and traveled on out into Gurley Street without so much as one good-bye woof.

I took that dog's opinion as a portent. He had been sent to do his work on me by *mi sombra,* my shadow.

The Mexicans say that a man's shadow not only follows him but goes ahead of him. It stalks his life but guides him

too. It was the same thing as an Anglo like me saying his
fate led him on. It was what I called "something strange,"
back when I had felt it push me along so strong in Santa
Fe. And it was what had meanwhile come to make me
understand that Tom Horn was an *hombre de sombra* for
real and forever; a man not truly responsible for his mis-
deeds and wrong directions.

Most won't believe that a growed-up fellow could lay
there in the freezing slush, peed on by a passing dog, and
have such thoughts to parade through his aching head. But
most won't believe anything of what happened to Tom
Horn, either. God knows they proved that. So it's no point
in trying to explain a cowpen Spanish saying like *hombre de
sombra* to them. All a man can do is tell his life the way it
truly went; and Tom Horn truly did ride his whole life with
somebody else's hands on the reins of his horse.

What drew me away from Scotland County, Missouri?
Lured me into that alley in Kansas City? Directed me onto
that flatcar bound for Newton, Kansas, with Staked Plains
Bronson aboard? What put me in the freight-wagon business with teamster Blades? Brought fat Mrs. Murray to
make her skinny husband hire me on the drive the Overland Mail? Steered Pajarita Morena into my cell, and me
to her red-lighted *casa numero tres* down old Calle Cantina?

I will tell you what; it was the same thing that got me
out of the wood-chopping venture at Camp Verde and bent
my tracks to Prescott where, as will be seen, my life took
its first deep set from me meeting up with the one man
who would change it all for me. The man my *sombra* had
in secret store for me six months down the trail from that
night the mutt dog peed me into getting up out of the
snow behind the Red Geronimo Saloon, determined to once
and for all give up hard liquor and take that fateful new
direction in my life.

Hello, Prescott, and good-bye! Tom Horn was outward
bound to find Al Sieber.

Seebie's Boy

Lucky for any damn fool to be caught sockfoot in December, I knew where I could totter to and at least be given shelter for the night. It was to the stage company I had spotted back out on Gurley, before the saloons began. I could tell them I drove for Murray and the Overland Mail people. There was a sort of comradeship mongst all stagers. Like with roundup crews in cattle country. Or old rodeo cowboys. They would take me in on trust. No question.

I began to suffer my first maybes when I drew up outside the place and spraddled back to gawk up at the company name. It took the whole of the front of the horse barn to spell out. My socks froze to the wagon-rut slush before I finished it:

THE VERDE VALLEY & MOGOLLON RIM, NORTH PHOENIX, BUMBLE BEE, OAK CREEK, COCONINO COUNTY & SOUTH FLAGSTAFF STAGELINE & LIVERY COMPANY, AMALGAMATED.

Christ Amighty, I thought. Might be that such a grand company would, after all, scowl at late-night shelter seekers from a puny outfit like Overland Mail. However, a man, like a gelded jackass, could at least try.

I walked out of my ice-stiff socks, leaving them standing side-by-each in the middle of Gurley Street. Barefoot, I hammered on the office door, still not quite sobered even with the half-mile hike up from the alley behind the Red Geronimo. Inside, I heard a lot of unfriendly language and wheezing coughs, and the office door was creaked open by an old man in his nightshirt, eyeshade, knee-high boots and carrying a 10-gauge messenger's shotgun, both outside hammers cocked.

This rheumy old rooster sized me up with one squint. "Git," he said. "If one more drunk wakes me up at three A.M. of the morning, I am going to increase his heft by four ounces of DuPont double-ought buck right square in both apples of his goddamn ass."

For emphasis, he triggered off the left barrel over my hat about three inches. I caught a part of the hot wad and some black powder chunks in my face. If that was the old coot's idea of where my butt was, there would be little telling where he might plant that right-hand barrel. In accordance, I did not take the time to ask any more of him, but took off and ran like a rabbit.

Once around behind the horse barn, I held up.

I was in the back corral, or "yard" of the place, where the line kept its busted-down and out-of-service equipment. Ah, yonder was the repair shed, a lean-to ramada, housing at the time the run's road-service wagon. This was actually a big toolbox on wheels and, shivering fit to loosen my rear teeth with the black cold, I figured that toolbox would do to spare my life from freezing. It took no more than ten minutes to chuck out the tools and bust a bale of hay open and dump it into the box. When I'd pulled shut the lid over my head behind me and snugged down into that soft-fine native hay, I was better off than a lost dog in a dry barrel full of butcher-shop sawdust. The hell with that old grouch and his 10-gauge. I was toasty as a tickbird on an old bull buffalo's rump.

When I woke up, it was to a jarring squeal of wagon axles and jolt of iron rims. By the time I could recollect where I was, the road-service wagon had hauled to a stop and its crew pried open the top of their toolbox. When they found me inside, rather than their rim irons, spoke wrenches, hub spanners, and the like, they were not happy. I tried to make up for their gloom.

"Why," I said, bright as brass, "where at ever can we be? This here surely ain't where I purchased my ticket for. This *ain't* North Phoenix, is it?"

The crew boss pulled a rim-springing bar out from under the driver's box. "No," he said, hefting it in my direction, "it ain't North Phoenix, it's South Prescott. This here is the wagonyard at Whipple Barracks, and we got a contract to maintain their ambulances and other rolling stock. Except that some young smart aleck done pitched all our handtools out'n the toolbox and filled it full of fresh hay. Which same half-growed, whiskey-pickled s.o.b. is right now going to get this here spring bar bent into a size-eight horseshoe square over the back of his cowboy hat. Up and out of thar, you damn bum!"

Whether or not he and his two mean-looking helpers meant to murder me was never contested. Just then, a herd of cavalry remount horses, leastways three, four hundred of them, came thumping through the yard on the whoop-and-holler run, hazed along by four riders. On the instant, I seen real trouble shaping.

At the back of the wagonyard at Whipple, there was an arroyo about twenty feet deep and sharp-filled with outcrop rock, sides and bottom. If those idiots driving those high-grade remounts didn't get the point of the bunch turned hard right in the next thirty seconds, Fort Whipple and the Fifth Cavalry was going to be out about fifty head of replacement stock.

There wasn't any time for debate.

The boss herder was sweeping by the repair wagon even as I saw the danger. I just bailed out of the toolbox and onto his horse's rump behind him without thinking it over any longer than to wind up and make the jump.

Next thing, I barred one arm over the boss herder's throat from behind, lifted him wide of his damn saddle, and dropped him like throwing off the mailsack at Bacon Springs or Crane Ranch without slowing the stagecoach. Into the empty saddle I went. That poor horse must of thought he'd been mounted by a six-foot cougar. I put the spur rowels into him to their shanks and nearly broke his ewe-neck turning him in full stride to his right. But he didn't fall, and we did get the point of the running bunch headed short of the sharp-rock arroyo. And by *we*, I mean me, Tom Horn, and that skinny-necked mustang I'd appropriated by long-jump from the tool wagon of the Verde Valley & Mogollon Rim Stageline Company. Those blasted other herders never even knew why their big remuda swerved so hard. In fact, one of the bastards kept right on going and wound up in the bottom of the arroyo himself. In further fact, I was still sitting my borrowed plug up on the rim of the gully and yelling down at this dim-brain that, if his horse had to be shot, he could figure to get the same medicine, and I would be just the doctor to give it to him, when up puffs no less than an oak leaf, or "light" colonel of the cavalry, on foot and mad as a dog-bit badger. He proved to be on my side.

When he had added his sentiments to mine in the direction of the banged-up herder down in the rocks, he wheeled about on me.

Colonel," I said in hopeful haste, "I'm right sorry I let him get by me. But it was all I could do to get the herd turned."

"I saw it all," the officer said. "How much do they pay you down at the stageline?"

I started to come up with some offhand yarn, then realized he thought I was working with the repair-wagon crew, out from Prescott. So I changed to a better lie.

"Seventy-five per, and found, colonel. But—"

"Don't but me. The army will pay you a hundred, no keep. Come on."

He started off and I held back only long enough to see the boss crewman coming our way on the quick-trot, still swinging the rim-spring bar.

"Yes sir!" I saluted the bowlegged little officer, and that's how I got to be chief herder for the U.S. Cavalry remount station at Fort Whipple, Arizona, in January of eighteen and seventy-six.

Early in '76, when I went to work for the Quartermaster herding the remount stock at Fort Whipple, all the horses came overland from California. They came in big trail herds of some four hundred head each. I was the boss of watching them all until the various posts throughout the territory sent and got their due consignments. Since Prescott was headquarters for the Department of Arizona, I handled every head that went into service the first six months of that year. It was some job of work.

There was but three of us to do it, too. Me and two Mexicans. One of them was half Apache, his mother's half, and he talked more Indian than Mexican. Neither one of them spoke English. Whatever I had yet to pick up of Mex or Apache lingo, I surely came by most of it in those five, six months handling horses by the thousands with Julio Vasquez and Tagidado Morales.

Morales was the half blood. Because I could speak his

tongue and was so dark of hide myself, he thought I had to be part Indian of some kind. From that, he trusted me. When it came time, along early in July, for the three of us to say *adiós*—the last horses for the year was allotted the Fifth Cavalry and we was out of work—Tagidado hung back when Julio rode away.

He was an older man, ugly as sin or, as his friend Julio said, as his Apache mother. "*Niño*," Tagidado said, touching my shoulder, "I want to give you something." He reached up and took off the turquoise earring he wore in his left lobe. I had marked it many a time as a most curious piece, but I had never asked him about it. That it was of Indian design was evident. But it looked terrible old too, and I knew it wasn't just Arizona Indian. Now he reached and put the bauble in my hand, closing my fingers over it mighty careful. "Keep it," he said, "but a condition goes with it; a prayer really, *Comprende?*"

"*De seguro*," I answered, "go ahead."

He told me I was a young man and that he knew I was spiritbound to the *Indios* and would one day go and live among them. He meant the Apaches, of course, and not the tame ones. "I had a son," he said. "The people of Mangas Coloradas took him as a small child. We heard they traded him to the Warm Springs people, but he was never returned, nor was it even known if he lived. When he was taken, he wore upon a circlet chain about his small neck the mate to this turquoise earring of the feathered serpent. Perhaps today, should he have lived, there somewhere rides a young Apache of your own tender years who will wear that earring in his right lobe. If you ever see him, show him your earring and tell him its story. The rest I will leave to God."

I didn't think too much of the story, as Mexicans are not to be believed except at considerable risk. I assured this old man, however, that I would be faithful to the trust and would wear the earring when it came to pass that I should go among the wild Apache.

"Remember. to do it," old Tag said. "It will preserve your life one day. That sign has medicine power."

He got on his runty Sonora mule and started off.

"Hey!" I yelled after him. "*Alto!*"

He waited, and I loped my horse up to him. "Listen," I said, "I am a shadow man, you understand?"

"Yes, of course," old Tag eyed me noddingly, "I knew that you were. We all are. But only some of us know it. Most do not. What do you want, *joven?*"

"Well, you are right, you see. I have always dreamed of *los Indios*. The *broncos*, the wild Indians, you understand, not the *reducidos*, the tame ones. Yet until this moment that you spoke of going to live with them, I had never thought of that. That was my shadow telling your shadow, eh?"

The old half-breed shrugged. "*Pues*, perhaps. But one does not require his *sombra* to inform him of your feeling for my mother's people. What is it, now?"

"I want to know what is the best way for a white man to find the *broncos?* I mean, without getting killed doing it. What should I do if I want to go and live with the wild Apache?"

"Easy," said old Tag. "Go and find Seebie."

"Seebie? *Quién es?*"

"Al Sieber."

He said it as though I would at once say, Oh! of course, Al Sieber! Now why didn't I think of that?

But I just frowned in my special dense way, and old Tag said, "What? You do not know Sieber? You never heard of the name?"

"Never. Not till this moment, *anciano*."

Later, men would say that I couldn't possibly have failed to hear of Al Sieber working at Camp Verde and then Fort Whipple all those months. Whipple and Verde were important posts. Anyone hanging around them must have heard of Sieber. The only alternative was that Tom Horn was a damned liar (again!) and never set foot in either place. He couldn't have it both ways.

Well, he did.

People forget that in 1876 Al Sieber wasn't of the same renown he was by 1886. You might as well say that anybody in that day who hadn't heard of Tom Horn was a damned liar and never lived in Arizona Territory. But who was Tom Horn in 1876? Nobody. And Al Sieber wasn't that much more of a somebody either.

Except to the Apaches.

And, ah! that was the difference.

Old Tagidado knew it.

"Well, *hijo mío*," he said patiently, "now you have

heard the name. And it is the one you must know if you are a white man thinking to find the true *broncos*."

"All right," I replied, "can you then tell me, *tío*, where I may find this Al Sieber? *A dónde está, amigo?*"

Old Tag gave me a mixed Indian and Mex look.

"Your *sombra* served you well in sending you to ride after me and ask this question," he said. "It so happens that Seebie has been in Prescott ten days, and what do you suppose he has been doing? Looking for someone to work with him. He has been given a big promotion to chief of scouts and requires an assistant now. *Qué tal!* And do you know what else, *chico?* No, you don't. Well, I will tell you; he is leaving today and he did not find anyone. If you hurry, you may catch him still."

"*A dónde?*" I repeated. "*Nombre Dios, a dónde?*"

"You know of the place called *Geronimo Rojo?*"

"Uncle," I said, wheeling my horse, "I know it well. *Adiós. Vaya con Dios. Wagh!*"

And I lit out on the flat gallop for Prescott and the Red Geronimo Saloon, not even thinking to say *mil gracias* to old Tag for his information.

Well, that was all right.

He would understand.

We were both *hombres de sombras*.

It wasn't our faults the way things happened to us, or that we got directed into doing them to others.

You didn't worry if you were a shadow man.

You just lit out.

You did, anyway, if fate had just tapped you on the shoulder to be Seebie's Boy.

Miss Pet

I had a good horse and outfit under me once more. I had earned myself back into a decent state, had money in my pocket, and a purpose in my mind. If I was out of a job, it was by hard work, not by prowling Tomcat Alley or drinking Whiskey Row dry. Moreover, I had good references. Matter of fact I was riding past one of them on my way into Prescott. This was the firm of Tully, Ochoa, & DeLong, beef contractors and general freighters for the military. Between horse herds from California coming in to Whipple, I'd filled in delivering beef herds for them to local Indian agencies. They were mighty good people, but I just waved at them now riding past on my classy blood bay gelding. The work paid cheap and wasn't steady. Nothing like good enough to compare with going to live with the wild Indians. *Wagh!*

Ah! that was a grand morning to be sixteen years old, yet grown tough and smart as a desert-bred mustang. There is no time in a man's life so glorious as that minute when he figures the boy in him has at last haired over, making him full-grown and ready to growl.

Not unless it's that other minute old Tag told me about, where a man is truly growed old but feels one brief day like he was a boy again and could pee his mark as high on the wall as any *macho* youngstud in Mexico.

Well, naturally I couldn't speak to that. I just reckoned nobody had better challenge Tom Horn to any wall-wettin' contests that particular sunfresh July morning of eighteen and seventy-six.

Wasn't I about to find the great Al Sieber down at the Red Geronimo Saloon? Hadn't my *sombra* sent me to him by way of old Tag? Wasn't I as good as hired by the new chief of scouts for the whole Fifth Cavalry, at San Carlos, the main Apache Indian reservation in the territory? Well, wasn't I?

No, as a matter of fact, I surely was not.

I never even got to the Red Geronimo Saloon. I was stopped on my way to it, going by Madame La Luna's New Orleans House, taking the shortcut through Tomcat Alley. Madame came stomping out into the street just as I drew up. She spooked hell out of my hot-blooded red bay gelding, and it was plain she was mainly unsettled about something. "Here, you," she said, spotting me. "You look like you had more muscle between your ears than compis mentis. Get down off that damn horse and come along. I've got a chore for you. Pays quick cash and no questions. Come along in, didn't you hear me? Don't just sit up there gawking with your mouth hung open fit to trap flies. Ain't you never seen a woman in a nightgown before?"

"No ma'am," I said, touching the brim of my hat, polite. "Not so close to high noon, I ain't."

She wasn't young but she had a body like she was, and she saw me admiring her splendid lines and she mellowed down a bit from that. Fact is, I swear she blushed a tinge.

"Goddamnit," she said, "foller me, boy."

Well, I went into her whorehouse with her and sure enough she did have a job of work for somebody laid out in there. It was a fellow built like *the* prize herdsire Hereford bull of the whole cow business. Big and blocky and thick-strong all over, and mean-looking like he would charge you on or off your horse. He was passed out cold drunk snoring on a tapestry settee in the red plush lobby of the place. And, saving for his stovepipe riding boots and Mexican cartwheel spurs, complete with pure silver jingle-bobs, he was naked as a new-hatched nest-bird. "Jesus H. Christ, ma'am," was all that I could think to say.

"Yes," she agreed. "And I will give you five dollars to haul this drunk son of a bitch out of my decent house without waking him up or scratching my hardwood floors. Here are his clothes, and when he comes alive you tell him he owes me for Clara, Bonnie May, Charlene, and Pet. And tell him Pet says if he ever again tries to bed her with his boot-irons on, she will cut off his cajones and mail them to his C.O. at San Carlos in a plain paper bag. Now get!"

I thanked the lady for the work, taking pause only to struggle on the man's pants for him and to ask Madame La Luna to please donate my five-dollar fee to Miss Pet so she might see the doctor about her spur cuts.

"You're a nice lad," Madame said to me. "Don't ever take up with the likes of this *lunático*. You would do better to join up with the Apache Indians."

"That's remarkable," I said, admiring her again. "How ever did you guess I aimed to do that?"

"Do what, boy?" she snapped. "Don't fret me."

"No ma'am," I said, tipping my wide hat again. "I

wouldn't never do that to any lady. I just purely was wondering how come you to know I was bound to join up with the Apache Injuns?"

"Oh, my God!" she cried, clapping hands to head. *"Two* lunatics!" Then, addressing herself to the half dozen disclad young females now peeking into the lobby at all the fuss. "Here, you, Pet. This young jackass won't take my five dollars for dragging this dead piece of meat out of here. Wants you to have the money for the doctor to tend your spur gashes. Ain't that rich!"

She commenced to laughing like a loon, but Miss Pet hipswung her way over to me with a sober face. And, oh but she was something! The most slimmest and beautiful blonde girl—and I mean all of her blonde—that I had ever dreamed to see in that life. She sidled up to me with a downglance look and murmured husky-voiced, "I want to thank you, mister. Truly I do." After which she eyed me up and down and in the middle, and she stopped there and sort of stared at me and added, "You can take it out in trade anytime, tall boy. Just put it on my bill, Madame," she said to the La Luna woman. "Oh, my!" With that, she touched me where she oughtn't to have, and all the girls giggled and I just grabbed up the Hereford bull man off the settee and drug him out into Tomcat Alley, sweating something fearful.

And that is how, of course, I met Al Sieber.

It surely may not seem a proper way, nor moment in a man's time, that he would choose to see printed of himself in the history books. Not neither for Sieber nor Tom Horn. But when you set out to tell of your life and have promised to put it down in a true way, then you don't stand short with your story.

That *was* the way that the Missouri farm boy ended his long journey to the West and came at last to live with the wild Indian horsemen of his rainy night dreams.

Book Two

San Carlos

I am certain I had no useful remembrance of anybody inside the madame's place having said who the bull-bodied naked man might be. Nevertheless, when I had propped him up against the adobe wall on the shade side of the alley and doused him with a hatful of water from the cathouse cistern, and he had come around wheezing and groaning like a gut-shot agency beef, it popped square out of me. "Excuse me, Mr. Sieber, but I have come to take the job. Here's your neckerchief and underdrawers."

He squinted toward my voice. "Awwhhrrugggl" he strangled. "Who led us into this ambush? Which way did the troops go?" The thick German tongue faltered, the eyes cinching tighter yet with whiskey pain. "Job, for Christ sake? Who are you? What day is it? We still in Prescott?"

I gave him his answers, naturally saving my name for last. I could see him wince again for some reason.

"Oh, by Jesus, yes, Tom Horn," he said. "I'd ought to have remembered. Why, anybody knows of Tom Horn. What day did you say it was? The seventeenth? My God, I'm due back at San Carlos day afore yesterday. Ach!"

He spoke with a heavy German accent but used American words strung together like any Anglo would. Now and again he would throw in some German for free, but never bothered to translate any of it or even appear to know he was using it. But of course I spotted that language right off. Neither of my sets of grandparents spoke good English, all being Pennsylvania Dutch and of German birth, using that speech mostly. I was the sole one of the Horn kids to pick it up, and that was from my gift with tongues. It always was that I could learn a language in no time.

67

So now I said again to Sieber that I had come for the job as his new "boy," and how proud I would be to serve him and learn from him all about the wild Apache Indians. But this time I said it to him in very good low *deutsch,* and he came up on his feet against the wall like he had got a letter from home. *Wunderbar!*

From that moment of our German bonding, I could do no wrong in the piercing black eyes of Al Sieber.

He was a man of the most uncontrollable savage temper and fighting spirit, really a terror when aroused. But in all of the coming sunshine years that we were together in the U.S. Cavalry's employ, and outside of it too in the Arizona Territory, Al Sieber never one time treated me in any but a gentle and kind manner.

Those who said in later days that he low-rated Tom Horn and those who denied the true things I told of our Apache scouting days are damned scoundrels and low thieves of a fine man's memory. Seebie was the stanchest friend I ever had. And maybeso the strangest, too. I will let that judgment make itself. For right then and there in Tomcat Alley, he merely cocked his bullet head on its oak stump of a neck at me and said, "All right, Horn. You're hired. Help me to find my mule."

The trip to San Carlos was well over one hundred miles. As well, Sieber had said that he was already a day late in returning there. He then proceeded to take ten days on the way.

We hunted deer, fished for trout, shot birds. We lollygagged and lay around our camps like we had the whole summer. But Sieber had his reason. He always had his reason. He was sizing up his "boy."

Although I could not have known it then, Tom Horn was to become the old German's young right arm for the next nine years of the ten-year Apache campaign. But Sieber understood it then. As he told me later, the Apache wars were going to go on for many years. He himself was aging and had been crippled for life by a friendly Apache gone *bronco.* If he was going to keep his job as chief of scouts for the Fifth U.S. Cavalry, he had to find somebody he could lean on. He had already discarded six or seven prospects in his search, when he "found" me, as he always told it, "lost and crying for his mother, outside a whorehouse in Prescott, Arizona."

He subsequently confessed he never thought much of me to commence with. I was just barely better than nobody to ride back to the reservation with. But I *was* young and willing to work. It was only two, three days out, he said, that he began to see I might do for his purpose.

Along the way he would test this idea. We would be riding along maybe an hour with not a word passed when, of a sudden, he would haul in his mule.

"Say," he'd ask, "you spot anything peculiar along the way here?"

"Not unless you mean them tracks we been follering."

"Tracks. What tracks?"

"Them three squaws."

"Squaws you say?"

"Yes sir. Two Apache, one Pueblo, maybe Pima."

"What the hell you talking about, Horn?"

"Apache women track with their feet close together. Pueblos and some others of them pot-maker Injuns walks wide. What peculiar did you pick up, Mr. Sieber?"

"Hmmmm," he would answer and kick his mule in the ribs and lope on out, leaving me to ponder the matter.

He didn't fool me long. If Al Sieber was watching me, I was studying him right back. And it was working. Sieber was not much of a talker, ever. Yet he would consider questions, I discovered, if they were put in a sober way. Above all, you must not get funny with him. He was hell on smartass answers, or camp pranks. "Don't jackass around," he would snap. "Some poor soldier may get shot while you're having your hee-haws. Simmer down."

And God help you if you went past that.

I never saw Al Sieber take kindly to a joke on him or grin off any wiseacre comment aimed in his direction. I got to understanding why. Life hadn't been all that funny for him. Born in the old country in 1844, one of nine children, he had left home to come to America and serve it on the Union side in the Civil War. He was many times wounded, lastly with a ball that shattered a knee and ankle that healed crooked and left him with a permanent twisting limp. Later, of course, that *bronco* Apache (the notorious Apache Kid, whom Sieber reared from a fondling) shot him in the same ankle, and it never healed. Sieber had to dress it two times a day the rest of his life. Officer friends from the big war had told him of the West, and one had given him a letter of commendation to General George "Red Beard" Crook, then in command of the Third Cavalry, in the Arizona Territory. Crook, who knew men, mules, hostile Indians, and rare bird eggs in about that order, hired on the powerful German in the line he had followed in the war. Sieber always proudly described this status as "battalion scout and horse troop forager." Whatever that meant, Crook soon made him chief of scouts for the Third Cavalry. He began at once to earn the reputation old Tag had been so astounded I did not know about. But, when later transferred to the Fifth Cavalry command, he had been going downhill, due to both the ignorance of the officers in that outfit as to what scouts—civilian employee scouts like Al Sieber—did and did not do, and also from his aggravating injuries.

When I met Al Sieber, he carried twenty major knife, lance, arrow, and gunshot wounds in his body. When he quit the service ten years later, he had garnered another eight serious scars. Also at that time of discharge or separation, he carried fifty-three knife cuts on the butts and stocks of his various guns. He said that twenty-eight of these represented those Apaches who had left their marks on him. People have called all that a lot of nonsense and hogdip. Not me. It remains my opinion that Sieber ought to have had a *hundred* and fifty-three Apache slashes on that gunwood of his. He easily killed more hostile Indians than the remainder of us put together. It was indeed from him that Tom Horn first learned that the surest way to guarantee the good behavior of an enemy, any skin color, was to kill him. "Explain it to him the once," the old German became wont to tell me, "then when he does it again, kill him. It is a system that never fails."

A system that never fails. Those five words were to mark my life. Yet when first I heard them, my guardian shadow was asleep. It did not warn me. When next they fell upon my ear, they were from my own lips. But that was twenty years and seven hundred miles away. By then, I did not even remember where I had learned them, but only why; it was to use them like Judas in the Bible, as pieces of silver to buy the death of a fellowman.

At the time that Al Sieber spoke them, however, I had not yet so much as thought of me killing anybody. Surely I wasn't dreaming of shooting or knifing Indians, as my aim was to live with them. True, I had a pretty hard view of life and was not a fearful sort. But that was concerning hardships and maybe not fretting about anybody else doing harm to me. Nobody sets out to just shoot down other folks. I know full well what's been said of Tom Horn, coming to that, but those that say such brutal things of me are fools. No boy of sixteen summers is hiring on as a killer. Not in his mind, he isn't. If his life comes to that in its ending, then that's why he leaves his story of how that happened. Of how a good man can turn to such dark ways and never understand that he has done it, or even that it is wrongful and wicked, played his way. And even say, as Tom Horn will say to his grave, that he never harmed an innocent man but once. And that one man was himself.

So, no, when Sieber said that about giving a guilty man one more chance, then killing him, that sixteen-year-old Missouri boy riding by his side over the Sierra Ancha range toward his new life with the Apache *bronco* Indians, did not "hear" the words as meaning exactly what they said. It was only the sort of thing rough men said on the western frontier. It was spoke as a way of thinking out loud. Just of warning those you did business with, or might, that they would not get two chances to "muddy the water at my camp."

I actually thought then that Sieber was letting me know, by saying such a thing, that I was to be mightily cautious how I answered to him in the coming work.

Certainly, there was nothing dark in my mind that last July morning when we drew near journey's end.

I could think of nothing but those Apache Indians and Sieber's gruff hints about their government home.

The big Apache reservation called San Carlos, he said, was two pony rides across and three up and down. Something in the practical order of a hundred miles by about sixty. But he was not talking of boundaries and blocks as they would be drawn on the army's maps, he warned. His meaning was that piece of the actual country that the Indians understood they had to stay on, or else. Now that land lay ahead twixt Salt River Canyon, the Gila Mountains, Escudilla Peak, and the south terminal of the Holbrook stage road, at McNary Junction. It was a "God-lonesome chunk of real estate for size," Sieber said, and of that quality described by the old scout as "the natural hell where mother rattlesnakes tell their babies they will go, if they ain't good."

Since to reach it the burly German and I had just come across the hidden pine paradise of the Tonto Basin, scaled the great Mogollon Rim, and loafed south along its precipice through virgin ponderosa and incense cedar timber watered by clear creeks bank-deep in mountain meadow grass to our mounts' bellies, you can imagine how that slag heap of bare rock, salt sage, and Gila monster turds hit my eager eye. I simply could not accept it when we busted out to our overview of it from the east shoulder of Aztec Peak, breathing our saddle animals there at about six thousand feet.

"Well," Sieber said, "that's it."

"Jesus," I said. "That's what? The back door into God's private brickyard?"

"San Carlos," Sieber grunted.

"No! Why, that is the forlornest looking goddamn stretch of snagrock granite and skeleton sand this side of the Jornado del Muerto on the Santa Fee Trail. It can't be San Carlos. We must have died and gone to hell."

"It's San Carlos," Al Sieber said. "Ride out."

So it was that I, Tom Horn, came to San Carlos Apache Indian reservation and the true beginning of my life among the wild bands of the *Chi hinne,* the red people of Apacheria.

Everybody knows my story in the Arizona Territory days, and nobody wants to hang me for what I done down there. But it all weighs in the final scale, and so what follows must be judged against the rest of it to end with a fair memory of Tom Horn.

My time mongst the *broncos,* both of Arizona and the Mexican states of Chihuahua and Sonora, went a ten-year run, and it came out about a even mix of hell and happy things, 1876 through 1886. And I would give all my life to live any one of those ten years again. To ride and raid once more with my blood-oath Chiricahua brothers, or campaign with my dear-remembered fellow scouts of the Third and Fifth U.S. Cavalry regiments, Department of Arizona.

Lord God, but those were times few white men then living knew, and no white man now living can ever know again. The times are gone, and the wild Apache vanished forever. I wish I had died in those grand years when Tom Horn rode knee-and-knee with names like Mangas, Loco, Del Shay, Nana, Kaytennae, Alchise, and Eskiminzin. And when he was the true *chi-kis-in,* the "full brother," to the Four Families of the Chiricahua people, the children of Cochise, Juh, Victorio, and Geronimo.

Ay de mí, as the Mexicans say.

Those were the hours of our lives.

And, ah! how swiftly flown.

Sieber's Mule

At San Carlos, Sieber got me put on the government payroll as what he told the army was "an interpreter of Mexican."

Since most everybody in the territory—white, Indian, and Mex—spoke and savvied enough cowpen Spanish to get by, I queried Sieber as to what sense there was in hiring an interpreter.

"No sense at all," he nodded gruffly. "But you got to

be something. You sure as bobcat sign smells bad don't think
you're a scout yet, do you?"

"No sir, but I mainly hope to become one. It has been
my biggest dream since I was a little tad, back in Missouri.
I would make a prayerful wish on it every night.

Sieber looked at me disgustedly. He had little stomach
for any fancy flying about with words.

"Well," he said, "hold your one hand in front of your
pecker-flap and take a good pee in it. Hold your other
hand out to the side and wish into it hard as you are able.
See which hands flows over first."

He glared at me three blinks of those eyes black as
obsidian rockglass, then growled, "Get your horse and fetch
up my mule. We got Injun business waiting."

You can imagine my excitement at that. Here was Tom
Horn actually at San Carlos Agency in the heart of the wild
Apache country. He was readying to ride out with the
chief of scouts for the entire Fifth Cavalry of the U.S. of
A. And that chief had just said that it was time for them to
get cracking at their dangerous work—finding Indians! I
could scarcely hold in.

I brought up Sieber's famous iron-gray mule from the
picket line, and we got out of there laying a handsome dust.
We went about half a day up into the White Mountains,
following the lonely course of the White River to its joining
with the Black. Here, Sieber drew in his mount. It was but a
mile or so more up the river, he said, to the rancheria
(Apache camp) of the noted chief, Old Pedro. Pedro's band
was a mixed one numbering about one thousand people.
The old chief claimed six hundred of these were men of
war age, a high percentage and risky, even though Pedro
tried faithfully to control them. The point, Sieber concluded,
was that this was an important band of Apaches to the
cavalry, as they could be visited in fair safety and much
could be learned of the renegade *bronco* Apaches.

These "bronks" were the bad Indians of course, and
the ones I yearned to join up with and learn about. So far,
I hadn't seen a solitary one of them and was accordingly
put out to hear the bunch ahead was tame Indians, or rea-
sonably like tame. Still, I listened close to what the old
scout had to say.

Pedro's people called themselves the San Carlos, he went on, which was a white man's name. There wasn't any truly bred San Carlos band. Not in the bloodline sense that there was Gila, Tonto, Mescalero, Jicarilla, and Chiricahua bands of Apaches. But Sieber stressed that, as an outpost or listening place for the army, the rancheria of Old Pedro was a duty post of great value to the cavalry at San Carlos and elsewhere in the Arizona Territory. "Of which fact," he finished, with an odd squint at me, "more may be made later."

For right then, another matter impended. Before we got up to the Apache camp, Sieber said, he wanted me to ride his mule aways so that he might observe if she was favoring her off hindside, as it felt to him she was. He got off her with his usual groan from the pain of his wrong-healed wounds and held her for me. I was some surprised, since he didn't ordinarily permit anybody to handle that she-mule, let alone to ride her. But I figured it best to do what I was asked, or told. So I slid off my bay right smartly and legged up onto Sieber's mule. Next thing I knew, I was laying down in the riverbank rocks mad enough to bend a cold horseshoe in my teeth.

"What was the idee of *that?*" I demanded angrily of Sieber. "You got a rodeo mule there?"

"Oh," said the German. "Now I am right sorry, Horn. But I forgot to warn you she has been trained to mount on the wrong side. She will pitch every time, otherwise. Try her again."

I limped over and caught up the she-beast, got around on her wrong side, and swung up on her again. And lit on the same pile of rocks that I done before, bucked off even harder than the first time. But I was too wobble-kneed to go to war over it.

"And *what,*" I pleaded feebly of Sieber, "was the extry added idee of *that?*"

Well, the old scout answered, I had hired myself out to cavalry and Indian employment, and he only wanted to show me how risky it could be carrying out orders that could get a man's ass in a permanent sling, without proper caution of forethought.

"You see," he said, "the mule is likewise trained to buck

unless the mounter walks alongside her a certain number of *pasos* before he clambers aboard her. The one trick guards her agin white horse thieves, the other agin being stole by Injuns. And there's your proper caution to it, don't you see."

"No," I grumbled, "I don't see. What has getting two times bucked off your blasted performing mule got to do with the Apache camp, or me getting started right in the Injun scouting business?"

"You've simply got to stay more on the *que vive*, Horn," he said. "That's what I've tried to show you. Question your orders, boy. Don't go and do a dumb thing because somebody has told you to do it. Back off and take a good look all about, every time. You *comprende?*"

"Yes sir, I reckon so."

"Well, no you don't," he snapped at me. "You're still short. You didn't ask me how many steps the mule is trained to go before she can be got on. Or how she can be mounted when there ain't time to walk her into it. Damn!"

He spit out his plug of chaw like it had gone rank on him. "Here's your horse," he said, handing me the reins. "I don't know if I will keep you on, or not. By God, I don't." He limped beside the mule for what seemed to me no less than seventy, eighty feet before groaning his way aboard her and turning her head upstream.

"Well," I said, after we had gone a proper ways, and me still smarting inside, "how *do* you get up on her without taking that overnight hike alongside her ass?"

"Oh," Al Sieber answered, seeming startled, "didn't I tell you that?"

And he left it dangling squarely there. As long as I knew him and rode for him, he never again mentioned it.

I wouldn't, to this day, know how to get on that damn mule, if I had to do it. She was a peculiar beast, fit mount for Al Sieber. Her name was Jenny. Really, it was Janet. But he only called her that when he was put out. Come to think of that, she was more Janet than Jenny, I reckon. But Sieber loved her. I never saw him ride a horse, saving by emergency.

He was a mule man.

He always said he learned it from General George Crook in his first tour with the Third U.S. Cavalry, in the Arizona Territory. Crook was a mule man. And he knew more about the Apache Indians than any other white man short of Al Sieber, or maybe a few of the other white scouts early employed by Crook with Sieber. Men like Will Rice, Mace McCoy, August Spear, and Jack Townsend. But Crook and Al Sieber were the mule men. Interesting. Of all the others only those two are remembered today, and they rode mules. Well, Sieber always said a mule will beat a horse every way but straightaway. By which he meant in a straight speed race. "A mule will go farther on less oats, climb better, get down better, carry more, is a sharper watchdog of your camp, has three times the sense and twice the sand of any horse, and, when whipped and clubbed on a reasonable schedule, will give faithful service to his master into advanced age."

Sieber ought to know.

He had come west in 1866, gone to work for Crook in either 1871 late or 1872 early, "found" me in July of 1876 —and he said he had got Jenny in the muster-out at Appomattox Court House, rode her all the way from Virginia to Arizona, wore out three saddles on her, and she was already six years old when he got her from General Grant by way of a crap game with a Confederate boy who'd been given her and sixty dollars to make a new life for himself and his family after the war.

So Jenny had to be sixteen, seventeen years old when she bucked me off on the way to Pedro's rancheria and, well, hell, Sieber was only thirty-two, himself.

Which will do it for mule men.

Myself, I always rode the best horse that money could buy or skill could otherwise acquire. All I could ever say for mules was that they roasted pretty good, and the *bronco* Apaches would rather eat low on a bony jackass than high on a fat hog. Matter of fact, they wouldn't touch lip to pork. Or to bear meat or fish. Which maybe made the old German pretty coy, after all; if he got caught by hostiles while on the scout, they would always eat his mule first before judging what to do with him, and any fool knows a full-fed jury

brings in the friendliest verdicts. An Apache *bronco* Indian
full of fresh-roast mule meat wasn't no meaner than a Pima
or Papago.

I suspect that's why Sieber survived.

Although I believe he used up more jennys in the
process than any white man will ever understand.

But mules always fascinated me. Them and the men
that rode them when they might have had a good horse.
You put your mind to the matter, and you can't help but
puzzle it.

Abraham Lincoln rode a mule.

So did Jesus.

Apache Bloodsmell

We had gone but a short distance toward the Apache
camp when a slender Indian of about my own age rode up
and halted us. He spoke in Spanish.

"Listen, Seebie," he said, "my father sends me to ask
you to turn around. The people have gotten a supply of
tizwin, and there has been a big all-night sing going on.
Some Cibicus (mixed-band renegades) are in camp and
talking lies against Jona-clum (John P. Clum, agent at San
Carlos). There may be trouble if you come on up there
now. All right, Seebie?"

The big German was angry to hear this. "Where did
they get the *tizwin?*" he demanded. "Don't lie to me."

The Indian backed his pony to turn away from us. "You
know where they got the *tizwin*, Seebie," he said.

"Chuga-de-slona," Sieber glared, "old Centipede."

"You did not hear me say that name," the rider replied.

"One day," Sieber rasped, "he will brew his last pot."

"Go back, Seebie. My father asks it."

"It will be his last pot," Sieber continued as if he had not heard the young Indian, "because he will be in that pot himself. I promise it. You will see."

"Go back," the Apache youth repeated. *"Por favor."*

In all this time, he had not so much as glanced in my direction. Now, still without "seeing" me, he dug heel to his pony's ribs and took off up the river.

Sieber sat there on his mule, scowling darkly.

"That was young Ramon," he said at last to me. "He is the prize mesquite bean in his daddy's soup. Damn."

I said, "And his daddy being Old Pedro, who we are bound to visit. Is that the fact?"

"Of course."

"And some outlaw Injun name of Chuga-de-slona is making and selling Apache whiskey, and we don't aim to tolerate that much longer."

"You have got your snoot square in the hoofprint," Sieber growled.

"We turning back?"

Sieber shook his head. "We don't never turn back," he said. "We only sometimes ride a little wide."

"Like right now, you mean?"

"De seguro," grunted Al Sieber, and he swung his mule off the trail, hard to the right and into the higher rocks. I and the gelding scrambled to keep up and just barely managed it. That old crippled German was onto a hot track. He had smelled out something that had not got to my greenhorn's nostrils. That was plain as warts on a scalded hog. When we held up to rest our mounts on an overlook eight hundred feet above the river, I asked him what it was.

"Horn," he scowled, "you got to learn that with Injuns it ain't what they tell you, but what they leave out that will spend or save your hair." He looked at me in a way to wither quartz rock. "Naturally, Apaches don't by custom cut scalp locks. I'm using simplemind terms so even you can surround the idee."

"What idee is that?"

"The idee that Ramon was acting bad scairt, back yonder. It wasn't that he was fearful something might happen if we rode on up to the rancheria. It was that he was walleyed shook that we would find out what had already happened up there."

"And what you suppose that might be?"

"Blood has been spilt for certain. Apaches are like green-broke broncs. Bloodsmell spooks them wild. Young Ramon, he had his nose holes so wide flared you could see clean to his butthole puckering string." Sieber cursed his way back into the saddle of his dapple-gray mule, settled there with a groan. "Come on, Horn," he said. "You got a beak the size of a cavalry bugle. "Let's see how good it blows out fresh Apache bloodstink."

"Yes sir," I answered.

Which, with Aloysius Sieber, chief of civilian scouts, United States Fifth Cavalry, San Carlos, was always the correct and proper reply.

Sieber brought us into the upper, unguarded, end of Pedro's village. We had ridden nearly to the old chief's wickiup before the Indians realized who we were. Spotting Seebie, they closed in behind us by the scores. In the time required to reach Old Pedro's dwelling, we were surrounded by uneasy, scowling, and some outrightly ugly Apache Indians. "*Anciano!*" Sieber challenged the silent brush hut. "Come out here. It is Sieber."

Pedro came out. He was very old. To me he appeared a breathing corpse. But he had been to Washington and shaken the hand of the white father, and he was a great Indian. His people called him a damned old liar, but they respected his wisdom and his many winters.

"What do you want, Seebie?" he croaked. "*Qué pasa?*"

"You know very well *qué pasa*," Sieber answered him sternly. "It is for you to tell me."

"There is nothing important. I asked you to stay away. Can't you see the trouble here. It is *tizwin*."

"I can see that. There is more trouble than that."

"There will be. Please to go, Seebie."

A bad rumbling ran through the pushing crowd of Indians. The whiskey was evident among them, and the threat to white scouts from San Carlos was self-exampled by a hundred hostile faces in any quarter of the compass.

Sieber looked around at the growling populace and

gave a growl of his own. *"Cállate!"* he commanded them. "Chiefs are speaking here. If you want to talk against chiefs, come up here where we are. Don't stand back there behind those women. Bah! I retract that advice. Stay where you are. You are all *ish-sons* ("women") anyway."

Fortunately, there was a rough laugh or three from the bolder men out front of the mob, and the tightness let up just enough.

"Quick, now, Seebie," urged Pedro. "There is a moment. Ramon, *aquí*. Ride out with them." He lowered his tones as the young man stepped toward us. "Smile and talk as you go," Pedro said. "Do not hurry and do not linger. Good-bye, Seebie."

As with Ramon earlier, the old man did not look at me. But, now, he did. He reached unexpectedly for my hand. "Shake," he said. "It will let the people think I know you, that we have met before, that you are somebody." As I obeyed, extending my hand readily enough, he said to Sieber, "Who is he for that matter, Seebie?"

"My new boy, like a son to me."

Only I might imagine what pain that falsehood cost the touchy old German, and I was properly beholden.

Keen-eyed old Pedro stared into my face, still pumping my hand. "Seebie's boy," he said. "Good, good." He released my hand and clapped me on the biceps repeatedly. *"Bueno, bueno, bueno,"* he kept chanting. "Seebie's boy, good boy. *Enjuh, enjuh,"* which last was Apache for "good." Then, right in the middle of this happy acceptance of Sieber's new apprentice, the rheumy-eyed old devil turned to the San Carlos scout, frowning, "What is he, half of a Mexican or something? He is as dark of hide as I am. Does he carry *In-deh* blood? Or just a Mexican mother, say?"

Sieber looked at me, trying to seem proud.

"You have guessed it," he told the old man, with quite straight face, "but his mother is not Mexican, she is Missourian. You can see that, surely."

"Ah, Mi-si-oo-ran, yes. Of course. A great Indian people. Where did you say they ranged, Seebie?"

"Far off, *jefe*. Between the Sangre de Cristo Mountains and the Sioux country, where Grey Fox has gone with all the Third Cavalry. You remember?"

Grey Fox was another Apache name for General George Crook, more commonly called Red Beard. Pedro had known him intimately. Indeed, Crook had made Pedro chief of the San Carlos mixed bands, or at least had put the government cement to that position for him.

Aha, aha! the ancient Apache said gruntingly.

Then, to me, "Your people welcome their half brother. We know all about your mother's tribe. Not so warlike as the Comanche perhaps, nor so bold as the Kiowa, but a fine people. I knew you were of our blood all of the time. I was but testing Seebie."

He stepped back, sizing me up.

"Here!" he shouted to the restless throng about us. This is Seebie's new son. His mother was of the great Mi-si-oo-ran band, up toward the Sioux country. His name among us will be Seebie's Boy. When he earns his own name, we will give it to him, of course. Welcome him. *Enjuh, enjuh. Wagh!*"

I thought to hear half a dozen grudging *enjuhs* and one questionable *wagh*. Then the meeting came down to cases, hard and ugly and rough as Sieber's growl.

"Horn," he ordered me, "take the corner of yonder tarpaulin and whip it back to show what's under it."

I looked at the filthy piece of government packing canvas on the ground beside Pedro's wickiup. It had a crust of green-blue blowflies on it thick as scum over an alkalied water hole. "You mean *that* tarpolean?" I specified. "The one with the lump under it?"

"You see any other, Horn?"

"Only showing a propertude of precautionary thought, sir," I replied. "Questioning every order."

"Whip it back."

"Yes sir!"

There could have been a side of venison, rack of antelope, or hind of mule under that tarp, but there was not. It was a man, an Apache, and he was stifflimb dead.

Sieber, staying on his mule, squinted at the corpse and said to me, "Brush them flies off the face." I took up a pine branch and did so. The buzzing cloud rose briefly, and Sieber said to Pedro, "Isn't that Zanny? It is, by God," he said, not waiting for the chief's agreement. "Your own son-in-law. Married that ugly girl of yours. Poor Zanny. He did you a favor, *jefe*."

"A drunkard," shrugged the old man. "No good."

"He's 'good' now," Sieber nodded. "Who did it?"

"A best friend of Zanny's and my daughter, also from Fort Apache, as they are themselves. He didn't mean it."

"Who was it?" Al Sieber said. "Was it Nol-chai?"

"You spoke it, Seebie. I did not."

"Have they gone back over to Fort Apache, *jefe*?"

"Yes. They went last night by separate ways. But first my daughter came to me and said, 'My father, Nol-chai has killed Zanny fighting over me. It was the *tizwin* that did it.'"

"Had to be," agreed Sieber. "Nobody would fight over that squaw sober."

"Her spirit is kind. She is a good worker."

Sieber didn't answer. He reined his mule around, forcing back the Indians who were pressing us. "Come on, Bucko," he said to me. "I will show you how to catch up to one bad Injun for good."

"We going after Nol-chai?" I asked, glad enough to be ordered back aboard the safety of my tall horse.

"Nol-chai? Naw. He's a Fort Apache Injun, not one of ours. They'll take care of him over there."

"What will he get of punishment?"

"The end of a rope."

"You mean the army will hang a man just for a drunk spree that got one of two best friends kilt brawling?"

"He's an Injun, he'll swing. But he ain't our Injun. Foller me."

The Centipede

Sieber kicked his Jenny mule into a lope in two jumps, scattering Indians like duckpins. You can believe that I did not waste a breath in hitting the bay a lick with my quirt. We dug out after the old German scout and Jenny like me and the bay was orphan strays and them our long lost mamas. We gained up to them in about four more cuts with the quirt, by which time the thickest of the Apache crowd was past.

We managed to make it on out of the camp in good shape, excepting for where one old squaw cracked me on my thigh muscle with a hard-hurled knobby club the size and heft of a pick handle. Damn! But Sieber only scowled and said, "Cheer up. You was a big hit back yonder. That ain't the only stick you'll get throwed at you. You are going to get the heaviest squaw play of any half-breed since Mickey Free. I been underestimating you, Horn."

We rode all that afternoon, coming late in the day to a desolate stretch of scrub pine and juniper brush high up on a shoulder overlooking the creek drainage that gave water to the corn and melon patches of Pedro's White Mountain rancheria. Despite the lonesomeness of the place, there was a good trail into it. When I asked about this, Sieber explained it was wore into the mountain by customers. When I then queried him as to what customers, he growled, "the ones that are going to be looking for another *brewmeister* come tomorrow morning."

He would not say more, except to order me to be quiet and do absolutely nothing I was not ordered to do for the next ten minutes.

"Ten minutes?" I said.

"Yes," he answered. "Five minutes to get where we are going. And five more to finish our business there."

I didn't like the feel of that empty mountainside. My *sombra* was punching me with its elbow. It was saying for me to look at Al Sieber. I did it, and it was a scary thing. His face was flushed and his back eyes burning like hot coals in the sundown shade of the place. I could hear his breath whistling out his nostrils.

"What the hell's the matter?" I said, forgetting.

But he didn't seem to hear me. He was pushing himself down off the mule, dropping her reins to ground-trail, and going forward afoot in his crawdadding, crimpled way. I had naught else to do but get down from the bay and follow him. When I came up to him he was bellied down in a rock outcrop giving view down into a little hollow below. Down in there was a brush wickiup built against a cliffwall with a cave running back into it. I saw two old busted-down burros and six, eight rusty ten-gallon cavalry water containers of the sort carried in field ambulances. Then there was the fire out in the middle of the hollow. And the vast black iron pot pole-slung over that fire and bubbling away full of a beautiful thick soup that any Missouri boy could smell was mash-whiskey makings, even dead against the wind, which was quartering across our front, down and away. "Christ," I whispered to Sieber, "Apache mountain moonshine."

For acknowledgment, he raised his near elbow and hit me in the mouth with it in a back-chuck of his bull shoulder that like to planted my biting teeth back amongst my grinders.

When I had swallowed the blood and got the green circles and bright yellow balls out of my eye-vision, he pointed down into the hollow with his thumb, hooking it two times, and nodding a whisper. "Yonder's our Injun. Bear in mind what I told you. We got six minutes left." He swept the hollow below with a last scanning look. "About right," he decided, "foller on."

I went with him down out of the rocks. The Indian, who had appeared out of the cavern to throw on more kindling for his mash cooker, dropped the wood and began backing around the blaze to get the huge kettle between him and Al Sieber. I could not see that he was armed. Sieber said to me out of the side of his mouth, "*A la izquierda,* circle to the left. Block him from the cave. Don't lift your rifle." He himself went to the right. The Indian held where he was.

Which was hemmed.

Sieber said to me in English, "I will use Mex on him, as he savvies it perfectly fine, and it will let you follow what's said. He will come back with some Mex and some Apache. Do your best to sort it out, as I want a witness that he was give his rights."

All the while he was saying this, he was not looking at

me but at the Indian. I was studying this man likewise. He was a mean one for certain. Heavy-built in chest and shoulder, long arms, legs bent in a bow you could have slid a cedar sawlog through, including the saw, and with a dark slab of a face that would give a Spanish longhorn bull second thoughts on charging it in a narrow place of the trail.

"Chug," said Al Sieber, "I have come to put you out of the *tizwin* business. You will kick over that pot of mash, scatter your fire embers, and go away and not look back one time at me or this camp. If you do not do as I say, you will wish that your mother had born you crosswise of her crotch and you had strangled on your own cord, as that will have been easier for you than to see me mad. Tip over that kettle."

Now this was all said in the lowest of *mestizo* Mexican, not your highfaluting Spanish, and it is a surety that Chuga-de-slona understood it perfectly, just as Sieber had said he would. But he didn't move to kick over the mash kettle. He just stood there, snake eyes glittering back in under the crag of his forehead and getting that crouch into his knees that lets you know you have got trouble coming with a big letter T.

"Damn you," Sieber said. "Turn out that garbage onto the ground."

"You are a meddlesome squaw," the Indian said, voice hoarse and heavy. "You do nothing but follow me and spy on me and you are always watching around all of the time." He picked up a small stick and tossed it on the ground between him and Sieber. "That is you, *Jon-a-chay*," he said. "See, I give you a new name, *jon-a-chay*, 'meddler.' And see, I spit on you and your new name. *Ih!*"

He hawked in his throat and spat a stream of saliva onto the stick. The spittle bounced and some of it hit on Sieber's left boot. He looked down at it.

"Centipede," he said, "you have called me *jon-a-chay* two times. If you do it a third, you won't do it a fourth. Now I have warned you. I have also given you opportunity to leave this place and never come back."

Sieber wheeled about and cupped hand to mouth and called toward the cave, in Apache, for those hiding within to come outside. I was astonished to see two old crones and a third, not unattractive, squaw emerge from the cavern. "Come over here," Sieber ordered them, speaking Mexican now. "You know me. I do not harm women. I do not kill children." The three came nervously forward. "That is near enough," Sieber said. "I want you to understand what happens here." He pointed at Chuga-de-slona. "I have told Chug to leave and I will not follow him, but he must promise not to look back, not to make *tizwin* to sell to the others anymore. Chug is still here. He did not leave. Remember that."

He turned back to the sullen Centipede.

"It is too late for you to go now," he said to the Indian whiskey maker. "I am going to take you to San Carlos again. It will be the last time, this time."

I later learned that he had arrested this particular man three or four times, with the evidence brought in to show in his trial against him. Each time, lenient authorities— civilian agents every time—had freed Chuga-de-slona. He had not done a day in restraint, or been punished in any way. So swore Al Sieber to me.

It was little surprise then that this Indian now laughed at Sieber. The sound, because so unexpected, jarred my nerves. It caused my belly muscles to shrink too. Nobody laughed at Al Sieber. The Indian had signed his final warrant, I was white-faced certain.

"You are an old female spying on true males," he told the dark-browed German. "You squat down to make water, and all you do is go about as a sneak-watcher, a liar."

Because the Indian was between me and Sieber, I could not see the scout's face, except by glances when Chuga-de-slona would move his big Apache head. But I could hear the danger in Sieber's voice. It was the same change that you hear in the snarl of a bear that has decided he is through warning the foolish human in his trail-path and will rush upon the poor devil. All skilled hunters know the chilling difference.

"*Hombre*," Sieber said, "*es verdad*. Yes, I do watch badmen like the Centipede. *Y, por Dios*, I will stop them from making *tizwin* to poison the brains of my Indians. Now don't make trouble, you son of a bitch," he concluded in plain-track English. "Put out your hands for my boy to tie up. Be very careful now." He bent his own knees when he said it. I detected the crouch of the brute and so, I think, did Chuga-de-slona.

"*Cuidado*," Sieber called out in Mexican. "Don't do it, Chug. Decide against it. Hold out your hands."

"*Jon-a-chay!*" screamed the infuriated Indian. "I will kill you!"

With the blurred speed of a horned rattler striking, his dark hand darted into the rocks beside him. He had a carbine hidden there. Sieber to my eye's knowledge was unarmed. The Indian, however, no more than got the lever of his old Henry rifle jacked open to load a rimmed copper shell into the chamber, when Al Sieber was upon him.

I simply do not remember the bulky German moving.

He was one instant standing no less than ten feet from Chuga-de-slona. None of the witnesses, not any of the three squaws and surely not young Tom Horn, remember that they saw him draw blade in the grunting leap to seize the whiskey maker. All remembered only that, in a blink of the eye, Al Sieber had Chuga-de-slona by the hair with one hand and a knife drawn back in the other. He bent the Indian's head backward to expose and make skin-taut as a drumhead the bulging jugular and bony voice box. He made one slash against that muscular target.

There was no outcry from Chuga-de-slona.

Only an escape of air, a shower of bloodspray, a hissing gurgle briefly stilled. The body of the Centipede fell away from Sieber's hand. My eyes fixed themselves in horror, not upon that poor, still jerking corpse upon the ground, but upon Al Sieber's hand.

When first I told this event in my accounts of the Arizona days, I used the words, "Sieber nearly cut his head off." A man will do that. He will soften a story to spare harsher judgments than he believes an action ought to suffer. But Al Sieber did not nearly cut that Indian's head off. He did cut it off. It was in his left hand. And the body was in the ashring of the whiskey-cooking fire.

The big German looked over at me and only nodded, letting his black eyes pass me to center on the weeping and mewing squaws. "*Anciana,*" he called to one of the old hags. "Do you have a sack for this, *por favor?* It is dripping on my good boots."

I found a rock to sit down on in a hurry.

I was sick to puking, but did not get anything up because we had not eaten since leaving San Carlos. For a man who detested knives as I did, and yet admired Al Sieber as I had already come to do, it was some unsettling shock.

But Sieber had no thought for my upset. He put the head on a clean stone nearby and took up Chuga-de-slona's two arms and barked at me, "Grab his feet." I did so, still shaky, and we stuffed the Centipede into his big iron mash kettle. A hand and both legs, from bend of knee, hung outside the pot, but the rest of him was already cooking when the old woman shuffled up with the sack for the head, or the next best thing she'd found for a sack.

It was an old nose bag stolen from the cavalry and would fit the jugheadedest mule or coarsest plug, but was still a tight fit for old Chug's outsized skull; I never again saw an Apache head like that, but Sieber got it into the nose bag and handed that back over to the old woman.

"Take it with you down to Pedro's village," he ordered the three squaws. "Show it to the people down there and tell them that Seebie is from now on hunting *tizwin* makers to kill them. It is no use anymore to run to San Carlos."

The women were moaning and screeching prayer songs for old Chug. They never let up, but they took the nosebag and lit out down the mountain. We could hear them for half an hour. We spent the time policing the Centipede's "whiskey camp." We towed the mash kettle with the Indian in it to a nearby drop-off cliff and kicked it over into eternity. We set fire to the wickiup and Sieber fetched a half stick of dynamite out of his pack and blew shut the face of the cave. When the powderstink had cleared out, we could no longer hear the squaws sorrowing down the trail, and we got up on our mounts and sent them out of there.

It was plumb dark by then.

"Where we bound?" I asked, so bone-weary of the saddle I could scarcely stand its feel, but certain Sieber was headed for some hidden camping spot nearby. "I trust it ain't distant."

"Awwhrrugg," answered Al Sieber.

"That far," I said, smart-assing him out of being wore down past caution.

"And then some," he rumbled, not jumping me.

An impossible thought wandered into my blind-tired mind. "My God," I said, "you ain't meaning we're going back to Pedro's?"

"Roundabout," Sieber answered.

"Roundabout what?" I gritted at him, still pushing.

"Roundabout twenty-two miles," he said.

Ah, what small store I yet had of knowing Al Sieber; I still thought he was heading for some nearby cozy blanket-spot.

"Oh, sure," I said, cheeking it out. "Let's see, that would make it about by way of Fort Apache, wouldn't it? Or may-beso Sawbuck Mountain. It's prettier that way."

"Stick with Fort Apache," Sieber advised. "That way you'll stick with me."

And he never said another word the whole night through of that staggering ride, by moondark, from Chuga-de-slona's whiskey flat, to the peeled-log gates of Fort Apache.

Sister Sawn

Do not imagine that Al Sieber wasted a mile of that grueling night ride to Fort Apache.

When, come dawn, we rode into the stockade, he sent me to where the scouts were having breakfast under a brush ramada by the picket line of ready mounts, but went on himself directly to the post commander's office. The whiles I ate with some of the boys I knew from San Carlos, Joe Yescus, (Mex name José María Jesús), Frank Monic, and Jaime Cook, Sieber reported the *tizwin* dustup over at Pedro's rancheria. It was a "good" report. Such had been our speed in "getting over the mountain" during the dark hours, that Captain A. R. Chaffee was able to collar poor old Nolchai before I finished my eats.

I felt sad for that little Apache fellow.

He could not believe that anybody might have beaten him to the fort, where he had come to pick up his war bag and spare horses. He was all set to take out for Sonora and the Sierra Madre, down in Mexico. There he could have lived out his years in what Sieber called "the Apache land of the free and home of the brave"—*broncos*, that was. But he never made it past the Fort Apache front gate. There, the Indian police grabbed him and slung him into the post jail. We were assured he would be carted down to San Carlos and given a fair trial. Al Sieber said to me that he would never see San Carlos, which I suspect he didn't. It was why I felt bad.

However, do not think that Iron Man made that all-night ride to get a poor little Apache buck hung.

That was but a side part of his mission.

He was not after the killer of Al-zan-ih, husband of Pedro's dark-skinned daughter; he was after the broad-ass squaw herself.

He wanted her for *me*.

I like to cut and run for Mexico myself; I could not believe Sieber was serious. But he was. Before I could recover brain enough to start tendering my resignation as interpreter of Mexican at San Carlos, we were both sent for by Captain Chaffee, the post C.O. at Fort Apache. "Be on your guard, Horn," the German scout gruffed to me as we obeyed the summons. "This will be about old Chug." He waved at two scouts walking by and continued, low-voiced. "Chaffee is a mean son of a bitch but one hell of a soldier. He will want to gumchew over the yarn I give him about Chug and will use you to pitfall me if he can. He *knows*, never you fear. So *cuidado*'s the word. Just let me answer wherever Chaffee will leave me to do it. *Comprende?*"

"Well, hell," I said, "you want me to lie, or what?"

We stopped walking. Sieber stared at me, thunderstruck. His face had a curious bewildered look, and hurt.

"Lie?" he said, aghast. "*Me* ask *you* to *lie?*"

"Yes sir. That's what you said, isn't it?"

The old German shook his thick-fleshed head. It was evidently more of a blow then he was prepared to contain and still not break down openly.

"Merciful goodness, Horn," he said to me, very loud, as we resumed our march to Chaffee's office, "you must answer as you think best. Every time."

Then, in a side-mouthing growl, just as we hit the first step of the stoop in front of the headquarters.

"Yes, and you better lie damned good, too."

"Now, then, Horn," Chaffee said, "let me see if I have this straight. Sieber and you went to this whiskey maker's camp, advancing openly and proper. Sieber advised him he was under arrest and would be taken safely to San Carlos. The man then went berserk, seized a hidden gun and commenced firing, point-blank. At which moment Sieber here, in total disregard for his own life, leaped forward and disarmed the Apache. In the struggle for the weapon, however, it discharged, mortally wounding the Indian. Is that precisely the way in which it happened?"

"Oh, yes sir," I saluted. "Only Mr. Sieber was much more braver than he makes out. Why, you ought to have see'd him, the way that he——"

"Horn!" yelled Sieber.

"Well, you was so almightily thoughtless of your own blood and bones, sir. When old Chug seen that you was bound to——"

"Goddamn it, sir!" Sieber bellowed to Captain Chaffee. "Cain't you order this idjut kid to shet up?"

Captain Adna Chaffee, who had about the toughest face a man could have and still not shatter his razor on it, gave a grin that blinked on and out like a lit match. "Yes, Horn," he said. "Please confine your answers to the questions. Yes or no will do nicely."

He then issued Sieber a string of profanity such as I never heard before nor since, ending up with, "And I will thank you, goddamnit, Al, if you keep your own testimony straight and short. Go ahead, boy."

Well, one way and another, I managed to limp through

Sieber's pack of stretchers without barking my shinbones too many times on the hard rock of truth. Captain Chaffee thanked me and said, "My clerk, here, has all of this copytrue in writing. Sign it where he tells you, and if you've not perjured yourself you're lucky."

"Yes sir," Al Sieber answered for me, knuckling his eyebrow in as near as he ever came to a proper saluting of an officer. "And he will be lucky if I don't kill him before the army puts him on the lovely shores of Alcatraz Prison for volunteering false testification against his superior, which is me. Thank you, sir!"

Out we went, and Sieber was mad enough to nail my hide to the log wall of the latrine, he vowed, and let the troops tan it with their military urine for their next six enlistments. But he cooled down when he remembered Alzan-ih's squaw and our urgent business with her.

"Forget it," he ordered. "Come along on. We got us some widow's weeds to water."

"You are daft!" I cried. "There ain't no human way you will euchre Tom Horn into taking up with no cow-hipped Apache squaw. Nor order him to do it, neither."

Which is of course the manner in which it came about that we left Fort Apache that same afternoon, tagged after by the squaw, her three Injun whelps running in age from ten down to five years, seven spavined and stringhalted pack horses, a one-eyed mule named General Crook, four ordinary Indian dogs, and a pet wolf cub named Snarler, which was sick with the epizootic. Sieber had bleated it about the stockade that his new boy was Indian-struck and determined, in the face of all fatherly advice from him, Sieber, to forthwith "take to the blanket and get himself a sleeping dictionary" on the romantic life of the nomad Apache people.

"What you mean," I overheard one sallow-faced old soldier say, "is that you've turnt the poor dumb kid into a squaw diddler, so's he kin spy fer you. Ain't there nothing so snake-bellied you civilian scouts won't creep beneath it to keep leaching off the guv'mint? If it wasn't agin orders, I would whup the—"

I suppose he was going to threaten to whip Sieber good, but he never finished the sentence. The powerful German sprang upon him and dragged him behind the nearby blacksmith shed and like to killed him with a bare-hand beating. He left the soldier there back of the smithy and we got our cavalcade under way out the gate, pronto.

Sieber never did know I heard that soldier's guff.

He said to me, "That son of a bitch has owed me a gambling debt of five dollars for three years. I finally caught up to him. It is a sorrowful thing that men cannot be honest and decent with one another."

I agreed that it was and tried not to look at the other troopers watching us file out of the fort with our fat-butt squaw and her possession of riches. It wasn't till nine miles out on the trail that I even knew her name. It was Sister Sawn.

Tizwin Trail

Even before we got back to Pedro's village, I had to change my opinion of Sawn. True, she was dumpy and duck-butted. She had a voice that sounded like a jack mule braying for his mate. Her face was flat, square, homely, and sun-fried as a cow pie. If you got close to her downwind, it was enough to clear out a head cold. But inside all that? Why, that Apache squaw was all sunshine and humor and good heart.

Funny? She made even Sieber laugh.

And work! Lord God, that woman herded all those kids and livestock and doctored the sick wolf pup and never lost a stride to the old German or me. More, she cooked for us, butchered out the deer I shot, dressed its hide, carried all the water for camp (we weren't hurrying), and even sneaked time in the dark of the second night to dip herself in the creek and show up alongside my bedroll spot with a sprig of sage back of one ear, ready, and I am certain fully anxious, to fill out the rest of her contract.

She was grinning wide enough for me to read newsprint by the flash of her teeth in the bear's-gut darkness and, moreover, she got halfways under my blanket before I could hoist her out with the two of my feet planted in the small of her wide behind. And, friends, that behind was naked as a baby's, and so was all the rest of her, which was a sufficiency amount of female parts anywheres you grabbed.

Sieber got wrathy with me over it.

Sawn was my ticket to get into Pedro's band, he explained. Why in hell did I think we went all the way over to Fort Apache to get her? If we two showed up back at the rancheria, having killed Chug and gotten poor old Nolchai arrested to hang, with only our sweet white selves to grease our welcome, we might easily earn our discharge from San Carlos in Apache writing. Which was to say cut up a bit and burned a lot, after the fashion of the *broncos* with *Pinda Lickoyi* ("White Eyes") who displeasured them.

But if we came into camp as the husband and best man to Pedro's daughter Sawn, why, tribal custom would require minimum courtesies, including the safety to close our eyes and lay down to sleep. After all, Apache widows were not that easy to remarry, and this one had been hard enough to get a buck for in the first place. It followed that Old Pedro would be happy to see us, while the Cibicus, the non-peacefuls visiting in from the out-country would be shut off from harming us. Leastways, on the rancheria.

"It's the best bet we got," Sieber concluded. "Now it ain't going to kill you to lay still for old Sister."

Of course I would not hear of it.

But when Sieber then grudged the information that he had done everything for me with a view to filling my boyhood dream of living with the Apache Indians and learning of their nomad life, why I had to weaken. It was scant use being stiff-necked over it. After all, the old scout had surely nothing to earn out of all this. He truly had done it out of a warm heart for me, "his boy." But, damn, that was one ugly squaw!

Sawn proved to have her red pride, however.

When I stumbled over to where she was bedded with her menagerie, she set the four dogs on me, and, in my scramble to back off from them, unbit, I stepped on the sick wolf pup and he nailed me good. The ruckus roused up the whole camp. The kids commenced to wail, the dogs to howl, the old packmule to scree-haw. My friend, Mr. Al Sieber of San Carlos, came up out of his blankets yelling in Apache and German, threatening, as I translated it, to kill Tom Horn on sight.

Instead, when he found out I'd been bit by the wolf cub, he settled for building up the fire and cauterizing my leg with his ramrod heated a cherry red and run two inches deep into each tooth puncture hole.

"I been watching the son of a bitch," Sieber growled about the wolf pup. "I ain't that certain he's got the epizootic. I don't like the way he acts. Could be hydrophoby."

"Goddamn!" said Sister Sawn, coming up just then and greeting us with her giant grin and the one English word she had learned at Fort Apache. "Everyone is awake and the wind is still. We could be home with the sun."

That was it. We broke camp and took the trail with some vigor and much silence. Somehow, I was given credit for the entire trouble. Sieber said not a word more to me until just outside Pedro's big camp. Then it was his usual word to Tom Horn in those learning days.

"Shut your mouth," he said. "You can bob your head if you need to, or shake it sideways. Otherwise, you ain't to open your trap wide enough to spit."

"*Sí, patrón,*" I sighed. "*Lo entiendo.*"

"You better understand it. Now smile and ride alongside your lovely bride. That's it. *Enjuh, enjuh—*"

The *tizwin* squaws from Centipede's whiskey camp had got over the mountain well ahead of us. This was precisely as Sieber had planned it. "An Apache ain't no different than a white man some ways," he said to me. "First off, when he hears something fearful, he gets the wind up fit to bust. Then when nothing happens to him, personal, he simmers off. Apaches are great ones for letting the other feller ride his own green horses. He don't borry a bucking off, happen he can avoid it without seeming to try to. That's ever the trick with Injuns; you got to give them the room to back down while seeming to be raising holy ned. It takes time to learn it."

In our case, we found it had worked fine.

The camp had flown into an uproar when the Centipede's women came into its haven. But that was near two days gone. The Cibicus had largely taken off for the back canyons to hide out whatever of storm might bring the soldiers up from San Carlos. And the rest of the people had had good time to think back on what a bum old Zanny had been, to figure out where they were going to buy their Apache whiskey now that old Chug was retired, and to reason that it would be fairly wise to listen to what Old Mad (one of their names for Sieber) would have to say about the *tizwin* business. Nevertheless, it was still a comfort to come into the camp with Sister Sawn siding us, laughing her famous jackass laugh, pounding Sieber's boy on the back, and announcing in Apache to anybody who would listen that here was her new husband and we were coming to live with her father's very lucky people and it was a fine day and she would buy a young mule and kill it for a proper sing and roast that night, if all went well with our reception home.

This calmed an assortment of the people, as a free mule feed was an occasion in Apacheria. Others had already said the hell with Chuga-de-slona and that, though it was a shame about Nol-chai, there was no Apache point in bothering Seebie, as the past had showed that to be a very bad investment of Indian time, indeed.

There remained a bunch of hardtails who collected about us and escorted us to Pedro's wickiup, with hardly hushed references to our chances, should we be caught outside the village after dark. But Sister Sawn joked and jibed with these malcontents, reminding them that her father was an important man and her mother a noted *gouyan*, or wise woman, of the Warm Springs wild Indians.

She did not need to remind them, also, Sister Sawn reminded them regardless, that the Warm Springs were the people of old Nana and the bitter killer Victorio. She was, through her mother, the own-niece to the latter famed chieftain, as well (Sieber said this was a pure pony marble), who was very jealous of her welfare.

I was not unimpressed with her performance, pony marbles and all, and said as much to Sieber.

"Well, sure," he said. "Now you are getting the idee.

What did I tell you?" He scorched me with that black-eyed stare. "You might make it yet, Horn," he nodded. "Just keep taking them notes along the trail."

"Yes sir," I said, as we dismounted outside Pedro's door. "I got my pad right here." I patted my Winchester rifle, and he seemed to think that was the right line of thought. He gave me two nods, his highest sign of approval. "What will happen now?" I finished off.

"Now," Sieber told me, pushing past the muttering bucks who were still trying to bluff us, "we deliver Old Pete his annual temperance lecture, only this will be the last year he hears it from Al Sieber. Shut up and stand close."

The ancient Pedro now came out of his adobe and stick-pole hut, and we three sat down under the brush-roofed ramada outside the door, and the talk was on.

"Is it true you killed the Centipede?" the old man led off.

"Killed him and cooked him too," Sieber said.

"It's unfortunate, Seebie; he was a part-devil."

"No," the German said, "he was a whole devil."

"The people are afraid when a devil is harmed."

"Let them listen, then, while you do likewise," Al Sieber told the wrinkled Apache. "Then let them go and talk this warning all about among the other Indians."

He then said that the Apache of those parts had better leave off making their Indian whiskey as he, Sieber, calculated to stop them from it. When he caught a man at it the first time, he would put him in the calaboose. But when he caught a man at it like the one he had just killed up on the mountain, then he would just kill him, for he had been warned before. There would be no mercy, let the squaws whimper their heads off. It was going to be *dah-eh-sah* on the *tizwin* business from then on, Seebie gave his word upon it.

Since *dah-eh-sah* translated "death" in Apache, Pedro was disturbed. In turn, he lectured Al Sieber.

He did not want his men, he said, either to make or sell *tizwin* whiskey. He would help Seebie suppress them every time. But he had six hundred warriors and some of them were as bad Indians as any Indians could be, and he couldn't do anything with these *hesh-kes,* these bad ones who had the wild urge to kill and hurt.

"These bad ones never get hurt themselves," Pedro complained. "They never grow old and never get killed, and they never, never turn good. They just remain what they are and are always into every trouble that comes.

"You see, Seebie," he appealed helplessly, "they are part-devils, as I say, or they would get old or get killed sometime. That is what frightens the people."

"Well," Sieber said, "I understand that. But if any of the people want to see one devil that is good and dead, let them go up and rope themselves down into the crevice at the bottom of the Cliff of the Cave, up there."

"They won't do it, Seebie."

"But you will tell them what I said. I mean each word, *anciano.*"

"*Schichobe,*" Pedro said, "old friend, I will do it. But the times are bad. It will be a long war this time, Seebie. The Apache will fight until the last wild one is gone. You know who I mean; Warm Springs and Chiricahua: it will last ten years, unless the soldiers go after them and kill every one. There is no other way."

"You know that, I know it also," Sieber said, "but the soldier chiefs aren't permitted to go after them and kill them, just like that. But I agree with you, *jefe.* You kill a bad Indian and he never is bad again."

"Yes," Old Pedro said, "and the same with a white man. Unless, of course, he is a part-devil."

I could see it was useless at this point, Sieber being likewise convinced. He changed the subject.

"Now," he said, "Sister Sawn has promised us a mule roast tonight. Will you come, *jefe,* and sit by my right hand? You know I would be honored. I want you also to talk with this new boy of mine; I have an idea in my mind for him, if he should please you."

Pedro said he would come. Moreover, he had two good young deer carcasses he would contribute and some late season cornmeal for pinole and for Apache bread. It would be a notable feast and we would all talk plenty.

"But now," he said, tottering to his feet, "I have a little

something inside." He held back the deerhide hanging of the door to his rude house and stood aside with a gracious gesture for Sieber and me. "*Entran, ustedes,*" he invited us, in Mexican. "*Haga me el favor, hombres.*"

We bent and went in. Sieber was under six feet but I was over, and the inside ceiling of Old Pedro's wickiup could not have been much over five feet. I banged my head a good one, then got smart and hunkered down on the mud floor. The old man dug out a jug and poured three tin army cups full of something smelling about as potent as mule piss, picked up his cup, and said some words in Apache, which I didn't catch but Sieber repeated. We all then drank her down, as they say.

I almost suffocated from mine, but managed to get back outside without either strangling or pitching up my breakfast, and Sieber and me got our mounts and rode off back out toward where Sister Sawn had our camp.

"What in the name of God was that?" I asked the old German when we were out of earshot of Pedro's hearing horn. The old rascal was very deaf and used an ear trumpet. "It like to et out my throat box."

Al Sieber looked at me.

There was a martyr's pang of endured suffering in the glance. A seething, too, of the white man's Indian ire. A cursing of the darkness of the redskin mind, and no candle lit to shine one ray of hope. But all overridden by the vista, seen close at hand, of the true place of *Pinda Lickoyi* in the grander scheme of Pedro's Apache world.

"It was *tizwin,*" Sieber said. "*Prosit—!*"

Talking Boy

Sister Sawn's "party" was a skull buster. *Tizwin* flowed like Moses had hit the big iron cooker in the sky with his rod and his staff. We got all kinds of stories from Pedro about how the juice was really only pulque or Mexican liquor which he couldn't help being sold, or it was "white man's whiskey" sold off the reservation by bad *Pinda Lickoyi* "living near Globe."

Sieber didn't auger it with the old chief.

But once a man has tasted *tizwin,* he would know it if even a drop of it splashed on a nearby rock, or a jug was uncorked and shook to pour in the next county.

It was sure enough the real stuff served at Sister Sawn's roast mule sing. Poor Sieber got so down in the mouth over it that he wouldn't eat. He just kept saying "son of a bitch, son of a bitch," over and over to himself, in German, and drinking from his own private jug, which he assured me contained "medicinal spirits" from the government supply of the post surgeon for the Fifth Cavalry.

Since the jug looked like the same one we'd swigged from in Pedro's hut earlier that day, I was suspicious. When, in pouring himself another tin cup of the brew, Sieber spilled a little on my bare hand and it burnt a red ring on the skin, I knew it wasn't what he said.

However, when he saw my hostile look, he shrugged and said, as mellow as he ever said anything, "Well, Horn, when you are in the camp of the enemy, you got to drink the wine of the country. Awwhhrruggg!"

Next minute, he fell square over on his side from where him and me and Pedro was squatting by the dance circle watching the fun. He didn't stir but laid there like he was froze stiff, and the old Indian shook his head sadly. "Seebie is not moving anymore."

"Not tonight," I said.

"Well," the old rascal said to me, "you are his new boy, and so I shall talk to you the same as I was going to talk to Seebie; I was going to ask him to let you stay up here in my camp for a while. What do you think of that?"

"*Muy bueno,*" I said. "*Mil gracias, patrón.*"

"Yes," he said. "Well, I hear you speaking Mexican to my people, and I thought you were a Mexican half-breed. But Seebie tells me now you are a pure American boy. It's just that you are dark in the hide, and eye, like us."

"*Sí, jefe,*" I nodded. "This is a true thing. Also, I think I am like your people inside of me, *en el corazón.* I would like to stay here and be one of you."

"A white man cannot be an Indian. Seebie joked with me about you and your tribe, the Mi-si-oo-ran. I believed him."

"Yes, *jefe;* yet my own-mother always told me that I was an Indian, different from her other children."

"Well, many strange things happen in this world. We will not worry about it. Yosen will decide what you are." He eyed me a moment, then added. "I hear you talking some Apache, too. Where did you learn that?"

I told him a brief story of my days on Beaver Head Creek, in Camp Verde, and the like. "Well," he said, "you have a gift of talking, so let us talk some Apache."

He began at once to jabber at me in his language, and I began to wish Sieber were conscious to help me, for I had the feeling the old man was trying me out. But to my amazement I commenced to jabber back at him, and in no time we were handing the Apache back and forth right decent. Pedro was almightily pleased. He whacked me on the back, with a string of *enjuhs,* and said, "Listen, tongue-speaker, we have got to wake up Seebie and get him to decide this matter."

"I thought you were going to leave it to Yosen," I grinned, carried away by my success. But Old Pedro did not grin back. He was turned earnest in the minute. "No, no," he said. "God is only God, but Seebie tells the soldier chiefs what to do."

"Ahh!" I said. And had the good sense to shut up right there.

To anyone contemplating the cavalry scout service in the Apache country, I would have the following advice: do not be taken drunk on *tizwin* where you will need to be "awakened" by Indian methods.

The Apaches put Sieber into a canvas packsling and drug him bodily down to the creek and rolled him into it. It was about four foot deep where they dunked him in, so he had either to surface or stay under and drown. He came up spouting water and terrible language, but Pedro convinced him he had only wandered down to the stream and fallen in all by himself. "Ask your boy. He saw it happen. Didn't you, *ish-ke-ne?*"

Since he called me boy, in Apache, I thought to be respectful and replied to him, "*Anh, da-go-tai,* yes, father." He beamed over that. "You see?" he said to Sieber. "This is a smart new boy you have, Seebie. I want to talk to you about leaving him with me a while."

Sieber waded out of the creek. He told Pedro they would talk about it. Meanwhile, he had had enough fun and was going to find his blankets. "Use mine," Pedro invited him at once. "I have that young wife now, the one from Mexico. I don't think you've seen her. Try her; I give permission." Sieber thanked him but refused, saying he was too tired to do well by a young wife. "Maybe my boy here would like to accept in my place," he mumbled to Pedro. "I give *my* permission."

He stumbled off to our camping spot, the one staked out for us by Sister Sawn, and I saw him no more that night. There was good reason for that. When I myself sought my bedroll in a few minutes, Sieber was nowhere in view of our rocky campsite. I bedded down weary to the bone, lulled into instant deep slumber by the monotony of the Apache chanting, stomping, gourd thumping, and sing-singing down at the village fires. I had no idea what hour of the night it might subsequently have been when something awakened me, and I came bolt upright, rifle to hand and at the ready.

There, not three feet in front of my dirty-socked feet, sitting on my saddle and studying me by the flare of a

match, was the most outlandish figure I had encountered
upon the frontier. There was a bit of a late-rising moon,
and that, aided by the brief flicker of the match, let me
etch the details on my memory.

I can see that picture yet.

He was about five feet and three or four inches tall,
if that. Squat in structure with arms dangling like those of
an ape, he had the high shoulders and no-neck look of
the Apache, yet he was not an Apache. Or not entirely
one. His hair, sheared off below his shoulder line, stuck
out from under his round-crowned, floppy dishpan of a hat
like the wild furze of some corn-patch scarecrow, and it
was as flaming red in color as a blood-bay horse's coat in
brightest sun.

"Are you the talking boy?" he said to me.

It was Apache that he spoke, and he spoke it with
all the Apache thick and slurring sounds, the way that no
white man could. Yet he *did* look like a white man. Or mostly like one. He wore white man's high field boots of military cut coming to the knee. His jacket was a cavalry
sergeant's blouse, and his baggy pants were of some ancient infantry issue gone out of Arizona Territory before
my time.

"Well," I managed to answer him, belatedly, "they call
me Seebie's Boy."

The apparition shook its wild head of carrot hair.

"I think your name is Talking Boy," the creature said.
"All the people say you speak the tongue better than they
ever heard a white man do it. Talking Boy. That's your
name. *Anh,* yes. Do you know me?"

He had dropped the burned-out match, but the moon
let me see his homely grin spread across the impossible
ugliness of that frog's face, and somehow I felt drawn to
him most powerful and strange.

"Here," he chuckled, "I'll light another match."

He did so and I could see that his single eye was an
intense blue, the missing mate of it being disfigured by some
angrily healed old wound. "A hurt spikehorn deer hooked
it out when I was twelve years old," he said. "Now do you
know who I am?"

"I am new to the country," I said in Mexican. "*Dispénseme, hombre*. I will learn."

"Sure," he said. "*Enjuh*." He sat there a moment, grinning still, then sobered. "I've come to ask you something, Talking Boy. You have a new wife."

"No, no. She but keeps my house and cooks for me."

"Good. I knew her as a girl. We feel strong for one another. I just saw her and she says she needs a man. She wants it bad. Says you have no bone in your penis and you sleep all the while with Seebie."

"It's true," I said.

"I'm sorry for you. A man with a soft ramrod is—"

"No, no!" I cried. "I am only saying that I camp with Sieber, yes. Not with Sister Sawn."

"Oh, I am glad. About your penis, I mean. *Enjuh!*"

"*Enjuh*," I said.

"You give me permission then, Talking Boy?"

"What?"

"Permission. I want to fornicate with her."

"Oh, of course. Yes, yes. Permission. *Enjuh!*"

He got up from sitting on my saddle, and naturally I found my own feet. He put out his hand and I took hold of it and we shook hard and quick. "*Schicho*," he said.

"*Anh, schicho*," I answered, and we were friends from that time and forever. And so it was that I met the sinister and storied Mickey Free, barring only Al Sieber, the greatest of all Indian scouts during the Apache wars of Arizona. So, too, was it that I acquired my Apache name, Talking Boy. Mickey Free gave it to me.

Later, Sieber was to say of him that he was half Mexican, half Apache, half Irish, and all son of a bitch.

Well, I suppose he was.

But he took the worry of Sister Sawn away from my blankets, and a friendship like that can never be repaid.

Our camp, from that night, was the happiest in all the rancheria of Old Pedro.

Wagh! and *enjuh!* Sister Sawn.

I love you still as I loved you then.

In Mickey's arms.

Into Apacheria

About five A.M., just with first light, Sieber came to my blanketplace. He moved noiseless as light wind. His hand was over my mouth as he awakened me. I got up and went with him. We did not disturb any of the children or dogs, and Sister Sawn wasn't there. Snarler, the wolf cub, saw us but only followed us out of our camp with his yellow eyes. I was glad to see that animal alert; it showed he didn't have the hydrophobia and would get better. I followed Sieber, feeling good.

When we were far enough up the hill, out of the rancheria, he whistled soft like the whitewing dove of that country. Mickey Free drifted in out of the morning mists. "Let's go," Sieber said. We went.

Down at the forks of the river, (the White River and the Black River), we found Lieutenant Wheeler and twenty troops of cavalry, from San Carlos. Mickey had guided them up the night before. There had been a story on the reservation that Sieber and me were in danger, held prisoners at the rancheria.

Mickey had left the soldiers at the forks to avoid exciting the Apache camp. He figured, too, that we would not be captives in Old Pedro's friendly hands. But the red haired Free had other and disturbing news for Wheeler. There were in fact a lot of bad Indians up in the rancheria and over in the Cibicu country beyond it. Mickey Free did not know why they were there, but the army would be well advised to keep Pedro's big encampment under discreet watch. Question: How best to do this without the Cibicus getting wind of it?

"I reckon I've got the answer to that," Al Sieber told

Wheeler. "But I've had a hard night and ain't et yet. You bring any rations up with you, lieutenant?"

Wheeler had, and he at once ordered breakfast prepared. As the troops roused up and set to fixing the eats— thick bacon and frying-pan bread—Sieber and Wheeler gathered to the fire with cups of last night's coffee smoking in hand and got square to it.

Mickey Free and me were included but not consulted.

This didn't bother me at first, as I was more interested in the smell of the bacon sizzling and the "Injun bread" frying. But when Sieber commenced to unload his answer for keeping tabs on the thousand Apache roaming Old Pedro's domain (the San Carlos Indians), plus the visiting Cibicus, Tom Horn's jug-handle ears stuck out straight. I could feel them lifting my scalp piece, almost, they was tuning so hard.

Mickey Free was harking close, too, and frowning.

Wheeler and Sieber were talking in English, knowing the one-eyed Irish half-breed did not understand ten words of that language. Naturally, this agitated him. Why he had never learned English is one of those mysteries of which there isn't decent explanation. My own opinion always was that he was simply too wild from his *bronco* upbringing (by the Chiricahua and Warm Springs bands, the very worst) and plain did not want to know the hated White Eye tongue.

However, this did not blunt his "Injun" curiosity.

He kept asking me what they were saying and I had to make up some potent stretchers for him, which I enjoyed. Lying was something I liked to do, and did it right well. Done proper, it could spare harm and bestow kindnesses, ease away pain and restore good feeling. I was to rue the art near unto the death on down the later trail of my life. But for that young morning at the forks of the White and Black it worked fine. Mickey Free didn't miss a word of what I whispered to him. Also, he didn't learn a solitary truthful thing from it, yet was happy as a small boy with the deception.

Fact was, Mickey kept me so busy translating this trash for him, that I missed the drift of Sieber's report to

Wheeler myself. The old German remedied this lapse the minute the confab ended.

"Now, Horn," he said, limping with me out of earshot of the fire, "I want you to do what I am going to tell you; it is the whole reason you got the job.

"Come full sunup, take your horses (I had purchased three head of good ones at Fort Apache) and go back up and live with Pedro. Pedro is a good man and has taken a fancy to you. You are picking up the Apache language swift as a snake seeks shade. In a short spell you will talk it like a Cherry Cow (Chiricahua). Your own mother told you you was an Indian, and she was correct. You was naturally born for a life of this kind and are just the right age to begin it. After a few years of it, you will become a good and valuable man in the Apache troubles, which will go on for years here.

"Now, Pedro has told Mickey to ask Seebie if Talking Boy could stay on as the government man in his camp. So you tell Pedro that Seebie says *anh* and *enjuh*."

He paused, studying me with those intent black eyes.

"Once I leave you here, you will be Pedro's Boy, Horn. You will live as they do and do what Pedro says to do, no matter the risk. But you must never forget you are there to take care of the government business."

Again the pause, the glitter of small black eye.

"Lieutenant Wheeler says your pay will be upped to $100 per month. In addition, you will draw your issue of beef and goods at San Carlos, same as the Apache."

The last pause, the final eye-glint.

"You can see that a spy gets more money than a interpreter of Mexican, likewise shot and cut up more: What is your answer?"

I stood there mute as a blasted stump.

Sieber had set this box trap for his boy all the way back along the trail. Every single thing he had done was aimed at getting me into the Apache camp as a paid sneak. Tom Horn the squaw man. Tom Horn the informer. Tom Horn the Indian traitor. "It is the whole reason you got the job, Horn." Of course it was! I saw that now plain as a cat cruller in a cougar track. Damn!

But it was away too late for weakling cusswords.

"Good man," Al Sieber said. "I knowed that you would do the right thing, Horn."

Wheeler's troop, under its sergeant, now mounted up and set off down the White for San Carlos. Saying not a word more to me, Wheeler then got to his horse, Al Sieber to his gray mule. Even Mickey Free, who I had supposed would return to the Apache camp with me, got on his shaggy mustang. The three of them rode off, just like that, leaving me there.

Sieber and Wheeler didn't even look back. The red-haired breed at least did that.

"*Cuidado!*" he called to me, with a parting wave and ear-split grin of his homely, half-Irish mug.

Which naturally meant that I had better be sleeping mighty light up there where I was going.

Look out, Mickey Free had warned.

So let it be.

I watched until the three riders were fly-speck dots against the rock shimmer of White River's falling course, then turned my horse and spare mounts upstream.

Behind me lay sixteen years, and boyhood.

Ahead waited ten years of my second life, as a young man in love with the wild country and fierce red horsemen of that unknown kingdom called Apacheria.

Chikisin, Brother

When I got off my horse up in front of Pedro's wickiup, he came out grinning and nodding his head.

He said, "Well, my son, you are an Apache now. But you need a brother to show you our ways."

Here, he called up Ramon, the boy who had tried to stop Sieber and me from coming up to the rancheria, just out of San Carlos. "Ramon will be *chi-ki-sin* to you, your brother. Ramon, Talking Boy here will be also your brother. Do you two agree on it?"

Ramon and I knew it wasn't a question but an order, and we both nodded, "*Anh*, yes."

"*Enjuh*," the old Apache said. "My camp is now your home and my lodge will be your lodge. I understand you have come to an arrangement with Mickey Free about my daughter Sawn and will no longer live with her as man of the house. So you stay with me until you find another girl. There are a lot of them, so Ramon says, that want to throw a stick for you to catch. *Anh!*"

Ramon gave me the eye in that moment, hitching his head to indicate we should ease away. We did so, me thanking the ancient chief—Apache people insist Pedro was a hundred years old and had forty-one children—and saying he honored me and I would not dishonor him.

He liked that, saying, "Nice, nice, very pretty," and Ramon and me got out of there.

"Listen," Ramon said, "word has come that a big bunch of Mexican horses, good ones, now, are over in Cibicu Canyon. Some *broncos* stole them. I hear they killed eight Mexicans who were with those horses. If you want some of those horses, we will have to hurry. When the soldiers hear about those eight Mexicans, *ih!*"

"*Por Dios!*" I cried. "You mean go over there into the country of the Cibicus and steal Mexican horses from those *broncos más feroz?*"

"I am not crazy," Ramon said. "We will mean to buy some horses from them. You have money, don't you?"

"Yes, a little."

"Well, I thought you would like to start being an Apache right away, like going to visit the bad ones."

"Chikisin, I don't know."

"Well, I can take you there."

"Hell!" I said. "*Vamos—!*" And away we went.

We got over to Cibicu Canyon all right and found our Indians who had the Mexican horses. They weren't in too good a mood, having just learned that old Chug was out of business and so no *tizwin* to be had. Had they dreamed that the tall, jug-eared white Apache riding with

Ramon was party to that shortage, I would still be in Cibicu Canyon. Or rather at the mouth of it, for we didn't get into the *cañón* proper. The *broncos* said the Cibicu was closed. A palaver was going forward in the wild camps. Big one. Great-name Indians up there. Chiefs with American prices on their heads. "Who?" Ramon inquired.

"Gokliya," said one of the Indians.

Ramon whispered to me, "Geronimo," and I got edgy.

"Is that all?" Ramon said, not wavering.

"It's enough; he's looking for men to go back with him. You want to go, Young Pedro?"

"No. My brother here and I, we are looking to buy some of your good horses, Ramon answered him. We have soldier money."

"Ahhh!"

"Yes, but say, who else is up there with Gokliya?"

"Josannie, Loco, Delzhinne, Juan Perico, young Chato, Kaytennae, Yanosha, Naiche, Eyelash. You want more?"

"No," Ramon said quickly. "I thank you, brother."

Since I later learned the list contained two brothers of Geronimo, a son of Cochise, a son of fabled Juh, and the others all *hesh-kes* ("ritual killers") except Kaytennae, the haste of my "tame" Apache companion was well directed. At the time, I merely felt that the mouth of the black, gaping chasm of the grand *cañón* of the Cibicu Fork was a premier place to be away from.

It developed that the Mexican horses were actually not for sale. They had been stolen and were being held to mount the men Geronimo hoped to enlist to flee from San Carlos to join him in Mexico, readying there for the big war that would drive the *Pinda Lickoyi* from Arizona for all time.

However, the increasingly restless Indian herdsmen believed that a few head would not be missed. Especially if the prices were tempting, with nothing later said of the matter in either camp. So the bargain was struck. I took eight fine animals, paying from $12 to $20 a head. I also gave $80 for the exquisite saddles and bridles of two of the murdered Mexican drovers. This took time, as the Indian is a passionate trader, and my companion began to get nervous.

"*Basta*," Ramon muttered to me. "Will you never quit your talking? These *bárbaros* cannot be bandied with. Come on, now. Quickly, but not too quickly. Ease away."

I nodded my understanding. In truth, I had commenced to get a little of the stink of danger into my own nose. Talking Boy had overdone it. Tom Horn had better return.

Carefully, we gathered our small band of horses and started away. We had gone perhaps a hundred *pasos* when it happened—and we froze where we were, looking back.

I can yet hear that keening cry. The eye of the mind retains the stark instant of its utterance. The taste of panic fear is a gall that is never forgotten. We choked upon it as we now looked back and saw what had sent up that pitiable wail.

It was a girl.

She was near naked under filthy ragments of a settlement dress, and she was running and crying for Chikisin and me to wait for her, to save her from *los bárbaros*.

Even as she ran, bursting up out of an arroyo beyond the Mexican horse herd, the Apaches opened fire on her.

"*Vamos!*" Ramon yelled. "God's name, we can't help her."

But I was watching the desperate girl and saw her stumble and go down, and I said to Ramon, "You run," and I heeled my horse around and sent him back toward the fallen captive. In the same breath of time, three of the Apache herdsmen got to their shaggy ponies and came on the digging gallop for the girl.

Sweet Nopal

Speeding in on the fallen girl, I yelled for her to "get up, get up!" Near as the three mounted Apaches were, there seemed to me time and distance enough between us that I might sweep up the girl and keep the tall horse running. But the girl did not get up, and I realized then she had either been hit by the rifle fire or knocked senseless by striking a rock in her fall. Now hell was to pay.

I slid the bay on his hocks to a stop over the motionless captive of the renegades. The last thing in my racing mind was to shoot any Indians. But Sieber had picked well when he picked me. He had "smelled," as he later put it, that young Tom Horn "was one that would do what he had to do, when he had to do it."

I do not remember pulling my Winchester '73 carbine from its saddle scabbard. I know it wasn't in my hands when I was coming in on the bay. It still wasn't when I hauled him into the hock-skid stop. But when my feet hit the sand of the Big Cibicu Wash, the Winchester was in my hands and blasting.

I shot the foremost of the three Indian riders at forty feet. I hit him square in the face, with his mouth open, yelling. His pony seemed to run right out from under him. His body dropped like that of a hung man going down a scaffold trap.

I missed the second Indian at ten feet, but only because his horse hit a snake hole and collapsed, throwing him clear.

My third shot was into the back of the third Indian, as he raced past me and missed with his own rifle. The weapon, a .50-caliber Spencer carbine, discharged so near my eyes I couldn't see for powderflash blinding. I fired after the rider on instinct, hipping the Winchester like a sawed-off shotgun. His god Yosen (or Ussen) wasn't mounted with him that day. My bullet took him about five joints up his vertebrae from his saddle. It was a hit of the purest outhouse sort, but I took it.

As Al Sieber had early taught me, "They all count one knife cut on your gunstock, lucky or otherwise." A dead Indian, the old scout observed, never did understand the difference. Regardless, I was left in a bad shake.

I stood there a moment, unwilling to believe myself.

In seconds, I had killed two Apache Indians, failed to kill a third only because his horse had gone down with him. *I* had done that. *Me*, Tom Horn, Jr. *Killing*

men. Men I didn't know and who had never done me harm.
It wasn't like real life. One fellow with his teeth mashed
into his brains in the back of his skull. The other with his
spine bones sharded through his bladder and blown out
the front of his breechcloth. *I had done that.* God, but it
felt strange.

It was also nigh the last thing I felt.

The third Apache's knife would have opened my kid-
ney meat but for the girl on the ground. Regaining con-
sciousness, she saw the Indian get to his feet and close
silently on my rear. Her slim hand darted to seize and trip
him by an ankle as he passed her. He stumbled and I
whirled about. Off-balance, he was exposed for the single
instant I required to pulp the base of his brainpan with the
steel butt plate of my Winchester.

I didn't give him a second glance. The soft, rotten
feel of a human head giving inward needs no experience
to judge. A man knows he has destroyed life.

The girl was meanwhile afoot. Indian that my closer
view disclosed her to be, she had captured the reins of
my gelding—cavalry trained to stand on a field of fire—
and now brought him up to me.

"Here, warrior," she said. "Here is your horse."

The voice reached into me, driven by the luminous
eyes.

Here, warrior; here is your horse.

Six words that made my world different. Six words
spoken in guttural, straight Apache. Words that I understood and answered, in tongue, not even knowing that I
did. Six words. And I had found my sweet Nopal, the
woman of my life, and we both but children in our years.

Children?

Well, strange children. Dark in more than outer skin,
or inner doubt of others. We were wild children, Nopal and
Talking Boy. We spoke a kindred language beyond the
thick Apache accents of our desperate greeting on that
bloody wash below forbidden Cibicu Canyon.

We were ourselves Cibicus, *broncos.*

Bunch-quitters.

"*Enjuh, nah-lin,*" was all I said to her, taking the horse,
"well done, maiden child."

And we mounted up on the rangy gelding, quick as two pumas going aboard the same big deer, and drove him out of there with Apache yells as wild as any Juh, Geronimo, Kaytennae, or Chato of the merciless white-hunting wolf pack gathered above us on the Cibicu Creek.

It was as well that we *were* quick.

Even as we wheeled the bay to go, disaster rode out of the yawning mouth of Cibicu Canyon.

"Behind you, behind you!" I heard a familiar voice crying. It was my brother Chikisin yelling at us. He had not ridden to save himself, but still had our band of Mexican horses bunched together, holding them until I might either pick up the girl or get myself killed trying it. It was all of bravery any man could offer his brother in such a case. It very well could have meant Chikisin's own death to wait as he had to help me, should such help prove of human provision. I shouted back to him, now, turning the bay to head in on the little herd that he guarded. Only when I had done this did I twist in the saddle to see what his warning cry concerned.

I had thought it would be the remaining two Apaches with the stolen Mexican herd of Geronimo. Likely, they had also found their saddle mounts by this time and were coming on to avenge their dead brothers. Well, surely old Chikisin and Talking Boy could handle them!

Alas, the ignorance of white Apaches.

It was not two Apaches but twenty of them. And they were not coming from the stolen herd but from the forboding entrance to the big canyon. And now, my white God forbid, Chikisin was yelling something else.

A name; one of recent memory for me.

"Gokliya! Gokliya!" the slender son of Old Pedro was standing in his stirrups to wave. The name did not on the instant come to me. Then it did. It was brought to me by the low voice of the girl clinging behind me on the back of the racing gelding. "He is saying it is Geronimo," she told me. Then, while my gut shriveled still to that information, she added. "Ride a little harder, warrior; I am Gokliya's youngest wife."

But for a whim of purest chance, we would never have returned to the rancheria of Old Pedro. We had, simply to make traveling easier, put our two grand new Mexican saddles on separate horses, cinched and buckled down. We thus had four saddled horses, with six un-saddled animals, to use in relay. As well, I had not wasted my dicker time with the *bronco* herders. We had got the best they had in the Mexican bunch, plus our own two mounts, ten prime horses for three riders.

The twenty Apaches, under Gokliya, failing to come up to us in the first mad race over Big Cibicu Wash, were outdistanced by the first relay of mounts, lost entirely at the second change. It was also by that time grown dark. We kept going. Terms such as *outdistanced* and *lost* have little meaning when Apache Indians are after you. The temper of our retreat may be judged by the fact that, until the high valley of our rancheria lay below us, we ex-changed no intelligence with the rescued girl. Even then, coming into the village, unannounced, we left the child with Sawn at my camp with instructions to "hide her out," until we could "cool the herd" and return.

Chikisin and me went on up into the overlook hills with our new Mexican horses and saddles and lay out up there in a far-lonely place called Fish Hawk Meadow. It was a sort of sacred place to the San Carlos Apache, re-served for cleansing the spirit. That was good for our cause. We wanted no company just then, and the spectacular drop-off cliff to the south gave a view near down to the Mexican line. We were looking for our *bronco* cousins to come after us along the track we had left coming home from visiting them. But they never came.

After a second long day of laying out and looking down, we whistled in our beautiful new horses and drifted on lower into the valley. We came into the village about noon with a fine story of buying the proud animals off a Sonora rancher up to trade at old Camp Grant. We said the saddles were won playing monte with the Mex cow-boys.

Nobody believed us, but Indians love a good lie.

We had a little more trouble explaining Nopal.

Finally, Old Pedro had an idea.

"Why not let the child tell her own story?" he suggested. "One can see she has been a long and a hard way. Go ahead, *nah-lin*. We are all friends here."

Nopal looked at Chikisin and me.

Especially me.

"Shall I do it?" she said simply.

I wanted to say, no, for God's sake, but the suggestions of Old Pedro were like the direct orders of Al Sieber, ignored or countermanded at certain peril.

"Yes," I nodded, fearing the worst, "go ahead and tell it as my father directs you to do."

Nopal was not long in the tale. She was not Apacheborn, but Yaqui, an Indian people wilder even than the wildest Chiricahua or Warm Springs renegades. Taken in a raid by the Nednhi band of Chief Juh when only a toddler, she had no Indian memory but that of her savage childhood among Juh's people. Then, another capture, this time by Mexican forces in a surprise (and most rare!) raid upon the Apaches, who were caught in a trading visit at Fronteras, Sonora. The now six-year-old Yaqui girl was taken, with the other suitable young females captured by the troops, to be sold into slavery, in Mexico, where such Indian girls were a regular item of frontier barter. She was bought by a family in Camargo, Chihuahua, and resold by them deeper into Mexico, to relatives in Durango state.

She had stayed a servant, a *reducido*, in Durango for ten years. Then, with a group of other Apache servant women, she had "gone into the chaparral" one night, nigh a year gone. This hopelessly brave little band, known in Mexico as *Las Gatas Alocadas*, "the Wild Cats," made their ways, together and separately, northward toward their Apache homelands, seven, eight, even nine hundred miles away, through settled Mexican land, under constant pursuit by government troops which, traditionally, made no distinction between the sexes when hunting Apaches.

The heroic saga of *Las Gatas* is well known in Mexico and should have its own book written about it, but this is not that tale. Nopal, so named by her Mexican owners because of her wild beauty reminding them of the fragile yet spine-guarded blossom of the *nahuatl nopali* cactus (which Arizona cowboys God-bless and condemn as the prickly pear), was one of three women to survive the desperate flight. The other four of the original eleven were either killed or recaptured. Of the five recaptured, four committed suicide. There is only a record of one who was sent back to Durango alive.

As to the three "lucky ones," they had split up at Casas Grandes, Chihuahua. The two older women had journeyed on toward Arizona, seeking Nana's Warm Springs band. Nopal had turned into the Sierra del Norte seeking the Nednhi. She never found them.

Instead, Gokliya found her.

He was bound north and had no time to take the returned "little sister" to the Nednhi, but carried her along with his war party. On the long ride up into the Cibicu Canyon country and the meeting there called to stir the San Carlos Indians into "going out" with Geronimo and his Bedonkohe band of Mexican Apaches, the great chief—ever one with an eye for women—had "seen" beneath the rags and filth and bruises and the hollow-eyed gauntness of the starved girl. When there was time, he had told her, she would be his youngest wife.

This thought had sobered the weary and weakened girl. Her years in the Mexican settled country had educated her mind, though her heart might remain as wild as any canyon creature. Watching helplessly the butchery of the Mexican cowboys with the stolen herd—the Apaches had unspeakably brutalized them before allowing the dignity of death—the Yaqui girl had of a sudden understood that she had not come this thousand miles from far Durango, still in the rags of her Mexican servitude, only to be sold into another slavery even more degrading as Geronimo's fifth woman.

She knew from dim memory the treatment afforded young wives by old wives in the Apache pecking order.

And Gokliya had a reputation as a *macho*, even among a people notoriously callous in their handling of horses and women. No, she would not stand to be mounted by this murderous Bedonkohe stud "at his convenience" and "when there was time."

Freedom, as desperately sought as Nopal's, must mean more than that.

"The end of the story of course you know," the girl finished, soft-voiced. "When I lay in that arroyo on the orders of the men with the Mexican horses and saw Talking Boy so tall and graceful riding away from there, my heart leaped up within me. Gokliya had ordered me to help the herders, the lowest work on a war party. I was still hurt and hungry and sick from the long running from Durango. My heart said to me, Go free. It said, Run, Nopal! Cry out to the tall boy and his Apache friend. Go with them. Go free—!

"And so I did it," she concluded, lifting her splendid eyes. "And I am free."

Old Pedro sat looking at her. The ancient head nodded. The rheumy eyes peered forth from their hooded folds of skin. His hand, all bones and shrunken sinews, reached out to touch her gently as a willow leaf will fall on sliding water.

"We will have something to say to Talking Boy and Chikisin," he told her, "but for yourself, Little Sister, you have found your people. This place is your place. You have come home."

Nopal took the old hand in her own firm young hands.

"Father," she said, "I am your daughter."

And that was the end of it.

Yaqui Bride

For four months, at the turn of the year, Nopal and me loved and lived the Indian life. Mostly we stayed with Sister Sawn and our Apache family, with all Sawn's kids and the animals, brother Chikisin, and sometime night visitor, scout Mickey Free, thrown in for full measure. It was wonderful times for all of us. And when it got too much for my Yaqui sweetheart we would go up into Fish Hawk Meadow to be alone for a spell. Those were the grandest times of all.

Nopal could stalk and shoot game with any young buck Apache. My passion for life of hunting and tracking kept us both out on the mountain. We were not just squaw man and squaw. Though, God knows, we shared what the Apaches called an "always warm" blanket. We were crazy to be at one another when the time was ripe for such play. We would roll and grunt and laugh wild as young creatures on four legs. Then, coupling, we would be wild and tender both, but mostly quiet and drawing it out. It seemed we knew what would come for our two lives, for Nopal had a shadow-spirit, too. Without ever saying a word on it, we used our time like it was gold or silver coin, spending it piece by piece. And when, with early spring, Nopal's belly commenced to round, we were deep-happy with the spending.

Then it came May of 1877.

A new agent was down at San Carlos, the first military man ever to hold that post. I had met him before. He was Captain, now Major, Adna Chaffee. When Chikisin came looking for me up at Fish Hawk Meadow that seventeenth day of May, he brought word that ended my loving time with sweet Nopal: Chaffee wanted to see me, Tom Horn; the hour had come to use what I had learned in my spy's apprenticeship among the Apache of Old Pedro.

When I got down to the village, word waited that the ancient chief wanted to see me before I should depart.

At his wickiup, I found him already mounted on his bony white mare. "I am going with you, Talking Boy," Pedro croaked. "You will need me." He looked around impatiently. "Now where did those two rascals go to?" he demanded of his wrinkled squaw, Na-to, "Tobacco."

"I don't know about the Mexican," Tobacco answered, "but the red-haired son of a bitch is off in the grass with Sister Sawn. I saw them going at it, when I was picking up firewood earlier. *Wagh!* No shame. No shame at all. *Pah!*"

I grinned at her. "Admit it, mother. You were peeping on them."

"A lie!" the old crone cried out. "I came on them by accident."

"Did you stay by accident?" her leathery husband inquired. "You are the one to be ashamed. Seventy winters, and the fire in your jacal still smokes!"

"Smokes, do you say?" the old woman challenged indignantly. "Ha! You should have some of the embers of my fire in your breechclout, *senita!* You would do a lot better job with that young Chihuahua wife, the bitch coyote! Let me tell you what I know of her—"

"*Cállate,*" said the old man. "Here is Mickey now."

He gave Tobacco a look to repay her having called him *senita,* "senile," and, with Mickey looking a little washed out in gills, off the three of us rode down the river. At the forks, a handsome young fellow came out of the alders on a magnificent black horse to join us. This was Merijilda Grijole, a pureblood Mexican caught and raised by Geronimo's Bedonkohe family of Chiricahua Apaches. Due to his kinship with the dangerous Gokliya, he made a habit of "laying out" of the camps like Pedro's to spare the nerves of the tame Indians who lived in them.

Geronimo was a name to jump a reservation Apache near as high as it did a white settler living too far out of Tucson or away from one of the army forts.

Me and Merijilda, however, hit it off on the spot.

He was a loner and a liar and an easy laugher the same as Tom Horn. Our shadows shook hands in the grin we shared on meeting up. Mickey Free of course saw how it was and said, *enjuh,* it was a good thing.

"You will need every friend you got, where you are going," was the exact way he put it. But I never was one to quibble a man's good intentions. Mickey always meant well. He just did bad at it now and again. That was of course his Apache moccasins tripping over his Irish cavalry boots.

Down at the agency, Major Chaffee had us in at once. His problem was one left him by the civilian agents that had gone ahead of him. The Indians, newspapermen, and merchant folk all over Arizona had said for years the

civilian agents were crooks outright. I, myself, had seen supplies meant for Indians hauled away by white freighters by
the wagon-train loads. There was supposed to be 12,000
Indians getting issued supplies. No more than 5,000 ever
showed up by my count. The "difference" went to
crooked white and Mexican merchants who bought the
"surplus" at ten and fifteen cents on the dollar that honest
Arizona traders had to pay. This graft was starving the Indians and the whites likewise.

The whole thing, Chaffee told us, had to stop.

His answer was to ask Pedro the old chief's help in
"getting to" the Indians of the entire country, carrying
to them the glad news that an honest White Eye was now
at San Carlos. One they all knew. If some feared him, all
respected him. It was Bad Talker Chaffee (the name taken
from his spectacular profanity). He was the oak leaf chief
who had been their enemy but never lied to them. Pedro's
role was to frame the appeal to the discouraged and alien-
ated Indians.

"Your job, Horn," Chaffee snapped, wheeling suddenly
on me, where I squatted against the wall with Merijilda
and Mickey, "will be to take Pedro's words into the Cibicu
country and preach it to the bad Indians out there. What
do you say to that, *jefe?*" he turned back to Pedro. "Horn's
been living with you. Why not send him to live around
with the Cibicu the same way? He could be able to influence them to come in."

Pedro, who so far had been sitting on a canvas camp-
stool in front of the officer's desk, now stood up. He always
arose when he talked to the army people or to anyone
important. This was to let everyone know it was not a talk,
anymore, but a speech.

"I say, no," he began. "He must not go there unless
you allow me to send at least one hundred good warriors
with him. Two hundred would be even better, and I offer
that many to you now. Soldier captain (all officers were
capitán to Pedro), you know soldiers. I am an Indian chief,
as was my father and my father's father. I have more influence with these Indians than any man on the earth. I
know the Apaches as you know your soldiers, too. But the
day you send this boy to the Cibicu country alone will

be the day he dies. I say this to you now, *capitán;* no white man can go among the Cibicus and return. They will put Talking Boy to the fire, roast him like a quarter of agency beef, and send you an old squaw to tell you to keep your flour and your sugar and your lies and send out some more of your warriors for them to burn."

It was my job—not very comfortable one!—to translate this long statement for Chaffee. Sieber was laid up sick with his old Civil War hurts, Mickey couldn't talk English, and Merijilda let on like he couldn't either, so I was stuck with it. But Major Chaffee surprised me.

"Son," he said to me, "the old man has made me see for the first time what kind of people we are dealing with in these Cibicu Indians. I will need to give it more time. But I am not going to send you up there, only ask you to be steady where you are, and keep prepared."

I thanked him, for I knew this man was a fighter.

"Major," I added, "you may count on me. And I hope, when it does come time to go after those devils, that you will remember Tom Horn."

Chaffee grinned, the smile lighting his sunburned face like noonlight on pink granite. "Goddamn it, Horn," he said, "one good thing about being such an ugly son of a bitch as you are is that you will get remembered. I could no more forget the natural beauty of your person than I could Al Sieber's."

"Thank you, Major Chaffee, sir."

"Don't give me any of that shit, Horn."

"Yes sir," I said. "I would never try that."

He eyed me, no smile now. *"Well, don't,"* he advised and gave me a parting shove and slammed the door so hard he caught the butt of my buckskin pants in the damn doorjamb, and a little of the butt along with them.

It was with some relief that I sought out Pedro and prepared to depart for the rancheria. But I was simple of mind to think that day was through troubling my small Apache world. We had no more than gotten our mounts untied from the rail in front of the agency office than here came an army ambulance up the street in a cloud of dust to halt right atop us. In it was the quartermaster of the Sixth Cavalry—which had relieved the Fifth in Arizona whiles

I had been with the Indians—and he got down from his wagon in some agitated state and went on the near-trot into Chaffee's office. I gave a uneasy sign to Pedro and said, "*Jefe*, let us get away from here, for my white man's nose smells army troubles."

The old chief only nodded and turned his mare.

"You have a good nose, my son," he said. "Noble and bent and big, like an Indian's. I believe you. *Vaya!*"

That was the *vaya* that came too late.

Even as I lifted my heels to drive them into my horse's flanks, the office door banged open and the florid granite of Major Adna Chaffee's face was split to bawl after me.

"Hold it, Horn. Get your ass back in here!"

I got down and went in and had my world changed again, all in under five minutes of that bright May morning.

The quartermaster's message was for me:

It was an order, effective immediately, issued that same day by General Willcox, from Sixth headquarters.

As thus:

> The QM informs no further funds supplied to meet civilian payroll. In consequence, all scouts & packers of this nomenclature are discharged on this date. Further, a general order accompanies, which mandates that no white person, not in active employ of the military or other arm of the government of the United States, will be allowed to live at the agency or upon the reservation. All those herein described are to be advised of the order and compelled to leave on receipt.
> Signed,
> WILLCOX
> ACG DA 6th USCAV

It may be imagined that this disclosure came as a knee buckler to Tom Horn. While it naturally affected all the scouts and white employees at San Carlos, I was the sole one of them with an Indian wife and living way off in the hills with her people. And I was for certain sure the only one of them with a wife but fifteen years old and five months pregnant. That was the cruncher.

I was still numb from it when I rejoined Old Pedro outside. I told him of the news as we rode down the agency street. He thought a bit, then said quietly.

"What will you do, Talking Boy?"

We had come to the chaparral at the edge of the agency clearing. Pedro halted his old white.

"I am going home," he said, pointing to the mountains. "Where are you going?"

"I don't have a home anymore," I answered. "If I go back with you, it will only bring trouble to the people up there. I wouldn't do that to you, or to them."

The old man looked at me a long time.

"I will tell Nopal," he said. "Is there a message?"

I nodded quickly. "Tell her I will come for her before the baby is born. She will understand."

"Yes," Old Pedro said. "She is an Indian."

There was a last stretching of silence. Only those know it who have suffered it. Two men parting, whose shadows are telling them that their lives together cannot be the same again, yet whose tongues refused to say such a thing aloud.

"*Jefe*," I said, turning my bay horse back toward the agency, "do you have any message for me?"

Old Pedro said, "Yes. I am still your father."

He rode away on the bony white mare, back up into the mountains of White River. I watched after him, feeling bad. At the last turning of the trail, he halted the mare and looked back. I saw him raise his left hand in the old Apache farewell. I returned the sign and said, "Good-bye, my father," but of course he did not hear me.

He was too far away.

Scheflin's Ledge

At San Carlos the other scouts, packers, and wranglers were getting ready to go. I found the most of them aiming to go over to Tucson, *the* place for white drifters from as far as Texas and California. If there was anything doing, you would learn of it in Tucson. It was the Denver of Arizona, or the Kansas City. So off we went to it, not one care amongst us.

Of our particular traveling bunch, out of the twenty-odd members of it, I remember there was Arch McIntosh; Sam "Bowlegs" Bowman; Frank Monic; "Some Long" Jim Cook (six feet eight inches tall!); Charley Mitchell; Buck, or Buckskin Frank, Leslie; Burt Sage (known as "the breed," which he wasn't); Francisco Bennet; Ed Clark (called Biggie); Joe Yescus; and, of course Merijilda Grijole.

Half the total was just packers, but most of my good pals named here was scouts and interpreters. We made a rough-feathered flock of birds, you may believe, and it don't need me to tell you who was the head turkey; it was naturally big Al Sieber.

Well, we hung around Tucson some that summer, but not long enough to molt. Along from California came old Ed Scheflin (Schieffelin), and, him and Sieber being campmates long before, Ed confides to Al that him and his California bunch has come back to make their millions. It seemed old Ed had struck a ridge of the pure *plata* over in the Cochise country sometime back, but been drove out by the Apaches, his partner Lennox kilt on the discovery site by the redguts, and so forth. Now, Scheflin was back with his tough *hombres* from the mother lode diggings of California. They was outfitted to go into the Apache country

126

and to stay there. Al and his boy was welcome to throw in and come along, but double-mum was the word otherwise.

Me and Al caucused on it for all of five minutes, voting to go as soon as the drinks were settled up.

By that time of the summer, most of our San Carlos packer pals had been forced to take jobs freighting for the private business and were gone on. There were but five, six left in Tucson. Sieber got the OK from Ed Scheflin to count these good old boys in.

The scowling German also had a word of last warning to the Silver Ridge Gang, as we called ourselves: we would not be on Scheflin's mother lode ledge twenty-four hours before every bad Indian in the territory would know that a "lone band" of white men had come into their Apache parlor, *without soldier guards.*

One of Ed Scheflin's Californy Boys, big as a grizzly and twice as gruff, answered for all the others of us.

"Ed assures us there is heavy mineral over there, and a lots of it," he growled. "If there is any bad Injuns to go along with it, they will just have to look out for themselves. Whichaway do we head out, Sieber?"

Al Sieber liked that kind of talk; it was his kind.

"Come on, boys!" he said. "Foller me!"

We camped that first night outside Pantano, a long thirty-mile day over toward the valley of the San Pedro River. Sieber and me lay out by ourselves and talked of a lot of things. The main drift of it was that Al advised me to think hard about some other business than cavalry scouting. He said to forget about my Apache wife, that her people would care for her and for my kid as well, when she bore it. "There is no next day for a white man with a squaw wife," he said. "It will hold you back wherever you go. Let her be, Horn. If we make a strike here, take your stake and ride away, a good long way, from them Injuns. Wasn't I so old and crippled up, I would go with you. But I will end here."

I thanked him and said I didn't know rightly what I would do about Nopal. Having been back with white men,

I was brought to see it different than up at Old Pedro's rancheria, or the solitudes of Fish Hawk Meadow.

"One thing sure," I said. "No matter I admire the Injun ways and with respect and love the good Apaches to the end, I ain't going to squander the rest of my life in squawing it, Al. But Nopal is carrying my kid and I still feel deep for her. I will go back to see that the baby is safe born, and its mother well off. Advice can't stop that."

Sieber nodded. He chunked a big piñon root on our fire that would hold the bank through the night.

"Well, Horn," he said, "study it. Here we are, fired out of hand again, and the Injuns helling worse than ever they was before. Why? Because of the Injun Bureau and them damn civilian do-gooders back east. Government hire don't make sense. Right when you're needed most, they can you. No, boy. Learn yourself another trade, cattle, horses—stay with this mining, if it suits you—but get out of the Injun-scouting business."

I was studying it, all right, but pulling blanks.

"Hell," I said. "You was the one told me I was born to that life. Was you lying then, or now?"

"Neither. You ain't like I thought you was, Horn. Not like me, nor Long Jim, nor Frank Leslie, nor Archie McIntosh, nor the others. You been forgetting you was born white. I warned you about that. So did Old Pedro. Now, here's my last word on it: remember who you are; forget who they are. Don't go back to the blanket."

Those gimlet black eyes of his, so natural to the human bear that Al Sieber was, bored into me for one final twisting scowl.

"You do go back to squawing it," he said, "and me and you will wind up hunting one another."

With that, he was done. He rolled over to tighten the cinch of his horse blanket about his bulk and was snoring inside half a minute.

But I knew what he had meant. It was that if Tom Horn wanted to run with the Indians, Al Sieber would make a gun-butt notch out of Talking Boy just as quick as he would any other war-age Apache.

I lay wide-eyed a good hour pondering it; I don't recall if I came to any choice, or not.

We made Benson with the second day's ride. But on the third day, getting deep into the Cochise country and cutting away from following the San Pedro south, to swing easterly, Scheflin lost his track. It took him three days more to get back on it. Then, at last, coming sundown of the sixth day, he stopped us on a high-lonesome salt-cedar brake, flanking down out of the Dragoon Mountains.

"Boys," he said, "we have arrived. Right here is where we was camped when Lennox was kilt." He looked around, a little wild in the eye, and us the same. "Come along on," he said, "and I will show you the very spot where I was digging."

It wasn't far off.

When we were there, it all lay as he had described it in Tucson. There was his exploration, twenty-three feet deep by our excited measurement. Its exposure was all ore, and high-grade ore. The men like to went mad.

When all had quieted some, Scheflin spoke out.

"We got our agreement," he said. "You all will get to stake, both ways from discovery. Every man will have a recorded claim. Each will pay me one-quarter for bringing you in, as signed to in Los Angeles. I will be filed as owning one-quarter of each claim, for the first fifty each way from discovery. Agreed, boys?"

"Agreed!" they all shouted, and he went on.

"Now, what will we call it? Got to have a name. Let me show you something first. Over here."

We all trooped behind him, leaving our horses. He led us off only about three or four rods. "See that?" he pointed. We squinted hard in the late light, all nodding. It was a slab of rock wedged upright, like a cemetery marker. There was a stake back of it, holding it firm and holding something else, too; it was a human skull. "That's Lennox," Ed Scheflin said. "I put my monument square atop where they kilt him."

That big bunch of hairy-eared miners and frontiersmen shifted around, uneasy. "*You* put Lennox's head on the stick, Ed?" one of them asked.

"Not hardly," Scheflin answered. "When I snuck back to bury him, the head was took. I put just the body under and got shut of this place *más pronto*. Come daybreak, I was thirty mile north and not looking back."

"How you know it's Lennox's skull?" another man said.

"Them three gold teeth and the twin bullet holes in the back of it. They turned him over, wounded, and shot him twice in the base of the skull piece. I *seen* that." Scheflin looked around through the glooming twilight. "It was just this time of day," he said. "It's how I got away. Bad shooting light. They plain missed me."

There followed a nervous stir of rough miners' boots and a wash of coughs and throat clearings.

"Well," Jim Cook said, "whyn't we call the camp after that headrock you put up for Lennox? That'd be appropri-ous."

Ed Clark snorted at that. "You mean Head Rock, Ari-zona?"

"Hell no, he don't mean Head Rock," Frank Leslie said. "He means Monument."

"No," Ed Scheflin said. "I mean Tombstone."

There was a spooky pause, then some burly hardrock gopher spoke out aloud, "Amen!" and yet another fellow prospector pulled a half-full quart bottle of Old Crow out from under his California coat, busted it on the outcrop crown of Ed Scheflin's twenty-three-foot vein of silver, and bawled out, "Tombstone, she is—!"

And, simple as that, the meanest town in the Arizona Territory got nominated, baptized, and deserted, all in about thirty-five seconds of that darkening summer's night, in the gut of the Cherry Cow country.

Tombstone Summer

Next day the whole camp (fifty-nine men) turned out in black dawn so as not to be left when light enough for "staking" streaked the east. Sieber and me was up with the earliest. But the bottle got to going around the breakfast fires, and Iron Man took his belts every turn. It was midday when I got him away. By this time, the only claims left were away up on the divide. For appearance' sake, we put in our stakes and piled up rocks for our monuments, with the regulation tin can wedged in at the top with our "description paper" tucked in it.

That was the official first day for Tombstone, Arizona. It would cut the story short to say that, within one year, those fifty-nine men had swoll to seven thousand. Claims were running out so far from discovery they made Al's and mine look like hot prospects. They were filed nearer the San Pete than they was Scheflin's strike and wouldn't mine a good grade of sand, let alone of stamp-mill silver. But Al Sieber had "been there before," as old mineral hunters say. He was able once more to advise me on "proper caution of forethought."

"Bucko," he said, "here is what we'll do. We can make us a better clean-up in this here camp by meat-shooting deer and antelope than by trying to outdig these hard-rock gophers. Let them handle the double jacks and bull-prod drills. Blisters ain't our style. Nor getting blowed apart by giant powder. I and you will just go up on the ridges and loaf around and hunt deer."

"But what of our claims?" I protested. "Maybe blisters ain't our style, but dying rich is my ambition."

"We can get two dollars and a half for every carcass we pack out of the hills. Maybe it ain't the short haul to owning the mint, but leave me tell you something: in hard-ass fact, them claims of ours ain't worth a dollar cash. We could work them all summer and come up owing ourselves money on payday. But, just wait till fall, when enough suckers collect and sufficient tinhorns show up, and we can sell out and ride away winners.

"Now you study it, Horn. It oughtn't to take you the rest of August to pick twixt hunting and hard work."

"No sir," I said, "that's a fact. Let's go."

It was the Sixth of October that me and Al was laying around our deer camp up in Middle Pass of the Dragoons, and a very old friend of the better days showed up to share our noon dinner with us.

"*Hola*," grinned Mickey Free, shadowing in out of the nearby bull pines. "*Qué pasa, hombres?*"

"Pull up a deer rib and squat down," Sieber told him. "*Qué pasa* with you, you little bandy-legged fart? We know it ain't good news, so save it till we've et."

"*De seguro*," agreed the wild-haired half-breed, cutting himself a slab of deer ribs off our roasting spit. "But you won't like it any better on a full belly. Guess who is up from Mexico again?"

"Oh, Christ," groaned Sieber. "Not him."

"*Mas suerte de la próxima*," Mickey grunted between wolfing bites at the hot deer meat. "Try it again."

"It *is* him," the old German scowled.

"*A ciencia cierta*, Seebie," Mickey Free nodded. "In the mining camp below is Lieutenant Von Schroder and a squad of six men, me guiding. He carries a letter from General Willcox. It says you and Talking Boy are under orders to report in at Fort Whipple, *más pronto*. Your pay starts when you do. *Enjuh?*"

"What the hell do you mean, is it good?" Sieber complained. "I ain't even finished my coffee yet."

Well, we chewed it over with Mickey, and Sieber reckoned he would do it. I couldn't come to it for myself that easy. I had made my split of the blanket with the Indians.

"Listen," I said. "From everything you tell us, Mickey, this here Sixth Cavalry can't even find the *broncos*, let alone whip them. They ain't ever been into the mountains, even. All hell's busted loose, you say, with the Injuns robbing and killing and raiding, and most of them drunk most of the time, and now you say Geronimo is back up here out of the Mexican Sierra ready to lead the Apaches square down the main stem of downtown Tucson. And me and Sieber is supposed to saddle up when Willcox blows the bugle? To go and ride naked out in front of a bunch of cavalry that's not so much as been fired on yet? *Hijo, hombre!* Let Seebie speak for himself. We are not both *lunáticos*."

Mickey Free wasn't grinning anymore.

"You don't want to go after Geronimo?" he said.

"Hell no. I ain't lost nothing in his camp."

The dwarfish Irish breed shook his mop of scarecrow hair. "Yes," he said, "you have. Your woman."

It was as direct as that.

Geronimo had sent a picked band on a side raid over into Pedro's country. They had come into the rancheria in the gut of the night, taken Nopal, gotten away back over the mountain, unscathed. A pursuit was made with daybreak and a rifle fight followed, when the raiders were surprised at a water-hole rest halt. Chikisin had taken a grievous wound, Al-chinne and Bobby Do-klanny been killed. Do-klanny had lived long enough to identify the leader of the Bedonkohe band. It was a young Mexican Indian named Hal-zay. He was a nephew of Geronimo, a grandson of old Nana, the only Indian worse than Geronimo in reputation. It was said Nana, who was still riding the war trails at seventy-eight years of age, had killed more white men than all the other Chiricahua chiefs of the hostiles combined. So Hal-zay was bred to be remembered, and I remembered him. But for that terrible moment of Mickey Free's revelation that Nopal was gone, I could think of nothing but her and our child.

"The baby," I said, when Mickey had filled out the stark bones of the raid. "My God, was it—did she—"

"No baby yet," the half-breed said. "Squaw all right."

"But it's past her time. Weeks past it."

Mickey Free shook his ugly head. "Baby still in her," he said. "You want to go chase Geronimo now?"

I got up and poured our water bucket on the fire.

Sieber kicked away the wet ashes.

"*Ugashe*," I said to Mickey Free in Apache, "let's go."

Geronimo Again

Back at San Carlos, the air smelt of trouble and the work pace was furious. Any man that rode for Al Sieber when the bugles blew would know what I mean. He became fevered with an Indian hunt in prospect. It was riding around the clock and then back around again, with no sleep, not stopping longer than to tighten a cinch, and as to eating, a Sieber scout had to be able to live on what a hungry wolf would leave.

You will understand of course that when Sieber got heated up to hunt Indians—and the same with me—it wasn't to kill good Indians but the bad boys that kept the decent Apaches from any chance at living peaceable with the whites. We knew, me and Sieber, what those poor damn "peaceables" never could seem to savvy. To be seen with bad Indians, made bad Indians out of all of them. And you just never could get at the bad ones but that some good ones was caught in the crossfire.

But I won't lie about it.

For me it was grand exciting times just like it was for Al. The "Injun fever" was in my bloodstream, too. Iron Man never took a step that Tom Horn was over a lariat toss away. Unless, that was, he had sent me on a mission as Talking Boy, where I could get into jacals and wickiups and under brush ramadas even Old Mad wasn't welcome in. It was some times!

The weeks flew and even months, and we was getting those Sixth Cavalry troops into trim and their asses saddle-toughed to where those tender boys could stay up with me and Al Sieber and Mickey Free and Merijilda.

But damn, where was Geronimo?

Where were all the "bad ones" up with him from the Mexican Sierra del Norte—the bastards that had been burning up the frontier when General Willcox called us back from Tombstone, the fall of 1877?

Good Lord, here it was the spring of 1878! Our boys of the Sixth was as ready as two-year-old bulls held out of the heifer pasture all winter. But Sieber and me and the others hadn't been able to find them one genuine bad *bronco* to chase, nor a solitary Cibicu to surround.

Then, midmorning of April 29, it broke. I remember the date because it marked the month coming (May) that would make it one year I had been away from my Apache wife Nopal. As a matter of fact, I was setting outside the agency building holding up its south wall—where the sun was best—

squatted in the dirt with Mickey and Merijilda and some of our purebloods, and we was talking about Nopal. I was telling them my hunch was that I would never see her again. They were wagging heads to the negative, insisting it wouldn't be Gokliya's style to settle for the kidnap. No sir. Old Saint Jerome would see to it that Talking Boy got hurt worse than that.

I knew who they meant by the Saint Jerome name. It was the beginning of the Mex name, *Jeronimo*, for Gokliya. The Americans then made Geronimo out of that. But the Mexicans hung Jeronimo on the Bedonkohe chief because Saint Jerome was known as the Orator. And God knows old Gokliya could orate something scandalous. Or at least that's what Mickey and Merijilda told me, and they had forgot more real *know* on the Apaches than a white man like me could hope to learn in his life, entire.

I still took pause on their story.

With Indians, names are peculiar items. For example, Geronimo's Apache name *Gokliya* was said by one branch of the Chiricahua to mean "the Laugher" and by another side of the Cherry Cow family to stand for "the Yawner." It was said to be taken, in either event, from his odd habit of opening his mouth from ear to ear as a baby still on his mother's teats. I don't know. It's a long stretch from liking jokes to being bored or sleepy. But I was only commencing to get my Apache education.

Right at the moment concerned, Mickey had just said, "Well, just be patient, Talking Boy. You will see that Cousin Merijilda and Brother Miguel are your best teachers. Seebie knows a lot and you know a little. But we know Geronimo. He is one bad Indian son of a bitch."

"Yes," Merijilda nodded. "Sieber calls Mickey a son of a bitch. But Uncle Gokliya? *Ay de mí! Sí, hombre,* you may believe it; Geronimo will think of some Apache way to 'show you' your wife again." He looked at me *con compasión.* "I hope she still has her nose," he said.

I had seen Apache squaws with their noses cut off for infidelity. Merijilda wasn't being cruel. Nopal had been named as belonging to Geronimo. And she had fled to me. The possibility spoiled the sun for me.

Merijilda Grijole was a pure Mexican raised by the Bedonkohe Chiricahua. Mickey Free was a half Mexican reared up in the Warm Springs band of Nana.

I had to believe them.

I did not, as the matter now developed, need to put that believe on a faith basis, however.

"*Miren ustedes,*" Merijilda said, pointing suddenly down the agency wagon road, to the south. "Do we not know that old crow flopping this way, Brother Miguel?"

Mickey peered southward, blue eyes narrowing.

"*Hijo!*" he said. "It is that old devil Mary Penole. Now we will learn something."

"Mary Cornmeal?" I said. "Who the hell is that? I see only an old crippled-up Apache crone hobbling this way on foot. And that packmule she leads! *Santissimo!*"

Merijilda and Mickey got up, and I with them.

"The old lady is a message runner," the Mexican scout told me, "from the *broncos.* Where Mary Cornmeal goes, the wild Indians will follow soon. You watch."

"And listen, too," Mickey Free added, with his grin.

A moment later the limping squaw halted in the road, squinting over at us. "*Hola,* handsome boy," she called to Merijilda, one of the most perfectly formed men. "Why don't you ever come to see us anymore? All the women ask for you." She drew her head to one side, eyeing Mickey. "*Hola,* ugly one," she waved. "How is the young jackmule today? Are you still frightening all the young squaws with that thing Ussen hung upon you? *Chispas!* Stand beside Gokliya some time, if you want to be embarrassed! *Madre Dios!*" She left off, staring at me.

"*Quita!*" she said. "What is this?"

"Seebie's new boy," Mickey answered. "The one that has been living with Pedro, up on White River."

The withered crone gave a start.

"Him?" she said.

"We apologize," Mickey nodded. "He is not much."

"Ha!" the old lady cried. "On the contrary, he looks good to me. Not pretty, like the Mexican there, but very tall, eh? And his legs are set wide out on the edges of his hipbones, but still no light shows at the crotch. You know what that means, ugly one. No wonder Sister Sawn followed him out of Fort Apache."

"Tut, tut, mother," Mickey grinned, "he is very shy about it. But just let me ask you one small question, eh? You talk about Gokliya! Hah! Why did that Nopal girl run away from him to go with this one, eh? *She* knew. She never quit smiling."

"Go to hell," recommended Mary Cornmeal. "You almost made me forget why I came up here. *Santa!* Come along, old mule of mine. Only a little farther, now."

She waddled on and disappeared into Major Chaffee's office. We continued to stand, watching after her. I think we all knew it would do no good to sit back down again. Something was up, sure.

We were right.

Next moment, Chaffee put his head out the screen door and bawled, "Horn, get your ass in here. Jesus Christ, these bastards never are around when you need them. Sieber," he yelled back into the office, "do you know where he is? Goddamnit, Al. Hornnn—!"

I stepped around the corner of the old building, throwing him my knucklebrow salute, copied from Sieber.

"Right here, sir. What do you need?"

"What you are paid for!" he roared. "Get in here and interpret!"

"Yes sir; I thought you had Al in there, sir."

"He wants you. Says the squaw's talking too fast for him. Too much Apache. If you ask me, I think it's too much pulque. Hike your butt, Horn."

Inside the office, old Mary Cornmeal proved eager enough to speak through me. All the while I told Major Chaffee what she was saying, the wrinkled creature kept patting my thigh and grinning, "good boy, good boy," in Apache. Or, "ah, if I were younger!" Or maybe, "who could blame Nopal?" And it got so bad the major had to put me on one side of his desk and Mary Cornmeal on the other. Then we got on with it.

The word the aged courier bore was not from Geronimo, as we expected. Rather it was Nana, that fiercest of them all, who sent the word. He, Nana, and his nephew Gokliya, were not happy living down in Mexico. Both would like to come and live on the reservation with all their old friends. They wanted to see Iron Man and have a talk with him about all this.

The old chief of the Warm Springs Apache said that neither he nor his nephew knew any of the new officers in Arizona. But they could tell that these officers knew nothing of what the Indians wanted and must have. It was up to Seebie to make the arrangement. There were no conditions, except one: Sieber must bring his new talking boy with him.

You may be certain *that* was received with interest by the interpreter! The old squaw never even looked at me, but kept right on rattling away, in Apache. It was all I could do to catch the key places and directions.

Sieber could bring one other with him, in addition to Talking Boy. It could be anybody but young Ramon (Chikisin) who, we would understand, was out of favor with Geronimo over a matter of some stolen Mexican horses.

Sieber, with his one or two companions, must be at the old maguey roasting camp in the Terras Mountains at the precise full of the May moon. A day sooner, or later, and the Apaches would become suspicious. Was all this understood? Sieber nodded yes and spoke his part.

"Listen, mother," he said to the old squaw, "you go back and tell Nana and Geronimo that Iron Man is coming. I will bring the talking boy and also the Mexican Merijilda Grijole. The people will know they can trust us with Merijilda along. Now, would you care to rest before you start home?"

Mary Cornmeal scoffed at the idea of rest, but she did let me fix her a right decent noon meal, make up a nice pack of meat and staples to take back with her and to feed her moth-bit mule. The last I saw of her she was hobbling down the wagon ruts of the road south out of San Carlos Agency, singing a cracked and crazy Apache happy song to the mule, which followed her like a pet dog. "A wonderful old lady," I said to Merijilda, standing with me. "I pray her a good journey."

"Thank you," the Mexican scout said softly. "She is the own-sister of Nana. She was my grandmother when I visited in his house. I will pray with you, *hermano*."

I never got used to the lack of emotion of these Apaches in public meetings. Privately, they were the warmest, funniest, and closest of people. Remarkable and marvelous friends. But in front of the white man they were all strangers to each other. The example of Merijilda and his Warm Springs grandmother was typical. In the Apache way, children of the wives of fighting men were turned over when weaned to the grandmothers for rearing. This was to free the mothers to go with their warriors on raids or hunts or the long foraging rides common to these nomads of the Arizona far places. So in reality the children were nearer to their old grandmothers than to their own-mothers. Yet, at San Carlos, Merijilda Grijole and Mary Cornmeal had passed as the merest of acquaintances. Only my chance reference to the dearest heart he held among the wild tribes had broken his Apache mask.

I loved the way of those dark warriors and love it still. They were truly *Tindé Ussen*, "God's people."

"On campaign," as the cavalry put it, we always moved sharp. No more laying around. No squawing. No bottles brought along. Easygoing Al Sieber turned into Old Mad and Iron Man the minute he told me to "bring up the Jenny mule, Horn."

And so we started from San Carlos, Sieber planning each day's march to the mile. Picking up the head of San Bernardino Creek, we followed it down to where it fed into the Rio Bavispe, in Sonora, over east of Fronteras on the sundown side of the Sierra de la Madera. Here, just as we prepared to cross the Bavispe, and were down off our horses letting them wade in and drink, Merijilda said softly, "*Miren, amigos;* we have company."

Sieber and me looked up and saw one Indian coming down a spur of the Terras range, opposite us. The man was afoot. He seemed not even to see us. Getting to the bank, he stopped and leaned on his rifle and watched our stock in the water. He was a magnificent-looking fellow, and I knew at once that I was staring at my first real-live *bronco* in his natural lair.

He was tall for an Apache, about six feet. Slender, wide shouldered, bowlegged. His copper skin gleamed in the late daylight. He was unclad except for a very skimpy, worn-low breechclout, Apache *n-deh b'keh* high mocs, and a brace of cartridge bandoliers sagging in the Mexican cross style from his lean shoulders. He seemed of a sudden aware of our existence and lit up his dark face with a smile that gave me glad relief.

"Hal-zay," Merijilda whispered. "Half brother to Natchez (Naiche, Nachee, Naches) and Taza (Tahza), the sons of Cochise."

"Ah!" I breathed excitedly. "Ain't he grand."

"He is one of the worst Indians you will ever see," Al Sieber grunted from the side of his mouth. "A real *hesh-ke* and a fourteen-carat son of an Apache bitch."

I could not believe it, watching the graceful and smiling savage across the stream.

"Come on," Merijilda said. "He will be all right with us. He is only down here to give us the direction Nana and Geronimo want us to take up to Mescal Meadow. He will lay back here by the water to make certain we don't have troops following us. Let me talk to him."

We waded out to our horses and got aboard them. I couldn't take my eyes off Hal-zay. Here was the Indian who led the band that took Nopal. He was of the blood of Cochise and the nephew of Geronimo and Nana. A *bad* Indian, Sieber had said. But I said, beautiful. And for a reason that my shadow was warning me of, I knew he was to play a singular part in my immediate life.

"Remember, do not ask his name of him," Merijilda reminded me, our horses splashing near the other bank. "If you ask his name you put a curse on him. You may ask *who* he is. He can then tell you what band he is from, or whatever else about him that he chooses."

"I know, I know," I answered a bit short.

"You *may* know," Merijilda nodded, "but out here you *must* know. We are five days south of San Carlos."

"*Basta*," warned Sieber. "Here we are."

We came out of the river and halted before the Indian.

He spoke first, addressing Sieber and Merijilda in that order. They returned his words, reminding him who they were and why they were here.

"Yes, I know who you are," he said. "I have seen you

both before." He pointed at me. "But who is this? Him I have not seen."

Sieber gave me a side-look which said to shut up.

"Oh," he answered Hal-zay, "he is a young scout we are breaking in. Very interested in Indian work. His father is very powerful. Merijilda can vouch for him."

This, the Mexican scout quickly did. But the Apache began to scowl. I was amazed at the sinister change in his face when the smile disappeared.

"Why did you come down here?" he demanded of me.

"He wanted to see the great Geronimo," Sieber said quickly. "You know, my brother," he shrugged, as if it were entirely nothing, "he is not grown as we are."

Hal-zay shook his head but spoke to Merijilda in Apache and then waved us to go on up the mountain spur he had descended. We passed on by him, single file, the way being narrow just there. "Don't look back," Sieber barked at me. "He expects you to do that. Keep going."

"Suits me," I said. "But where *are* we going?"

"*Too-slah,* the Apaches call it," Merijilda answered. "To the Mexicans and gringos, it is Mescal Meadow. I know the way, but we are riding late. *Ugashe.*"

Ugashe was the Apache term for "go!" or "let's go," and we obeyed it willingly. The trail was steep and dangerous and night was coming down. But we had an Apache invitation. "Be in the *Too-slah* grazing place when the May moon slides around the shoulder of the Terras Mountain." The dangerous old chief Nana had sent it. No other urging was required.

Not if you were one of two white men following an Apache Mexican up the blind side of a strange mountain, five pony rides from the nearest troop of U.S. Cavalry.

Wagh—!

We saw the light of their night fires five miles away.

"Christ Jesus," Sieber said, "we've struck a hornet's nest of them."

"More like a mud daubers' wattle," Merijilda amended, "than even you imagine, Seebie. We will find a thousand Indians up there. But it's all right. They don't burn bright fires like that in a war camp. *Vámonos, amigos.*"

Half a mile from the camp, a small Apache boy came out in the trail. He had been sent to guide us to our camping spot, he said. We thanked him and followed on, very glad to see him. They don't bring children of such an age to camps where weapons are being cleaned.

The boy found us an excellent place out on the edge of the biggest encampment of Apaches of any kind I had ever seen. To know that every last buck, squaw, and pup of them was *broncos* sent a thrilling up the small of my spine that I remember yet. "God Amighty!" I breathed to Sieber. "They can't all be hostiles, can they?"

"Cherry Cows to the last dangerous bastard," the old German growled. "Either Warm Springs Injuns with Nana or Mexican Injuns with Geronimo, plus kinfolk slipping over from the Cochise country. What's your count, now, Merijilda?"

"Over a thousand," the Mexican said. "Twelve hundred anyway, and more coming in. I never saw so many women and children. Business must be good in *Méjico*."

"Merijilda," I said, pointing, "look who's coming to see you. How in God's name did she beat us here?"

It was, of course, the old grandmother.

Old Mary Cornmeal, who had brought us the message, *por Dios!*

Merijilda laughed at my question about a crippled ancient like that outmarching three top scouts of the United States Sixth Cavalry, and on foot!

"She knew the way," the Mexican said. "We had to find it. *Abuela mía!*" he shouted to the old lady. "It is you. *Ya lo creo!*"

Merijilda swept her up in his arms, and the gaggle of other squaws and kids following her laughed and clapped their hands to see such happiness. But the old lady was kicking at Merijilda and commanding that she be put down. "*Tonto!*" she cried. "Do you think I was coming to see you! I had enough of putting dry moss in your pants and keeping the flies out of your eyes when you used to come visit us and made yourself the jacal pet of that old *sentto* Nana. Put me down this instant, and let me at that tall boy with the ears that stick out and no firelight showing through his crotch. Here!" she yelled at me. "Don't try to get away!

I see you there sliding out into the dark. Stop him, Seebie. That is *my* boy. *Hoo-hooe!*"

Hoo-hooe is a sound the Apaches make when they are rounding up ponies, driving cattle, chasing pigs, racing horses, or trying to catch a fat pet dog to put in the family stewpot. It means almost anything but mostly is a pursuit yell which has the spirit of I'll catch you, you son of a bitch, never fear!

In this case, Sieber reached out and nailed me with his grip of iron, hauling me back.

"Stay put," he said, "and smile, Wide Crotch. You have taken the eye of the chief's little sister."

"*Mierda,*" I said. Which, not being either very elegant, or original, I won't bother to translate.

"Nevertheless," Al Sieber said, "you're it."

He was right. The old lady, Mary Cornmeal, would have it no other way. As soon as the rest of the squaws had made Sieber and Merijilda a fine camp, I had to go along with her to her brush hut. I simply wasn't going to do it, but Sieber made it an order. I went along mad enough to dent a horse-blasting cap, or bite a bobcat, using my own teeth. But I had old Mary wrong.

It came to pass that she had spread a lot of stories about how nice I had been to her at San Carlos—feeding her a good meal, giving her a fine pack of meat and flour and sugar, haying down her old pack animal—and that I had done all this out of desire for her, well along in winters though she might be.

The truth was that Major Chaffee had commanded me to butter up the old hag. She knew that as well as I did, advising me of the fact with an evil but twinkling look of pouchy eyes. "Boy," she said, "all you need do is behave as though I had told those nosy women the real thing. See them following us? If you will but go with me through the entry-skins of my poor home, yonder, they will cluck their foolish tongues loose with envy."

She gave me that impy, wiseacre wink again.

"If you should see fit to pat me on my old rump bones as we bend to go in the hut, it would keep the silly hens awake on their roosts the whole night. *Ih-hah!*"

Here, she laughed her cracky, cackling laugh and gave

me a tweak in the front of the breechclout that like to
pinched me off into a shorthorn. *"Hombre!"* she snorted, loud
enough to be heard by every Apache in Mescal Meadow,
"the things you say to a woman! *Wagh!"*

Cringing, I came on with her up to the dog kennel she
called her wickiup. Still cackling and chucking me with elbow
and stabbing me with bony finger, she pulled aside the moldy
deerhide door-drop to her castle and yelled, *"Entra, en-
tero—!"*

Since this meant "come on in, studhorse," I felt the only
decent thing to do was play it her agey, crazy old way. Her
squaw friends were still peep-tomming at us from over back
of some other brush-heap huts nearby, and Tom Horn was
damned if he was going to disappoint them.

"Ai, mujer!" I shouted.

And picked up the old lady, tucked her under one arm,
stooped down with her, and went into her hut.

Inside, I put her down a little rough and began to say
something like, all right, that's the end of the ponyplay, old
crow, but I never got one word out. I was lucky enough to
see, by the shine of the old Indian oil lamp she had left
burning—a copper bowl with free-float wick—that tears
were streaming down her face.

"Boy," she croaked, "a very old woman thanks you; it
was no game for her. You recall for her other nights when
she was not as you see her now. It is a thing of the heart, of
the pride. Ussen will repay you for it."

"Mother," I answered, "it was nothing. Neither Ussen
nor the very old lady owes any debt to repay. Nor did I
play it for a game, either. You are still beautiful. What do a
few winters mean to us, *linda mujer?"*

She commenced to sob out loud at that. I placed an
arm about her hunched shoulders and gave her a squeeze.

"Go ahead," I said. "Your friends will only think I am
doing a good job in here."

That returned her wide, wicked grin and the happy
laugh. *"Hijo!"* she said. "You are right!" And immediately set
up such a yammer of weeping and crying out as would flatter
the meanest *macho*. While she was carrying on this make-
believe, she pointed out to me a hole in the brush at hut's

rear. "It backs up on the chaparral, *cortejo grande*. No one will see you leave. *Adiós*."

I squeezed her again and then, because she had called me "big lover," fetched her a smacking kiss. Apaches don't like kissing, but Mary Cornmeal forgave me with a kick in the shins and a Chiricahua curse. I went out the rear brush-hole of her hut on my all-fours, *más pronto*. When I snuck back into our camp, Sieber was there alone, Merijilda being no doubt off visiting kin. The old German didn't stir, and I didn't stir him. You can bet he was wide awake. Old Mad never slept. He just didn't want to embarrass the big lover.

"Come on, Talking Boy. Wake up. Geronimo is waiting for you." I came up to a sit on my blankets, and there was Merijilda standing over me. Sieber was setting on a salt box dressing his bad left foot-wound for the day. He was all clothed other than for his one boot, and the sun hadn't even crope over the edge of Terras Mountain yet. Something was moving, sure.

"Where did you drop in from?" I grumped to Merijilda, feeling around for my own boots and yawning.

"From Uncle Gokliya's jacal," he answered, which naturally was the end of my yawn.

"You mean Geronimo really is waiting up on us?"

"On you," the Mexican scout said. "We're ready."

I glanced over at the old German and saw that he had got on the left boot, with its entire vamp and toe cut out to free his bad foot, and knew that it was "going" time. Jamming on my boots and hat, I said to Merijilda, "Lead on, *batidor;* the troops is right behind you."

"You got any more fun in you," Sieber growled at me, "blow it out your butthole, right now. Geronimo don't understand anything short of dead serious."

"Yes sir," I said and shut up.

Minutes later, we was in our places outside Geronimo's brush shelter. "Look sharp!" Merijilda warned with sudden lowering of his voice. "He's coming out now."

And then Gokliya was there.

Mary Cornmeal

Geronimo came out of the wickiup and stood there looking at us with his arms folded and his great head held with the heavy chin jutting out like a marble statue of a Roman headman. He was something to see.

Others have said, and I, too, that he was six good foot tall. Looking back, I know he wasn't. He just seemed it. I would guess, by the inches I had on him, he must have been about five ten, as I was then six foot and two inches tall myself.

Somewhere, somebody called him the Daniel Webster of western Indians. They weren't just meaning he was an orator but that he genuinely resembled Webster. I don't know that. Can't recall seeing any picture of old Dan that looked like Geronimo. Still, when once you saw Gokliya, you never forgot the view.

Mouth was like it had been cut with a knife. Almost no lips and way wide, with downturnings at the outer corners. Nose, high in the bridge, wide at nostril but not the bony arch of it. Eyes was set in under head-jutted brow bones, where they gleamed out of the dark shadows. Those eyes stayed with you, wherever you moved or let your own look wander. You could *feel* them. It was the same as being watched by a wolf, where you were ganted up and weak in hock and he was just waiting for one wrong, careless flick of your attention or stumble in your gait. He made a man shaky, even in broad sun.

Suddenly, he dropped the folded arms.

"How are you, young man?" he said to me in Apache. "What are you doing here?"

"He will interpret for me," Sieber said quickly.

Geronimo nodded, never taking his gimlet eyes from

146

me. "I speak fast," he said. "Can you interpret as fast as I speak, young fellow?"

I was actually trembling from nerves, but said I would try. "I have one mouth and one tongue inside it, *jefe*. They are only ordinary and cannot keep up with a great chief's, but I will do my best, *patrón*."

"Well spoken," he rumbled. He looked on at me for another moment. "It is too bad," he said, "that you didn't know me before."

At that, Al Sieber traded looks with me. I could see he didn't like it. "*Jefe*," he said to Geronimo, "the boy is nothing. I came to hear Gokliya talk."

Geronimo then turned back to Sieber and began to talk in earnest. This is all he wanted:

The agents at San Carlos had done him great wrong.

The soldiers hated him and mistreated him.

The White Mountain Apaches lied about him forever.

The Mexicans cheated him and killed his people.

He wanted to come back to San Carlos and live happy with his friends. He wanted two Mexicans hired full time to make mescal liquor for him. He wanted the government to give him a lot of new guns. He wanted, with them, all the ammunition he could shoot up. He wanted four bolts of calico for each woman, five sets of shoes for every child. He wanted bacon every day, beef every night, warm fires for all when the snow was on the earth.

He would have other ideas, he concluded, but for this agreement we could begin with the things put forward.

Well, Sieber turned to me, breathing hard.

"Horn," he said, "you tell Geronimo only what I say, to the word, *exactamente*." He then answered the chief.

Geronimo had asked for everything but to have these Terras Mountains moved up into the United States to live in. Maybe, now, *el jefe* would like to add in those same mountains. Sieber would wait, if Geronimo wanted to go talk to his people about moving those mountains up into the American country. For, if the great chief believed he was entitled to those other things he had asked for, then just as surely he was entitled to have the Terras Mountains moved up to San Carlos.

The old German quite abruptly broke off his talk.

He nodded to Geronimo and stared him back.

"Now you think about it," he said, and he turned and walked out of the council.

It fell to me to give a small lie about what Iron Man had meant, against what he had said, but Geronimo didn't need the bull tallow to smooth him down.

He pointed admiringly after Sieber and said, "Anybody's business that is in that man's hands will be handled as he says, or it won't be handled at all, *ih!*"

To me, he added, "We will meet here again when the sun goes."

"*Si, jefe,*" I said and retreated after Iron Man.

Sieber stood looking out over the crowd that had gathered to the big fire. Night was hard down, and we had come, as bid by Geronimo. But it was Old Mad, the storied Iron Man Sieber, who held the Indians silent.

In the morning meet there had been but a handful of subchiefs, Geronimo, and the three of us from San Carlos. Now we estimated between three and four hundred bucks were waiting for Sieber to begin. Not a squaw, not one pup or older child, even, was in sight. Merijilda whispered at my side, "I have never seen so many Chiricahua big men at one place; I am worried for Seebie." To this uncertainty I gave full accord, yet we needn't have bothered. Old Mad knew where he was.

"Geronimo," he began, "I will address you, with respects to Nana and all the men of reputation who have honored the government to come here. I speak to you because of who you are and what you have done before.

"I have no true idea now that you will do as I say this night—return to San Carlos and obey the government—for you do not love peace. You are a man of war and fighting, a battle chief of the Chiricahua. Will you listen to anyone?

"You could go to the reservation and stay maybe one winter, and more likely one moon. But within your camp here may be some others who do really want to come back, to settle down finally to peace. And all of these I will take back in safety. Sieber promises it. But you, Geronimo, two times already I have taken you there, and two times you have become fearful and left. You had food, shelter, good blankets. You did not ever say to the government that you did not. But someone would sell your people whiskey and you would all—a great many of you—get drunk and away you would go again. This thing cannot go on."

The old German let them wait again, then resumed.

"In my opinion, all of the Chiricahua in this world, one by one, will be killed by our soldiers if you stay out on the war trail. Aha! you say that you can always go to Mexico and be safe from American pursuit? Don't you know the *mejicanos* hate you worse than the gringos? Have you not heard that the two countries are making a treaty that will permit the Americans to chase you into Mexico! Ai! believe it. Never have I told you one lie; you all know me: I do not talk two ways. Listen to me!

"I leave in four days for San Carlos.

"Who will come with me? Who will die out there in the dark, nobody to claim his bones, nor remember him?

"Come back with me, old friends.

"Four days only. *Enjuh!*"

There wasn't a sound when he finished speaking. Nor any when he turned away and walked out. I stood in a trance with Merijilda, not leaving. We saw Geronimo take note of us and send Hal-zay over with a message:

The Apaches would be alone.

This was an order for us to leave the area, and we did so quickly. Merijilda stayed with Sieber and me that night. The fires stayed burning until daybreak. When we were cooking breakfast, we saw scores of bucks just going home. They had talked the night away.

But in vain.

Four days later, when Sieber was set to depart for San Carlos, sixty-two Indians were all of the twelve hundred who came to our fire to go back with us. The old chiefs Nana and Loco, both so ancient they had to be helped up on their horses, came with these people. Of Geronimo there was no sign. Sieber said, "We will wait a bit for him; he would never miss the chance."

I studied the two famed old chiefs and tried talking with them, at Sieber's suggestion. I got them going pretty good, as they were nervous and downhearted to be coming in, finally. Both said they were grateful to me for my interest. Both took me aside at different times and warned me to "watch Gokliya" but would not tell me why. I gave them both a twist of good Burley chaw and a long pull at Sieber's "medicinal" bottle. Then there was real gratitude!

Nana, then about seventy-eight years old, was as tall as I was, maybe taller. Even stooped with his rheumatism, he looked level into my eyes. His hair was snow-white, his skin smooth.. He was a grand, fierce old Indian.

Loco, nearly as old, was crippled by the attack of a grizzly bear as a young man. The bear had torn off half his face, including one eye. His expression was horrible to see, but he was in truth a mild man and sober. It was the pain from those terrible wounds of the bear that drove him to strike out, he told me.

Still waiting for Geronimo, I struck up a trade with a young nephew of Chief Juh, of the Nednhi Mexican Apaches. I later learned he was not so young as I thought, being thirty-four years old. But Indians are hard to tell age on.

Anyways, this Kaytennae Indian had two of the most splendid racing horses and a brace of elegant mules that he seemed anxious to be done out of. I got them off him for two handwove Culiacán Mex blankets. As the blankets cost me six dollars each in Tucson, I made a sharp trade. Kaytennae did even better. The horses and mules hadn't cost him ten cents, being fresh-stole in Mexico.

We shook hands, vowing we were *chi-ki-sins* for life, and he rode off to go with the hostiles and I never saw him again. Maybe it was just as well. One of the "race" horses was a wind-roarer, and both mules had hock-splints so bad they'd go lame just from seeing a packsaddle coming at them. The other horse lived a long time, but you couldn't shoe him due to thin horn on the feet, and soft; a nail just wouldn't stay in it.

I heard Kaytennae later prospered in business.

I have no reason to doubt it.

Geronimo waited until Sieber and me and Merijilda had our sixty-two Indians all mounted and lined out ready to trail down to the Bavispe. Then he showed.

He patted Sieber on the back and thanked him for taking all those poor, broke-down, and agey Indians off his hands, as they hampered him on his raids, etc. Sieber patted him right back and told him not to fret over it, as those agey Indians would be in fine fettle long after Geronimo had been cut down by a soldier bullet. "But of course, *jefe*, that is what you wish," he said. "A war chief goes to war. He likes to die."

Geronimo behaved like he didn't get the point, turning his back on Sieber to smile on me.

"Look out," Merijilda said in my ear. "He is coming to it now. I should have told you, *hermano*. But I was afraid you would get us all killed."

"What in God's name you talking about?" I said.

"You will see," Merijilda Grijole replied. "*Lo siento mucho, hombre*. What could we have done?"

"By God," I said, the thought draining me, "it's Nopal, ain't it? You've learn't something!" I accused him. "She's dead!"

Merijilda shook his head. "Be still, *hombre*," he warned. "Listen to Gokliya, and don't talk."

In the stillness following that, Geronimo edged his mount forward. He brought him almost to my boot toes.

"I have a reward for you," he said to me. "Some payment for your good work you did here and in other places I remember." He put a meaning on the part about those other places he remembered, staring it into me. Then, he turned to the knot of hard-faced bucks who had come with him to say good-bye to Iron Man. "Bring it over here!" he called in Apache. "Bring out our gift for this young interpreter."

Out of the group of Chiricahua scowlers rode Hal-zay, the magnificent Indian from the crossing of the Bavispe. He bore a bundle before him on the horn of his saddle. I could not imagine what variety of present it might contain, being of no familiar shape or dimension. But, in the silence of Hal-zay's approach, a hint came plaintively from the bundle itself. It was a cry, muffled but yet distinct and singular enough even to a fool like Tom Horn.

That was a baby they had in those wrappings—my baby.

Merijilda, standing faithfully with me as he ever did, saw my struck look. "Yes, it is yours," he said, "but think very hard before you do anything with it."

Before I might query him on that, Hal-zay was there holding out the bundle to me.

"We don't want it," was every word he said.

Al Sieber, who had meanwhile gotten up on his mule, moved that animal in between us, blocking me.

"Don't take it!" he said sharply. "Once you accept it, it can never go back to these people. You refuse it, and it's still theirs."

"But, my God, Al, it ain't theirs; it's mine!"

I butted up past the Jenny mule to come at Hal-zay again. "Where is the mother?" I demanded. "Where is my young wife Nopal? The child is hers alone to give!"

"She does give it!" barked Hal-zay angrily.

"Where is she?" I insisted. "Let me hear her say it."

"No."

"I knew it! She *is* dead, then."

"No."

"What, no? Then how? Safe, happy, sick, what?"

"Take the child."

"No, now I will say it to you. No."

"If you do not, I will smash its head." Hal-zay raised his gun butt as if to do the very terrible thing, but again the old German was before me, shoving Jenny once more between us. His face was a dark red, like beef liver.

"Warrior," he rumbled from the chest, "if you touch that baby, your own brains will be splashed on your fine saddle." He stood in his stirrups to yell past Hal-zay, to Geronimo. "Now, I am getting mad, Gokliya. You let this cub of old Cochise's come up here and make a fool of me, threatening my talking boy, holding up my Indians, here, who want to be on the trail to their new home. I want to know, right now, what is your purpose?"

Sieber was getting one of his famous "mads" on. Geronimo knew it and answered him quick and straight.

The child's mother, the Yaqui girl known as Nopal, was now the wife of his nephew Hal-zay, he said. He, Geronimo, had given his concern in the young squaw to Hal-zay as a wedding gift. The woman was presently home down in Mexico, carrying Hal-zay's baby. She had "given" the other baby to be taken to Terras Mountain, when she heard Talking Boy would be there.

Geronimo flung up a hand to make an accent.

"She said that Talking Boy only talked. He promised to come back for her and her baby, but he never did it. 'Give him his child,' she told me. 'I will have my own. Tell him Nopal waited a long time for him. Tell him the baby's name is Sombra, after its father's shadow. Tell the father that the mother never thinks of him anymore.'"

The famed chief lowered the unflung arm.

"Now you have the truth," he said to Sieber. "Hal-zay loved the woman, after stealing her from Pedro's village. The woman is in good health. I think your talking boy is lucky to be the same. We don't want any trouble here. Do you?"

Sieber now raised his arm.

And quick.

"No trouble, *jefe*," he said. "Ease your men."

I started forward at this point, determined to take the child before it might come to grievous hurt. The old German reached out with his good foot and fetched me a kick in the chest, going by, that like to caved in my wishbone. "Stay out of this, Talking Boy," he said. "There's a current settin' in here that's running deeper than you been trained to get acrost. Backwater, damn you!"

Hal-zay upreared his rifle butt once more.

"You will not take the child?" he said.

"He can't take it!" Sieber flared at the Indian. "You know that would spoil the child for being received again by its mother's people. What are you trying to do, warrior? Kill a little baby? Is that the great fighter we've all heard about? The famous hesh-ke half brother to Tahza and Naiche?"

Instantly, Hal-zay reined back his horse, crying out, "I will kill you, Iron Man!" and the clot of warriors with Geronimo surged forward to back him with their guns. It would have been one more "dark and bloody ground in Arizona" right then and there, but for one person brainier than the lot of us added together, red and white.

"*Idiotas!*" screeched old Mary Cornmeal, hobbling down from the side of the nearby rise, where she had been waiting to go with the Geronimo people back to their stronghold in Sierra del Norte. "What is all this *cháchara* about the giving law and killing small babies with gun butts?" She puffed up to Hal-zay, confronting him with raised walking cane.

"You want to make laws, do you, big baby fighter?" she snapped. "I will give you a law. Yes, and you, too, simpleton," she said to Geronimo. "Don't try to hide from me behind this braying burro who says he is the seed of Cochise. I wiped your bottom often enough when you were a baby this size, Yawner. I can still do it!"

She whirled back upon Hal-zay, almost falling down with the vim of the turn.

"Here is your law," she rasped. "If another Indian of the people accepts the child for the alien father, the child remains of our people. You recall that rule? Well, you had better!" She brandished the walking stick. "I accept this child for its father; give it over to me, at once."

Hal-zay looked helplessly to Geronimo.

Geronimo made an angry sign, meaning yes. Was not Mary Cornmeal the own-sister of Nana, and an elder of the Warm Springs tribal keepers and council on laws? *Santa!* They were helpless. The old magpie had them by the cajones. Give the brat over to her. *Ugashe!*

Hal-zay obeyed, glaring at me as old Mary took the whimpering bundle to her scrawny breast.

He didn't say anything.

Neither did Tom Horn.

Geronimo and his war bucks rode away, Hal-zay going last behind them. They took a "Mexican" direction, southeasterly around the shoulder of Terras Mountain. Sieber ordered our remaining sixty-plus Indians, now including Mary Cornmeal and the baby, to move out at once down the Bavispe River trail. We reached the crossing for noon-halt but went on over and kept going. We were deep into

Mexico, and Sieber wanted to get back into U.S. country *más pronto*.

It had been a bad journey for him.

Getting back over the border with our Indians, few and mostly aged as they were, was the best he could hope to get out of it, now.

As for my lasting memory of it, it was seeing old Mary Cornmeal coming along on her ratty-ass mule, Mangas, holding Nopal's and my baby in her arms and singing *"Pajarito Barranqueno"* (Little Bright-eyed Bird) to it, in a fifty-fifty mix of Apache and Mexican.

She was a grand old lady.

The baby, Sombra, was a boy, about eight months old when we got him. He was near-dark as a pickaninny for hide, very ugly, and with jug-handle ears that stuck out from under his thatch of black wild hair, to brand him mine, then and thereafter, amen.

The last I heard of him, he was living with old Mary and her grandson Merijilda Grijole, somewhere down in Sonora state. Near Fronteras, I think. There was even some story that his mother was with them, later on, Hal-zay having been killed by an old man blind on *tizwin*. Nopal never coming up out of Mexico to surrender, it may have been so that she joined Mary and Merijilda, as commonly told around San Carlos. I scarcely know.

That was some many winters back, even after I looked for them before leaving Arizona. The boy would have been seven years old at that time. I mean sure to find him and his mother, when I get home again to Arizona.

I know it won't be too late. Not ever.

People can always start again.

Closing Up

Going almost up to the Mex line with our sixty-odd Apache "peacefuls," we veered over to the Bonito Canyon and hid in it until American troops could get down and "escort us in" officially. Our boys showed up in time to bluff off some Mexican Cavalry that had got on our tails, and we went on into San Carlos with no trouble. There, we done good, too.

Another batch of hostiles, forty-nine of them, came in right after we did, and on their own. They were from the Mescal Meadow meet, and thus were credit on Al Sieber's ledger. Which naturally meant on Tomasito Horn's, also. For the next months of that winter of 1878–79 small bands of wild Indians dribbled into San Carlos, all of them driving stolen Mexican horse stock ahead of them. We picked up another couple hundred hostiles with these winter dribbles. Fact was, I spent all of my time running down to the border to bring over these horse thieves (including their stolen animals) in a way to get them through (around) the U.S. Customs station at San Bernardino. There was a heavy duty on Mex stock to prevent just this kind of Indian thieving, but the U.S. men had to look the other way and the Mexican owners to foam at the mouth from despair.

The Indians would not come in without their horses.

And we had to get the Indians in.

I think they call it politics.

The main Mex paper in Tucson, *El Fronterizo,* suffered editorial stroke every edition for months, but I don't know of a solitary case where the government paid over a dollar of proper duty to any of the Mexican horse ranchers. But what could the poor sungrinners do? The U.S. had the soldiers.

The spring of '79, a really big surrender of hostiles took place. Hundreds of them came in by day and by night, for weeks on end. The winter had been fierce in Sonora and Chihuahua states, bitter cold, with the Mexican Army driving after the *bárbaros* without letup. The U.S. was the "lucky" winner. Old Loco, for example, had 650 Indians with him, at San Carlos, by that spring. Sieber had me secretly run a herd count on their stock—just this one band now mind you—and I made it something over five thousand head of horses and mules! San Carlos was running over its Apache cup. Only Geronimo and Juh were still down in the Sierra Madre del Norte fighting the Mexicans. And of course we considered them hopeless anyhow. But them and their Chiricahua aside, it seemed to Sieber and me that we had about cornered the Apache Indian market for the San Carlos Agency, come that early summer.

We were precisely right.

In June 1879, all the scouts and interpreters were again cut loose and fired off the reservation. The excuse was the same as before; appropriations had run out and the Quartermaster department was broke. Good-bye, Al Sieber and son! They had done it to you yet once more.

They had also lied to us again.

The real reason for our turning out was that the soft-on-Indian people back east had got control again, fired Major Chaffee, and put in a damn civilian, name of Tiffany, as agent at San Carlos. He was the bastard had us run off, and no wonder. In his first year, starting August of '79, he came up short $54,000 in his accounts, and was the next several years in the territorial courts explaining "how" he had done it.

Me and Sieber already knew how it worked.

Tiffany just sold all the Apaches' supplies in the private market at five dollars a hundred for flour, ten dollars a hundred for sugar, and like prices for everything that ought to have gone to his Indians, and he was undercutting the civilian merchants by about 120 percent, the way Al Sieber and I worked it out for ourselves. Tiffany got rich and got arrested. The Indians went hungry and raised hell about it and got shot. Tiffany to my memory never served a day in jail. The Apaches served life sentences, every one of them, and died by the hundreds for their wrong of being born Indians, and free, and wanting to stay both.

It did not seem to me their human spirits could bear another winter of such justice; the Apache had finally to fail. Swift-off, it appeared I was right.

In December, Geronimo and Juh, with 108 men, women, and pups of all ages, asked unexpectedly to surrender through the old friend of Cochise, Tom Jeffords. The place was agreed as old Camp Rucker, a supply base in Cochise County. Neither Sieber nor me could go down, of course, being fired. Archie McIntosh, General Crook's old chief of scouts, was the one did the interpreting. The officer who took the surrender for the army was a Captain A. S. Haskell, aide to General Willcox. It did now look to be for undeniable certain that the "broncos had been broke." Al Sieber knew better.

"Wait," was all he said.

One month later, almost to the day, January 1880, Victorio, rumored to have with him 350 fighting men of mixed Chiricahua, Mescalero, and his own Warm Springs wild ones, swept up the Rio Puerco Valley burning, killing, and looting through the San Mateo Mountains. The raid went 90 days and 900 miles, and when it ended with Victorio safely back into Mexico, the Apache war blood was stirred into a six-year killing fever.

From that day and date it was war to the last warrior. The army knew at length what Iron Man Sieber and Talking Boy Horn had been telling it since 1876. The Chiricahua, the bad Apaches, whether Warm Springs, Nednhi, Bedonkohe, or Cochise bands, had got to be destroyed. The only way it could be done was by blood-trail pursuit right on into Mexico. But it was to require another two years of unavoidable *dah-eh-sah* for the good Apache, and ambush body counts of their own dead by the cavalry, to convince the government back in Washington, D.C., of the same thing. And we who had to hold off the hostiles, meanwhile, did not have two years to wait. Not for what we scouts called our "Hot Trail" Treaty with Mexico, nor for anything from Washington, D.C. We had to do the job with what we already had of weapons—nothing but our guts against the Indians' guts, our Winchesters against their

Winchesters. Our officers had their orders, and passed them on to us: *Keep after the devils; run the last Cherry Cow Indian out of the U.S. of A. "dead or killed;" build a cavalry bonfire under the Chiricahua that would burn out every last jacal, wickiup, rancheria, or secret camping place known to the wild Indians.*

And then burn the Indians.

Naturally, Tom Horn and Al Sieber was called back for the torching.

We didn't go entire because of the pay. $150 a month.

We could have made as much or more meat-hunting for the mining camps. But we had got infected with the six-year fever. Killing a human being that had to be killed got to be like that. Me and Al Sieber, we couldn't stand to stay behind when "Boots and Saddles" was sounding, the ammunition being issued, the packmules diamond hitched, and our tame Apaches that was going with us to run their bad brothers starting to cry out and ki-yi like redbone hounds.

We had to go. The trumpets was blaring again. I ran for my rangy bay, Sieber limped for his Jenny mule. Hostile Apache trail had been cut, and we must run it to the kill. "Mount up! Mount up!" the sergeants bawled, and "Forward ho!" the lieutenants. Column twos and column fours, the salty troopers rode. Some would die and some get wounds and all grow older in a hurry. But that was how they drew their pay. The same as me and Sieber. Find the track of those "bad ones," run it down, start the rifles barking. Let the dust fall. Have a smoke. Check the dead and kill the crawlers—living wounded—count them all alike, "good Injuns," and go home, true heroes.

When the Apache undertake a journey of the people one man is appointed "closing-up rider." He is the one who keeps the nomad marchers bunched and moving to their ending place. Now it had come time for Tom Horn to be the closing-up rider on his own journey with the Apache people. What remained must be bunched and moved along.

There was six years of Indian fights to come, the ones where I was in them myself. These I mean to note in their order, and the bare bones of them only. Call it a

Tom Horn field book maybe. It will be some mistakes in it here and there, and things left out deliberate to spare decent folk still living. But the meat of it won't shine of taint, nor stink from being spoilt; it will hang prime.

Here is where the guidons flew that followed me and Sieber on that six-year march to kill the Chiricahua *broncos.*

Cibicu Creek

In May of 1880 Victorio came back up out of Mexico to set things off. He raided thirty days through the Black and Mogollon ranges, killing to our count thirteen American Mexes and seventy-eight Anglos, including soldiers, settlers, and travelers.

Me and Sieber, with a lean troop of our Apache scouts, pursued Victorio's main bunch for three straight weeks. We got into five shooting scrapes with them but got only three Apache dead to show for it, two of them squaws. We did not, as was accused, kill any of the Indian kids and never did except through accident of fire.

Good old General Willcox was in career trouble now, regardless. The newspapers and the damned Indian apologizers in Washington, D.C., lied about our low casualty claims, saying, "The notorious Tom Horn and the Prussian Sieber are said to have 'accounted for' no less than two-score of the fleeing Indians, over half of them helpless children." Such miserable falsehoods were naturally credited to Willcox's command. We saw one eastern report that actually accused the general of "trying too hard to kill Indians." No commander can win a war like that where the real enemy, the lying reporters, can make up their own battle blamings and bogus body totals.

But, by damn! old Orlando Willcox wouldn't buffalo. "Push harder," he ordered all field commands.

We heard him.

Troops out of Fort Bayard ambushed Victorio and the main band as we drove them hot from behind. They killed close to fifty of the Apache. One of the dead was a big one—Victorio's beloved son, Washington. Victorio himself fought clear and made it away.

That coming fall he wasn't so lucky.

In October the Apaches, running for Mexico bad-scairt ahead of us, blundered square into the Mexican troops of General Terrazas all laid up in the rocks and waiting for them. It was a frightful kill. Only a few of the Indians got free. One who did not was Victorio himself.

The Warm Springs chief had been a fearsome fighter; his death ought to have warned his people of what was certain to come. Sieber knew them better than that.

"Wait till winter goes," Al said. "Give them the spring grass to fat their ponies. They got short tempers and memories to match. Summer will see them back."

"I don't know," I frowned, still doubtful from the terrible casualties in Mexico. "My hunch is they're whupt this time."

"Your hunch is just like the way they'll show up here," Sieber scowled, "full of piss and *tizwin*."

I laughed but Sieber didn't; he knew it wasn't funny.

July 1881 brought the Cibicu Creek Ambush, in Cibicu Canyon, and the Apache war was on again. It began when the army ordered troops into the canyon to arrest a renegade Dreamer calling himself Do-klanny, real name of Noch-ay-del-klinne. This Indian was preaching the old trash that all the dead Indians and killed-off buffalo were coming back to wipe out the white man. The advice me and Sieber gave the cavalry was to let Do-klanny preach. "Don't, for Christ's sake," Sieber pleaded, "send no troops into that hole."

Captain Hentig, who had been given the assignment, said the time had come to teach the red rascals a lesson.

Sieber looked at me and said, "Well, Horn, let us go and visit our friends in Tomcat Alley, over to Prescott. Or maybeso mosey down to Tucson and rest in the cool of some good Mexican saloon. I ain't of a mind to die so young, nor in such infernal heat. Where's my mule?"

But the army, having ordered Hentig into Cibicu Canyon, had shred enough of brains remaining to insist that Horn and Sieber go with him.

History ordered it from there.

The three Indians who were our guides were traitors and led Hentig into a set ambush just inside the black bore of the canyon proper. The Apache rifles blazed like summer lightning from the rocks, rivening the stifling heat of the canyon. The entire command would have died but for the fact I was in front and went full out, at first crack of Apache Winchester, for the high ground to our left— where a knob of the wall rock commanded the throat of the canyon, both ways, in and out. In the same jump I went for the knob, Sieber saw it from column's rear and likewise went for it. We got up there about the same time, me first by about two magazines of my Winchester. I never shot better and hit an Indian every squeeze, the last half dozen shots knocking red climbers off the canyon wall to their deaths below. Sieber was with me then, and half a dozen cursing, white-faced troopers. Our combined fire broke the Apache apart, and they fled on into the canyon, taking their dead with them.

When we came again below we found Captain Hentig dead, with eleven men wounded and the horse stock badly shot up. It was no good place to linger. We buried Hentig in the canyon, not grieving over it. It was officers like him that me and Al Sieber hated. And their men hated, too. Those troopers hardly put Hentig in deep enough to fend off a lame coyote. When we rode off and I looked back, I swear I saw one of the dead officer's hands protruding from the rocks of his mound. More, it seemed to wave, as though in farewell, or some hopeless plea from past the grave to wait for him.

I don't know. The light in canyons plays quirky tricks with a man's eyes. I kept going. Like the soldiers ahead of me, I didn't care for the grieving sounds of the Indians, moaning and crying out softly for their dead, on in the bowels of the Canyon of the Cibicu.

The year turned and, in April 1882 Albert Sterling, chief of Indian police at San Carlos, was killed by a band of sixty bronks up from Mexico with Geronimo, Juh, Chato, and Nachee.

They used a log-mill buzz saw to cut off Sterling's head, which the squaws and their yammering pups then used to kick around like a football. Whiles this game went on, their menfolk took turns pumping lead into the stump of the corpse. It was later counted 123 recovered bullets from the beet-pulp body of Sterling, a decent man who was a good friend to the Apache.

There followed a thirteen-day chase of the guilty broncos by seven outfits of troops in the field around the clock. Dust and blood and the whine of bullet lead got our own Indians crazy. Hundreds of them deserted the agency or their own peaceful camps to flee with the Mexican hostiles. It made the greatest—me and Al said the grandest—flight of the Apache people in one bunch ever seen in Arizona. We figured, counting them past us from high rocks where we lay scarce breathing, that there was upward of one thousand Indians in that wild cavalcade. A thousand mad and angry Apache Indians running desperately for the Mexican line! And Sieber and me the chief scouts for all of our cavalry that was following them. What a time that was for us!

But what a dark one for the Apache.

Sieber and me scouted up close to the Indians and one night found them camping early. We got back to our commands and jumped the column making camp, scattering the Apache something fierce, putting them on the wild drive deeper into Mexico. Unbelievably, it happened again; we hounded them head-on into a big Mexican force under the Mexican commander, Colonel Lorenzo Garcia. Garcia killed seventy-eight Indians, fifty-four of them squaws and kids. Since, just shortly previous, our own troops had killed some eighteen of them in the skirmish that spooked the band into the Mexican ambush, it was a sober and sad Apache time that sunset in Mexico.

We were later in grief over it ourselves.

Colonel Forsyth our ranking officer near lost his commission for this high-casualty chase across the border. Al and me was only punished by short paychecks and some due-bill hard looks from agency Indians that had lost wild kin.

We survived both, knowing spring would pass. It did, bringing summer, July again, and Apache weather.

A new Dreamer was active in the renegade camps; he billed himself as the ghost of Do-klanny, although we knew him all too well as Na-ta-i-osh, a real bad one. He went out one scalding midnight with sixty tizwinned braves on a raid the Verde Valley still shudders at.

Sieber and I were on leave but was called in special to go after the killer broncos. We did so, angered at the need, and caught them in Chevlon Canyon where they could only get out crawling up the far wall of the cut.

We shot them off the face of the cliff rock. I had made the trap for them by a long, long shot which killed a gray pony that fell down into the trail of the cliff, blocking it. As the poor devils would dismount to pass this blockage afoot, we would drill them. It was target-butt practice.

Liars since have claimed it was a sergeant of Major Chaffee's "I" Troop did the fancy shooting that day in Chevlon Canyon. The sergeant tried for the gray pony, all right. And missed him thirty feet. I didn't miss him by nothing. The credit wouldn't have mattered, excepting that the rider of the gray horse happened to be Na-ta-i-osh. The pony pinned him falling. I think it was Sieber scratched him finally.

Bedonkohe Breakout

The rest of 1882 ran quiet up to September.

Sieber and me made some scouts of our own naturally. We had to catch up on our serious drinking in Mexican Tucson and from there, each time, ride home by way of

Prescott to make sure Miss Pet and Madame La Luna was all right and safe from Indian raids.

The last time we got back we were met by big news.

General George Crook had come back to the Department of Arizona. And this time he'd brought with him a *real* Hot Trail Treaty, one that let the U.S. cavalry cross into Mexico any where, any time. It was the death sentence for the four wild bands of the Chiricahua, especially the Bedonkohe of Geronimo. Old Red Beard would surely kill the Cherry Cows now. But not with me and Sieber along.

We had had our fill of the killing, we figured; remorse, I reckon, and maybe some outright disgust. When Crook sent for us to report in, we saluted proper and told him, "No thank you, sir; we are gone again on business."

I don't know what Crook said.

But we heard it blistered his pet mule's nose and set a brush fire to smoking in his adjutant's chin whiskers. One way and another, we felt it was time to go. We saddled up and went back into business for ourselves, prospecting over in the Dragoons. Such grand luck could not hold.

In March of '83 came the Chato raid.

This young Chiricahua, whose name meant "Flat Nose," rode a six-day circuit up into Arizona, out of Mexico. He went a hundred miles a day. Killed twenty-five white men and murdered one woman, carried off the son of a New Mexico judge from a stagecoach burn-out, stole seven hundred horses and cattle, burned twenty-three ranches, outrode ten companies of U. S. Cavalry, and got safe back into Mexico.

But Chato gave Red Beard Crook the fuel to fire up the Hot Trail Treaty, and Red Beard laid his fire careful.

First off, he asked every one of his commanders who were the absolute best scouts in the territory. He was told they was still Al Sieber and Tom Horn. Forgiving us, the general sent once more to Tucson for us to "come in."

Al and me had got us a new mine going in Tombstone by then and were making it pay. But Sieber couldn't stop his ears to the blare of the cavalry bugle. Away he went again. I felt Tom Horn owed the old German at least that much as to go with him and watch out over him. I still was sick of shooting bronco Indians for a fact. But the need hadn't changed for somebody to go after them. I figured I could do a better job of *not* shooting the good Apaches, than the other scouts, and so went with Al.

We had great luck to open with. Riding over to Willcox, where Crook was readying his Mexican column, we caught us a half-pint hostile loner buck name of Pa-nayo-tishn, or The Coyote Saw Him. Sieber nicknamed him Peaches, which is the name that stuck to him. This little fellow told us he knew the secret trail to the Apache hideout in the Mexican Sierra. Sieber so reported to Crook and advised the general to trust Peaches. He did so, and the big column set out down into Mexico following this one little bandy-legged Apache drifter. He never failed us.

It took weeks of frightful trail to locate the Apache retreat but, with Peaches to help us we found it at last for Crook. Going in hard, the red-bearded general caught near all the hostile Chiricahua, and those he did not catch promised by messenger to come in peaceful and pronto. Some of these did and more didn't. But we had us our great victory anyway.

We come back into the United States with the likes of Chato (he spelt it Chatto) and Bonito and Kaytennae (Looking Glass) and Loco, Nana, Chihuahua, and Nachee marshaling their bands along behind us. Only Geronimo did not follow, and he promised to do so as soon as he found his missing squaws and children. The count Al Sieber and I made for Crook of the captives came out at 389. Chato and Chihuahua later disappeared when no more word came from Geronimo, but it was still finish to the main Cherry Cow bands, even if yet again Tom Horn was fouled of the part he played. I will gladly confess that little Peaches was our "scouts' scout." But without me to watch him and Sieber to watch me, he could have led us anywhere, and to our deaths, among other places.

Wagh, Peaches!

But you were still an Apache.

In February of the following winter of 1884, Chato came in from Mexico surrendering with a small band of nineteen people but a big packtrain and many cattle. In March, Geronimo at last appeared. The great fighter came in with but eight followers but, lo! with 350 stolen Mexican cattle and a thirty-seven-mule packtrain staggering under plunder raped from the ranchos over the border. Both him and Chato were taken to San Carlos under armed U.S. escort. Many other hostiles continued to drift in that spring and summer. By late August, Crook was able to say for the newspapers, "For the first time in the history of these fierce people, every member of the Apache tribe is at peace."

"Well," Al Sieber said, "maybe."

Come April, his doubts took on heft. The politicians of the Indian Bureau had got through a secret order to have them "administer" the San Carlos Agency, their scheme to rob Crook of running the show. The Apache, somehow hearing of the Bureau's return to power, looked at Red Beard Crook, the respected "Old Clothes Soldier" of a hundred honorable chases after them, and felt sorry for their once-powerful friend-enemy. They began, as was natural, to look past him. Crook knew what was happening but was helpless. His orders had not been altered by a comma, but the dark-skinned children of the desert had already demoted him.

The winters, oh Lord how they fled. It seemed but yesterday that Red Beard was pridefully reporting his Apache children at peace. But that was a year ago, and now another spring had burgeoned in the Arizona high country, and it was suddenly May of 1885.

Down at San Carlos, sly new civilian agent Ford (an Indian Bureau man) worked to shackle the cavalry troops and set the civilians free to again plunder the Apaches of all the great father in Washington provided to them for keeping the peace. It was suicide, Crook warned. No one heard him but the Indians. And of their number, Geronimo listened the hardest.

What was this? Red Beard reduced in power again? Confined with his Hot Treaty troopers to the ranges of Fort Apache. Aha! Ussen be praised. All was not yet lost of freedom's call to the Apache.

Geronimo raised the war whoop in the middle of the night of May 18. With him, fleeing San Carlos, went forty-two war-age bucks, ninety-two women and children. All vanished without a trace into the Arizona mountains, south-bound for the Sierra of Mexico.

Nor did the implacable Gokliya disappear with only his personal Bedonkohe tribesmen in the ghostly breakout. He took Nachee, Mangas, (own-son of the great old Mangas Coloradas), Nana, and the ever-wild Chihuahua, with all their meanest fighters. It bid to be and proved to be Indian hell set fire again.

By June, five cavalry units from Fort Apache and adjacent posts remained in the field casting for the Geronimo fugitives, reported to be still in Arizona, and desperate. Twice we got our particular troops up to rifle range of the rear guard of the Indians, but no casualties either side. But as we pushed them, the toll mounted of their kills—twenty whites in Arizona alone. Then, crossing into New Mexico, they pillaged and burned a hundred-mile swath. On one ranch they killed the rancher, raped and strangled his wife, killed an older child with a hay scythe rip between the legs, left the other child, a blonde-curled three-year-old girl, hanging alive on a meathook outside the kitchen door. With that for farewell, they swept back into Arizona, attacked the supply dump at Guadalupe Canyon, near Fort Huachuca, killed the five soldiers guarding it, made off with seven muleloads of rifle ammunition. Two days later, we lost their trail for good. They simply disappeared. Birds of the air couldn't have made it into Mexico with less sign. Not me, not Al Sieber, not any white man who ever lived came to understand such Chiricahua medicine.

Apaches could literally vanish.

White men who doubted this had a habit of vanishing with them. Al Sieber accepted such things. He glanced over at me, looked south down into the broody stillness of the empty desert, and nodded his bull's head uneasily.

"They're gone," he said. "Let us be likewise."

The land lay quiet, then, all of the summer and until late fall. In November, a new raider appeared. He was Josanie, also called Ulzanna, younger brother of the wild one, Chihuahua. He and ten men got into Arizona through the Florida Mountains. They killed thirty-eight people, rode 1,200 miles to do it, lost but one man of their own band and were never once sighted by soldiers. This brought Crook looking for Al Sieber and Tom Horn again.

We could have anything we wanted, the general said, and had only to name it. It happened it was for me to say, as Sieber was down with infection in his bad foot, and could not go. "All right," I agreed. "Let me have Mickey Free and forty Apaches from Old Pedro's village, and we will go and get them for you."

I found Mickey, and he got ahold of Merijilda and Tissnolthos. With our forty Indian "war dogs" from Pedro's rancheria, we rode out in grim certaintude of coming up with the killers, likely inside forty-eight hours. Ah! the advices of ignorance!

We cast and rode, recast and rerode, the southeast quarter of Arizona Territory for five starving-cold weeks, and never saw a moccasin-print of Josanie or his men. All we ever found were blowing ashes of dead mesquite fires, and pony droppings dry enough to rattle on the icy ground when kicked. And we *were* the best Indian scouts alive.

Finally, along into December, the cavalry took pity on us and called us back in from the field. But pity proved not the idea, at all. A big excitment was in the winter air.

General of the Army Phil Sheridan was in Arizona talking with Red Beard Crook on how to finally kill the Chiricahua "bad ones." They had selected their troops to go into Mexico and do the job. There would be two columns, under Captain Emmett Crawford and Captain Wirt Davis, the two best Indian-hunting officers in the territory.

And what about us, what had we to do with it?

Easy.

Crawford wanted Tom Horn for his scout, Wirt Davis insisted on Sieber for his.

We were going to be in on the kill.

Contrabandista Spring

It was only after we had been called in and told of our assignments that me and Al Sieber were given the rest of the excitement. At long last, the army had got around to chasing Indians with other Indians, as the old Iron Man and his "boy" had been trying to tell them for seven years. Wirt Davis's command was to have only one company of white troops, three of San Carlos and Fort Apache Indians. Crawford's force was even more thumping to the pulse; but for its chief scout and its white field officers, the entire one hundred riders of the command were to be my enlisted Apache scouts.

Now Geronimo and his Bedonkohe *broncos* were done for.

Gokliya was finished, and the rest of the Chiricahua bad ones with him.

Our columns went into the field at once. We moved apart but in continual touch, pushing always deeper into the wild Mexican *monte*. January of 1886, mid-month, Crawford located the main stronghold of the Chiricahua Apache in a mile-deep, uncharted canyon south of Janos and west of the Rio Casas Grandes. Tom Horn and Al Sieber, with Merijilda Grijole, were the three scouts found it for him (and Tom Horn is still waiting to hear the Army say so).

The Chiricahua scouts discovered us early, but Crawford's one hundred Apache troops were real war dogs, and we got the entire enemy horse herd, along with a big surround of squaws and children all ages. While we regrouped our scattered Indian riders to follow up the main bunch of hostile men who had made it away, in came an old squaw saying to Crawford that Gokliya (Geronimo) had sent her and wanted a meeting set for his surrender the next day. Our stout captain agreed, but brave Emmett Crawford was never to see Geronimo.

It was not the Apache but the damned Mexicans that brought the tragedy on us.

A big bunch of their sungrinner cavalry jumped our camp before daybreak, to get at our troops because they were composed of Apache Indians. Poor Crawford, than who no braver officer nor finer man ever saw Indian service, took a bullet into his head which let out a part of his brains onto the rock against which he fell. Lieutenant Maus took over, and we retreated some miles in a fair disorder, but gathered again. We made camp that evening, prepared for anything. It was a scary night and cold as rim ice.

But next morning our young lieutenant got a happy relief along with his hardtack and hot water.

The Mex irregulars who had jumped us had been hounding Geronimo and the Chiricahua hostiles right hard previous to our arrival, and for once we got the benefit of *their* drive. For, lo! who was that up in the sunrise rocks above our nervous night-camp? Could that six-foot devil looking eight foot tall posed up yonder on the slope like Moses be who he looked to be?

He was; his deep bass voice soon enough rolled down to let us know it.

"You know who I am. You know my name. I am ready to talk."

As he spoke, a number of subchiefs, warriors, and fighting women with some older children began to appear out of the same rocks, forming a red phalanx about the feet of their granite-faced messiah. There were a mort of them, many of substantial reputation, and young Maus was shook to his muddy spurs. "For God's sake, Horn," he said to me, "what will we do? What would Crawford have done?"

"He'd have talked to them, lieutenant," I said.

"Yes, yes, of course. Tell them that, man."

"Hold the men steady, sir," I said, and I moved out a little away from Maus. Looking up that mountainside into the morning sun, I quivered a bit in flank myself. Goddamn but those were rough-looking Indians up there. And Geronimo the most ominous of all.

"Gokliya," I called out, "do you remember me?"

I thought the answering silence would never end.

But Geronimo laughed of a sudden and said of course he remembered me, he always remembered young men who stole prize young wives from him. "How are you, Talking Boy?" he said. "Where is Seebie? Where is Captain Crawford?"

"Seebie is with Captain Davis," I said. "Captain Crawford is resting. This is Lieutenant Maus. He will talk for Crawford."

"I won't talk to him."

"Talk to me then, Gokliya." I made him the Indian sign of respect, touching the brow toward him. "What is it you came to say? We will be quiet for a chief."

That reached him. He seemed to grow another foot taller up there on the mountain.

"Listen, Seebie's Boy," he rumbled down, a sudden anxiousness upon him, "we hate these Mexican people as you do. We want to go home with you to your country. We are all done fighting down here. We will put our families in your care so that you may see we do not talk two ways. Go and tell that to your officer."

I went quickly back and consulted with Maus.

He knew Crawford had come to trust me to interpret for him, as Wirt Davis trusted Sieber. When I told him he must let me talk for him, to set up the surrender with Geronimo, he agreed at once. "Hit me on the shoulders with both your hands," I told him. "Then point to me and point from me up to Geronimo and back from him to yourself. That tells him you name me to talk for you. Your boy. Your talking boy. All right, hit me."

He did so, smartly.

On the mountainside we heard the audible "Ahhhh!" of the waiting Apaches. They all moved, unbidden, farther down the slope, halting finally just above us. And God but they were a fascinating and beautiful sight. Seeing them so close sucked my breath away. It was a long minute before I could speak.

I asked Geronimo if he was ready, and he was.

The following is precisely the words and the way that it went, written in the eye of my memory as firm and clear as any parchment scribed with ink and pen.

HORN: To begin, be very careful what you ask; little can be given.

GERONIMO: All right, yes. Nana will go with you now, right now. Nachee and I need time to gather our people and to influence Josanie and Chihuahua to come in with us. We will put our wives and children in your care and will, the others of us, all come north in two moons to talk with Red Beard. We will not speak with any other. Now let me tell you what place we will come up there to meet Red Beard in.

HORN: Wait now. Do you think that Seebie taught me to be a fool?

GERONIMO: Say what you mean.

HORN: I mean I would be a fool to let you pick the place. We will pick the place. Now say yes or no.

GERONIMO: I don't see you speak to the new soldier chief (Maus). I think he doesn't know anything and you are bluffing for him.

HORN: The place will be Cañon de los Embudos. No other place.

GERONIMO: Well, all right. But no soldiers. Is that heard?

HORN: Agreed. (The Indians did not know we were out of ammunition and food, and Crawford in a coma dying.)

GERONIMO: I mean not even the few soldiers that you have here now.

HORN: You did not mean that. These are Apache scouts. You meant white soldiers. Talk one way.

GERONIMO: (laughing) You have learned well from your father. (Sieber) I like that. Yes, no white soldiers.

HORN: It is done then.
GERONIMO: *Anh,* yes, all done. *Ugashe—!*

And that, indeed, was the end of it there on the sun-lit mountainside in Sierra del Norte, Mexico. The Apache remaining with Geronimo went south. Those staying with us turned to the north. I never saw that country again.

Nor wanted to.

The Indians were another matter.

In March, General Crook, talking through Lieutenant Marion Maus—whose tongue was Tom Horn—met with the Chiricahua, as agreed, in Funnel Canyon, called by them Cañon de los Embudos. Geronimo, Chihuahua, Josanie, and Nachee all came in as promised by Geronimo. Nana, the old Warm Springs killer, we already had in custody from the talk on the mountainside.

Their friend Red Beard Crook spoke—again and always through me—with an unexpectedly harsh, because bluntly honest, tone. He offered the Apache only tears and punishment for the sorrows they had brought both Mexico and the United States. Terms of the surrender were crushing: the Apache must give up unconditionally, they were to understand that they would be sent to Florida, the dreaded "Hot Place."

It seemed an exodus of the wild Indians would follow, but it did not. The Chiricahua had been too long driven, had lost too much tribal blood, were too weary and starved and lost in spirit to continue.

A compromise of sorts was arranged: they would surrender on Red Beard's terms if they could spend but two years in Florida. Crook accepted this limitation and climbed on his roach-maned army mule.

"All of this is over now," he had me tell Geronimo. "You have given me your last promise. Remember that."

This was his entire "speech" at Cañon de los Embudos. Delivering it, he turned the mule and rode out of the canyon, bouncing and jarring to the rude gait of the lop-eared charger some say he loved better than any man.

His departure, with all his staff, left Lieutenant Maus and Tom Horn to supervise the march of the Chiricahua from Cañon de los Embudos to surrender site.

For two days all went well. The last night we camped the lot of them—upwards of 125 of them, mostly famous or infamous wild bronks—just to the south of the U.S. border. It was there that rotgut hell caught up with Cherry Cow destiny.

Charles "Swiss Charley" Tribolet was the bastard's name. He was running an Indian trading post on the line but some miles off from where we were. He was a notorious fence for the stuff the Apaches stole on both sides of the border, but he mostly did a cash business in skull-buster whiskey at $10 silver the quart.

Tribolet was likewise a known member of the Indian Ring in Washington, D.C., and worked for them as Sieber and me could easy prove. Sieber had documented evidence which I had seen that Swiss Charley was given his orders by the Ring. And more. He had also a letter intercepted by our Indians at the San Carlos post office which showed that the whiskey runner was explicitly paid by the Ring to do the hellish thing he done that night. Why the old German chose never to reveal this letter, only he knows. I think it was to let the dead past bury its dead. Seebie believed in tomorrow; he always rode with his shadow behind him, toward the day.

But Tribolet didn't wait for any sunrise; he did his labors in the dark. That night of our last camp in Mexico, he voyaged toward us through the chaparral with a double mule-load of kegged whiskey, plus a big pannier of cheap squaw gimcracks to grease the celebration. At a spot not far off from our fires, he set up his floating whiskey camp in a tangle of lonely brush called Contrabandista Spring. It became then merely a matter of letting the Apache leaders under our guard know that the drinks were on Swiss Charley.

Business was brisk, once so advertised.

And all sales were final.

Tribolet soon had the worst of our Indians, Geronimo, Nachee, and Chihuahua—all known bad drinkers—well into the staggers. When he saw that he had the three of them "fired up," he let drop to them that he, Swiss Charley, had learned that Lieutenant Maus and the traitor Talking Boy Horn were leading them into a trap set by General

Crook just over the American border. They would be put in irons, placed in unknown soldier jails, never see their loved ones again. Well, Christ Jesus, that was it.

Geronimo and Nachee, with twenty-one men and nineteen squaws and pups, stampeded. As Al Sieber later wrote of it, "they lit out back down into Mexico, fetlock, gunstock and whiskey barrel." Tom Horn had no comment for the occasion. They had been his Indians and had got away from him. Bright remarks wouldn't bring them back.

We got the details of the treachery of Swiss Charley the next day. It came from Chihuahua. The old boy had gotten too happy the night previous. He could not in fact stay on his pony, but kept falling off, and so didn't make it away with the others. We found him with his aching head dunked into the cold water of Contrabandista Spring, one moccasined foot still hung up in the stirrup of his faithful pony, which stood patiently by him cropping mesquite beans and dropping horse apples on the fallen chief. But Chihuahua gave us the line on Tribolet and on the vanished Geronimo. We thanked him for that and pulled him out of the horse apples. He seemed grateful.

Back at camp, I asked Lieutenant Maus for the loan of Merijilda and a permit to go after Swiss Charley. Maus understood. "Go get him," he said. "Unofficial."

We ran the bastard trader three full days and damn near got him, but the Indians were helping him lay his trail, and they mighty close to killed us from a dry-gully rifle pit down on the Mexican side, and me and Merijilda figured we had done our duty. We went back and picked up Maus and our remaining Chiricahuas, some seventy-nine of them, as I remember it. We got them on over the line into the U.S. and then safe up to San Carlos. They were restless as hell and there was some fair doubt we would have come off so good, but that crusty old Nana had persuaded Chihuahua and even crazy Josanie to pitch in and quieten down their people.

They were Judas goats, the poor wild devils.

Every one of their seventy-nine kinfolk that followed them into San Carlos, and themselves with them, were seized and sent onto the train for Florida "for life," routed for Fort Marion to an existence of whipped dogs, lied to, cheated, and shamed to the end.

General Crook did his level best to fight the double cross of their sentences. But the government broke its word to him, a sorrow he bore to the grave.

Nor was that all.

But twelve days after we got home from Mexico with our Indians, General Nelson A. Miles was given the command in Arizona and arrived at Fort Bowie to assume it.

Crook was sent off back up north to the Department of the Platte. The Ring had got him at last. He was the best friend the Apache had. His end forecast their own. The day of the Chiricahua had come to twilight.

So neared its close the field book of campaigning that brought me and Al Sieber to the grits of our own last decision. Like always, it wasn't us that made it. It was our shadows. The ones we cast that night at Contrabandista Spring—or that Tom Horn cast there alone—and cost George Crook, "the old clothes soldier," his honorable peace with the Apache people.

Skeleton Canyon

Let it not be said amongst his friends that Tom Horn then took, nor now takes, the entire fault for what happened to let Geronimo and Nachee get away from Lieutenant Maus at Contrabandista Spring, Sonora. It was a great many things involved there. But I knew, for my enemies even then were letting me understand it, that Talking Boy was going to get the main credit. Sieber warned me so.

This was in the immediate days, of course, of Maus bringing our Indians in. None of us knowed then that Crook was going to go, or who would replace him. Moreover, my mind was already looking back on other times, trying to think where Nopal might be, or my boy from her, now that most of the hostiles had "come in," with yet no sign, nor Indian word, of neither of them.

But then came the news that General Crook had resigned in despair of the Indian Bureau treachery to his Chiricahua charges. When their Red Beard went away, however, the Apaches mourned as for a friend. When Bear Coat Miles showed up to take his place, Old Mad and me joined the Indians in their sentiments.

"Horn," Sieber said, hearing of the change in command, "this will wash out the riffle box for both of us. We mighten as well take our clean-up and git."

But I still had one more try in me.

"Nope, Al," I said. "It would be going back on the boys with Maus and me. I owe the lieutenant one."

"For what?" Sieber demanded, bluntlike.

I fished inside my vest and brought out a crumpled piece of paper. "For this," I answered, full proud.

Al took the paper and unrolled it, squinting to make out the hand print of it, and the signature. His lips moved like it was painful to form the words he saw.

To Whomever May Be Concerned:
I cannot commend too highly Mr. Horn, my Chief of Scouts; his gallant services deserve a reward which he has never received.

Sgnd. *W. P. Maus*

Marion P. Maus
Lt. 3rd Cav US.

Sieber recrumpled the paper careful to get the right creases back into it. He handed it back.

"That and five cents," he said, "will buy you a good nickel beer anyplace that sells it."

"You're sore," I said, "because you was with Davis."

Al Sieber did not get mad. He just looked sort of used up and shook his head with a vast sigh.

"No, kid," he said. "For once you read the trail sign

wrong. It's that I am coming up on forty-four years old, and you ain't yet hit twenty-seven."

"I still don't read your sign, Al."

Again the sad, slow nod, the flinch of pain over the jowly, square face that I had seen across those many hundred campfires from me since 1876.

"*Enjuh, ish-ke-ne,*" he said, "that's good, boy."

I had the sense to let it ride.

Sieber proved right as Sieber always proved.

Miles's first act, mighty near, was to fire me and the old German "out of hand." That was April. Me and Al took off for our other home, the saloons of Tombstone. There we prospected some, kept up with "the war" in the papers, let old Bear Coat run his tongue hanging out chasing Apaches with his white "super troops," as his press officer called them. By July, Miles was truly desperate for a victory —he was in line for making major general and instead the Apaches was making a fool of him—and he sent at last for his one real "Injun captain," Charles B. Gatewood. "In the name of God," Miles said, "what must we do, Gatewood?" The captain had his answer ready.

"General," he said, "you must do two things; you must get me old Al Sieber to scout for me and let me have young Tom Horn and his war dog scouts for my troops—not one white soldier squad in sight anywhere."

Miles didn't care for that. There'd been words betwixt him and Sieber when we was layed off. And likewise, Miles did not think of Indians as Crook did, as human men and master cavalrymen. But he was trapped.

"Very well," he said at last, "recall them."

Thus it was the word came once more to Tombstone for Tom Horn and Al Sieber to report "back active."

But Al would not go. His rheumatism was terrible on him just then, and he could not get up into the saddle of his ancient gray Jenny mule to even report for the duty. "Horn," he said, "go and take my place. It is your time, at last. You will do the job."

And so I came alone to the last grim running of the Chiricahua. It went short and mean and dismal.

The command was actually under Captain H. W. Law-

ton, but Gatewood called me aside and said to go and get
my old war dog troop out of Pedro's rancheria and meet him
on the trail to Haros River, where Lawton and his super
troops was then camped, having lost the line on Geronimo's
fleeing fighters. "Don't worry about Lawton," the officer con-
fided to me. "We will get around him." And he was right.
He never went near Lawton (like his orders read) but
crossed Haros River and, on a hot track found by me and
Chikisin and Merijilda Grijole, drove eighty miles down
Fronteras way. In three days we arrived at the Chiricahua
camp in the Terras (Torres) Mountains. Me and Merijilda
went in alone and arranged for Geronimo and Nachee to
meet with Bay-chen-day-sen ("Big Nose"), which was their
name for homely Captain Gatewood.

The Cherry Cows were done in and, moreover,
honored Gatewood as a good man and friend of Red Beard
Crook.

At the end of two days interpreting (by Tom Horn)
Geronimo stood up and made the talk that got into the
history books, ending with those fateful words: "We will
go with you to surrender to General Miles. Send that word
to him. Ask him to meet us in the Canyon of the Skeleton,
and say you will travel with us to that place."

On the next day, August 25, Geronimo and Nachee,
with twenty-two warriors and fourteen women and children,
began the long march back with Captain Gatewood. Miles
met us at the canyon, took Geronimo and Nachee in charge,
and transported them by army ambulance to Fort Bowie.
There we found out that Bear Coat had traitorously arrested all the Chiricahua—382 Apache souls—under false
pretense of a routine "head count" for rations, at Fort
Apache, while us and Gatewood had been in Mexico.

Within that same week, Miles arrested most of our
loyal war dog Apache scouts, as well, and threw them all
on the same train for Florida. Just ten days from Geronimo
surrendering in Skeleton Canyon, him and all the Chiricahua
was in irons and "on the cars" for Fort Marion, in Florida.

As the prison train left from Bowie Station, the band
from the Fourth Cavalry played a nice rendition of "Auld
Lang Syne."

So the Arizona days drew down for Tom Horn.

With Geronimo gone and Nopal disappeared, I could see clearly the track ahead. The Indian trail was not to be the ending place of my life, as I had dreamed it to be. I had ridden out its dimming page of pony hoofprints and had read on it the footnote that despaired me most:

My old German was failing.

His Civil War and Apache war cripplings, the agony of rheumatics that they caused in him, the unhealable great open abscess that was his pitiful left foot, all had grown ever more intolerable both to him and to the army. Each painful day now brought him nearer to the end of his employment as a scout. Already he had lost his chief-of-scouts ranking to me, and the changing made a hurt that I could see far back in the deep black eyes. Our time had dwindled down to its own ending place.

Should I, his boy, have left Al Sieber in his decline, before he himself knew that Seebie's day was twilight lit, it would have been no different than abandoning a hit comrade under battlefield fire. God will know, and my true friends, also, that I would never do that to Old Mad. He was the parent to me that my own father never was, nor could have been. As long as Iron Man could sit the saddle, Tom Horn would side him out. But when the day came, as now it had, where he could no longer get aboard his Jenny mule when the bugles blew, that day would be the last one in Arizona Territory for his son Talking Boy.

Thus were the campaigns ended that brought Al Sieber and me to our final parting. They faded away with Geronimo run to his dying earth, the Chiricahua wild ones scattered forever. It seems like nothing to see these notes. But, ah! every word of them was a splash of Apache blood.

Every line an Indian life.

Chi-ki-sin, forgive us.

Ending Place

I had now been eleven years away from Wyaconda Creek and the Horn farm, in Scotland County, Missouri.

Ten of those years had been spent in the Arizona Territory with the Apache Indians. A man just doesn't saddle up and ride off from such a span of his lifetime, but I was determined to do it. A rumor had come that Miles was disbanding the scout force, firing the civilians first. Well, I had about my fill of that. I went up and resigned from the service, then and there, before they could order me off the reservation again.

In the office of Miles's aide, I ran into Al Sieber.

He was feeling some recovered, and I was pleasured to learn the army had offered to keep him on.

When I told him what I'd done, he just nodded and said, "Yes, I envy you. You're young. That's the time to ride away." He shook the bullet head, now showing iron gray, the old growl but an echo. "I waited too long," he said. "Now I can't do it. We ain't up to it, me and old Jenny. They're pensioning us both, Horn."

He stopped, looking down south toward the Sierra Madre and Mexico.

"Ride out, bucko," he said. "If you hear hoofbeats coming behind you, it will be me and Jenny, but don't look around. It'll only be our shadows follering on."

Nothing I could say would cheer him. Finally, we made our parting. It didn't no way match up to what we wanted to say of good-byes. It don't never.

"Yeah, well," I managed, swinging up on my restless horse, *"hasta la vista."*

Al Sieber nodded, raised one gnarled hand.

"Cuidado," was his single word to cover the ten years of it.

I went up White River to Pedro's rancheria and was aiming to say good-bye, but there wasn't anybody there I wanted to touch the brow to. The chief was sick, over to Fort Huachuca seeing the army surgeon. Chikisin had gone with him. Sawn, my Apache "sister," had gone off down into Mexico somewheres with Mickey Free. Her nine kids, by at least four fathers, was along with them. I finally asked for Na-to, (Tobacco), figuring she was too old to be traveling, but the eldest wife of Pedro had taken her journey the spring before. It was to visit Yosen in his great *kinh* ("house") up above the moon. The Apache who told me this said, as I was leaving, that he had just remembered an old friend of mine who *was* at home. "In fact," he said, "he's staying with me."

I went with him to his wickiup, glad enough.

It's a wan-gill feeling to come home and find all of your friends have gone away. At least I would get to talk to someone who could remember me with sufficient kindness to care that I had come. Whoever it was, they would help me lighten my burden of *chin-da-see-le*, homesickness. But I had forgotten that Apaches count all things as old friends.

My guide, Choddi, (Antelope), told me to wait outside his house, *por favor*. "It is a very old friend who waits in there," he said. "He might not recognize you in the darkness." I heard a jangle of chain, a rasping growl, and out came Choddi dragging a bundle of moldy bones and falling hair and trembling hindquarters that at first I didn't realize was a stone-blind timber wolf.

But the poor thing got a whiff of me and quit growling and went to making circles with his mangy tail, and I said, "My God, is that you, Snarler?" and when he heard my voice he commenced to whimper and bawl and, well, it was all I might do not to join him, I was that choked.

"Yes," Choddi said, "Snarler."

"Well," I said, rubbing the old wreck's ears, "I am happy that you are taking care of him."

"I have been meaning to," Choddi nodded, "but other matters have interfered."

"What?" I said. "Tell that again."

"I promised Sister Sawn I would shoot him, while she and the children are away. But I haven't done it yet. To tell you the truth, Talking Boy, I haven't got a bullet for my gun."

I took the rusted chain from the Indian. "I will take care of him for you," I said. "You tell Sister Sawn that I did it. Tell her Snarler remembered me."

"*Mil gracias,*" said Choddi. "Ussen guard your horses."

"*Y lo mismo a usted,*" I answered, touching the brow.

My horse was trained, as all I ever rode, to walk behind me, off rein or on. Now the animal was following me and Snarler down the river to the forks of the White and Black. I wanted a pretty place for the old tame wolf, one where he could watch the game trails and hear his kinfolk howling off over in the Sawbuck Mountains. I knew the spot.

We climbed to it, and him and me sat up there a spell. He couldn't see a lick, but his old white muzzle worked that upriver wind better than most human sets of eyes, and he give a soft moaning sort of sound that I knew was his thank-yous for bringing him to a decent place. I eased out my Colt's .44 and shot him in the back of the neck, and he just gave a little sigh and sunk down right where he was. I left him lay there, head pointing down the wild lower canyon of the White. My last Apache friend.

Down below, I got on my horse and gave him his head.

He was a rangy tall bay of the kind I liked, black legs, a star and no snip, eyes full and dark as an Arab's, a reaching easy gait that ate the miles like magic. He was what the Mexican hotblood breeders called a *kehilan*, a Barb or Turkey word that meant "drinker of the wind." I called him Sheik, and had given four prices for him off a Sonora breeder down Fronteras way. Now I didn't call him nothing. Just turned him loose with me on him.

But he knew the way to go.

Upriver was Indian country and would be for our time. Downstream lay the trail out.

Sheik just gave a low whicker, blew out soft through his nostril bells, and struck out down the river.

I was to wander three more springs in Arizona, and search through as many winters, looking for Nopal and little Sombra, yes, and trying to find something of my own-self somewhere in the long ride, but I never made it. The new grass followed every snow, and Tom Horn followed every new grass. When that last spring of 1890 came along, I had found nothing. But that summer something at last found me. It was a letter from the Pinkerton Detective Agency's home office, in Denver, Colorado. The "Pinks" had heard of Tom Horn, and decided he was the man hunter they wanted to hire that August, *Enjuh, ugashe,* so be it.

That night, me and Sheik left Tombstone in the dead of the two-A.M. darkness. I didn't want anybody to know we had gone, nor which direction we had took. There was no more good-byes for me in Arizona. My *sombra,* my shadow, was warning me. Get out! Get out! If you don't, you will be like Sieber, staying too long. *Adiós muchachos. Enjuh, schichobes.* Ride away, Talking Boy, ride away. If you hear hoofbeats following you, remember what old Al said. Don't look back. Only shadows are there.

So it was me and the rangy bay went north.

We thought it was Denver we were bound for, but Denver was not our north. We had another place to go up there, old Sheik and me. It was to be our ending place.

History called it by another name.

And wrote it dark for me.

It was Wyoming.

Book Three

Pinkerton Detour

I went by way of Tucson, the Pinkerton letter having advised that route. I was to meet their man in a certain saloon there, down in the Mexican quarter. Idea of that was to save me the long ride up into Colorado, if their contact didn't figure I was all the Arizona papers libeled me into being. Which was to say, liar, cheat, Indian lover, ambusher and bushwhacker, bullshitter, ladies' man, big talker, and top tracker. The last proved to be what the "Eye That Never Sleeps" was interested in, lucky for the liar and cheat and bull thrower.

I got me a chair and drug it to the front wall of El Coyotero, the cantina designated for the meet. I have a working suspicion of such meetings and never took on one full face. I would lay back in the dark against my wall and let the other fellow walk into the lamplight and show himself first. I would then contact him. Or I would if he looked safe. That is to say, appeared to be looking to hire a man and not collect the bounty on him.

If I didn't take to his cut, it would be either gun or run, depending on which "out" I was offered. I did not ever shoot my way out of any set, or deadfall, where I could escape it *sombra*-style. To "shadder out" of a scrape, as they say, is second nature to a scout and hunter like Tom Horn. The idea of a market hunter, and that is what I had been for the past ten years, whether stalking whitetails or muleys for venison, or Chiricahuas or white cow thieves for blood money, the idea, to repeat, was to "bring home the bacon." If you didn't fetch back the game you had gone after, or furnish cold proof it was dead meat where you'd left it, you didn't get paid. And Tom Horn never worked free.

That night, however, I didn't expect any trouble; my

sombra wasn't twinging me any. After all, the Pinkertons were not pony apples. They had run the U.S. Secret Service during the Civil War and were "the law" most feared by the guilty throughout all the West. When you got a letter from them, handwrote by Mr. James McParlan, the Denver superintendent—and the man who had busted up the outlaw coal miner gang, the Molly Maguires, single-handed—you didn't look to get cut down by their agent.

You could get outflanked, though.

"Hello," said the low voice behind me. "If you were already on salary, I'd fire you."

"Yes," I said. "And if you hadn't of spoke up just now when you did, your wife would of had to buy a black dress. You made more noise coming through that window than a drunk going up a gutter pipe to get into his house without using the front door. What kept you?"

It wasn't a cold bluff, it was stiff-froze.

I did remember there was a paneless window cut in the adobe wall on along from where I was. And I did figure he had to have crawled through that. But mostly I was betting blind. Which sometimes works.

He laughed a low chuckle and said, "You're hired."

And that was how I met W. C. "Doc" Shores, the sheriff of Gunnison County, Colorado. He introduced himself, saying he hoped I was Tom Horn, but if I wasn't, I would do. Naturally, I admitted I was guilty. Shores nodded and said, "Come on, I will buy us the bottle. They got to have a back room here, where we can lay this thing out."

I knew the El Coyotero like the inside of Sister Sawn's wickiup. Being Mexican, it was my dish. I liked the people and their cooking and the real way they looked at life and had I a second choice to being born a Chiricahua Apache, I'd have made it sungrinner Mexican. So I said to the owner Manuel Arroyo, "Don't let anyone disturb us, *hombre*. Just send us in a bottle of the best you got. We are going into the back room and don't need any *compañeras de cuarto. Comprende?*" I winked. "*No chanza esta noche.*"

Manuel nodded. "*Lo entiendo,*" he said. "No fun tonight."

"Yes," I specified. "And no roommates."

"*Sí, amigo.* Only the girl who brings your glasses."

"*Bueno.*"

"*Gracias.* Enjoy the night."

"*Sí, bueno. Lo mismo. Saludos.*"

"*Suerte,*" Manuel said. "Where is that damned girl?"

Shores stood aside, holding the cowhide curtain for me to precede him into the alcove.

"I can see," he said, "why the Indians named you Talking Boy."

"You talk, you learn things," I answered.

"Talk can kill you," he said. "Remember it."

I was to remember it, God knows. But that was yet years to the north. For now I was sitting pretty tall on my horse. People knew of Tom Horn. Big people. Important ones. Even the Pinkertons. In the man-hunting business they didn't grow no bigger nor more important than the Eye. And they had sent to find Tom Horn. Who was Doc Shores to schoolteach me? The sheriff of Gunnison County? Hell, I had worked for Buckey O'Neill, of Yavapai. And Glenn Reynolds, Gila County. Yes, and Commodore Owens, over in Apache County. Real lawmen, gun packers, shooters, cold trailers. The best. Yet had the Pinks sent for them? *Even* for them? Hell no.

They had sent for Tom Horn.

"Tell you what," I said to the Gunnison sheriff, meeting his eyes across the rickety table we settled to inside the alcove. "You keep quiet and I'll keep talking. It ain't my style to sing low. Was it, I reckon Mr. McParlan wouldn't never have heard of Tom Horn."

Shores stared back. He had the palest blue eyes I ever saw. And he was a big cuss, like me. Six two, maybe. Going close to two hundred pounds. All catgut and baling wire. It occurred to me a little late in the evening that maybe Mr. Sheriff W. C. "Doc" Shores had also ridden down a few men in his own time.

"Horn," he said, not unpleasant but no grin to crinkle the edges of it neither, "McParlan never *had* heard of Tom Horn. It was me told them who to write."

"You did? I'll be damned. Well, thanks." I frowned after a moment's thinking it over. "Say," I said, "how come you to hear of me?"

"It's my business to know who will kill a man if he has to. I keep a list. You're on it."

"Be damned if I am!" I bit back at him. "I ain't never killed anybody. Not white, I ain't."

Shores tapped his vest pocket. "There's a New Mexico warrant in here says you did."

"The hell!"

"And a Texas."

"Christ Jesus, I ain't ever even been in Texas!"

"Tell that to them. They think you have."

"That's just talk, goddamnit."

"In Texas they call it testimony. Juries believe it Judges sentence on it. Same for New Mexico. But the rope now, it don't say a word. Never."

I knew those stories about Tom Horn in Texas and New Mexico. Every time some poor son of a bitch was found shot out in the lonelies, Tom Horn was given the credit. I got to be like I was running out hanging warrants for old Lucifer. Whoever got hit, it was my bullet. I had always more or less let those lies ride, seeing how pale they turned folks faces who was watching me. It made a man feel dangerous. Mysterious. Big on the land. Yet he knew he hadn't done the things they said. None of them that involved white men. So what harm could come of letting people scare themselves? They enjoyed it too.

Shores was watching me, waiting on me.

I reached for the bottle, wondering where the hell Manuel's girl was with our glasses. Uncorking it, I took a long pull, slid the bottle over toward the Gunnison lawman. He caught it and tilted it without wiping off the neck of it. It gave me a minute.

Trouble with those Tom Horn killer lies was that they had followed me out of the Indian scouting service. The most of the past three, four years out of army work, I'd put in punching cows and busting bronks for the big outfits like the Chiricahua Cattle Company and the Hash Knife (Aztec Land & Cattle Company) and suchlike. I had even rode a little for smaller ranchers, of the stripe of Ed Tewksbury, until him and the Grahams got into it in the Pleasant Valley sheep fight. And, damn it, no matter if the outfits were big or small, knowed or unknowed, if a man got it out in the chaparral, no witnesses, no sign left about that even an Apache Indian could follow, why it was just automatic that "Tom Horn done it." Several of those lonesome corpses had been white. Those were the ones you didn't want added to your score. But there was those Texas and New Mexico *fábulas* again. With me letting them grow, grinning over the starts they gave folks, they had taken such root that they'd spread five hundred and a thousand miles, over the years, springing up finally right here under my feet in Arizona.

Damn! And Doc Shores had those bogus warrants and I didn't dast contest them, and he was still peering at me out of those frosty blue eyes, and I threw in.

"You are right about judges and juries," I conceded. "I found that out working for the Chiricahua Cattle people and some others of the big outfits. We would bring in our rustlers and horse thieves, with the goods on them cold turkey, and they would, by God, nine times out of eight, walk away from the courtroom laughing at the law and at us boobs what caught them busting it and drug them in to stand before the bar. Shit."

"Which is to say," guessed Doc Shores, "that you will take the case."

"It wouldn't be fair to the Pinkerton folks not to."

"If there's anything I admire outrightly in a man," nodded W. C. Shores, "it is that he's fair. And I can see that fairness shines forth from you in a quality to blind the eyes of Diogenes."

"Must be new in these parts," I said. "I ain't heard of him." I scatched my head. "Greaser or gringo?"

"Greek," said Doc Shores.

I pushed back from the table. "You have got the wrong boy," I said. "I ain't working with no curlyhair foreigners. This Diogenes feller may be all right, but I—"

"Chop it off at the shoulders," the Colorado lawman scowled, interrupting me. "Shut up and listen."

The job was to go after a Colorado horse thief who had been costing the ranchers up in Doc Shores's county thousands of dollars. Doc had been hard after him, on a special assignment for the Pinkertons, when he had lost the trail in Arizona. That's where I came in. The story was that this bastard had got over the line into Mexico, and the Pinks, by damn, wanted him back. They still hung horse thieves up in Colorado, and they meant to hang this one high. His

stringing-up would serve to be like the coyote hide hung
on the bob-wire fence. It would warn off other coyotes
(horse thieves) to stay shut of land where the Pinkertons
was employed.

Shores knew nothing of the fugitive, except that he
was a Mexican. He used the name Sancarlos, which ought
to have told me something, but didn't. Of course, that
wasn't his real name. He was said to have friends among
the Apache Indians, particularly in Sonora. It was this part
of the case that had suggested Tom Horn to Sheriff Shores.
If anybody in Arizona could go down into Mexico and find
a Mexican and haul him back for hanging as an American
horse thief, it ought to be Talking Boy Horn.

I tried to tell Shores I had cut the lead rope twixt me
and the Indians. He rightly argued that you could never do
that. "Being a squaw man," he finished, "puts a st—" He
started to say puts a stink on a man that is forever in his
hide, but changed it to, "well, you know, Horn, puts a strange
mark on a man. It won't come off in water, nor wash out
with settlement soap. You can go among them where I
would be dry-gulched the first day. What do you say? The
Pinkertons pay first-rate and on the date. You bring this
man in, I can get you on the payroll permanent. How old
you now, Horn?"

It hit me like a blunt arrow; I had to think.

"Thirty," I finally said. "I don't believe it!"

"Time to think past pickup cow work."

"God, yes. Jesus. Thirty years old!" I shook my head
like a wolf trying to scatter a bad mouthful of poison bait.
But the bitter taste scalded still. "All right," I said, "give me
the warrant."

He gave me the document, and I never glanced at it
but stuck it inside my vest. "Where do you want him
brought?" I asked.

"Here," he said. "I'll wait three days."

"Three days?"

"I've a tip he's over in the San Pedro Valley. Never
went into Mexico. A half-breed name of Nino Pinto spies for
me up in Gunnison. Knows this fellow we're after and has
located his track down past the Pantano Wash. Says it runs
westerly, into the Santa Rita peaks. Pinto's over there in

Pantano now. You know where the Santa Rita lateral comes into the main wash? He'll be there."

"How come you and him don't run this track, if it's so all-fired hot and near?"

"I told you. This Mex is up in those rocks with some Apache friends—maybe. Neither me nor Nino Pinto is apt to last long enough to climb the first ridge. You can get in there. At least, I told McParlan you could."

I wanted the job. That thirty years old reminder had spooked me bad. Could be that detective work on the range would be my true life's calling. I better find out.

"I'm gone," I said, starting up from the table.

Just then there was a tinkle of glasses on metal outside the cowhide curtain of the alcove. Doc Shores whipsnaked around the table, caught the guilty girl, and drug her into the alcove so fast I was yet bent over getting up. I didn't even have time to turn to see our eavesdropper, face-on.

"Well now, little *espía*," the Gunnison sheriff accused her, "how much did you hear out there? Come on, *dígame*."

"*No, no, patrón*," the Mex girl denied the charge. "*Yo no persona que escucha a escondidas lo que no debe oír.*"

She was saying that she was never a person who listened to the "hidden things" of others. But I did not care what she said. I knew that voice. I had heard it a hundred times in lonely dreams since Santa Fe and the address of *numero tres*, Calle Cantina. I swung hard around, and it was her. "Lord God," I said. "Pajarita Morena."

"*Hombre!*" was all she whispered back to me.

The Horsethief

There was a raggedy sky of buttermilk cloud, shot through by a three-quarter moon. The sand still held the heat of the day. Perfume of sage and cactus and piñon made a grand smell all about us. Our horses went eager and easy, the borrowed black mare nuzzling Sheik and whickering she-horse things to him. I commenced to hum. Pretty quick the words came: *Pajarita, Pajarita, Pajarita barranqueño, Que bonitos ojos tiene, Lastimas que tengan dueno.* I trailed off; my friend laughed.

It seemed strange to be riding through the young night with a woman. Tom Horn, the great man hunter. Bound after a Mex desperado with a hanging price on his head. And being sided by Pajarita Morena, his "little bird" from the *juzgado* in Santa Fe. But happy? Christ, I hadn't been so at peace inside myself since laying with Sweet Nopal up in Fish Hawk Meadow.

Shores had been decent enough to understand the reunion in the El Coyotero's back room. He had gone out and paid for the bottle, saying only to me, as he ducked past the cowhide, "Three days, Horn. Good luck."

I had paid Manuel for Little Bird's night off, and we had gone to her place. It was at the livery barn next door, a miserable lean-to of a hut tacked onto the hay shed and not fit for a good dog. But the years had not been kind to Pajarita Morena and this was her life now, a cheap whore in a Mexican saloon in old Tucson.

"Tomasito," she had sighed, "forgive it, this place that you see me in. It is not like *numero tres,* eh?"

"Nothing ain't like it was, *querida,*" I'd told her.

"No," she had whispered, dropping her shawl and loosening her reboza. "Not except that we make it so, Tomas."

And we had made it so, for that little time.

I dropped Pajarita off in the town of Pantano where, as all good Mexicans have in every town, Little Bird had "cousins." I left her outside a dobe shack on the outskirts, promising to see her there in two days, and rode on down the big Pantano Wash, south, toward the Santa Ritas. In the gray dawn I found the campfire of Doc Shores's spy, Nino Pinto, sneaking in and putting the muzzle of my Colt's .44 in his ear to awaken him. He calmed down when I showed him the warrant for the Mexican. With first good daylight, he said, he would take me up the sidewash and put me on the trackline of the horse thief's mount, but he would not go with me beyond those hoofprints.

"*Dispénseme, patrón,*" he apologized, "but only a little past this point where I will take you, you will see that unshod horses come in to join the shod horse of the Mexican. I would guess six at least. My father was one-half Jicarilla Apache," the breed said. "I know those unshod pony prints. *Están los bárbaros.*"

I forgave him and told him to lay out in the chaparral beyond his campfire for two days. If I did not come back, he was to go tell Sheriff Shores that his Mexican horse thief wouldn't be coming in.

"*Suerte,*" the little *mestizo* nodded, when he had put me on the trackline of shod and unshod horses later that morning. But he was only wishing me luck as a courtesy. He knew he would never see Senor Horn again. *Los bárbaros* would see to that. And for a fact, they damned near did. Well, trim that down a little; they *could* have seen to it.

I ran the tracks all that day until the light commenced to fail. It was late sundown when the Apaches rode out of the rocks on either side of me and said, in Spanish, for me to not move myself or my horse, lest we both be shot from the two sides, *más pronto y más despacho.* I answered them in their own guttural tongue, saying I understood the need for delicacy. This delighted them, and one of them, the apparent leader—who somehow seemed vaguely familiar to me in the thickening darkness—said to the others, "Yes, this must be the one. Who else would speak our tongue? *Enjuh, enjuh. Ugashe.*" And so they herded me up the final twisting ascent of the Pantano lateral wash and brought me, in the full of night, to the camp of the horse thief.

I ought, by this time, to have been ready for anything. But I was not.

When they had dragged me off my horse and over to the fire, where the Mexican stood alone, it came as a total disbelief to face him across the smoky flames.

It was Merijilda Grijole.

I was struck mute, but still the first to speak.

"But you cannot have done it!" I objected to Merijilda.

"They have accused the wrong man. You, a horse thief?"
It was *lunático,* I added, moon-nonsense.

"You have the warrant," he said. "Look at the name
upon it."

I had forgotten the paper in the excitement of finding
him there. Now I took out the paper and he was right;
his real name was there along with the alias Sancarlos. I still
could not accept it. Merijilda assured me I must do so. Listen,
he said:

He had gone up to Colorado when Miles let us all go
back in '86. There was work up there at the mines for a
man who knew mules. A large trade went forward freighting supplies to the high camps by mule train. Merijilda
had risen to be head packer for the A.L.&M. Syndicate,
operating above Boulder in the Ward, Jamestown, and
Utica #1 strikes. He had done well. Then a number of
ranches in the area began suffering big losses to a master
horse thief who had defied identification. But one midnight a friend had come to Merijilda, saying the horse thief
had at last been found. He was a head packer for the
Syndicate and Utica #1, a Mexican named Grijole.

Merijilda had fled in the night and been running each
night since. He was trying to reach Sonora, to live with the
unsurrendered Chiricahua of Juh. On the way he had met
these good comrades and fallen in with them, as they, too,
were attempting to reach home in the Sierra Madre del
Norte.

"*Hijo!*" Merijilda said, concluding, "you remember
this fellow don't you?" He pointed to the leader of the
Apaches. "He remembers you."

I turned, and the muffled figure of the Apache stepped
into the fire's full light; it was the half brother to Naiche
(Nachee) and Tahza, the sons of Cochise—my enemy,
Hal-zay.

"Those were other years," the resonant Indian voice
greeted me. "I remember you but I have forgotten those
bad times."

"It is best to see ahead," I agreed. "Only old men look
behind them."

"Yes." He lapsed into silence, looking down.

"Are there any others here that I might know?" I said

to fill the stillness. "Anyone from those old days none of us remembers?"

"There is one," answered a slender figure, moving forward. "I am still here, brother."

That voice. The slight body. The music of the soft words. My heart leaped.

"My brother!" I cried. "It cannot be you!"

"Yes," Chikisin said, "it can."

And we wept to be there together, even though white men know that Apaches never cry.

Of course I could not arrest Merijilda. But I had that warrant with his name on it, and I had come to take back a Mexican horse thief. Here, Chikisin had a thought.

Hal-zay had a prisoner he was guarding back to Sonora, a bad man who had murdered his squaw and fornicated with a war chief's wife. By Apache law he must die. Therein, my brother Chikisin saw the opportunity.

"I think Hal-zay will let you have this man cheap," Pedro's son told me. "We are all tired of watching him all the time. And feeding him, too. Also, he makes his dirt right where we chain him at night. An animal. Make Hal-zay an offer. Anything at all."

"But I don't want him!"

"Take him. Hal-zay will be reasonable. Cowboys and soldiers both have been pressing us. This man killed a white woman, too. It was over near old Camp Rucker."

"Damn it, brother!" I exploded. "He is an Apache. I require a Mexican."

Chikisin palmed his hands. "Did I say he was an Apache? He is not. He only had the Apache wife that he slit the throat of, who was the sister of Hal-zay. He himself is a Mexican, raised by the Nednhi, Juh's people. *Hi!*" he called over to Hal-zay. "Bring out the Mexican. There is a buyer here."

I had not a *peso* on me, but Hal-zay proved insistent. When, casting desperately for some trade item, I remembered the turquoise earring old Tagidado Morales had given me at Fort Whipple, and I mentioned it as a "fine piece, possibly Aztec, even Tehuantec." The muscular brave grunted, "*Enjuh*, let me see it, I'll take it."

I dug the bauble out of my doeskin personals bag
and held it out for inspection. The fire made it glow like
blue ice in my hand. Merijilda, seeing it there, gasped
aloud. "God's name, look at this—!" He ripped open his
shirt. Gleaming against the dark chest, worn as a pendant
on gold chain, was the other earring. I had found the lost
son of old Tagidado Morales.

When I had told the story, Merijilda was unstrung
with emotion, but he gathered himself to placate Hal-zay
with a favorite palomino horse in trade for the earring,
plus three boxes of .44-40 Winchester shells I had in my
saddlebags, for which I got the prisoner and a safe conduct
out of the Santa Ritas.

It was also arranged that Merijilda would go to Pantano
and say to Pajarita at the house of her cousin that the
tall boy had to help Sheriff Shores take the Mexican horse
thief to Denver, but that she might go with Merijilda to
Mexico, where I would find them when my work up north
was done.

Before dawn, I and Merijilda rode out, north. Chikisin,
with Hal-zay and his *broncos*, headed south. The last I saw
of Merijilda "Morales," he was wearing his two earrings of
Tehuantec turquoise, waving to me from Pantano Wash outside the town as I cut away through the chaparral for
Tucson with my "prisoner."

I don't know if Merijilda ever found Pajarita, or if she
went with him. I only know that old Tag's earrings were
strong stuff, just as he said. Maybe they didn't save my
life; then again, maybe they did. *Something* guarded me
all the ten years that I rode among the wild *broncos*.

One thing I do know; they surely saved a son for old
Tagidado, and found a father for Merijilda.

Oh, yes, one other thing I lay to the power of old Tag's
turquoise earrings. The Mex prisoner worked out just fine.
He talked only Apache. Couldn't speak a damn word of
English and only enough Spanish to deny he understood
anything said to him, or of him. Including the fact that his
name was Merijilda Grijole, and he was a dirty murdering
Mexican horse thief wanted by the legal law in Colorado.

I can't recall if they hung him, or not.

I rather doubt it. Those days were passing. I did give

Nino Pinto five American dollars, and some chaw tobacco that was getting too old for me, to identify my boughten prisoner as the man that was wanted in Colorado. But I don't figure that was perjurous.

I gave the son of a bitch more than Hal-zay's Apaches would have given him; I gave him a chance.

Having attested to which fact, I will tack on one last p.s. to this Pinkerton detour affair with Sheriff Shores. It is put in here to prove one thing. That is how banefully little true history tells of a man's real life as he himself knowed it and fought it out.

I must have seen half a dozen print accounts and had another six sent me, clipped out of the *Pantano Wash Scout*, and they all give it like this, total:

> Sheriff W. C. "Doc" Shores, of Gunnison County,
> Colorado, met Horn in Arizona and asked him to
> help catch a well-known Mexican horse thief,
> which Horn did. . . .

Well, maybe that's fair enough.

Somehow, I don't reckon that old Greek fellow Diogenes, that Doc Shores was telling me about, would agree.

Yellow Journals

Sometimes a man has to laugh, even though they're after his life.

That's talking about newspapermen and the double-hung tongues they got. How they can lie the way they do and get it printed for the gospel passes the limits of a simple cowboy's mind. They will shrink a thing up to nothing when it's the truth, blow it up like a dead steer's belly when they've invented their own private history for the front page; the bastards.

But sometimes they do a decent job.

One reporter's account I recall—it sure wasn't from th[e] *New York Herald,* you can bet—crammed the next ten yea[rs] of my life into two, three columns for his paper's Sunda[y] edition and managed to get it close enough to the bor[e] that I will enter it here. It will close up the straggle [of] those mean years, 1890 to 1900, that brought Tom Horn [to] look across his last river.

Somehow, the name of the paper never came to m[e] nor of the reporter. But it was an eastern paper. That [I] remember. For they was all against me from the outset.

Except this here one fellow.

And even he had to start out with what they call [a] "lead caption" to sell newspapers for his "sheet."

BORN TO HANG, it said in the big print, with unde[r]neath it, in littler letters, but still bold enough to bite yo[ur] eye in bad light, *Tom Horn's Decade of Death.* With whic[h] it set sail square out through the sage, as given here copie[d] in my own hand and signatured:

> In his Arizona days, as a cavalry scout for Crook and Miles, Apache mothers used to frighten their children by telling them Tom Horn would get them if they didn't obey and be good. By the time this "Man of the Dark Shadow" got to Wyoming, white mothers up there did not need to use his name to get the kids to come in and eat their suppers. They were already "in," being afraid to put their noses out sod-house doors to begin with, when it was known the ominous horseman was in the area.
>
> Leaving Arizona—many accounts claim at the request of the government—in the late summer of 1890, Horn went to Denver where James McParlan, famed "Molly Maguire" suppressor for the Pinkerton National Detective Agency, put him in hire as a "range detective." In this capacity, Horn worked all cases, train robberies, bank jobs, horse and cattle thieving, every capital and petty crime in the western "bad brand" book. But it is safe and indeed accurate to say that 90 percent of Horn's "detective" work for the Pinkertons was

"detecting" cattle rustlers for wealthy rancher clients of the renowned man-hunting agency.

In its Colorado and Wyoming connotations, "detecting" a rustler meant anything from the routine and proper arrest (with subsequent fair bringing to trial) to the kangaroo-courting on the spot of the unfortunate poor devil apprehended "eating the boss's beef."

At this dangerous work Horn became so proficient in the skills learned from Hash Knife and Chiricahua Cattle Company days in Arizona that the demand for his services began to exceed Pinkerton's capacity to pay him. After four years, during which Horn is said to have made the murderous Charley Siringo's work for Pinkerton to have "appeared benign," the big agency was forced to "lease out" its best-known bloodhound to the highest bidder, the vast Swan Land & Cattle Company, of Wyoming.

In the following two years, alone, 1894 to 1896, Horn is alleged to have "cleaned out of rustlers the whole south of Wyoming."

It was during this "campaign" that he met his to-be great friend, John C. Coble, an easterner of means turned western cattle rancher (personal friend of Teddy Roosevelt), and a man whose "spread" lay in the middle of the Iron Mountain country, "a fifty mile square area containing more rustlers per square mile than any other part of Wyoming."

Horn's original employer in this bloody business was John Clay, not John Coble, however. Clay, a Scotsman, holds vast feudal lands along the drainage of the Chugwater River. One of these holdings, alone, the Swan L.&C. Company, is capitalized at over $4,000,000, the main stockholders being in Scotland. Clay was president of the all-powerful Wyoming Stock Growers Association at the time he hired the killer Horn. He is rumored a heavy holder in the Chicago Union Stockyards, as well as the Wyoming properties. A worthy king to armor such a deadly knight, it would appear.

Over the subsequent two years, 1896 to 1898, small cattlemen (the "enemy" to Horn and his baronial bosses) interviewed by this reporter in the field accused the "Association nightrider" of no less than eleven (11) "coldblood executions" among their helpless number. Of these, two are documented cases of record, the celebrated Powell and Lewis slayings. But the prologue to these famous "detections," as Horn still calls them, was of more note than the murders themselves; it is the first appearance of, or rather immediate cause of, Horn's dark statement to the irate Wyoming Stock Growers board meeting that he had "a system that never fails," with regard to rustlers.

Horn had just spent 13 weeks gathering evidence of cattle stealing against the so-called Langhoff Gang, in reality a "nest" of small owners, called squatters. "They 'squat' to eat our cows," as Tom Horn defined it in testimony. The evidence he brought into court, in Cheyenne, would have "hung the governor's mother," according to the disgusted members of the Stock Growers Association, Horn's employers. But the jury, itself composed of small owners, "winked at the proof and turned the guilty rascals loose."

Actually, one man was sentenced properly, one lightly, two fined an amount that evoked titters from the spectators. The remaining rustlers, all arrested single-handedly by Tom Horn, got off "free as tickbirds flitting off a clean-picked heifer's backside."

Leaving that trial, Horn is quoted in the Cheyenne paper as saying, "That's the last of the sons of b——s that I will bring in. You couldn't get a conviction here if you cut the critter's belly open in court and found the rustler inside your cow, eating his way out."

It is scarcely doubted the quote is accurate. Horn is a man who expresses himself freely and often, a habit which has cost him dearly of both friends and liberty in this tragic situation.

1898 brought "Teddy's War," in Cuba, and of course Tom Horn must go and serve his country, being as Rough a Rider as any in that famed brigade. But Horn, by his own admission, never rose above "head mule packer" nor got any closer to San Juan Hill than the beach at Daiquiri. There he was, in his words, "took down with the yeller fever, and shipped back sick to die in New York City." He outlived the latter fate and "took the cars for Chicagy and home," home being the Iron Mountain ranch of John C. Coble, where he had a long recuperation.

Ah! the readers say. But you forgot to account for the "celebrated Powell and Lewis slayings," before the war. What made them so celebrated? Well, only one thing: they marked the turning in Tom Horn's detecting policy; they were the first two "tried alongside the evidence." That is, shot and killed as they bent over somebody else's beef. No more courtroom losses for Tom Horn's employers. His reputed comment, en toto, of the assassinated pair's preparation to meet their Maker, was, "They was the worst scairt —— — ——— you ever see."

Following his recovery from yellow fever, Horn resumed his range cleaning work, operating out of Coble's Iron Mountain Ranch.

"I was by then," Horn says, "thirty-eight years old, and still some shaky in health from the yeller fever.

Evidently the realizations of middle age, plus the conditions of first doubt of his cast-iron constitution, reduced his pace afield. For in the period 1898 to 1900 not a solitary notable "detection" is credited against the "system that never fails."

When your correspondent interviewed Tom Horn for the last time in the spring of 1900, he was nearing forty years of age. He was balding and quiet, soft to speak, and had the look of a man more hunted than hunter. He told me that he had worked mostly for Mr. Ora Haley, millionaire owner of the famed Two Bar ranch, since 1898, although staying much with Haley's neighbor, John Coble. He said he believed his work was about finished in Wyoming, and he was planning to go down to Arizona the coming winter, to "live again with the onliest true friends I ever had," by which he meant the Apache Indians. He was "getting too agey" for stock detective work, he said, and had moreover been bothered a great deal by something he called his "sombra." This was a man's inner spirit, he explained, taken from the Mexican word for "shadow." His *sombra* was what guarded a man from harm, he said. When it "took to twinging him" and he didn't saddle up and move on, he was running "crost prairie full of dogholes, in front of a dark-night stompede." A man ignored his shadow-spirit, I took it, at the express peril of his mortal connection.

When we shook hands, I noted the famous outlaw's appearance, understanding that his was a story that would carry into legend.

Horn was tall, over six feet, slender and of dark complexion, good forehead, kindly expression, smiling sadly or brightly, by mood, but withal of a sanguine, hopeful nature and absolute steady nerves. His long legs were set upon a short, muscular upper body, notably wide of shoulder and flat in the hips. The legs were visibly bowed from a lifetime in the saddle. He walked with an Indian grace, unlike most cowboys—of which, by the way, he was a rodeo champion roper and bronco rider—and when mounted had a spellbinding, unforgettable "look."

As we said our good-byes, the pressure of his grip upon my hand tightened.

The dark eyes, and eagle's intensity in them, searched into my face, into, it seemed to me, my very mind; it was unsettling, even unnerving, and suddenly I understood something that the sad smile and soft laugh had masked from me.

These were the last eyes looked into by dead men whose true number will never be known. Far back in those eyes, deep beyond the crinkly

brown and friendly face, lived another creature
than this celebrated cowboy and honored Indian
scout.

It was the *other* Tom Horn.

The one who would kill you for $600, as he
had—they say—those others without number who
had "squatted to eat the boss's beef."

It is not clear at this printing where Horn is.
He told me had had "one more job" and then was
going home to Arizona. But one wonders if any
man may "go home" after dealing *a decade of
death* to his fellowmen. It would seem that the
only home Tom Horn will truly find is at the end
of a hempen rope. May God rest his search.

Well, there it is; the fairest to me of any of the big
newspaper "yellow journal" stories on Tom Horn. Yet think
what it says! Mothers telling hobgoblin and fantod lies to
their poor kids that "Tom Horn will get you if you don't
look out!" Small ranchers "interviewed in the field" giving
reporters herd tallies on my murders like they was counting
ducks shot over decoys. It was outright bald-ass bull
hockey, all of it.

Didn't those "mothers" ever stop to think what I was
going to do with their kids when I "got" them? Skin them
and eat them? Sell them to the Apaches? Start my own
orphanage? And how come those tally keepers on all them
corpses I strewn over the whole of south Wyoming stopped
at only eleven? Why not thirteen, or thirty-three? Hell,
eleven don't even make a jury. Except if you're judging
Tom Horn, I guess.

All right; it's over and did with.

But lies sell newspapers.

Facts don't.

In all of the time that I was accused of being a hired
killer, no single capital crime was ever proved on me. Not
either by legal-swore witness, nor any other reasonable nor
lawful rule of evidence.

That's the facts of it.

Jim Hicks

The people hated Ora Ben Haley.

When a man said "the people" that lulling summer of 1900, he meant the nesters and squatters that plagued the working ranches. If you were worth over thirty-dollars cash, or held title to so much as a quarter section of thin grass, you weren't considered people. Neither were you if you hired on for wages or paid your proper taxes.

You were only people in Sweetwater, Carbon, Albany, or Laramie counties if you were one of three things: busted-gut broke; on the dodge; or working for state or county.

If, like such a mort of the nobler citizens, you were all three, then you were blue-ribbon stock, qualified to set on the juries that tried your friends, the cow thiefs.

Contrariwise, if you ran enough cow stuff to hire riders, you were a rich son of a bitch. And if you were Ora Ben Haley, you were the *richest* son of a bitch. It followed that you was the meanest and most hateful.

But even the people testified honest once in a while.

"We thanked God for our bread," they said, "and Ora Haley for our meat."

Which is where I will leave it.

I didn't see Mr. Haley, but his ranch manager for the main Two Bar, Hi Bernard. "Tom," Hi said to me, "we are taking a terrible loss over in the Hole. Mr. Haley wants somebody to go over there."

The Hole was Brown's Hole, Colorado, properly called Brown's Park. It was where the Big Vermillion Creek and Green River came together to empty out of Lodore Canyon down to the big Colorado. It was rustler heaven, and you could not pay a legal lawman to go down there. Ora Haley's Two Bar boss was naming a stiff order. I hesitated.

"You know anybody?" Hi Bernard said.

I quit looking at my boots and said, "How about Jim Hicks?"

Bernard nodded, quick. "He will do just fine," he said. "When can he leave?"

I give him a grin. "About now," I said and got up from the office chair and went out the screen door and to my horse, Old Pacer, hitch-tied outside.

Me and Pacer was in the Hole six weeks before I had broke anything. But it takes time. You have to work yourself into a country.

I hired on as a drift range rider with Old Man Spicer, a pioneer in the Hole. For the first five weeks I rode sixteen hours a day. I slept dirty, lost weight, ate muddy water, never shut both eyes all the way. But at the end of it I had met with and been accepted by the citizens (cow thiefs) of the basin as just another wolf of the same pack as their own. They let me be to do my work and, with July pushing in, I had learned who was running the rustler show in Brown's Park, Colorado.

I'll not name the party, for her folks can't help that she is coyote-wild. Yes—she; for the first time in my range-detecting work I was up against a woman cow thief! The idea of it sweated me bad. Could it be that the system that never failed was about to fail? Damn. There must surely be another way to cut down this lady rustler than leaving her with a stone under her head the way they said Tom Horn marked his "victims." In fact, there *had* to be another way. Where to look for it was the next question for Jim Hicks.

The Saturday night dance is the place to learn about any cow country settlement. Sam Spicer told me about a big one the coming Saturday at the Lodore School. It was certain to draw from the whole of the area, Diamond Mountain, O-wi-yu-kuts Plateau, the Zenobia Basin, Cold Spring Mountain, Clay Basin, Cottonwood Draw, even Pat's

Hole down on the Yampa. The main bait was a new girl from over across the Utah line, who could be "braced easy." And she had a little sister, of like convenient virtue, that she was bringing with her. Their names was the Misses Arabella and Lucine Pratt, of Pot Creek, Utah.

Other attractions were scheduled.

The fiddler would be the renowned Nigger Isam, with Mex guitar played by Madison "Matt" Rash, the high-rolling Texas boy that was going to marry Ann Bassett, of the Brown's Hole pioneer Bassetts.

It was likewise speculated that Miss Icy Nice herself would attend. As this was the Hole's name for the lady rustler I was looking for, Jim Hicks naturally pricked up his jug-handle ears. I'd not dared push too close to her place under Zenobia Peak, but if there was a safe spot to study the outlaw lady, the Lodore School dance ought to qualify.

Saturday noon, I went up to Old Man Spicer's shack and asked to borrow the buckboard and team of pinto mustangs. I told him I wanted the buggy for my fair try at the Pratt sisters, from Pot Creek. Sam Spicer blinked at me and said, "Ain't you a little gray in the muzzle, Hicks, to be bracing young she-stuff at the school dance?"

"The muzzle, maybeso," I grudged. "But it ain't spread to the trigger yet."

"Cowflops," snorted old Sam Spicer. "I will rent you the rig. Five dollars and damages. No spurs nor square-corner conchas wore while using. Daybreak return."

"All right," I said to Old Man Spicer. "It is highway robbery, but I will pay it. Maybe I will invest it in Miss Icy Nice, instead of them Pot Crick tramps."

"Hicks," the old man said, "stay shut of her; she's Matt Rash's girl."

"The hell! He's engaged to Ann Bassett, ain't he?"

Sam Spicer looked at me. "Hicks," he said, "you ain't tall enough to touch bottom in that quicksand. Don't try."

"Well, maybe she won't show, Mr. Spicer," I laughed. "I'll be spared and you'll make money."

He shook his head. "She'll be there if Matt Rash and Nigger Isam are. They're her two shadows."

"Ahhh," I said. Then, covering it, "They'll be there, sure. They're the two-man band, ain't they?"

The old man gave me a hard Brown's Hole look.

"They are," he said. "Gimme the five dollars for the rig."

I was glad to pay him. The musicians hadn't even tuned up yet, and he had told me the names of the rustler lady's two main riders. He had given me the way to go around the unfailing system.

Jim Hicks had only to circle Matt Rash and Nigger Isam and come in on them from the rear.

You cut the hocks, the heifer dies; but *you* don't have to kill her.

The dance went good, even though the rustler lady never showed.

I bought four drinks for Matt Rash and we sung snatches of good old Texas tunes. I let him know I was leaving Old Man Spicer. Did he know anybody else in the Hole that could use a hand till maybe September? He did, he said. Him and Anne Bassett was building a house along Matt Creek, next the Bassett homeplace. So he could use somebody to look after the 700 head he was running up on Cold Spring Mountain, the while he was putting up the new place.

"Well, Matt," I said, "you have found your summer hand."

Matt Rash looked at me a little sideways. "Let's pick another tune and we will see," he said.

He struck a lick on the guitar, getting into "Red River Valley." Nigger Isam slid in on the fiddle. I grinned and dug out my old French harp, which most never knew I owned, as I played it mostly when out in the hills making the long dark rides of my trade. But I was fair good at blowing it and after I joined in Matt Rash asked if I knew any Mex songs, as he was homesick for the south Texas border.

Well, I knocked the spit out of my harp and played him two choruses of *"Pajarita Barranqueño,"* and Rash said to me, "Hellsfire, Jim, I will go up there to the Cold Spring camp with you in the morning and see you settled in, personal. You got the job and can even have some meat with your beans." He fetched me a clap on the wingblades and said, "Naturally, it ain't going to be my meat!"

We all laughed at that, and I put up the harp.

The schoolhouse was filling up, by then, with the folks hollering for the music to start. I floated out on the floor to find out if the famous Jim Hicks charm was still shaking up the ladies after all the years. It first appeared it was. I had the dumb little sister of the two free-teasers from Pot Creek all het up and sent out to wait for me in the Spicer buckboard in way short of an hour, but I had already conquered about a straight quart, and some scoundrel handed me another bottle as I was following her out. I don't rightly recall ever getting to the rig.

Evidently I did, though.

For I was still in it come five o'clock next morning when Nigger Isam woke me up and said we were home but had better leave again right quick.

I looked around half sick and seen we was at Spicer's, parked in front of the harness shed. The pintos looked terrible used up, and one of them was shy a hind shoe and the other going limpy in the off foreleg and, well, hell, the nigger was right.

I got Pacer and my saddle and we led the pintos into the shed. Just as we got shut of them, we heard Old Man Spicer strangling on his wake-up cough-and-wheeze and spotted the first blue smoke puffing out the tin-can stovepipe over the kitchen lean-to.

"I am purely beholden to you, Mr. Nigger Isam," I said to the waiting black rider. "Let us be long gone from here."

Isam only laughed in his soft, happy way, and said, "yes suh," and guided us down out of Spicer's Draw.

He was all right, that Isam nigger. Him and Matt Rash was both good Texas boys. It made a man feel fair downmouthed to think on what might need to happen to them up on Cold Spring Mountain.

I cheered somewhat as we climbed steadily up to Rash's high range through a pretty jack pine and red cedar country. Before long, the sun had burned through the early cold mists. It felt good on your back. Yes, I told myself. Jim Hicks will think of something else; there has got to be another way this time.

Fortunate for me, and my chances of finding that other way, I was left alone up on Cold Spring. Isam had to go back down below to help Matt. "Be up nex' Sattiday, Mr.

Matt and me," the nigger said. "Likely in time for noon dinner."

This being Sunday, it gave me five days. It would be enough, providing my luck held and I wasn't seen leaving Cold Spring Mountain, or caught away from it by Rash or Sam. My plan was simple and I had worked it many times. The first part took just plain hard riding.

Five settlers (rustlers) that last week in June found warnings left at their places in Brown's Hole. It was a fifty-mile spread to cover them, and Old Pacer damned near gave out on me coming up the Cold Spring slide late that Friday afternoon. But we made it and I wasn't seen.

Mel Tripplet, over on Talamantes Creek, would find a crude note nailed to the planks of his door. It contained a skull and crossed bones and was printed YOU HAVE EAT YOUR LAST TWO BAR BEEF. GET OUT. ONE WEEK. That was all.

Al Goncher, up past Crouse Creek, would see his notice stuck to the inside of his outhouse door. He could read it easy sitting down. TWO BAR BEEF IS POISON FOR YOU. YOU WILL SHIT BLOOD.

At Marco and Pete Arbolbides, up Hoy Canyon, it was a little different. The brothers would find an empty salt bag hanging from the lamp over their kitchen table. In it was two smooth stones about the size of good water-skipping rocks. Them and a print message:

ONE ROCK FOR EACH OF YOU. PUT THEM UN-DER YOUR HEADS. SAVE SOMEBODY ELSE THE TROUBLE.

It went like that for all five of the rustlers me and Pacer hit. It was a good feeling to know this as I fried my meat in the Matt Rash line-shack the early evening of July 1. Yes sir. Come tomorrow morning, Saturday, Brown's Hole was going to be whispering a name that had nothing to do with Jim Hicks. It would be Tom Horn.

That would be the name that Matt Rash and Nigger Isam would hear at the Lodore Store and bring with them up to Cold Spring Mountain to me next day.

I was trailing straight, except for two things.

It wasn't them that brought me the name up the mountain, nor was it brought the next morning.

"Don't move, you son of a bitch," the lovely voice said, *"or I will kill you."*

I set down my clasp knife and bent fork alongside the tin plate of Two Bar beefsteak I was eating, spread my hands atop the table, and looked up slow.

In the doorway stood the most leanly handsome woman ever born or bred. And in her hand was the biggest goddamned long-barrel Colt's .44-40 revolver ever bored or blued—pointed right square, and cocked, into my belly.

"I mean it, by God, *Tom Horn*," she said.

And I answered, "Yes, ma'am, by God, I can see that you do."

And I kicked the table up into the air from underneath with my knees, caught it by its turning top, and drove it across the room at her with every uncoiling force I had.

I had her figured right, thank Christ.

She got off four shots into that table in the time it was in the air coming at her. Unshielded by the flying furniture, I would have been as dead as a plucked dodo. As it was, she got a glance off the forehead from the edge of the table and was knocked silly. Bringing her around with cloths cold-wrung from the spring gave me time to think. When at last she opened those gray eyes, however, I couldn't think of nothing. I never had a woman to hit me like that one. Never. No wonder Matt Rash hated so to give it up to marry Anne Bassett.

"I'm sorry as hell, lady," I told her, "but I wasn't aiming to set still and get gut-shot for Tom Horn."

I had put her on Matt's bunk. She was still dizzy and a little sick from getting hit. But she sat up and swung her legs to the floor, giving a soft groan.

"Goddamn you," she gritted out, "I know you're him."

"You're crazy, lady. Name's Jim Hicks. Been working all summer for Sam Spicer. Ask Matt. Or Isam."

She shook her head, wincing at the hurt of it.

"They're both stupid," she said. "They believe you."

"So do I, lady." I went over to the bed. "Leave me get you another of them cold cloths. You ain't thinking straight."

"You go to hell!" she seethed at me, pulling away.

"Where's this Tom Horn talk coming from?" I asked her. "Damn if I like it, wherever. Man could get shot."

"You know where it's coming from, you bastard."

She didn't talk nor act like a lady but, God knew, she was the greatest looker of all time for me. I just could not get my eyes off her. She had glossy red hair, sheeny as beaver. Her body was trim and hard and beautiful; her face, well it was the same, so to speak. And the looks she gave!

A man just knew how she would go, could he get at her.

Of a sudden, I felt all cold toward Matt Rash.

The son of a bitch. He had played and daddled with his queen of all women. Rolled her around and pawed her no different than I'd done Lucine Pratt and such trash. Goddamn him. Down there in the brakes sweet-talking the Bassett girl, whoring all the while over to Zenobia Basin with this cat-bodied redhead. And what about me? Getting my ass shot at, that's what. And for what? Trying to get an honest job done on this bunch of goddamn cow thieves in Brown's Hole and still not have to headstone any of them. Well, damn that. There was real danger in this woman saying I was Tom Horn. That had to stop. Right now.

"Lady," I said, "your head cleared yet? Me and you have got to talk. If I *am* Tom Horn, then I'm going to have to kill you, ain't I? If I'm Jim Hicks, and you keep running around calling me Tom Horn, you're going to get *me* killed. Now what's it's going to be, your way or my way?"

She had quit wincing and plainly felt better.

A light got into the pale gray eyes.

"I will make a dicker with you," she said. "Call yourself anything you want, but get out of the Hole and don't come back into it. *Somebody's* been giving people a week to leave their land hereabouts, and I will give you the same." She took a breath, and I noted the rise of the high breasts under the riding jacket. "Matt is going to the rodeo up to Rock Springs for the Fourth of July," she said. "Be gone when he get's back."

"That's it?" I said.

"Flat-out final," she said. "No little notes pinned up in the crapper. No little rocks hung up in salt bags over the kitchen table. Move out, or else."

"And meanwhile?"

"Meanwhile, I won't call you Horn."

I eased back from the table.

"Well, lady," I said, "you're wrong as a five-legged jacksnipe, but right as rain in August. I want to say you are the most beautiful woman God ever fashioned and Matt Rash is plain crazy. Was I him, I would throw you crost my horse's withers, jump the Lodore Canyon, and thunder of inter Utah with you, forever and ever after."

Her eyes flashed a glimmer like heat lightning far of in a summer storm. "That was purely fine of you, Jim Hicks," she murmured. "If you were Matt Rash, I might get on my own horse and jump the canyon with you."

There was something wistful in the words. It was like maybe, met some other way, we could have changed it all But we both knew who we were.

I got up from the table, and so did she.

"*I* thank *you*, ma'am," I said. "Hicks or Horn, I will see that *he* gets out. It'll be tomorrow. No need to count any days. Maybe I'll go up to that rodeo in Rock Springs myself Once upon a time I could tie off a calf with any of them.'

"Do you expect Matt tomorrow?"

"Yes, him and the nigger. I will wait until they ge here. The stock is all fine."

"Thank you. Good-bye, Mr. Hicks."

"Good-bye, ma'am."

She started out the door, then held up just within it She was a woman and had been reached. She gave me look I will never forget and said in that low voice, "I've no been Matt Rash's, nor any man's, if it matters." And she went on out into the night to her horse and was gone.

Saturday, Rash and Isam showed up early. They had news of the "Tom Horn" notes, and "salt-bag killer stones." had to move one foot ahead of the other, not knowing i they had talked with Queen Zenobia. I waited till Rash had spoke his views, then said, "Well, I am glad you don't spook at notes, for you've got one of your own. Had to be placed some time last night, after your girl left."

"What the hell you saying? What girl?"

"The one from Zenobia Basin."

"Oh, sure; what of the note, Jim?"

I got it out of my pocket in a crumpled ball and

handed it over. "Looks the same as you describe the others, don't it?" I said.

He spread it out: M. RASH. STAY *IN* ROCK SPRINGS. OR YOU WILL STAY *ON* COLD SPRING. PERMANENT. THE NIGGER SIMILAR. XXXX.

"What you reckon them x's is for?" the Texan said.

"Kisses, maybe," I answered. "I didn't get none on mine." I dug out the second note, tossed it to him. He gave it a quick scowl: P.S. JIM HICKS WON'T KICKS IF HE STICKS.

"What's that supposed to mean?" Matt Rash asked, returning the note to me. "You won't kicks? You won't complain, or what?" He was getting very edgy.

"Either way," I said, "you ever see a dead man that could kick *or* complain?"

"Oh," he said. "Yeah."

It went uneasy the rest of the morning, the three of us working his cow-and-calf herd up till noon dinner.

At that time, Isam announced that he had imperative reasons to "go down the hill." We both watched him go over, get his sorrel gelding out of the pole corral, and depart. "I mentioned to Isam earlier," I said to Rash, "that I would pay him three prices for that sorrel. He laughed and said nothing could buy the horse. You suppose that's so?"

"Don't know," Matt Rash said. "But it's some horse. I mean to get him for a lady I know."

I didn't ask him which lady, figuring I knew.

Pretty quick, the nigger gone, Rash said, "I hear there's another stomp at the schoolhouse tonight. Want to go down and give her a lick?"

I laughed quick, to cover my hunch feeling, and answered him, "sure, let's ramble."

Matt Rash said, "All right," but he wasn't laughing about it. Something had spooked him. There wasn't any more talk. We just got our horses and pointed them down the hill, and let them go.

It was strange the way it went then.

Matt Rash and me were coming down the last draw off the mountain when our horses went to pitching on us. We got them quieted, but they wouldn't go ahead. I made a sign to Matt and we got down and tied them and went in, walking careful where we put our feet.

But not careful enough.

"Hold it right thar," ordered a voice we both knew. "You cain't come on down here. Ride around."

"Isam," drawled Matt Rash. "You black bastard. Get the hell out of my trail."

The tall Negro rustler levered his Winchester.

"Cain't leave you to pass this way, Mr. Matt," he said. "Please, suh, ride on around."

Before Rash could answer, the wind switched in the draw and came at us from behind Isam Dart. Old Pacer humped his back again and made a noise down in his chest that I knew meant one thing. Bloodsmell. The nigger had killed something, or somebody, and we had rode up on him doing it.

"Will he shoot?" I muttered to young Rash, never looking away from the black man and his rifle.

"Well," Rash said, "let's find out."

I am fair with a handgun myself. Not many could get their piece out ahead of mine. I never saw the Texas boy make his move. I just heard the crack of the Colt .45 long that he carried and saw the buttstock of Isam's Winchester go to kindling splinters between his hands. "Now, you black son of a bitch," said Madison Rash, "stand out of the trail." And he went forward, me following him.

There in the brush, just off the draw, lay the big carcass of a roan shorthorn.

"Christ Jesus," Matt Rash said, "you've killed old Sam's prize herd bull. God Amighty, why for?"

The nigger didn't really know. It had just come to him to do it. There'd been trouble twixt him and Old Man Spicer over lies told by Spicer against Isam. The bull had just seemed the meanest way to get back at the old devil. Rash couldn't believe it.

He raked that poor nigger up one flank and down the other for being so stupid. Isam flared back at him and, in the next three, four minutes the two of them washed more dirty rustler underdrawers in front of Jim Hicks than his six weeks of dangerous riding had shown him on the entire Brown's Hole clothesline.

These two were the pair that sided the queen of

he rustler war against the Two Bar, no question. What had
een only hearsay evidence against them now was what the
ourts call *prima facie,* or cast-iron clad. No way out. Not
or them. Nor for their friend Jim Hicks.

The close of their argument came when Matt Rash
lemanded that the nigger pay over to him his beautiful
and-raised sorrel horse, for Rash keeping his mouth shut
bout the bull. Isam Dart at once turned ugly. "Mr. Matt,"
e said, "if you wants to start telling things you know on
ne, ain't the half of whats I could tell on you. You ain't
ever getting that sorrel horse away from me if I has to die
or him."

They left it there. Matt Rash and me rode on. Isam
vent his own trail. At the dance that night, I spread the
tory of the angry meeting. Before the substitute fiddler
vore out and went home, half the people in Brown's Hole
new that Matt Rash and Nigger Isam had "fought" and that
he nigger threatened to die before he would give in. The
un-in between the two gave Jim Hicks what he needed
o draw suspicion away from himself for distributing the
iotes warning the rustlers to quit the Hole. Now, should
omething befall Matt Rash, *neither* Jim Hicks *nor* Tom
Iorn would be given the blame for it.

Isam Dart would be.

Grim and printed proof of this was swift to come. It
howed first in the *Routt County Sentinel.* The date is tore
n my clipping, but I make it out to be July 11, 1900:

> Mr. Rash had nearly finished eating when a
> man materialized in the doorway to his Cold
> Spring cabin. The Brown's Park ranchman did not
> even have time to stand up before three shots
> came in succession. After a few moments of
> silence disturbed only by the hum of summer in-
> sects, a fourth shot sounded outside; the killer who
> had fired on Mr. Rash had taken time to shoot a
> fine sorrel horse tied to the doorpost of the corral
> gate. It was just after noon, Monday, July 8.

Thus reason the two witnesses who found the
flyblown corpse, as taken in their testimony to
Routt County authorities.

Two days after the murder the witnesses,

"Uncle" George Rife and Felix Meyers, a fourteen-year-old boy, chanced to ride past the Rash cabin. Rife waited while the Meyers boy went to say hello to the dashing Texan, who was the cowboy idol to all the boys in the Hole.

Mr. Rife says that he next heard a terrible scream from Felix and went to the cabin himself.

He describes Matt Rash as lying on his bunk but not answering to any hail. The stench in the foul-aired cabin was awful. Rash's body was badly decomposed from the July heat.

George Rife testified that the victim had taken off his boots after being shot—strange behavior in a mortally wounded person—gotten somehow over to his bed, and fallen thereon. He had gotten an envelope from somewhere and tried to dip a fingernail in his own blood and write on it the name of his destroyer. He died in the effort.

Charley Sparks, Routt County's fine deputy sheriff, who led the investigators, reports the stink so overpowering that to get the body out it was necessary to soak clothes in carbolic and tie them loosely over the nostrils. The burial, Deputy Sparks says, was sickening.

Every effort will be made, Sparks assured, to track down the killer, who fired a .30-30 rifle and walked up to the cabin without his boots on. However, Sparks warns, the matter will prove difficult. No other trail, either of ridden horse or man on foot, was found.

"It was in every way a professional job," says Charley Sparks. "Witnesses confide it was likely Isam Dart, but no charge has been brought, nor arrest planned."

Mr. Rash will be reburied in Hood County, Texas, his home. His father and a brother are coming on the cars to claim the body.

The natural thing to come of such finger-pointing at a well-known local figure sure enough did come. In this regard, some will say the paper never printed Isam's name. Or that Deputy Sparks didn't give it and was misquoted.

Sparks was a damn fine man. I wouldn't say against him in any such matter. But the difference would never have saved Isam Dart. If Sparks or the paper didn't name him, everybody else in Routt County did.

Including the *Craig Empire-Courier,* October 5, 1900:

There was company at the lonely Summit Spring ranch of the I-D Bar. Owner Isam Dart, the well-known Brown's Park pioneer, had with him for a hearty bunkhouse breakfast the following visitors; George Bassett, Sam Bassett, J. Dempshire, Alec Seger, and the popular Griff Yarnell.

Unknowing of any danger, the six men sauntered from the Dart ranch house, going to the corral to get their horses. They went spread out and in a single file. George Bassett was in the lead. Isam Dart came second. He was laughing at some joke the younger Bassett had told him when the first bullet struck him in the face.

In this way the *Courier* learned from Griff Yarnell, one of the witnesses, of the ambush execution of the notorious Negro "character" Isom Dart. Dart, known in Brown's Hole as Nigger Isam, spelled with an "a," was an ex-slave, from Arkansas, freed by his owner during the late war.

Dart was shot two times by a man posted behind a large ponderosa pine less than one hundred feet from the ranch house door and but seventy-five from the corral. It was in broad daylight, but such was the fear of the others that no one of them saw the assassin fire or flee.

Indeed, as Mr. Yarnell is big enough to admit:

"We was all so panicky we collided at the cabin door trying to stompede back into the house. Young Bassett was so inspired he did two full laps about the place before he found the door. I think the lad might be sprinting yet but that Alec Seger stuck out an arm and snared him going by the third time."

The men stayed in the house all the day, sawed their way out through the back of it by dark that night, and came away.

Deputy Sparks being out of the county, the Brown's Hole people made up their own posse to go up to the Dart place. Josephine Bassett, of the prominent settler family, is said to have led the investigators up the mountain. Now Mrs. Josie Mc-Knight, the Bassett woman said she believed the killing was the work of the same man who murdered Madison Rash. This man, both she and her sister, the noted "Queen Anne" Bassett, have maintained from the beginning, was the Two Bar employee, Tom Horn. Hi Bernard, Two Bar spokesman and resident manager for owner Ora Haley, labels such "wild charges" as ridiculous and unsettled.

Dart was shot twice, the second time while still falling with the fatal head wound of the first bullet. He was dead instantly. The date was October 3, two days past. Two .30-30 shell casings were found at the base of the pine tree. There was no trail going away, and no other clue was found. The Bassett sisters have insisted that Tom Horn is known to have the only .30-30 rifle in that part of the country. Tom Horn could not be contacted for his view of the matter.

Dart was buried on the place.

His coffin was a blanket. The sermon was said by Anne Bassett, who prayed for the hand of God to strike the guilty.

Well, all right, and bless the *Courier*.

People will believe what they read in a newspaper. I make no comment against that, except that I will say my facts and theirs are viewed from far apart.

Like so:

On the eighth of July, when I was supposed to have killed Matt Rash, he got a letter with that date on it from Jim Hicks, mailed in Denver over three hundred miles away. Might not the friends of Tom Horn take that to mean a man still can't be in two places at the same time? Maybe someday my enemies will explain it better for me.

Coming to October 3, where all them "witnesses" saw not a damned thing come out from the back of that ponderosa pine but two .30-30 blasts that they say blowed away the top of Nigger Isam's black head, it was the same thing of me saying I was somewheres otherwise. Put exactly, I was the very next day—and early—in line over to the county seat, at Hahn's Peak, Colorado, swearing to an affidavit for a complaint charging the same Isam Dart with altering brands on Jim McKnight livestock. That was of course October 4, not third. A day's difference they will yell. You had time to slip into the Hole, shoot the nigger beforehand, and still be first in line next morning over to the county clerk's office. Well, maybe. But I would like to see any of those fat-seat newspaper reporters make it by horse back from Summit Spring Mountain in Brown's Hole, to the clerk's office, in Hahn's Peak, from morning to morning of October 3 to October 4. Yes, and turn the ride without leastways a dozen witnesses seeing them along the way.

The hell, mister.

If I done it, there's not even a top-riding cowboy alive to tell you how, nor to equal the trip on his own horse stock.

Meanwhile, that document of affidavit is yet on file in Routt County, Colorado, and it is signed with a "Tom Horn" never questioned but being mine.

Yet, demanding "prove it" of those that accuse me of killing Isam Dart is not the same as claiming any false sorrows over Isam's sudden judgment day; I am grateful to whoever done the nigger in.

Like the *Steamboat Springs Pilot* put it:

> Immediately following the murder of Isom Dart, several Brown's Holers discovered they had urgent affairs elsewhere. Young Sam Bassett put a great deal of distance between himself and Mr. Hicks— he went to Alaska!
>
> He hasn't returned to northwestern Colorado, even for a visit.
>
> Joe Davenport, who helped track down Harry Tracy, also took his departure on a "Horn's Holiday," concerning which Joe says, "It got too tough in those parts with Tom there. Many of us left. I went to Missouri for the winter."

Old Joe had it right.

And the *Steamboat Pilot*, likewise.

But there was another clipping I saved from the papers that hit it even closer:

> Mr. A. G. Wallihan of Lay, Colorado, reports as follows regarding his (Jim Hicks) subsequent movements (fleeing Brown's Hole):
>
> "Horn stopped here at my roadhouse on his way to Juniper Springs. He had got cut pretty bad in a fight (with Newt Kelly) in the Bull Dog Store Saloon, Baggs, Wyoming, and he thought the springs might help him.
>
> "He wasn't a bad appearing fellow to me. Whenever he looked at you, he always looked down, though. If you spoke to him, he would look at you a moment, then his eyes would fall again.
>
> "I didn't like him.
>
> "My wife had lived all her life on the frontier, and she was not afraid of God, man, or devil, but she was scared to death of Jim Hicks."

Well, that was the business of a stock association range detective. Fear. That is what he sold. Delinquent accounts were treated accordingly. They was all warned once, then went after. We never had a bad debt, Jim Hicks or me.

Which was why, I reckon, the Rock Springs paper printed this finish to it:

> Following a period of recuperation at Juniper Springs on the Middle Yampa, Tom Horn rode out of Colorado never to return. Horn, alias Hicks, knew whereof he spoke. His system never failed, and it surely will put an end to the old large-scale rustling of cattle in northwestern Colorado for all time.

It also put an end to Jim Hicks.

He quit the Two Bar, and Hi Bernard, and Ora Ben Haley, and truly was never seen again.

His horse, Old Pacer, showed up the following spring

at the John Coble ranch, Iron Mountain, Wyoming. His rider was an old cowboy and cavalry scout from Yavapai County, Arizona. He wanted work, and Mr. Coble put him on. He was a fair-tall man, getting bald, with a bad knife scar shoulder to chin. He said his name was Tom Horn.

Big Pasture

That spring and summer were easy doings. The work fitted me, and the life was good.

I stayed up at the main ranch house with Mr. John C. Coble. He wanted me there and it was all right with the other hands, as my employment did not send me with them. Mr. Coble was an easterner of some substance who loved the western way and country. He had started in the range cow business with $10,000 borrowed off his mother, which he paid back with all the interest in under two years. This was some fifteen on more years back. He had owned spreads at Plum Tree, Nebraska, and Powder River, Wyoming. The winter of 1886–87 wiped him out, like every other big outfit in the north. He then moved down to Iron Mountain and went into horse ranching but switched back to cattle when "he got his nerve back." Lately, after doing right good, things in that business had got tight for him again.

It wasn't blizzards this time, but buzzards.

And them, we could do something about.

But John Coble held me off.

"Not yet," he kept saying. "They are bound to see the light, if we just keep after them."

So I kept on riding the "pasture line" and letting the "people" see me doing it.

It was some pasture that I covered. Look on your map of Wyoming and find a placed called Fort Laramie. It is on the Platte River, over near the Nebraska line. Now you will see that the Laramie River empties into the Platte there. Follow the Laramie up and you will see it breaks into a spider web of forks and various creeks with names like Fish Creek, Bluegrass Creek, Richeau Creek, and then two bigger forks, more like rivers, called the Sybille and the Chugwater. Ponder the space twixt Sybille and Chug, east to west and north to south. Then figure my work also took me up and down both banks of both streams, and you will have some little idea of the miles rode under by me and my main two saddle mounts, Cap and Old Pacer.

Those horses deserve some mention.

Both was gifts of Mr. Coble and his general foreman Duncan Clark, who knew my job and what it required of an animal. Cap was a black bay, big, flat-boned, rangy, like all my horses. He took his name from the brand C A P burned on the forequarter. He would go close to 1,100 pounds, all of it lungs and heart girth. He was a doing horse, and the one I rode on the darkest ride of my life.

Pacer had once been the private mount of Mr. Coble. He was a big-barreled snorty horse. Very dark bay or brown horse. Handsome appearing. Had a kind of racking shuffle of a gait up to when he would strike his run, in which no horse could hold to him. He had a very high life to him and always acted like he had got himself a little touch of the jimsonweed. You might call him kind of crazy, snorty, or flighty, but you would saddle him for risk work every time.

Him and the Cap horse, both, was the using kind.

Pacer was a TY-branded horse, out of the remuda of Duncan Clark.

The two mounts figured in what was left of my life as that summer of 1901 wore on; it is fit that they be remembered as the horses of Tom Horn.

There is one thing sure: the people of the valleys of the Chug and the Sybille remembered them. Whenever I would appear in a vicinity on either of those "dark horses," you could practically hear the slamming shut of cabin doors and window shutters. I would be met fair enough if it was day and there was no reasonable getting away from me. They would treat me decent, and many times I stayed with various ones of them for the night. But a man knows when people are afraid of him, just like an animal knows it. It's a smell, almost. With some, the ones with cause to sweat cold, it was a rank stink.

Some of them stinked to hell.

Kels Nickell was one.

He was a small cattleman who had brought in sheep and was hated for it for fifty miles around. He was a mean bastard. His wife, though, was different. Mary Nickell had a sad look to her, but I liked her, and she was a good kind. Of the two boys, Fred was all right. Slow, but his mother's blood. The other, the older one, took after Kels. Willie Nickell was the kind of kid you would want to kick the whey out of for his own good. But in his case he would need to wait his turn, as his pa was such a son of a bitch before him.

Kels Nickell went back ten years with my friend John Coble. The *Cheyenne Daily Leader* for July 24, 1890, puts it better than I might, who wasn't there. Mr. Coble had the clipping and give it to me. I put it under the band of my hat, for remembering. It said:

J. C. COBLE CUT: SLASHED WITH KNIFE BY KELS P. NICKELL: TWO QUITE SERIOUS WOUNDS ARE INFLICTED: BADLY SLASHED ...

J. C. Coble of Iron Mountain was seriously stabbed at that place yesterday by Kels P. Nickell, another ranchman, and is under treatment of Dr. Maynard at the physician's Cheyenne residence. Sheriff Martin has the assailant in jail.

Nickell and George Cross, a foreman for Mr. Coble, quarreled over the trespassing of some cattle. Nickell, without a word, dashed at Coble with the knife and made two effective slashes. The wounds are ugly cuts in the abdomen, and while they are serious, Mr. Coble will recover. Nickell was arrested by another ranchman and brought in on Sheriff Martin's instructions. ...

Maybe it was my own knife scars from the rascal Newt Kelly that was burning me when I looked at Mr. Coble's long red wounds done by Nickell ten years gone. Whatever the reason, they rankled inside me. I always hated the man with a knife.

Yet I don't say that Kels Nickell was a rustler.

I didn't find him stealing Iron Mountain, nor any other cattle. Likewise, I deny it was his sheep led to what happened. Roundabout, it was the feud. That was the fight him and his neighbor Jim Miller had going. It came out of the bad blood between the Miller boy, Victor, and the mean Nickell kid, Willie. But that was only the back scenery of it. Direct on, the cause of it was that Kimmell foreigner woman. Hadn't she come to live with the Jim Miller family, teaching at the Iron Mountain School, Tom Horn would never have rode into the trap he did—the trap that was swung wide for him when Willie Nickell opened his father's pasture gate.

But that was down the road.

And the schoolteacher wasn't; she was only down at the "railroad." She had just arrived from the east and was waiting at Iron Mountain depot, on the U.P.R.R., for some Samaritan to come and get her.

Guess who was the Christian that I-M foreman Dunc Clark handpicked to take the Coble company "spring wagon" and go fetch her out to the Miller place?

That's right; you may shine the teacher's apple.

It was Tom Horn, the famous stock detective.

Naturally.

Miss Kimmell

It was the fifteenth of July that I set out to get Miss Glendolene Kimmell at the Iron Mountain waterspout station on the U.P. line. I had got a little late due to disliking the kind of work and wanting everybody concerned to know it. Especially the schoolmarm. I had her in my head for having metal-rim specs and a flat bustle, with a walk like a mud-hen coot with the strain.

I seen her standing trackside from afar and weakened a tad. She looked so small and total alone. Which you can't be any more alone than to be left trackside in south Wyoming. But when you're likewise fresh out of the East, never west of, say, Kansas City, it can show you spooks out there. Particularly it can in a late dusk like the one I came through toward Miss Kimmell.

Well, she was that glad to see *anybody* that I feared she was going to cloud up and rain all over my good shirt.

But crying wasn't her style; style was.

I could see it on her the same as you see it on a leggy filly or good-backed heifer, as far off as they can be made out. But this was only a little ways out on the Iron Mountain road, just near enough to the depot to show my eagering eye that this "little girl" down there had a set of eating titties on her that would water the mouth of a ninety-year-old mummy and a backside that was all hers and no part bustle. I tucked in my damn shirt and whistled up Buck and Becky. I dug in my pants pocket for my Sen-Sen. I scuff-shone my boot arches on the legs of my Levi's and set up in that nifty rig straight as a Sunday-morning pecker. Of a sudden that hot sagebrush smelled like French perfumery. The sunset was no redder than my woke-up blood. I wasn't pushing forty-one years old but was young as the summer night.

I swooped those damn mustangs up to that trackside like Ben Hurt cutting his chariot short on the last corner. I stepped down out of the rig whiles it was still moving and swept off my four-gallon stetson and bent her a bow that would have broke Sir Walker Rawley's back.

Then I rared back upright and took my handclose look.

It hit me hard, and I spit out my Sen-Sen.

She was a damn slant eye.

Miss Kimmell sat beside me. There was still a lingering green twilight of the luminous sort that summer brings in the West. The red of the sun is gone, but there is yet this lovely pale gloom all about, peaceful and calm and still as

trout-pool water at the foot of the riffle. It is a time of day
to stir the soul of a rock, or soften the heart of a damned
fool.

"Ma'am," I said, "are you all right?"

We had not either of us spoke a word since introduc-
ing ourselves back by the U.P. water tank spout. I had
packed her duffle into the trunk of the rig, let her climb in
by herself, whipped up the mustangs, and built a dustboil
away from the tracks that I could still see, looking back.

Now she turned those Jap or Chinky eyes on me and
answered in a low and husky voice, "Yes, thank you, Mr.
Horn. I will never forget this night, this twilight. You cannot know what it means to me."

She talked in that manner. Like a schoolteacher. Each
word set apart from the other, careful, somewhat slow, as
if fearful she wouldn't be understood. She had some kind
of foreigner accent, too. Just a small touch of it, but it was
an odd one. Sort of made you quit thinking she wasn't
white, was maybe even part nigger. Got you to listening
to her. And more. Got you to taking a second, sidelong look
at her there on the seat next you. Then deciding you were
right, you had been a damned fool to put off on her as
you'd done back to the depot.

"Well, Miss Kimmel," I said, "maybe I do know how the
country hits you. I can tell it in your voice that you've
dreamt about coming out here. I done it myself. There
was whole nights of my life that I never closed my eyes
for thinking about being 'out west.' I didn't know nothing
whatever about it. But I was born wanting to go west. 'Out
there,' I called it." I shook up the team to cover a dip
down and up out of a cross-gully. "Folks mostly don't com-
prehend what it means—'out there.' You would know it,
though," I said. "I seen you from the top of Four Mile Mesa,
coming in. You was standing looking off south, and all
around, while there was yet sun. You was looking 'out
there,' wasn't you, Miss Kimmell?"

The little slant-eye lady gave me a look.

She put out a hand, no bigger than a child's, and
let it light like a butterfly where no lady's hand ought to
settle on a strange man's leg.

"Mr. Horn," she said, that soft I had to cock my head
to hear it, "I *was* looking out there. And do you know what

saw? I saw a man who was the one I had seen in all of my own nights of lying sleepless, thinking of the West. I old myself then that I would know this man when I saw aim. It is a little frightening, Mr. Horn. I don't know yet what to make of it."

"Of what, miss?"

"Of you," she said, and the small hand tightened, just before it fluttered away. "You *are* the man in the dream."

Well, I flushed up some, which she couldn't see due to he dark, then got a little riled. This had gone about us far as was decent. I wasn't going to try throwing a leg over the new schoolmarm her first night. Nor was I aiming o let her see I was *thinking* of it, which I sure was. She was emale female. Slant eyes or not.

"Well, ma'am," I said, slapping Buck and Becky with he lines, "don't make nothing of such oddments of the mind. You need a Apache Injun to tell you what dreams mean, and the nearest one is a week's train ride from Albany County, Wyoming. I learnt to read visions living with them Injuns, and I can tell you your case ain't unusual. You're likely one of us shadder people"

"What people, Mr. Horn?"

"Shadder people; you know, what follers you around when there's sun to see it by."

"Oh!" She squealed it like it was something great. "You and I are shadow people! How quaint."

"Maybe," I said. "I got to know you better before I'm sure you're shadder people. But you got the feel."

She slid that hand back onto my leg.

"And so do you have the feel, Mr. Horn," she murmured. "I just know we will get better acquainted." She stopped and leaned over toward me, anxious. "We will, won't we?" she said. "I mean, get to be friends?"

I shook up the team again.

"We will, and right fast," I gritted out twixt fixed teeth, "happen you keep putting your hand there."

She give a fluttery gasp and lifted her hand like she had fried it on a stovelid.

"Mr. Horn! Such talk. I would never think to—"

"Yes ma'am, I know you would never," I said. "That's how come I said it. You just hang on now, Miss Kimmell. I am going to make up some time along this here level

stretch." I give Buck a shot with the popper of the buggy
whip and cracked Becky in the butt with a loop of her
line. "Hee-yahh!" I yelled. "Hi-yup, hi-yup!"

And there wasn't anymore said until we had got
around to the good-nights and thank-you-so-muches in the
ranchyard of the Miller place.

Then I said the wrong thing, forever sure.

Gun Talk

I will never know why I said yes to Dora Miller when
I was already getting back in the spring wagon to leave.
Lord knew I was well shut of the slanty-eyed schoolmarm
and she of Tom Horn and the ideas she'd fired up in him.

But Mrs. Miller urged me to stay the night, saying her
boys Vic and Gus wanted me to. They had heard of Tom
Horn, naturally. You know how kids are. They will follow
you like tramp dogs, if you carry guns and ride fast horses.
So I give in to the invitation, sort of flattered.

After a good supper, it set out to be one of the nicest
evenings ever for a man of my calling. It is not that many
fine summer nights you get to sit with a family of good folks
in their pioneer ranch house and be the center of the talk
and attention. I confess it favored me of the Millers. But it
also let Glendolene Kimmell take side-look liberties with
"my western man," as she sniggered it a little too loud, and
cozy; it was getting close in there.

I was glad enough when Gus, the younger boy, informed me I was to sleep "out in the yard" with him and
the other boy, Victor. They had a tent out there fixed for
summer bunking. I wasn't specially ready for bed, but I was
of a mind to get away from Miss Kimmell. She looked ever
better in the candleshine and coal-oil lamplight than out on
the prairie by star-view. In fact, one time Jim Miller caught

my eye and rolled both his up in his head toward the ridgepole of his shack, like as to say, "Oh, my, ain't she somewhat!" And I had to nod back and wink to answer him, yes indeedy. "I'm right glad," I told him, aside, when he come out with me and the boys to the tent, "that it's you, not me, going to have her in the next room all winter. I will bet your good wife don't close her both eyes till Miss Glendolene gets took back to Iron Mountain depot. Was I you, I would spend the summer out here with the boys."

Jim Miller give me a knock in the ribs with his elbow.

"And was I you," he chuckled, "I wouldn't waste no more summer nights sleeping with boys in tents. From them smoky looks the schoolmarm was fetching you, all you got to do is snap your fingers."

"Well," I grinned, giving my fingers a couple of pops, "I will commence practicing. But tonight I promised Gus and Vic to tell them about the Cherry Cow Injuns, and how I caught Geronimo for General Crook."

"I thought it was General Miles?" Miller says, kind of cutty. "And time afore that, General Orlando Willcox."

I didn't take him out on it. No man likes to be made small of before his kids. Especially boys.

"It was Crook," I said. "Miles come later and Willcox earlier."

"Oh, well, whichever, I won't stay for it," the ranchman said. "The boys won't limber up in front of their pa. Yonder they come with your bedding." His voice went cautious. "Listen, Horn," he said, "be easy with the gun shooting and such in your stories. We've got fresh neighbor trouble, and there's bad blood here enough already that it wouldn't be wise to fire them up any. Particularly Vic. He's scairt halfways sick now."

"What you talking about, Miller?" I said. "Kels Nickell?"

"Him and his crazy kid Willie."

"It's that serious twixt them and you Millers?"

"Horn," he answered, and the tone left no question of his fearfulnesses, "it has become the hell of my life, and I can't tell you the hurt it's brung me and Dora, already." I thought he was going to weep, he was so sudden atremble with remembering whatever it was of hell that Kels Nickell had brought the Miller family. But he steadied, and I said, "All right, Jim. I understand. Don't fret about the boys. I'll not stir them any."

Jim Miller shook my hand without another word and went inside again, and me and the boys got ready for bed.

It was fun with the boys after we was stretched out on our soogans, the juney bugs bumping the net outside and the crickets sawing their leg bones off, and way over on the Sybille a loafer wolf howling lonesome and long, and, down on Little Piney Lake, a loon hollering its wild, shivery cries.

"I would give my saddle and summer savings to be like you, Mr. Horn," Gus, the younger boy, said. "Riding at night out yonder there with all them sounds and scary things, only not scairt of them."

"Well," Victor said, "neither would we be scairt had we guns like Mr. Horn's. Specially that Winchester."

"If you'd like," I told them, "I will show you how to shoot it in the morning. We'll go down to the meadow and let her rip. I got two spare boxes of ammo that is getting old, and I will want to buy some new for it, anyway."

"Cripes!" Gus said. "You mean I can fire it myself?"

"Sure, if your pa will let you."

"Gawd Amighty," the older boy said. "Shooting Tom Horn's own Winchester. Wait'll I brag on that!"

We fell still, the three of us, and I reminded them we would do the shooting only if their father said. "He don't like guns, it seems," I finished, "so we got to work him up careful. It'll be our secret plan."

They liked that fine. Boys just naturally love guns and secrets. I had no fear they would peep.

We quit talking again. After a spell, Victor said, "Pa's all right. It's just what happened with him and his rifle that's soured him; he kilt our little brother."

"Oh," I said, "that's mighty sad. I didn't know that."

"Yup," Gus said. "Kilt him pretty bloody. It wasn't apurpose, though."

"Cripes, Mr. Horn knows that!" Victor was ired.

I reared up on an elbow. "No, Vic, I didn't know anything about it," I said. "How come Little Brother to get shot?"

Well, they told me, the two of them, one breaking in

patch up any part of the tale that the other forgot, how had gone to bring Little Brother Miller to his death.

The Miller and Nickel places butted against one another, and there'd been constant hazing of stock back and forth over the common boundary, each rancher protecting his grass from outside animals. Then Nickell had brought in ,400 head of sheep. The Miller pasture began to grow white woolballs all over it from the Nickell sheep, and the Miller cows wouldn't eat proper because of the smell of the stuff. As for Nickell, Miller's cows muddied the creek above Nickell's sheep pasture, and the damn-fool woolies wouldn't drink from the stream. It got bad, with threats going both ways.

Then, one day, Victor Miller was herding some strayed sheep off Miller grass, afoot. Willie Nickell had showed up riding a snorty horse and had tried to run down the Miller boy, and nearly did so. On one pass, the running horse hit the dodging Victor and knocked him spinning. Victor was on the ground and Willie trying to make the horse go back at him when Jim Miller hove into view with his rifle and fired a warning shot that busted the horn off Willie Nickell's saddle, which happened to have been borrowed without consent from his father's hook in the barn.

Well, old man Nickell had come storming over that night to demand payment for a new saddle horn and apology for shooting at his boy, and Jim Miller had just said, "Goddamn you, Nickell, you son of a bitch, you keep your idiot kid away from my boys. He comes on Miller land again, or puts that horse at either of my lads, here, one more time, and it won't be his saddle horn that gets shot off. Now you better get off my place and stay off it. I will have a gun in my hand from now on."

Kels Nickell wasn't the one to back off.

"I won't come again without a rifle, either," he warned rancher Miller. "Somebody is going to get hurt, sure."

It wasn't two days later that Jim Miller, loading his old .38-40 Winchester in the house before going out, had accidentally let the hammer fall on a live round. The bullet struck Little Brother, playing only six, eight feet away, and splatted parts of him all over the kitchen table.

"Ma went loonyheaded for a week," young Gus said, as Victor finished the gruesome tale. "Pa just picked up baby brother, what he could of him, carried him out of the house and put him in the oat bin in the barn, and come back out and stood there in the rain looking up into the sky. He said in a loud voice that me and Vic heard—we was hiding in the loft because the grief of ma and pa was so fearful—that God would surely take his vengeance on Kels Nickell. Then he shook his hand up at the falling rain and yelled, 'Lord, you hear me? You don't strike down this man who has killed my baby boy, I will surely kill him myself!' "

"He did say that?" I asked, to make certain. "That he would kill Kels Nickell?"

"Sure, but he never would do it." It was Victor Miller. "Pa ain't that kind. He grieves worse nor a dog over dead puppies. But he ain't going to shoot Nickell."

I let the juney bugs butt their shelly heads against the netting for a spell. I could hear Victor Miller breathing hard and could understand his pa not wanting him worked up. "How about Willie Nickell?" I said. "He ever come around again?"

"Nope, but he's done shot at Vic two times," Gus said.

"Where?"

"Over the yon rock outcrop, in the milk cow pasture."

"You mean where the one-mile gate is? That ridge?" I scowled. "Hell, that's Nickell pasture and their gate."

"Sure it is. But we always let the latch post down careful and close it tight with the loop wire. Shucks, they ride our pasture!"

"He missed us and we run like hell," Vic broke in. "I was by myself the first time. Then Gus was with me the other. It was Willie doing the shooting, all right. We know that old Henry rifle's bark. It's a .44 rimfire. His pa lets him use it on sheep guard. Willie goes out with the flock when the dago herder spies a coyote or loafer wolf hanging around. Willie's a damn good shot, that's why."

I nodded, frowning. "If Willie's such a deadeye," I asked, "how come he missed you both times?" I put it to Victor Miller, since he'd been the one to get two times fired on. "You know," I went on, "it ain't a bad idea laying out up on that ridge. Happen you want to kill somebody coming through that pasture gate, it ain't."

Unthinking, I idled along. "You got good cover to take a hold and brace a aimed shot. There's hard-rock trail coming and going, so's you won't leave no tracks. No sir," I shook my head. "Maybe your friend Willie ain't so crazy, after all, boys." I paused, eyeing Vic. "You ever think about it that way, boy?"

"Cripes!" the older lad breathed, face in a flush.

"Yeah," I nodded. "But you're saying he missed you both times by accident. Or hoping that's it, ain't you?"

"By damn, I don't rightly know," Victor Miller said. "Maybe it *was* just too long a shot. Maybe he *was* trying to kill us and didn't miss by no accident. But then maybe he was only meaning to scare the shit out of us, like our pa done to him when Willie run me down with his horse."

"Yeah, Mr. Horn." It was young Gus siding his older brother. "Willie's not right upstairs, you know. He is scary to look at when he gets mad. Turns white and his eyeballs roll opposite ways. You know, like a bronc being drug to the snubbing post." Gus paused, and it was plain he was roused. "Vic's some older than Willie, but he is bad scairt of him all the same, ain't you, Vic?"

Victor admitted he was much afraid of the Nickell boy, who was but fourteen to Vic's eighteen years of age. "Willie always has to get his 'evens,'" Victor said. "Onct at school, he told me he figured I was to blame for all the trouble twixt our kin. Said his pa told him that. Willie, he vowed to me that he would pay me good for what I'd done to him. I asked him what that was, and he didn't even know. Said to never mind, that he would get his evens on me and I had better look out for him."

"Yeah," young Gus echoed again. "He's crazy; you got to be afeered of somebody crazy."

"I reckon," I said, pondering it. "But you boys just take him at his word. Stay shut of him. Don't egg him on or rile him unneedful. Person that has got his brains working wrong ain't to be reasoned with, nor run a bluff on. You both of you do as Willie says; keep far away from him. I don't like this business of him firing shots at you and him hid out to do it. I am going to check into it with Kels Nickell. Meanwhile, you two keep it quiet twixt the three of us." I give them a nod, man-to-man style. "We'll be working on the case together."

They liked that grand, but Victor saw the hole in it.

"Cuss it, Mr. Horn," he said, "meanwhile could be our ass. Willie's got a gun he can get to, and we ain't. Pa won't even let us clean his .38-40."

"Yeah, that's so," agreed Gus, the lighter spirited of them. "But, hell, Vic, we can kipe that old .45-90 of Grandpa Miller's. I know where pa's got it hid."

"Shit," Victor said, "you cain't hit nothing with that blunderbuss. It ain't even got a blade in the front sight slot. Nor it won't lever the second cattridge in, neither. No sir, by God." He stopped, and I didn't like the look, nor the continuing flush of his face. "We got to get us a new sizzler of a cattridge like Mr. Horn's thutty-thutty; with a gun like that, you could hit the son of a bitch, I will bet. We'd ought to do it, too, by God, before he gets one of us. Hell, it would be nothing to it. You know, Mr. Horn, just like the way you said a minute ago."

I didn't care much for the sound of that, either.

"What the hell you mean?" I said, sharp and quick.

"Well, you know, like you said to do it," the boy answered. "From up on the ridge. Laying your sights on him square in the middle of one-mile gate. Hell, Willie comes through that gate near every day taking the milk stock to grass and back. It would be a turkey shoot, sure enough." He skipped his pace to take a gulp of breath and winced me again. "You know, like you said, Mr. Horn."

Well, being cautious not to overpush it, I shushed that line right there.

"Vic," I said, "I didn't 'say' to do *it* that way. I said it was one good way to take that shot, happen a person was serious. Now, I've told you I'm going to talk to Willie's pa about the shooting, and I don't want to hear such nonsense from you, meantime, that you're aiming to ambush Willie Nickell, or that Tom Horn done told you how to do it. If we cain't talk without you grabbing the bit in your back teeth and running off as locoed as you claim Willie is, we will blow out the candle right now."

I did it, too, huffing like I was ired and putting out the tent candle with one magnified snort.

In a way, I wasn't shamming, though.

I had gotten onto uneasy ground with the boys, and

I'd done it through my own weak spot of talking too much when I'd ought to be damned tacit. Accusing Victor Miller of not understanding what was said, and babbling on too much as I had about their made-up boys' yarn of the Nickell kid trying to kill them, well, it was Tom Horn doing what he done next best to what he got paid for doing —whicht was talking too much about what he got paid to do.

"Tell you what," I offered to the boys, who were both laying too quiet and breathing too short to suit me. "Sometime soon, when I get back, say, we will the three of us go up on that Nickell ridge and see if we cain't spot us something of clues. You know, like maybe if Willie forgot to pick up his empty brass. You'd be surprised how frequent that happens."

"Cripes!" Victor said. "I never would of thought to do that."

"You done the right thinking and the right thing, too," I assured him. "You got out of there, *pronto*."

"Cripes," was all that Victor Miller answered me. "Them empty cattridges. Think of that!"

"We'll do it," I said. "Remind me next time I ride this way. Meantime, don't talk to nobody."

"Never would," Victor swore.

"All right. Get to sleep now. Got to be sharp eyed for our target practice tomorrow."

The boy reached silently in the tent's gloom to touch the cold steel of my Winchester, where the rifle slept by my side. "Thutty-thutty," he said sleepily. "And always pick up your empties—never leave your brass behind—that's right, ain't it, Tom—I mean, Mr. Horn."

I didn't need to answer him. He trailed it off, and I lay there a good while after they were both breathing easy and deep, as asleep as only boys can get.

It bothered me that young fellows like the Miller brothers would know of me and of the system that never failed, and that it excited them to where they would come right out and talk about using it themselves. My God, I thought, just to settle a feudy neighbor grudge twixt their two fathers? And giving me the credit for the idea? Well, Christ, it was enough to keep a man awake nights. Good Jesus, they was only boys!

Well, of course that was it; being only boys they was
only talking: they wasn't going to do nothing, only talk of
it. I had to remember that. And remember who it was they
were talking for. It wasn't for some clod-busting farmer like
their own pa, or Kels Nickell. Hell no, and not quite. It
was for me, Tom Horn, the great manhunter. The one who
did use the system that never failed.

Somehow, the reassurance fell short.

I didn't sleep good that night. I couldn't get it out of
my mind that I had made a bad mistake somewhere with
these Miller boys.

Or with one of them anyways.

Caliber .30-30

Next morning—it would be a Tuesday, July 16—came
off very hot. We all was slow to get up. Miller was to
take Miss Kimmell over to the Iron Mountain School, which
they called the Miller-Nickell school. When they'd gone,
Mrs. Miller took into the family wash, leaving me with
the two boys. Naturally, they hadn't given me the least
chance to dodge them, as they expected their "shooting
lessons."

Well, I didn't want to get to fooling with that business when their dad wasn't there. Neither did I want to fret
their ma with it, whiles Jim was off the place. So I just
had to tell them it was off for the morning, and maybe we
could get to it after noon dinner. They understood about
the problem (with their pa) but nonetheless insisted I
had promised them "something" to do. Seeing they wasn't
going to leave off trailing me, I gave in.

"All right," I said, "how'd you like to learn a little
scouting? It's more important than shooting anyways. You
got to scout any job you do beforehand. That's so you
don't give your cow thief the drop on you."

I saw them fetch a funny little look back and forth betwixt the two of them, and I backtracked quick.

"Course, rustlers is only part of your range detective work," I said. "But it's the part everybody talks about, rustlers. You know," I said, "like them damn thieving Nickells."

They both fair glowed at that. Cripes! By damn! Shit yes! Why them dirty Nickells even stole Miller beef, and that wasn't fair!

I nodded but said no more here.

The truth was that Miller was more generally suspected for raising his family on free beef, than was Kels Nickell. Kels's problem was mostly Kels. Every cowman in two counties hated him. All would be happy to see him "spoilt" by any big outfit's pasture rider. But I wanted these two boys to get it back to their father what I said; so he would know Tom Horn hadn't ridden Miller grass just to bring the new schoolmarm up from Iron Mountain depot.

"Any particular place you'd like to scout?" I asked Gus and Victor.

"Nope, you're the leader," Gus said. He talked more and sooner than Vic did. It should have warned me, the older boy's quiet, but it didn't. My *sombra* was asleep again. I rode square into it.

"Vic," I asked, "what do you say?"

"I'd like to scout the Nickell ridge," he said, quick enough this time. "Maybe see where Willie laid up to potshoot at us. Mighten be we could find them empty shells you said about."

"It might be you're right," I agreed. "Let's ride."

Gus bounced along behind Victor for a few strides, then called to me, "Hey, what if they see us?"

I lifted a hand to him, gesturing him to not fret.

"They won't," I told him. "That's where the scouting comes in. You ain't *never* seen, unless you aim deliberate *to be* seen. The Cherry Cow Apaches learnt me that."

"Cripes!" said Gus Miller. "Just like the Injuns!"

His older brother Vic shook his head.

"No, by God," he said, "just like Tom Horn."

We didn't stay long on the ridge, once I'd found the three empty copper-case .44 rimfire shells. There was no mistaking the raised-up H headstamp on the shells. Nor the bulge up where the bullet seats that all them old Henrys put in those soft copper casings. But the Miller boys fooled around long enough that I got the fantods.

There was something about the ragged, dark granite of that outcrop looking down three hundred yards away, on one-mile gate of the Nickell milk cow pasture, that turnt me hunchy and spooky. It wasn't like I was proving that Willie Nickell likely had lain up here and lobbed those missing long shots down at the Miller boys. Nor it wasn't just like me being up there answering Victor Miller's intent questions about exactly how Tom Horn would lay up in those rocks to take his bead on a cow thief coming through one-mile gate. Say, one who had a fresh-dressed beef in the bed of the wagon he was driving. A beef that Tom Horn could see through his field glasses was the crumple-horn long yearling he had only yesterday branded with the I-M iron. No, it was scarier than that. It was like Tom Horn really was laying up there glassing that gate. Like Tom Horn really was lining up the front blade in the buckhorn rear sight. Jesus, it was eerie, and I didn't like it worth a damn.

"Come on," I said, something rough, "let's drift."

"No, wait," Victor frowned. "Where *would* you lay your sights from here?"

"Well, one thing," I answered him, short, "I wouldn't lay them nowhere at all from this distance with a damned Henry .44 short. I would get me another gun for openers."

"A .30-30," said Victor Miller, not as a question.

"It's what I carry, kid," I said. "Now you know that." Then, growling my uneasiness. "I told you, let's git. So, goddamnit, let's git—!"

We slid back down from skyline and went for the horses tethered in some bull pine clumps sheltering the west rise of the Nickell ridge. It was then about eleven A.M. We made it back to Miller's for noon dinner, just as Jim and Miss Kimmell rolled into the yard from school.

Dora Miller had made some spit-roasted beef ribs over the pit in the yard. There was potato salad, pickled snap beans, hot corn dodgers, and a molasses skillet cake that plain melted on the way to your mouth.

I noted Miss Kimmell didn't stow much away and remember wondering how she had got all those nice plump things under her trim white-collar gray gingham dress without she et better than that. Being sparing by nature, I put away sufficient for the two of us.

My appetite didn't go unnoticed.

By jings, Tom," Gus Miller said, "I will bet you don't pack in any such vittles when you are tracking down a rustler! No sir. Your old Cap horse would bust his ass—well, excuse me, uh, he would surely strain his crupper some. How do you manage?"

His mother broke in to remind him I was Mr. Horn, not "Tom," to children, and Jim Miller sent him to the house until he could remember not to say vulgar things with his mouth full and in front of the new schoolmarm (who I could see was having a struggle to keep from laughing out loud, and I liked that in her). But Victor Miller was still present and he said, "Yeah, how *do* you manage, Mr. Horn?"

I answered him straight enough.

It was a way I had of not letting such chances slip by, where I could use them, in a safe way, to advertise my Tom Horn trademarks. In that manner, certain habits of Horn could be used to do the work of Horn himself. That is to say, instead of laying up all night watching somebody's place that was a known cow thief, you would just scatter around a cheese rind, some raw bacon bits, and a crust of rye bread. When the "rancher" seen that, the nape-hairs of his neck would lift up and spike into his shirt collar and he would say, soft to himself, "Jesus Christ, Tom Horn," and likely he would be moving to some new part of the country with not a shot fired in anger, or a note nailed to his door.

So I said to Victor Miller, "Well, boy, you know me; I carry some rat cheese, hunk of salt bacon, loaf of rye bread. That's if I'm on the stalk. If I'm just riding, I always add coffee and sugar. But on the hunt, it is just cold water and no fires." I saw the looks going back and yon with Miller and his wife, and I give a laugh and patted Victor on the shoulder. "Shucks," I said, "don't suck all that in like it was the Gospel. You find any old moldy bread or cheese rinds in Mr. Coble's spring wagon yonder? Well, hardly!

Ain't I done told you that 99 percent of a pasture rider's work is riding pastures? Next time you see me going by, you look for that old coffee pot tied back of my saddle. You'll see it."

They let down, with that, and we finished the meal in a good spirit again. Jim Miller even agreed when Victor asked if we might now have the shooting practice that Mr. Horn had promised to show. "Yes," the rancher said, surprising me. "Go and fetch your brother. You ladies excuse us," he said. "Dora," he added to his wife, "you and Miss Kimmell get dressed for it, providing you want to go to town. I am going in, when we finish shooting."

Dora Miller sort of looked puzzled.

"What you going to do in town, Jim?" she frowned.

"Get me something," was all he told her. "Be ready."

There was a swale down back of the house. We went down there and the boys set targets for me and I busted them, shooting from hip, shoulder, free of body with two hands, and one-handed, cocking the lever by throwing the rifle out and back and firing it dead on. They got their turns on some easy tomato cans on a rock ledge. I took note that Victor was a careful and close holder, a natural, too, on shooting free. Gus could not hit the ledge, let alone the cans. Jim Miller was little better. It was plain to see how his poor other kid had got hurt by his handling of firearms. But now he was dead serious.

"Horn," he said, when we had used my two boxes and put up the rifle, "let me see that piece again. I want to study it." While he turned the model 94 this way and then that, he asked questions about the new .30-30 caliber, muzzle velocity, recoil kick, distance carry, fall of trajectory, various bullet weights, everything about my gun and what I loaded in it. I never see a man so intrigued of a gun. Particularly where he was so edgy about them, and sorrowed.

He could see me studying him. He gave the weapon back.

"I suppose it's the best," he said, "or you wouldn't have it."

"The best I know, Jim. It comes either soft point or the metal patch bullets, 160 grains, with the new Winchester powder that hops either load along at about two thousand or so feet per second. That's 30 grains of powder, mister."

"Smokeless powder, eh?"

"Yes sir, not like your old .38-40."

"Must be the most accurate, too."

"Some cuss it, some kiss it," I said. "Depends what you want it for. On thin-skinned game it's a killer."

"Thin-skinned game, Horn?" Miller was eyeing me uneasylike.

"Sure, Jim," I said. "You know, like rabbit, antelope —a man."

I caught Victor Miller looking open-mouth at me and nodding his head to every word I was saying to his dad.

"Thutty-thutty, pa," he said. "Got to be."

His father scowled and looked off. "Go on up to the house, boys," he said. "Harness the wagon for the women-folk. I'll be along. Tell your mother to fetch—" He turned back to me. "What's the gun cost, Horn?"

"Don't know right now. Mine was $14.75 with the octagon barrel. Round barrel's cheaper and just as good."

"Tell your mother to bring fifteen dollars, boy. No, wait." Again the turn to me. "What's the shells, Horn?"

"They was $.67 for a box of twenty. $3.32 per hundred."

"Tell your mother to bring another five dollars," Jim Miller said to the flush-faced Vic, "and hop it!"

He stood behind with me a minute, whiles the two boys galloped for the house.

"Horn," he said, after another moment, "did the boys tell you about Little Brother?"

"Yes."

"I appreciate your help with the rifle information," he said. "I can't stand to look at the old gun and today pitched it down the Clay Crick bluff. But I must have a new one or be helpless to them goddamn Nickells."

"Go careful," I advised him. "Kels is dangerous."

Jim Miller looked at me, shaking his head.

"I don't fear him," he said. "He the same as killed Little Brother. I never carried a gun about before then. It was Kels Nickell made me do it."

"Better leave it sleep with the little tyke, Jim."

"No, they owe me a life over there."

"That why you want the new rifle?"

"No, that is only to defend my family."

"Would you gun down Kels?"

"I don't know. I don't see how I could."

I nodded, watching him. "How about Willie?" I said.

"No, no, no! My God, Horn. A child?"

"Just wondering," I said. "We'd better get on up the rise. Yonder's your missus waving her shawl."

We walked up together and I seen only Gus and his ma in the Miller wagon, with Vic fussing with the team's headstalls and bit chains. "You got the money, mother?" Jim Miller said. Dora Miller said she had, and Jim got in the wagon and took up the lines without another word to anybody. Victor swung up beside him, and Jim whipped the team out of the yard. I was still watching them go when I heard the kitchen door fall to behind me.

"Is that you, Mr. Horn?" said the deep soft voice.

I stood there a minute before turning. I had begun to tremble. I knew I was trapped. I could *hear* it in the way she spoke to me. Hardly over a murmur. Husky in the throat. Damn her anyways. I had to get going.

"Mr. Horn—"

I turned about slow, holding my eyes down the way that was my manner to throw people off.

It didn't throw her off. "Look at me," she said.

I brought up my eyes.

And flinched clear down to the loins.

She was standing there in the late summer afternoon breeze, with the button-front gray gingham dress on.

Only it was unbuttoned.

And blowed apart by the light wind.

There wasn't nothing under it.

Just Miss Kimmell.

Smooth People

Glendolene was what any man would dream to play with. She was a tiny thing but the loveliest without clothes that I ever seen. Her spirit, too, was forward and full of excitement. She was not afeared of a man. Yet neither was she ever loose that I knew of. With me, she had just met her "western man." To the rest of Wyoming she was that "dark little schoolmarm" and proper and prim as some convent girl. There was never a breath of scandal to her name and, saving again for me, I don't know that she so much as batted an eyelash at other men.

But that day in that old July-hot ranch house, with nobody to home and nobody likely to come calling, she was a woman so heated to have a man that I could scarcely stay with her. I never did know, and do not now know, how I felt about Miss Kimmell. I was ma'aming her the first and last days that I saw her. But those that say I was cruel to her, or treated her low down, or laughed at how she hung after me, are damned scoundrels. I did call her a slant eye and say some other unkind things about her later. But I never made cheap of her, nor so much as hinted of our secrets.

If I never loved her, I surely liked her a lot.

But she was one of those women who lacked her ordinary pride with one man, and it was me that was the one. Other than for that, she went about the country with her small chin elevated and looking Wyoming square in the eye. I will sure remember her well.

She was smooth people.

The Millers hadn't got home by suppertime. Me and Glendolene was hungry as wolves. I had to cook the feed as she didn't know a stewpot from a Dutch oven. I made

247

a stew from some cold roast beef. We had white potatoes, hot biscuit, canned corn, and coffee with real cream. The schoolmarm couldn't get over how fast I got it all whipped together. I had my reasons for the haste. All the while I was being the chef, she was sort of laying and sashaying about the place in a kind of negligee bathrobe she had ordered out of the Sears catalog. It was called *La Parisienne* from the label in its neckband. Glendolene said it made her feel like a French *fille de joie* which she explained was not a happy female foal but a high-class "lady of the evening," in Paris talk.

I told her I didn't know what it felt like, but I could sure as hell tell her what it looked like, and that was a short, light supper, and then back into Jim and Dora's backeast feather bed.

"It shows everything you got," I told her, "and you got everything."

She laughed easy and a lot. It made a delicious sound when she did. Sort of gurgly and shiny eyed, like a kid would laugh from purely being tickled. But she was no kid. God, but that body of hers. It made me think of Pajarita Morena, that first time at *numero tres*, in Santa Fe. I never forgot that night, or the filmy *La Parisienne* that clung to Glendolene Kimmell close as the ivory skin it covered. I think of Pajarita and Santa Fe. I think too of sweet Nopal and Fish Hawk Meadow. And a hundred forgot names and faces in between. But remembering Pajarita I am sad, and dreaming of dear Nopal my chest hurts with love of her and what we lost. The others were just women to be had as men have most women, for a night, even for a morning, but then spun away like a good or poor cigar, whichever it had been, but left to smolder out in the dirt of the back trail. Glendolene, silk-bodied, cowboy-struck little Miss Kimmell, wasn't like any of them.

You don't have to love a woman to know when she loves you and to give her, for that, a special place with Pajarita, the little bird, and sweet Nopal, my Apache bride.

We made up the feather bed and straightened the shack to look like it did when Dora Miller left it. Then we went out on the front stoop to watch the moon rise over

Iron Mountain. Likewise, we watched the road for first glint of the Miller wagon lantern. But mostly we just lay back easy on the warm boards of the floor, bracing against the wall planks, smelling the night, and resting. It had been some afternoon, fierce and fun and soft-tender by turn. We was both just plain loved out. And satisfied to hunker there in the coming breeze, catching each other up on who we were that had been so fevered of each other the past six, eight hours.

She had been born far out in the Pacific islands, on the big island of Hawaii, itself. Her father had been a German, Helmut Kimmell, of München, in the old country. Her mother was what she called a Polly Neezhun, which she spelt out for me, p-o-l-y-n-e-s-i-a-n, and she was part Japanese and some Korean, as well. Miss Kimmell had read the Wyoming schoolteaching ad in a Chicago paper, whiles living in Missouri, with German kin.

It was then my turn to tell, and I quick found out that Glendolene had already heard all the old rustler killing lies that littered my life in Wyoming, getting them from the Millers even in the short day there with them. It was particularly from Victor Miller who, Glendolene said, had his own eyes to follow her with and was thus jealous.

"Now, Tom," she warned me, "young August is all right, but you must watch Victor. It is pathetic the hungry-calf way he tags after me, and it's very plain what he suffers."

"You meaning to say he's horny-dog serious?" I grinned.

"A boy that age? They're the most serious. Worse yet, he knows I'm fond of you and that upsets him."

"You been talking of it, you two?"

"No, no, I talk only as is required about the house."

"Keep your ears open." I had not had a right feeling about this Miller stop, all along. Miss Kimmell seemed to have sensed it, too. "How about Miller, hisself?" I asked. "He done or said anything off-color?"

"You mean to me? Or about me?"

"You," I said, "and me."

"With me there has been nothing. Oh, he *looks*, but that's all. As to you, I would have to guess."

"Guess then."

"Be careful of him, Tom; it is a way he looks at you when you are walking away or when he thinks you're not watching him. But he hasn't said anything that I have heard."

"I'd rather bet your hunch," I said. "I get the same feeling. I will clear out soon as they show from town."

"Oh, no," she said quick and in that throaty way of hers. "Stay the night, Tom; oh, stay the night."

I thought I was plumb wearied of her up to then, but I wasn't. The blood begun to get thick in my wrists again and to pound along the sides of my neck cords.

"How?" I said. "You're in the house with them. I am in that blasted tent with Gus and Vic. It ain't workable."

I saw a wink of pink-yellow light down at the bend of the road, passing the Nickell place. "Yonder they come, anyway," I said. "Don't say a word of what we've talked. These people are maybe not my friends, remember it that-away."

"Oh, Tom!" she cried softly. "Have you any friends?"

"There's you," I laughed.

"No, no, you know what I mean."

I did know and lost the laugh. "There's John Coble," I said. "He is the whitest man and best friend there is."

"One friend?" she asked, small voice doubting.

"Iffen he's the right one, you don't need any other," I answered her. "Johnny Coble's the right one."

The wagon was turning off the road, we heard voices.

"Tom," she said, "when the house is asleep, I will come out to you. Where will it be?"

I didn't know where *it* would be, but I knew where I would be; I wouldn't be *there*. Still, I gave her a place. I wanted her calm and content, not flustering in front of the Millers.

"The little shed off the main barn," I said. "It's fresh filled with prairie hay. Bring a blanket, as it's summer-cure, and prickly. It will stick you like thistles."

She laughed the teaser laugh. "I thought you 'hands' slept in hay and straw and thought it 'prime fixtures.'"

"Fixings," I said. "Prime fixings. But we don't sleep like you do."

"Oh? How is that, western man?"

"Well, ma'am, we leave our clothes on."

"Mr. Horn—!"

"Smooth people," I said, "hold it down; they are here." And I stepped off the low plank veranda to hand Dora Miller down from the wagon. I wasn't that total attentive to it that I missed the long flat cardboard carton propped on the seat beyond her. I knew that box.

It was a Winchester rifle, model of 1894.

Jim Miller thought he had the box covered with his missus's lap robe. He never caught me spotting it. Nor did I leave on that I had. I didn't need to. I could mind read those end-label stickers. I knew what would be stamped on them, along with the serial number and the length of the barrel: it would be the caliber.

And it would read 30 W.C.F.—.30-30 Winchester.

The killer's caliber—just like Tom Horn's.

Dark Horseman

It was a bad dream.

I was with Victor Miller and we were tracking an Apache hostile. I couldn't recognize the country. It was one minute like the Chugwater or Sybille, next it had turned to the Gila or San Pedro or White River, only to plunge into a strange, dark hole in the rock and it was Lodore Canyon and I was with Isam Dart and Matt Rash. But always it came back to me and Victor tracking the Indian. Suddenly, there he was.

"No!" I yelled. "Christ's sake, don't shoot!"

I could see it was the wrong Indian, wasn't even any Indian, was instead the old German, Al Sieber. But the Miller kid shot true, and the poor crippled Old Mad was down and we were off our horses bending to turn him over onto his back—and, Christ Jesus—it was Willie Nickell.

Next morning, before leaving for school, Glendolene Kimmell said no word about me not keeping our meet the past night. She had to be hurt over it; you cannot do that to a woman you've been with. But I was in a position that morning "neither to defend, deny, nor tell a fancy lie," as the poem goes. I had lain out the whole night up on the ridge watching the ranch. Miller had got the new .30-30 rifle he'd gone to buy, but who knew what else he had "bought" in town? Or sold. Just before day, I had slipped into the tent with the boys, and they never knew it. But things felt "closing in" on me, that fine morning of Wednesday, July 17. I wanted to get clear of there. And did so. The dust from the schoolmarm's buggy hadn't settled back before I was in the I-M spring wagon, going the other way.

At the home ranch, I found Mr. Coble away, in Cheyenne. Duncan Clark was there and told me Coble had left word for me to "loop the Sybille and the Chug," as beef was again counting some short up there. I-M beef, that is. I told Clark I knew it. When the foreman then asked me about Jim Miller and Kels Nickell, I told him there was so much hate between the two of them up there it made it hard to dig out the truth. "I will tell you one thing, Dunc," I said, swinging up on the big dark Cap horse. "Somebody is going to get hurt up there. I will ride wide of it this trip, as I do not care to get caught in the cross fire."

"You afraid of them farmers?" Duncan Clark squinted.

"It's a blood feud," I nodded, turning Cap away. "A man's a fool not to fear such fights. You ordering me to go that way again?"

"Go your own way, Tom. You know the pasture."

"All right. I will check Billy Clay's place on Mule Creek. I may go by Johnny Bray's, up the creek. I will cross on over to the Sybille and check Berner Creek. Tomorrow I'll turn around and come home over Marble Top. I may be in Friday, Saturday for certain. Anything else?"

"Yes, we would like you to check the Colcord place."

"I can do that today, going out."

"Be careful, Tom. We don't want you seen over along the Sybille. Work back of the settlements along that way, but stay low. There is a lot going on over there. If it is known you are on the drainage, you won't see a cow of any brand. You know those bastards over there."

"They won't see me, Dunc. *Hasta la vista.*"

Contrary to what I told Duncan Clark and to my own hunches, I did go back up by way of the Nickell place. I kept getting these twinges from my *sombra*, the first hard ones in two years. But all I saw up there was Victor Miller on his ribby plow horse crossing the Nickell back pasture. I frowned over it some, as the kid was carrying a sack of grub and an old pair of field glasses. Playing at being Tom Horn, I guessed, and I gave it a wry grin and circled on to miss him. I wish to God I had done it different.

But for then, when it ought to have been warning me at its lifetime sharpest, my *sombra* failed me.

It let me set there unseen on my horse watching young Miller skulk toward the rock ridge above one-mile gate, on the Nickell place, permitting the lad to go past me without halt nor hail to let him know he'd been spotted. Whether or not Victor Miller was guilty—and it was never to my mind proved either way—of the terrible thing that happened next day at one-mile gate, I, Tom Horn was certain-sure guilty of letting the boy ride on when I should of least have suspected he might be bound on some such dark business, and when I might thus have stopped him so easily from it.

Well, we all know the brand of pitch the road to hell is tarred with. Likewise, that if wishes was dealers, everybody would draw to his inside straights. The way it works, no man has eyes both ends of his head. He saddles the best horse he's got and hopes the son of a bitch won't stumble in front of the stompede.

It ain't in me to hate a kid.

Nor to hold against him that what is the fault of his father. As to Jim Miller, he may see me down another road. When he does, he had best have his things in order, he won't get home to straighten them out.

That day that was to change my cowboy world, though, I just rode on checking my pastures until dark. I camped late, making no fire on Mule Creek.

Next day, Thursday, July 18, the fatal day, I went on still riding directly away from the Miller-Nickell ranges up into the Sybille country. I was up there most of the day. Even rode as far as the Divide and to the heads of the Chugwater. In all the time not one soul, except a young cowhand drifting through, saw Tom Horn that ever came forward to testify to it. That lone other rider was unknown to the country, just my luck. He said his name was Charley Starrett, but he was shook bad by recognizing me for an I-M Ranch pasture rider when he rode up on me, and he took off without leaving no address.

Other than for this one Starrett fellow, God picked a mighty bad time to let my Apache training protect me so utter perfect from being seen. But as I told the court later, I was being extra careful to stay low and at the same time comb that whole country for Mr. Coble one fine and final time. It was knowed to both him and me at that time that Tom Horn had worked himself out of a job in the Sybille and the Chug country, and I wanted only to be certain there wasn't any more cow thiefs to "notify," before traveling on to some new country and some other employer.

I guess I dawdled over the ride, not wanting to get home and ask for my time. I didn't make it back to the home ranch until Saturday afternoon, having started that morning from Blue Grass spring. The date was July 20.

Duncan Clark wasn't there. Mr. Coble was yet in Cheyenne. Jack Ryan and his missus, the caretakers, was up at the main ranch house. A hired hayer, fellow name of Carpenter new to me, was at the barn and horse corral. I turned the Cap horse into the corral, thinking Carpenter and his hay crew were looking at me a little dark. At the house, I went into the kitchen. The Ryans was there and looked startled to see me.

"What the hell's going on?" I asked. "Them fellers down to the hay barn staring at me like I had the smallpox, and now you folks backing off as if I'd stepped in something and walked it on your kitchen floor. What is it?"

"You ain't heard?" Jack Ryan said.

"I ain't even been seen, let alone heard, since leaving here Wednesday noon," I answered. "Heard what?"

Mrs. Ryan, pale as a bed sheet, answered.

"They've found little Willie Nickell murdered up to one-mile gate," she said. "Been dead since Thursday."

"Shot in the back," Jack Ryan said. "Three hundred yards paced off. He was wearing Kels Nickell's coat."

Mrs. Ryan raised floured hands, wiped at her nose and eyes with wadded apron.

"He wasn't but fourteen years old," she said.

I looked at the two of them, and they was looking back.

Jack Ryan set his jaw, fearful but determined.

"Where was *you* Thursday?" he said. And we all three stood there and let the kitchen clock tick.

Gravel Blood

I didn't care a damn bit for Ryan's question.

I told him so and he said, "Why, hell, I only meant I hope you wasn't near the Nickell place Thursday."

"Was I you, Jack," I warned him, "I would watch my mouth. Things are apt to get a little tight around here."

I went back down to the hay barn, thinking I had best get into Cheyenne and talk to John Coble. But Carpenter told me he understood the boss had gone on East, and so I decided to ride into Laramie instead. There, I could at least get the "town drift" to this Willie Nickell shooting. It was getting to me that others than Jack Ryan might be asking where at was Tom Horn last Thursday.

"What horses have you got up in the barn?" I asked Carpenter. He told me there was only some broomstick ranch mustangs mostly, but that Pacer was ready. "Get him out for me," I said. "Tell Dunc Clark I took him."

"Anything else?" Carpenter said, eyeing me.

"Yes, tell him I've gone into Laramie to learn what I can about the Nickell murder. Who the hell would kill a fourteen-year-old kid? Son of a bitch."

"Maybe," Carpenter said, "they wasn't meaning to kill Willie. He had on his dad's old sheepskin coat, and was riding that plug Kels generally uses. Feller could have thought he was shooting Kels."

He was watching me funny, and it made me more than

ever want to get to town and sort the thing out with whoever might be looking for me. "Get the Pacer horse up," was
all I answered Carpenter. When he did so, I piled on the
big gelding and kicked him into a high lope for Laramie.

On the way, I ran through my mind the places I had
been on Thursday, and since. Clay's ranch, the Colcord
pasture, Johnnie Bray's place, the Allen and Waechter
ranches near Mud Spring, the main Two Bar pasture, Ru-
dolf Hencke's home grass, a part of Dr. Stevens's outside
range and, damn, it all come out the same in every solitary
instance: not a person who could helpfully testify to seeing me had done so. Of course there was the drifter,
Starrett. But hell, I needed—or damn well might come
to needing—local people. Ones that the folks hereabouts
might know and incline to listen to. And maybe even such
good witnesses couldn't have helped me, or might not have
wanted to, God knew.

The lame words of Jack Ryan came back to me. And
the funny looks of the hayer, Carpenter. Damn again. These
were friends of mine and John Coble and the Iron Mountain ranch company. What might Tom Horn expect of suspicion among his enemies? Or even just among the people
who didn't even know him but hated the Wyoming stock-
mens association and all its members, and them that rode
for them? I shook my head and hit Old Pacer a lick with
the braided Mex quirt. My *sombra* was starting to talk to
me.

And more. Chance was starting to run against me.

I rode into Laramie the entire way twenty-two miles
of it, and never saw another person that Saturday afternoon. It is of course a wide and lonesome country. But you
will not ride twenty-two miles of it on the main Laramie
road one time in fifty of a Saturday and not see somebody either coming or going along it. I came within sight
of the city feeling edgier and edgier.

Who in God's name had killed the Nickell kid?

And how could I prove it wasn't me?

In Laramie, I left Pacer at the livery barn and worked
about the town. I didn't hear a thing that would make me
any glummer, however. Quite the opposite. People I trusted
told me various encouraging things. There was naturally

some talk of Tom Horn but nothing like I had expected. I was pleased aplenty but did not let down. It was still way early for getting careless. Meanwhile, I listened:

Willie had been sent the early morning of July 18 to catch up to a sheepherder Kels wanted to hire. He had not come home that night, but the family thought little of this as Kels had told the boy to go all the way into Iron Mountain if he needed to, to come up with the man.

Morning of the nineteenth, young Fred Nickell found Willie's body at one-mile gate below the ranch house. Mary Nickell had collapsed. A man had ridden hard into Iron Mountain to telegraph the law. Sheriff Shafer and county coroner T. C. Murray had got out to the Nickell place within a few hours. They had taken stenographer Robert Morris to record findings. Deputy Pete Warlaumont was along.

The officers went over the ground and came up empty.

They had gone back to Cheyenne with no clues, filed no charges, made no arrests.

Willie's body was carried to Cheyenne by rail. Dr. Cook and undertaker Alex Trumbull escorted it the whole way. Burial services had been private, but turned out a huge crowd.

The coroner's inquest got under way directly.

Main findings as follows:

Kels Nickell and surveyor John Apperson examined the body. It was on its back but twisted sort of sideways, like it had been turned over. A ragged brace of bullet holes, not three inches apart, was in the back about opposite the heart. Bleed marks showed the boy to have run about seventy-five feet after he was hit. Where he fell, the spurt of the blood squirted a four-foot circle.

Dr. Amos Barber, assisted by Doc Conway and Dr. G. P. Johnston, did the postmortem. They said: "The body was in an advanced state of decomposition when examined, being swollen and discolored. Death was produced by two gunshots, either of which these examiners jointly feel could have been fatal."

Time of death was laid at approximately six A.M. to seven A.M. the morning of Thursday, July 18.

It was believed the assassin inspected the body after the fact of the shooting. Loose gravel from the road was found stuck by dried blood to the face and front of the shirt. But as the body was on its back when discovered, the killer must have come down to it and turned it over from the way it fell, which would have been facedown. The coat and shirt had also been pulled away in a manner to expose the exit holes of the bullet wounds, as if for inspecting to be certain of fatality. A little rock was said to have been wedged under the head of the boy, but the officers rejected this, as no such stone was found by them.

It was established directly that Willie's brother Fred Nickell had gone through the one-mile gate only minutes before Willie was shot down there. Indication of this was that the killer was looking only for Willie Nickell. The finger of that circumstance pointed to Victor Miller. And, if not him, then *some* Miller. Meaning Jim Miller the father. The feeling was given that this would match in an eye-for-an-eye vengeance, being a son for a son.

For me, the most interesting testimony of the coroner's inquest was Kels Nickell's: "Tom Horn will get the blame for this, but he never done it," Kels stated.

This was in answer to repeated effort under oath by small ranchers to drag me into the picture by name and reputation alone. Chief among these Tom Horn accusers was Jim Miller. But all he succeeded in doing was to rekindle doubts of his own whereabouts the day of the murder. Nevertheless, I could not shake my own uneasiness about finding who did kill Willie Nickell. Me knowing I didn't do it was not going to help anything but my conscience.

I sought advice of parties at the stock growers association, whose names will never appear, and was told that it would be wise for me to find a little daylight work that would take me away from Albany County for the time.

Meanwhile they, my stockmen friends, would be able to prove I was on the train between Laramie and Cheyenne on Thursday, July 18. Or at least they would contend this story to be a provable alibi. And, as I knew I was entirely innocent of the terrible crime, I could accept their alibi as they offered it, with a clear mind.

I first argued that, hell, I had a real alibi and that all they had to do if they wanted to help me was go out and collar the wandering cowboy, Charley Starrett. This they made a brief run at doing but came up with nothing but a handful of lost trail dust. Nobody out in the country had ever heard of a Charley Starrett, and Starrett had certainly had opportunity and time to come forward. Maybe I had better quit telling them about *my* alibi and grab a good hard tail-holdt on theirs. I agreed with a deal more of uneasiness. But it was a good thing they took the precaution of "urging" on me their extra alibi of me being on the cars for Cheyenne the time Willie got shot. The inquest was opened up again suddenly and without warning, and we were all back under oath. A bombshell had been fired off. We might damned well *need* that bogus alibi!

Miss Kimmell wanted to change her testimony.

She had sworn previously that Victor Miller was at home, with her and all the other Millers, the day of the Willie Nickell killing. Then the Millers had double-crossed her. They had begun to go around telling it that Tom Horn was the real murderer and that they had witnesses ready to swear and testify to that fact. This was of course a vile lie, and Miss Kimmell was forced to reveal her former falsehood under oath.

The little schoolmarm now said that she had testified for Victor Miller on the promise of the Miller family that neither Tom Horn, nor any other innocent party, should be charged with the crime or, might God in heaven forbid, tried and convicted for it.

Well, Coroner Murray wanted to know, what did Miss Kimmell wish to depose differently at the present time?

"I lied to protect a confused and frightened young boy as I would do again given the same circumstances of misguided vengeance that warped the lad's heart," Glendolene answered in a good clear voice. "But I cannot now stand by and see an innocent man crucified for this heinous murder, the fault for which must be faced by this entire community."

Coroner Murray sensed something strange and dark here, but he held steady.

"What precisely are you saying, madam?" he asked carefully. "And I must warn you that testimony you now give may be entered against you, yourself."

"Your threats do not affect me, Mr. Murray," the little battler said. "What you will get from me is the truth I would to God I might have hidden. Victor Miller was not at home at the time of the killing of Willie Nickell. He was not there, not can it be else than falsely proved that he was." Miss Kimmell arose from the witness chair, fixing Murray with her slant-eyed, smoky look. "But I can tell you where he *was* at that exact time," she said.

"Miss Kimmell I must warn you—"

"And I must tell this court the truth, Mr. Coroner."

"Order! Order!" The bailiff rapped his nightstick on the railings of the witness box.

"Miss Kimmell!" Murray was getting red.

"Victor Miller confessed to me that he killed Willie Nickell. He did it to avenge his father for the accidental death of Little Brother Miller. The father's sins have been visited on poor Victor. That is why I lied for him. But no more, Mr. Coroner. Tom Horn is innocent!"

At once, the court was in a bedlam.

"The witness is excused!" the bailiff yelled, on a cue from Murray. "Step down, step down."

"He wept like a child of eight, not eighteen," Miss Kimmell continued, as if unhearing. "Victor was fond of me and I believe had been coached not to speak to any living soul of the crime. His relief at telling someone, was profound and touching. I asked him if anyone else knew of this and he said, yes, his father did."

"Order!" the bailiff shouted. But Miss Kimmell was not to be ordered by him or any other hearing officer.

"Moreover," she swept on, "Jim Miller himself told me Victor had confessed to him the killing of the Nickell boy."

"Clear the room!" the bailiff yelled. But again Miss Gledolene would not back off.

"Nor is that the end of it," the dusky little teacher of the Iron Mountain School concluded. "When Victor then saw his father coming into the house where we were, I asked him to repeat what he had told me, to Jim Miller.

"Victor did so; Jim Miller knows, as well as he knows his God is in heaven, that the boy committed the crime, and only he committed it. Yet he, Jim Miller, has been going about the community saying it is Mr. Horn and that he has witnesses who saw Mr. Horn do it. I challenge this court to bring Jim Miller forward and demand of him the names of those witnesses!"

With that, little Miss Glendolene Kimmell stepped down at last. She swept right on up the aisle and out of the stuffy fly-buzz of the hearing room, and the court permitted her to go, I suspect, damned glad to be shut of her.

The ruckus among the spectators that followed her sensational charge against Victor Miller lasted something over five minutes. It was a heady, remarkable feeling for me, as I believed I was now out of it.

How "innocent" I really was! Miss Kimmel's entire testimony, first and last times, was thrown out of court and she herself threatened with an indictment for perjury! My situation was murkier than ever.

Worse than that.

My other witness, the missing cowboy Starrett, now showed up out of the sagebrush, full of apologies for his late appearance, and demanding to be heard then and there. Coroner Murray wanted to go home to his noon dinner, but the crowd in the hearing room started growling and he called the bailiff back, and had Charley Starrett sworn.

It was plain inside of two minutes that Charley was full of more than his sorrows for not showing up sooner.

He had been at the bottle for some time—I later was told that the Millers had got wind of him being in town and had "oiled him up" good and proper before turning the poor younker loose to speak his piece for Tom Horn.

By the time Starrett, who would become a staunch friend and sober witness after the inquest, had been on the stand long enough to get his name spelled right in the records, he had convinced the noisy crowd *and* the hungry coroner that he had never before that minute seen *or* likely even heard of Tom Horn. He could not remember if we had met on the Sybille or the Chug, and, as with Glendolene's loyal and God knows *I* knew true story of my innocence, my case suffered grave damage. After the laughs and guffaws, came the scowls.

The little ranchers and rustlers, in town from their hideout draws and ratty homesteader flats, especially didn't like the taste of Glendolene's reversed story. She was known to be "in heat over Horn." She was showing her "furriner blood." She had been paid by Coble to change her story.

She had lied flat-out to villify the Millers and put Tom Horn in a white-knight light, and on and on.

The stockmen's association didn't like it. They put me on the train for Denver that same night, advising me to not get off in Cheyenne, nor even stick my nose out the vestibule of the smoker. I didn't. And I hadn't hardly found me a room in Denver before a news headline made me mightily thankful to be in Colorado: somebody had tried to kill Kels P. Nickell, Willie's father!

Kels had been shot walking out early in the morning of August 4 with his little daughter to get in the milk cows. Kels was unarmed, the girl toting the bucket. The ambusher fired seven or eight shots. He hit Kels three places, left elbow, left hip, under right arm, the elbow hit shattering the joint. Mary Nickell's brother, William Mahoney, took Kels to Cheyenne for treatment. There Kels, tough as they come, accused Jim Miller and his sons Victor and August, of the attack. He made it flat, saying he *saw* them as he ran for his life.

A second edition of the Denver papers the same day told something else:

> Later that day (of the shooting) it was learned that about seventy-five sheep owned by Dr. Bennett and Mr. Geddes, run by Kels Nickell, were killed when four masked men fired into the herd of about one thousand head. The sheepherder, an Italian immigrant, told a confusing story but maintained his life had been threatened, and he knew two of the voices. He is said to have walked the entire distance to Cheyenne from the Nickell pasture.

That was all right news for me.

It seemed to point stronger than ever at the Millers and away from Tom Horn. Why the devil was it, then, that I kept getting *sombra* twinges? Move out! move out! my shadow was telling me. Don't go back, don't never go back to Wyoming. But the temptation to return was on me.

All I could do in Denver was drink, which I done, see some women, which I likewise accomplished and found

a new special one name of Big Blondie, and in general
stayed up nights and spent my money.

Well, Denver was growed to eight, ten times the size
it was when I knew it in the early days, and had elec-
tricity everywhere. Moreover, they was throwing a great
Colorado Carnival, and I had brought some outlaw horses
for its rodeo on from Wyoming with me. These were
John Kuykendall horses. And were my alibi, too. So I stayed
where the carnival was, drank my fair share of old Overholt
bourbon, Baltimore Rye and Wilson Whiskey, and tried to
stay up with Big Blondie. But the outlaw horses was easier
to board and stay on. About three days of this was two too
many, and I was thinking of a ticket to Cheyenne all over
again, when I got a clipping dated August 8, from the *Laramie Boomerang*. There was no name from a sender, nor any
letter inside, just the newspaper story tore out:

> The first man to step from the cars was Special
> Deputy Sandy McKneal. He carried his Win-
> chester and was followed by James Miller. After
> Miller came his son Victor carrying a Winchester,
> then August with another rifle. Special Deputy
> Brown brought up the rear with a short rifle.
> The crowd was orderly. Miller looked uncon-
> cerned. The boys appeared very nervous. At the
> sheriff's office, the door was slammed in the face
> of the curious.
> A crowd of over 200 met the train returning
> with the prisoners.
> The Miller men were arrested in connection
> with the wounding of Kels Nickell and the killing
> of 75 head of sheep he was pasturing. . . .

Good, good. Just what I wanted. Now they would
quit talking Tom Horn, and I could go home to Wyoming.

I decided I would wait another day.

It must have been a hunchy decision, for next day
came another envelope to me, no letter, no name, and another clipping from the *Boomerang*:

> Feeling in the Nickell matter is running higher
> than ever in Cheyenne. Sheriff Shafer, seriously

ill, has asked Deputy U.S. Marshal Joe LeFors
to come in on the case. LeFors, a seasoned sleuth,
says he has heard of the shootings and is anxious
to go to work on them. He insists, he says, on
no fanfare in the work that he will do. His first
act has been to visit the Nickell place. In his typical way, he went out there and came back with
no one knowing of it. His sole companion, Deputy
Warlaumont, says the guilty party is known to
LeFors and will be brought forward in proper
time ...

Now I did not care for that. I had never met LeFors,
but he had a hardcase reputation as a bulldog who never
quit. He was a southerner, fearless as a rutting elk, nervy
as a riverboat gambler. He was the kind, I suspected,
that would mean real trouble, or might. I went out on
the town that night and got the drunkest of my life. The
last thing I recall of it was the lights spinning in my eyes
at a Blake Street saloon. I woke up in my room at the
Windsor Hotel, just conscious enough to put a call out on
the telephone for John Kuykendall.

The hotel found him, and he come over and told
them who I was and had me ambulanced over to the Saint
Luke's Hospital, where I was for the next nineteen days
with a multiplied jaw fracture. Mr. Kuykendall told me I
had made the poor choice of loudmouthing and then trying to land a punch on a member of a party of professional
boxfighters then touring the West. Among the number was
one Gentleman Jim Corbett, a dapper younker aiming to
whip old Jim Jeffries out of his heavyweight champion-
ship. Having learned something by this far in my life of
the grand luck of Tom Horn, you will not need to be told
who it was I picked out to swing on.

Well I had always had trouble with whiskey.

But those broken bones in my face were to prove
the least I lost to the bottle and Mr. Gentleman Jim Corbett
that night of my staggering drunk in Denver. Before the
fight, I had been to God knows how many other saloons
talking free about who I was and what I had done in the
world that ought to be remarked and remembered. Loose

talk like that—talk of ten invented killings for every real one Tom Horn was party to—had dogged me all my days. I used it as a way to scare off men I didn't want to come to shooting, sure. And it worked grand for me that way. But only to a point; the point being a whiskey bottle.

Once blurring, thick-tongued drunk, like I was that fatal night on the town in Denver, Colorado, I would say and claim anything to draw attention to Tom Horn. Down uncounted such bottle-bragging trails, I must have said I killed a hundred men I never even saw, or was tied in to a dozen big-name murders of range rustlers that I wasn't in three days' ride of.

It was my way, drunk and oft-times even sober, of building my name to a place of dread where, when it was signed on a note nailed to some cow thief's door, that man would saddle in the night and be gone with daybreak.

But in the end of it, trying to spare other men their lives in this way like to cost me my own.

Somehow, past belief, I said something that night to the head barkeep at the Scandinavian Saloon, in Denver, that could hang me. And, God help me, to this day I do not know why I said it, nor where the terrible thought of it could have crept into my brain. But Mr. Kuykendall got it from the barkeep direct; I had to have said it.

It was about the Willie Nickell killing:

"It was the longest shot I ever made," I told the Denver barkeep, *"and the dirtiest trick I ever done."*

Through those long days in the Saint Luke's hospital, I tried to think back on the night that had put me there. I even tried talking to the Lord in the middle of the long, bedpot-banging nights that followed each of those days. I was figuring that being in Saint Luke's care might gain me some listening up above. It didn't. I could never unravel any reason why I would say what I did to the Scandinavian's barkeeper. Finally, I gave it up. I took the easy trail away from it, telling myself that the Scandinavian man, and anybody else hearing it from him, would put it down for drunktalk and forget it.

That being that, and my nature never the one to lose sleep over what was done with, I forgot it myself.

But I had learned something in Saint Luke's.

I celebrated getting out of the hospital there by shipping home, cold sober, on a string of cattle cars scheduled to make Cheyenne by Frontier Days.

It is no use to trust the further claims of a man who drinks, so I will not boast of my success in the rodeo contesting there. I will leave it to the newspapers and to at least one honest reporter who saw me take the top honors in all the roping on the big day and who wasn't interested in accusing me, between his lines, of shooting little boys in the back.

The *Laramie Boomerang*, September 1, 1901:

ALBANY COUNTY BOYS DID GOOD WORK ON FRONTIER DAY:

Tom Horn easily won first honors in the riding and roping contests Frontier Day in Cheyenne.

Otto Plaga did some fine work in bronco breaking and was given first money in bareback.

Duncan Clark was high up in fancy roping and is one of the best; he has money to put up if anyone does not believe it.

Frank Stone rode Bay Devil, the noted outlaw horse, and rode him straight, fanning both sides.

Little Flowers

That fall of 1901 was open weather and fine for the most part. I worked steady for the Iron Mountain company on both the I-M and the Bosler ranges. This was regular cow work, not stock detective assignments. It was largely gathering, separating, branding, and shipping cattle out of all the pastures I rode for Mr. John Coble. It was the time of the most hopefulness and contentment that Tom Horn had known since the grand days with old Al Sieber, Merijilda Grijole, Mickey Free, and all of them, down in Arizona. And during that spell, I growed a lot different, or anyways a little so, than my hard man-hunting life had taught me to be.

Mr. Coble was purely set to help me, for he knew what I was going through, and he was then, as forever, the stoutest friend Wyoming ever gave me. Moreover, John Coble was smart. He understood that Tom Horn's day was sundownbound, and he did what he could to put me onto other grass, and finer, while there was time.

In this direction, we had many campfire and ranch-house yarnings, him with his calabash pipe chuffing away, me usually spinning him a tale of some desperate men I had never known and killings by Tom Horn that never took any real man's life, excepting as they was invented to lead on John Coble. I never saw another to take such head-cocked, pipe-puff interest in the work of the western range rider. Mr. Coble was a cowboy in his eastern citykid heart, and he never outgrowed the yearn to be a Tom Horn himself. Naturally, he could never have made it. There wasn't in John C. Coble nothing but gentleness and honorability. And the fact he hired me to, well, push on rustlers from his legal-owned grass did not change that part of it. He knew these rides got rough. He also knew they had to do so now and again. But he trusted me. And I never let him down. I could say to him, and did, just what I had told a hundred others before and since; there was never a man I shoved on, or bid to stay permanent where he was, that I couldn't have proved legal in court was a damned cow thief, or a hell of a lot worse. Nor was there ever a one of them that wasn't warned, not once, but two and three times, to, for *God's* sake, if not for that of his woman and little ones, get out of the country and to do it alive. Most of them listened. Some didn't.

But John Coble believed to the last day I knew him that I got my job done by scaring the lives out of them that needed moving on and not by taking those lives in dark blood. Above all, he believed that I was innocent of the Willie Nickell killing, and he spent a great or at least good part of his personal fortune on that belief.

John Coble was a handshake man, always.

He looked you in the eye, and you looked him in the eye, and you said, "By God, John, I didn't do it," and that was all the bond he needed, all the word he ever asked. You can't over-glory a man like that.

There was but one thing we tested back and forward on, and that was women. He knew that like most cowboys I held a female to be worth whatever she said she was worth. Happen she was a lady, she got high respect. Providing she wanted to play, and was still quality about it, she likewise got treated careful. Was she just a trampy thing, she would be handled about rougher than a bawly calf at a branding fire. Mr. Coble didn't hold with that, being a man who bowed to all ladies, shady as well as sunlight brand. "They are glorious things, Tom," he used to tell me, "like the little flowers that come up in the May rains. Here a day or three, then gone. We dassn't pick them or tromple on them, but must gentle them and treasure them. There is nothing God makes so well as He does a woman. Find yourself one, Tom, before it is too late. And gentle and treasure her, always."

Well, fine, but the trouble with that was that he had a particular female all picked out for me. He was head of the Albany County school board and had been the one to hire Miss Kimmell. He'd been partial to the little dumpling lady from first sighting. When he found out she was gone on me, well, he thought he saw his duty clear and went to work on Tom Horn for her. He was still at it that autumn of the coroner's hearing, arguing that I'd ought to see her for several reasons other than the fine set of her busts and, as he put it with a brown-eyed wink and a wave of his pipe, "the rustle of her bustle."

The excuse he gave was that "we" ought to talk to her about our case; if she had been bold and loyal enough to do what she had done for me, the least I should answer with would be to thank her in person, letting her understand she was important to me in every way and that I was mightily aware of it and grateful to Glendolene Kimmell, my brave friend and maybe more.

Hell, I could see he was right. We hadn't any real argument to it. Finally, I give in.

"Listen, Johnny," I said. "I will do it, but you must front for me in the matter. Me and Glendolene ain't been seen public since she was at the Millers. It seems all quiet now in the Willie Nickell business, and let's tread light to see it stays that way."

"It is just that quiet that I don't care for it, Tom," he answered me. "We must do what we can, while we can, to find out anything that may help us. This is a mean thing you're into. If Miss Glendolene can tell us something, we had better hear her out on it."

"All right," I agreed. "You go and get somebody you can trust to pass her on a message. It will be from me and will say only "meet me at our place" and set a night to do it. You got somebody to trust with that?"

"I think so," he nodded. "How about John C. Coble?"

It was some full-of-the-moon Indian summer night that Glendolene Kimmell showed up on at our place that September of 1901. It, the place, was where I had taken her on some other nights I would likewise remember to my twilight years. This night, though, went different. It had to. Both our lives had changed since those other nights. I wasn't the same "western man" that I was then. Nor was Glendolene any longer "my little private slant-eye lady" that I had said she was before.

"This world turns," she said to me, in that low, husky way of hers, coming up to me there in the moon shadows. "We can't go back, Tom. But we can go on. Will we, Tom?"

She had come right to it. I understood it. So did Glendolene Kimmell. It was her way. She never backed off nor played bat-eyes with a man when the matter was earnest, or the time growed short.

"I don't know, Glennie," I said. "I reckon that's why we're here tonight. To find out."

"I want to go down by the water, Tom. To our fire rock, and the cave. Can we do that?"

"Sure, come on. We'll have a fire, too."

We had met up on the headland above a craggy loop in the Sybille which nestled a postage stamp of a pine-shored lake. It was the home of loons and fish hawks and eagles, of the coyote brother and, in shadowed times, of the lobo wolf and even of Old Ephraim, the great silver-tipped bear. Hard on the shores of this tiny water, we called it Wolf Pond from an old near-white loafer we'd seen there one night, was the fire rock and the cave Glendolene spoke of. It lay above the lap and moon-twinkle of the lake, sheltered alike from wind and man, and it was there that we had "our place." Going down to it now, leaving our horses hid in a grassy swale of the crags, our minds was going back, hers as well as Tom Horn's, I knew, and our hands held tighter, for the way was steep, and we didn't say anything more all the way of the climb down.

Once down, I made the fire. The wondrous smell of the new pine chunks taking flame in the old ashes rose to mix with the needle-scent of balsam and cedar. We sat side by side, backs braced on the warming rock of the cave's wall, watching out over the water. Under us was a bed of pine duff maybe hundreds of years in the gathering there. Back in the cave I knew, and had showed Glendolene, there was Indian markings, both painted in colors and drawed in lines. It could be that a thousand autumn nights before this one, Indians had lived here, maybe even one man and one woman of them climbed down to set as we was setting.

I said something of it to Glendolene, and she had been thinking the same long-ago thoughts herself.

"Tom," she said, "could we live like the Indians? If we do go on together, if we ever do, would it be possible, for a little while, at least, for you to take me with you, far, far into the wild country, and find the Indians again?"

"I don't rightly know," I said, surprised at the turn of her mind and the stir of the question. "But, by God, it's an idea, Glennie. Maybe we could."

I felt the tiny hand squeeze hard, holding mine.

She leaned into me, the smell of her coming to me with the smoke and the rock and the pine smells.

"Tom," she whispered, "let's do it."

I laughed, sort of low, sort of chuckling, the feeling of the place and the soft small woman good within me. "I said maybe we would, Glennie. Or leastways maybe could."

"No," she said quickly, "I mean tonight, Tom. Right now. There's time yet. They haven't caught you and, oh, Tom! I know they will try. They *are* trying!"

"Do you know *that?*" I said. "That they *are* trying?"

"Yes, I know it. I see it and hear it all the time."

"Who is *they*, Glennie?"

"All of them, all of these miserable people in this terrible country. They are going to hang somebody and they have let the Millers go. That leaves you, Tom, don't you see that? Who else would it be?"

"The one who shot Willie."

"They don't care who shot Willie. They want to get Tom Horn. We *know* who shot the Nickell boy. The Nickells know who it was, too. Just as they know it was the Millers shot Kels and killed all those sheep. But that's changed, Tom. Now both Mary and Kels Nickell are saying you did it. They've gone completely around. The whole thing has changed. I don't hear any talk of the Millers now. It is all 'that damn Tom Horn.'"

"Who you suppose is behind it?" I asked.

"I don't know and can't find out. I can only tell you what I hear. Oh, please. I will go anywhere with you, Tom. Now, tonight, tomorrow at the very latest."

"But I ain't guilty. Damn it to hell, don't nobody care about that?"

"Nobody," Glendolene Kimmell said. "Not one."

I couldn't believe it, but she told me things to anchor what she said of the tide shifting against Tom Horn.

The Miller boys, Victor and Gus, had made much of my telling them how to shoot from the ridge at somebody coming through one-mile gate. Of how I had told them the right gun, the right caliber. How to get on and off the ridge without leaving tracks. How to be certain to pick up empty brass after the ambush. The whole stupid and dumb "advice" and "scouting hints" on man hunting that my simple mind had carried me away into giving those damned kids, both in the backyard tent and up on the ridge next day. It was like I had deliberate set a trap for my ownself. Then stepped square into it.

All we were waiting for now was for it to go off.

I thought of my original hunch, and then doubts, that Victor Miller had really done it. How could a kid have shot that good?

Yet I thought, too, of my hunchy fear that day when we set up on the ridge looking down at one-mile gate, and how Victor kept asking me how I would lay my sights, how much to hold over for the long 300 yards distance, all of that nightmare stuff of how to kill *anybody* coming through that gate. And then how, inside my mind, it wasn't Victor Miller I saw laying up on that ridge to frame Willie Nickell in that pasture gate, but me, Tom Horn. And me who shot. And me who killed the boy. Christ Jesus, I was in a cold sweat all over again and told Glendolene to quit talking, that I had heard it all before and it didn't change nothing.

Sure, maybe there was a lot of them wanted Tom Horn strung up. But, hell, that had been tried before. It didn't work then and wouldn't work now. Wasn't it all quiet now? Wasn't that because they had no real case against anybody, since they dropped the Millers?

Why, hell, sure it was.

Forget those Laramie and Albany County bastards. They hadn't, none of them, seen the day they could hang a guilty Tom Horn, let alone one that was innocent. Let all that be. It was running down now. In a few weeks or months it would all be a bad memory. Meanwhile, I *was* going to do some changing of my own to make a different life for me, and maybe for somebody with me. I surely would rather talk of that than of running away to live with the Indians.

And what with the wind fallen still and the lake like a glass sheet out yonder, the fire died back to red coals, and Miss Glendolene Kimmell smelling so sweet of woman-smell and feeling so soft and close against a man, why, God, had we to talk of Indian hunts and Tom Horn's troubles to be run away from?

Wasn't there something else to say?

Something else to call back?

It was quiet then and we held each other. We said gentle things, made long vows and tender promises, all the little-talking that goes with a man and woman loving in a natural way. It was good, and we both knew that it was and was grateful each to the other. For a fleeting while there on fire rock over Wolf Pond, we were again the western man and slant-eye lady. But then the moon went low, the ashes to blowing in the dawn wind, and the chill rose up off the lake. Glendolene and me parted like we had come. Climbing the crag footpath hand to hand, saying no word but understanding we wouldn't see our place again, nor ever find those Indians, nor raise those kids, nor travel on from there together.

Miss Kimmell never really knew Tom Horn.

She was bright and sweet and kind and full of a courage and love away too good for my lonesome, troublous breed of drifting man. She would fight for me to the mean, bitterweed end of it. She would know I didn't kill Willie Nickell, and she would know who she thought did and try, in face of the cruelest low and sneaking treatment, to so testify. God never made a braver nor better little lady. But He didn't make her for me or, putting the blame of it where it really rode, He never made my kind for Glendolene.

When we topped out and stood panting atop Big Loop crags, above the sweep of the Sybille, I did my best to say it out and leave it straight with her.

"Miss Kimmell, ma'am," I said, bowing to her with a lift to my voice that made it light when it wasn't, "I reckon you know, being a schoolteacher, and all, that I don't talk too good."

"Oh, Tom!" she said. "Don't talk. Not now."

"Got to, little slant-eye lady."

"I know, I know."

"I'll say it in a tongue I speak better, ma'am." I was still touching it with that playgame smile you use when it's damn serious but neither wants it so. But she wouldn't look up at me, and I reached and took her gentle by her both arms and kissed her on the forehead.

"*Hasta la vista*, Glennie," I said to her, soft. "It means 'until we meet again.'"

She raised those lovely, dark-deep eyes, at that.

Nodding, she answered me just as soft.

"*Aloha*, Tom Horn; it means the same thing."

Glendolene's Letter

I never saw Miss Kimmell, close enough to touch her or call out to, but once after the *aloha* on the Sybille crags. By then, things had altered so ugly and bewildering that I let her pass by. With her went the last, best chance I would have to leave Wyoming.

But for the rest of that September I lived the life that the Lord had sent me west for. It was to be out on the open, unfenced land. Me and my horse tending our cattle, ranging pasture grass, camping with a fire every night, going free as the eagles that I saw nesting on the crags of the Sybille, running wild as the waters of the Chug, where she falls ten foot in a quarter mile, ah, God! A man that hasn't rode western cattle country by himself, out yonder 'neath that sky higher than the main Rocky Mountains, dry and sharp as champagne wine, grass smell in his nostrils, why, dear Jesus, he ain't drawed the breath of true life yet. He don't know what riding free is like. If he did, he would know, like Tom Horn knew in those dwindling precious days of his life, what price he would pay to stay where he was; to never give in or to go in on a charge that was false and would cage him away forever from the eagle and the morning wind.

No man was going to close the bars on Tom Horn, and no law ever to make him say he killed a poor damned little fourteen-year-old kid by shooting him in the back from ambush. Christ Jesus. Not while Tom Horn could still ride on and find his own place to die, "out there," where he belonged.

So went my September days, and soon.

Early in October, it was learned Kels Nickell finally had got his fill. He healed good from his wounds but realized the next time he would not be so lucky. He was

274

the oldest settler south of Iron Mountain, yet he sold out his place at a loss, moved his family into Cheyenne, and opened a steam laundry there. He said he was on the Nickell place twelve years. I don't know. He was there the whole time I was, beginning in '94.

For another spell then nothing happened.

The matter seemed more than ever to have wearied itself out. I commenced to think of that happier future.

Then, on December 2, a doubtful letter addressed to Tom Horn came to the Wyoming Stock Growers Association, care of its secretary, Miss Alice Smith. It read:

> Madam,
> There is a gang of thieves in this neighborhood killing cattle and stealing horses and I want a good man to help me watch and catch them. Can you send me Tom Horn, or please send me his address for reference to my standing.
>
> Very respectfully,
> J. E.
> Esterbrook, Wyo.

Miss Smith, a fine if sober-sided maiden lady, told me she answered the inquiry, thusly:

> Sir,
> In reply to yours of December 2, would say that we think a letter addressed or directed to Tom Horn at Bosler, Wyoming, in care of the Iron Mountain Ranch Co., will reach him. You of course understand that he is not in the employ of the Assn.
>
> Yours truly,
> Alice Smith, secty.

I don't know why, but something was bothering me about that letter, and I never responded to it, or to Miss Smith. I was still pondering whether I ought to look up rancher J. E., of Esterbrook, when another letter came to me, and not through the association. I will not give it all here, for it is an embarrassment in a personal way. But had I heeded it and its devoted sender, all my life would have been different, and finer, than it was.

"You must take heed of this warning, as your life is in serious threat," the letter claimed.

"Joe LeFors has been at Millers and Nickells and every ranch in the vicinity. He makes no secret wherever he goes as to whom he thinks 'did the job' on Willie Nickell. He has turned your onetime friend Mary Nickell even more against you than I told you. He has done it by telling her that *Tom Horn* is the one who 'killed her little boy,' and saying she is 'not to worry about Horn getting away with it, as justice will be done and the guilty caught and hung.'

"Tom," the letter concluded, wrought up, "be careful! LeFors is after you and has been from the beginning. He is the one I didn't know, to name, when I warned you the night at our place that somebody was stirring the country against you. LeFors is the one. You must believe me.

"This man will never quit on your trail. He does not care that you are innocent or guilty. Tom, get away while you can. And for God's sake, Tom, and for mine who loves you, watch out meanwhile for Marshal Joe LeFors."

Well, naturally, such a pleading, overwrote letter could come only from Glendolene Kimmell, mixing in over her head again.

But help like Glendolene's, like she had given me at the inquest, say, was hardly wanted anymore by me, or by my friends at the stockmen's association. And this letter—it got mighty heated up in the middle of it—gave uneasy promise of more of the same sort of flashing-eyed but harmful defences of me getting made public by her.

Likewise, the letter showed she had not given up or got over mooning after Tom Horn. And I surely did not wish to see her doing herself further hurt on that account. She just wouldn't admit, or couldn't come to admitting it to herself, that I wasn't worth it. The fairest thing Tom Horn might do for the little schoolmarm *and* her letter was to ignore the both of them.

But just when I had decided my mind on that course, I got down to the end of Glendolene's letter.

There was a P.S. on it that turned my hair: "It has

just been learned, Tom, that LeFors can prove you were not on the train between Laramie and Cheyenne on the day of the killing."

That was a shaker for certain. But then I false-calmed myself out of it. After all, what the hell? I already knew I wasn't on that damned train. There wasn't any danger in it being knowed I was riding the backlands when Willie was shot. That fact wasn't going to convict me. Not even a jury of cow thieves would vote guilty on that kind of "evidence."

Yet, I confess I was edgy.

Something in all this, not Glendolene Kimmell, not Joe LeFors being so busy, not Mary Nickell failing me, kept hammering at me. The small voice of my *sombra* seemed stuck on the two words, *ride out! ride out!* and they were in my ears continually, those two words. But I knew how to shut them off.

I still had money for whiskey, and Big Blondie had come up from Denver, and all my friends and everybody in Cheyenne, it appeared, wanted to talk to the famous Tom Horn and to buy him another round for the privilege and to so get his "view" on the Willie Nickell mystery. It got especially so, when it was learned that Sam Carson, the head of the Laramie County commissioners, had got LeFors a leave from the U.S. marshal's office and hired him on to take charge of the investigation into the shooting of Kels P. Nickell, not that of little Willie.

Again I thought of Glendolene's letter.

Willie had been shot July 18. Kels was ambushed August 4. Considerable over two weeks' lapse there. Then Joe LeFors had got on the case *after* that. Maybe a three-week span or lag. So why was he going out to investigate Kels's shooting but only asking questions about Willie's? The schoolmarm's letter said not one word to hint LeFors was after who got at Kels. It was all Willie Nickell killing answers he wanted. As a man hunter, myself, that ought to have read like darkblood sign for certain.

But the friends of Tom Horn were standing by to set me up to all the Old Overholt I could guzzle, and, well, Tom Horn was still Tom Horn. The hell with Joe LeFors. What I had heard of him didn't scare me. I hadn't shot the kid. Where at, in such a fort-up, did I have any real reason to fret? No sir. It was a pat hand I held. I would sit on it.

Besides, me and Big Blondie had business to settle.

We was in fact settling some of it in the back room, of this saloon in Cheyenne which I will call the Bull's Horn, when, through the fringe-and-spangle draperies I seen somebody come in the front that I surely didn't want to see me in the back. It was Glendolene Kimmell. Talking to the barkeep.

I saw the damn-fool barkeep point back toward the rear room. I shoved the blonde off my lap and said, "Yonder comes a crazy woman that follers me everywheres; get shut of her, right off." With which, I slid back of where they had the wine bottles racked and held onto my breathing like I was gut-down in some outlaw gulch with the killers searching six feet away.

There was a red glass tulip shade over the light in the musted little wine room. Glendolene come in partway through the spangles, stopped, and stared around.

"Oh, I'm sorry," she said. "I was looking for someone."

"We all are, honey," the blonde said.

"But the bartender told me he was back here." Glendolene looked around again, and even half lit I could make out she was bad agitated.

"Maybe he was," Big Blondie shrugged, after her good-natured way. "What's his name, honey?"

"Tom Horn," the schoolmarm whispered, guarding it. "Please, if you know where he is, won't you tell me? I must find him. You must help me if you can. Mr. Horn's life is in danger."

"He's not the one, honey, to flinch at that."

"You do know him, then! Oh, please, please—"

She faded the words away, waiting for the blonde to help her, but Big Blondie just shook her head.

"Who don't know Tom Horn, honey?" she said.

Glendolene stood there, face twisting, hands doing the same. I blinked and squinted, peering at her.

I could see her good from where I was hid.

The view didn't help none.

It looked to me like she had put on fifteen pounds. She was sweaty with fear, and her skin was yellow as a chuck wagon biscuit. Her poppy eyes was bugged out to where you could have knocked them off with a stick. She didn't have no color on her face, her shirtblouse had big perspire rings under the arms of it, and, in that whiskied light, she appeared about four foot tall and homely as a pockmark Paiute Indian squaw.

That, naturally, was the booze-blur of it.

The booze-blur and my interrupted lather to get at the big blonde.

It made me see some other Miss Kimmell than the dear husky-voice little loving one I remembered.

A man and his whiskey bottle. Christ Jesus, the woes and wrongness that pair had wrought to my life.

I slunk there back of the bottle rack and watched Big Blondie tell the schoolmarm to forget Tom Horn, as neither him nor any other man was worth such fretting, but to do her forgetting of him in some other back room than the one at the Bull's Horn, where Big Blondie had business lined up and waiting.

Glendolene sounded to me like she was crying. But she bucked up, said something of apology to the blonde, and backed awkward out the spangled curtain. I seen her stop and pester the barkeep again, showing him some kind of a letter. But he was smartening up. He give her the directions to find the Inter-Ocean Hotel, where he said Tom Horn generally stayed in town, and Glendolene bolted out the front of the Bull's Horn on an actual trot. I remember the last view I had of her was of that perky little red hat she always wore square atop the black bun of her hair abobbing out the doors. And I remember my last feeling for her to be one of vasty relief that she was gone, and nobody had got bad hurt over it.

Nobody?

Ah, Christ! how late I forever was to learn.

Had I but known, even dreamed to know, what she had brought to show Tom Horn—the handwrote hard evidence she waved at the barkeep that Joe LeFors, with the Cheyenne police and the county sheriff, was setting a deadfall trap to drop on Tom Horn in twenty-four hours— God alone can say how far off and free I would still be riding. But that's like saying that, if I had listened to her that one decent, small, kindhearted minute, I would not be where I am now, with my sunrises cut down to the few more coming, and every preacher in Laramie County wanting to set me right with the Lord whiles the time remains.

Instead, I went back to the blonde and the bottle. Of the two of them, it was the bottle got me.

I don't even remember the big blonde woman's name; likely she never give it to me. But I can see the label on that last bottle—it was OLD OVERHOLT, my favored brand of them all. And the fellow setting crost from me buying that final bottle for Tom Horn was U.S. Marshal LeFors.

Deputy U.S. Marshal *Joe* LeFors.

The little sandy-haired lawman I didn't know, and wasn't any way scared of.

I can see that bottle yet. Every chip in its uncorked mouth, every bar stain on its label, every fly speck on the tumblers coming with it.

And I can see Joe's hand, as he picked it up to pour for me.

"Have another, Tom," he smiled, *"and tell me how you done it."*

Joe LeFors

Sometimes, when a man is running, he must back up to get the right start. Sometimes he doesn't even know he's running yet, but backs up anyways, on instincts. I done that then, and do it now.

I was, on this day before LeFors bought the bottle, over at Frank Meanea's saddle shop. Frank had been sewing me up a saddle scabbard for my .30-30 Winchester, and I had the rifle with me. I saw shadows in the shop door from one eye-corner and moved around quick but easy. It was Laramie County lawman, then chief of police in Cheyenne, Sandy McKneal. He had a short, wide-shouldered man with him. The man was of a roany blond complexion, stiff short hair, and he spoke a rich southern drawl. He didn't look to be another lawman, and I let down according.

"Tom," McKneal said to me, "I want you to meet Joe LeFors. Joe, this here is Tom Horn."

Well, we both settled in our boots, sizing the other.

"Horn," LeFors nodded, pleasant enough but not offering any handshake.

"Marshal," I nodded, returning his failure to put out a hand. "I've heard of you but had you pictured a bit different. Our tracks were bound to mingle, eh?"

"It seems," the marshal agreed.

"I got to go along," Chief McKneal said. "I will leave you two to your talk."

I watched him leave, wondering why it was assumed me and the marshal was going to palaver.

"Your rifle?" LeFors said, pointing to the .30-30 on the hide-cutting counter.

"Yep."

"Thirty-thirty, I see."

"Yep."

"How do you find that caliber?"

"Good." I gave him the ballistics of the round, together with the character of the rifle, and he just kept nodding, very pleasant all the while. "It will put all them other calibers out of business," I finished. "You will find it in a class by itself, marshal."

LeFors looked at me.

"Yes, very nearly so. Not too many thirty-thirties around."

"Not too many, marshal, no."

"Name is Joe, Horn. We don't know one another, in spite of what people think, but that is no reason we must be so formal. We are in the same business."

Something warned me to go along *muy cuidado*, and I fell into his invitation as if not in any way spooked.

"Well, Joe," I said, "if that's the way it is, then it's Tom and not Horn. You are right. If we are going to do business, no use walking around it stiff-legged."

"No use at all. Tom, you are headquartering up to John Coble's Bosler ranch at this time, if I am right. And George What's His Name is bossing there now."

"Yes, that's so. We are moving cattle up from Iron Mountain. And some over from the Wall Rock."

"I want to talk about a time before Willie Nickell was killed. About what you were doing then."

"Yes, all right. If I remember."

"I have a letter here which may help you, Tom." He pulled out a letter wrote by John Coble, dated ahead of July 18, handing it to me. "Just read the last of it there. About the sheep. And you."

"Hell," I said, straightening the paper. "How'd you find out I can read, Joe. I ain't even supposed to have sense enough to sign my name."

"Well, we know better than that. What does it say?"

I read it for him:

" 'The Iron Mountain, Wall Rock, and Plumbago pastures look woolly and are filled with sheep. . . . When the sheepmen attempt to drive or handle our cattle I will at once have them arrested. But they are scared to death, are hiring all the six-shooters and bad men they can find. I want Horn back here; he will straighten them out by merely riding around. . . .' "

I give the letter back to LeFors, watching his feet and keeping my glance down in my way.

"What do you think? the marshal said.

"About what? Riding around and straightening people out? That's my work. It's how I draw my pay. Same as you."

"Yes, well, somebody straightened out little Willie Nickell, Tom, and I wanted to let you understand that if you learn anything I would like to hear of it. This man will be caught, but he is very cute."

"The schoolmarm says it wasn't no man did it," I said, bringing my eyes up. "She says Jim Miller told her Vic did it, and Vic later admitted it to her that he did kill Willie and was woeful sorry for it."

"I heard she said that."

"Well, I done better than that; I heard her say it."

"Tom, it's only hearsay evidence. It's no good."

"Well, what you want of me, Joe?"

"Tom, we can do a lot of good if we can work together on this thing. You know, setting a trap for this fellow."

He was a very engaging man. Made you believe him and want to believe him. And the next thing he done there in Meanea's pace convinced me like a cold rain.

He had just come in on the train from taking a convict to the pen at Rawlins, he said, and on that train had run into some information he knew I would want to act on. And he wanted me to have it first.

"Go ahead on," I told him.

"Come outside in the sun," he said. "We'll set on the bench and let folks see us talking, and they will think everything is all right."

By that, I knowed instantly that everything was not all right, of course, and followed him out of the shop.

"Tom," he began, "I will be careful with this, as I want you to take it in the proper way. The flag was up at Bosler station, when the U.P. #39 come past with me aboard, from Rawlins. Fellow got on that I recognized for George W——, your boss up there. I went and set by him and told him I wanted to talk about the killing of little Willie Nickell.

"I said, 'George, what are all the Pinkertons doing around Cheyenne? I've seen three of them in as many days. The ones I saw were following Tom Horn around; Tom was drinking and, I understood, talking about the Nickell case. Why don't you send him out of the country? Horn is going to get someone in trouble yet by his talk.'"

"Hold off," I broke in. "What the hell talk is that?"

LeFors grinned at me friendly and said, "That is exactly what George W—— asked, and I told him."

"Told him what, goddamnit, Joe?"

"Tom, you remember the night you got your jaw busted in Denver?"

"Shit. Does a bull calf beller when you cut his balls off?"

"Well, all right. Do you recall what you said about the Willie Nickell killing that night? It was in the Scandinavian Saloon. To the head bartender, I think."

"That was before the fight, Joe."

"Yes, before that."

I started to deny the barkeep and me had even talked. But the memory of it twisted in me.

"The bastard was pumping me," I said. "Yes, and priming me too. He would say a thing and then I would agree to it, or add onto it. You know how I am, Joe."

"Yes, and I take it into account, Tom. But the man is serious about it. He will come here to testify against you, and says he has a witness, as well."

I scowled and switched trails, backing him up.

"We was talking about my Bosler boss," I said. "Go back to that. It was about me talking too much."

"That's what I'm getting to, Tom." LeFors touched me on the arm like an old friend will do. "When your boss man asked me, just like you did a minute ago, what talk it was that I had heard that would get somebody in a lot of trouble, I had to tell him it was what you said about the Willie Nickell killing to the Denver barkeep."

We sat there in the late December sun.

It was warm and very still.

I never said yes or no to Joe LeFors on that twisted barkeep story. I wanted to forget it. I just studied the boards of the saddle shop walk and said, "Joe, why are you telling me all of this?"

"I haven't told you all of it," he said.

"It's enough," I answered.

"No, I don't think so, Tom. Your Bosler boss man answered me that 'if Horn gets to talking too much more like that, we will have to bump him off ourselves.'"

"The hell!"

"He also said he had paid you for other jobs but not this one. He said the pay was made on the train between Cheyenne and Denver, always in gold or fresh paper bills."

"Jesus Christ, it seems to me they're the ones that is doing the talking, not Tom Horn!" I snapped out.

LeFors nodded, thoughtful as could be. "Seems that way to me, also, Tom. It is why I've had this talk with you."

"Well, Joe, I am grateful to you."

"I know; but you have got to do something, Tom."

"What is that?"

"Well, let me show you another letter."

Joe LeFors brought forth a thicker document this time. I saw the seal of the Montana Livestock Inspector's office on the envelope. "It is from W. D. Smith," LeFors said, seeing me frowning at the seal. "He's their chief investigator. He wants me to send him a man for detective work in northwestern Montana. I am wondering, Tom, if this might not be a good place to get you out of sight for a while."

"How do you mean that, Joe?"

"Well, George has said you are clean in the Willie Nickell case. He didn't pay you for that. He also told me you were not paid in the Kels Nickell shooting."

"Hell, I know that, Joe."

"Sure, and every time I can help a man who is clean, I will do it, Tom. The trouble here is that the people think you did it, and they want it that way."

I opened the letter quick then but trying not to seem shook or spooked. I was both, and bad so, by that time.

The letter looked to me like a fresh horse and a fair start away:

Joe LeFors Esq.   Miles City, Montana
Cheyenne   Dec. 28th, 1901

Friend Joe

    I want a good man to do some secret work. And want a man that I can trust. And he will have to be a man not known in this country. The nature of this, there is a gang over the Big Moon River that are stealing cattle, and we purpose to fit the man out as a wolfer and let him go into that country (and wolf).

    And if he is the right kind of a man he can soon get in with the gang. He will have to be a man that can take care of himself in any kind of country.

    The pay will be $125 per month and I believe a man can make good wages besides.

    Joe, if you know of anyone who you think will fill the place let me know. There will be several months' work.

                  Yours truly,
                  W. D. Smith
                  Ch. Insp.

I handed back the letter to Joe, but he said if I meant to answer it, and avail myself of its opportunity, I had best take it along with me. I did so, putting it away.

"I am not sure what to do," I told him. "I will go back out to Bosler and see if I can find John Coble."

"I saw him in town today, Tom, and he said he will be on the Bosler ranch tomorrow sure. You will want to talk it over with him, I suppose?"

"Yes. He should see the letter."

"I agree."

I went in the shop and got my Winchester from Frank Meanea and come back out. LeFors was still there.

"If you decide to write Smith," he said, "better do it through me, Tom. I can cover for you on it. Otherwise it might get out somehow."

"All right, Joe," I nodded. "I will get to you by the first of the year."

He didn't say anything, and I went on down to the depot in time to hook onto the 3:05, for Bosler Station.

I et on the train and met some good old friends of mine who had a bottle, and it was a fine trip home. All of them said I had nothing to worry about. Everybody in Laramie and Cheyenne knew what case Joe LeFors had, which was no case whatever, unless he wanted to bring up the Millers and issue a bill of indictment where one belonged. We drank to that, and the conductor came down into our car and told me we was slowing for Bosler, and I got off the cars and found Tack Cowans, one of the boys from the ranch, there to meet me in the rig.

It was blowing up to storm on the way home.

It was a mean sky and took some of the glow off me and off my prospects. "She's switching," Tack said.

I can't remember it so goddamn cold for December.

Nor bleak.

I didn't say anything back to Tack.

Yours Truly

Mr. Coble read the letter for me and said he felt as though the marshal was right, and that I should answer him to that effect. He knew, as firmly as ever I did, he told me, that I had not done such a cruel murder as to kill the Nickell boy. Johnny Coble was with me and would stay with me, but he still believed I ought to try Montana.

"There is a poor feeling to this entire affair, Tom," he said. "Be very cautious up there (Montana), and do not write back here through Joe LeFors. Send everything to the association, and Miss Smith will see it gets to me."

"What do you think they will do, Johnny?" I said.

"Nothing," he answered prompt. "They have not an iota of hard evidence and cannot find any. Scoundrels though they are, (the people), they have a curious respect for law, where it does not bind them."

"I don't like it, Johnny," I said. "I've turnt hunchy and will do as you advise. When I drift back, the whole thing will have blowed over."

"It must!" Coble cried, with his unquenchable spunk. "The rascals will suffer for their impudence. Kels is already gone. The others will think about that."

"Yes, well I reckon we still suspicion mighty strong who done it, Johnny."

"We do, Tom."

"And they will go as free as we do."

"Miss Kimmell saw to that unfortunately with her contradictive testimony. But that is done now. We cannot call it back nor, as Omar the tentmaker said, cancel half a line of it."

Coble got up from his desk, where we were sitting in his game-head room and ranch office. He came over to me.

I got up out of the big morris chair and set aside my Habana cigar. He patted me on the shoulder roughlike.

"But there is something we *can* do, Tom," he said, in that special quiet way of his.

He pointed to our map of his Iron Mountain ranges—Wall Rock, Plumbago, Bosler—and I saw his finger settle on a place along the fairest flow of the Chug. It was homesteaded land, the old J. K. Brister place at Four Mile fork. There was no better grass nor water nor winter shed on the Wyoming range, and I had often told John Coble he should move there in his old age. But he had it figured different. It was for somebody else's old age.

"I want you to have the Four Mile pasture, Tom," he said. "I mean to deed it over to you, and I will when you come back. It is time to put away the Winchester and take down your detective shingle. Four Mile will make you a nice start. We will see if you can't brand a few fat head for yourself. How would you like that?"

I had never until that moment thought of such an idea.

My own place?

Tom Horn rooted to one spot?

No more muddy water, rat cheese, stale rye bread, and raw bacon?

My God, I must be getting age on me; it sounded damn good. "Johnny," I answered him, "I reckon I would like that fine. Lord bless you, and if he don't, tell Tom Horn!"

We left it there and I figured out my letter to Joe LeFors: I told him in it that I would take up the work and felt sure I could give Mr. Smith satisfaction. I said I didn't care how big or bad his men were, or how many, I would handle them. They could not be any worse, I pointed out, than the Brown's Hole gang where I had stopped cow stealing in one summer. I told Joe he could assure Smith that I would handle his "work" for him with "less expense, in the shape of lawyer & witness trouble fees, than any man in the business." I closed by adding, "You yourself know of my reputation, Joe, and what it is, even though we have never been out together." I signed it like I did most anything I ever wrote, "Yours truly, TOM HORN."

That was January first.

In a few days, here come another letter from Joe

LeFors dated January 6, saying mainly that he had forgot to tell me that the "Montana man will have to report to Smith in Helena, for the job."

I frowned over it a bit. Wasn't it off-trail for him to send a whole other letter just to say that?

The *sombra* feeling stirred again.

And I said, oh, the hell with it. This here is Wyoming, not Arizona. It ain't *sombra* country up here.

So back went my last letter to Joe LeFors.

Joe LeFors Esq.   Iron Mountain
Cheyenne, Wyo.   Ranch Company
                          Bosler, Wyo.
                          Jan. 7, 1902

Friend Joe

Rec'd your Jan 6th today and contents noted. Joe I am much obliged to you for the trouble you have taken for me in this matter . . . I will get the men sure, for I have never yet let a cow thief get away from me. . . .

I will come to Cheyenne to get my pass on the railroad as I can get one on the U.P. to Helena from there. I can go at any time after ten days. I will see you in Cheyenne when I come in. . . .

                          I am yours truly,
                          TOM HORN

When I had sealed up that letter and put it on the train from Bosler so LeFors would have it next day, I figured I had my calves all in the barn for the winter.

But I had forgotten one small thing.

I didn't look to see that the barn door was shut tight. It wasn't.

There was a two-inch crack under it.

Just enough to let out a man's life.

Bad Business

I had told Joe LeFors I would see him in Cheyenne in ten days. But some days after this another letter followed from him, saying I must come in before that time. It was necessary, he said, for him and me to have a meeting. He called it an interview. The idea was that the "Montana people" wanted him, LeFors, to "give Horn a final look," as to his qualifications for the work.

Well, it was only January 11, but I went immediate and got him off a telegraph from Bosler. It said I would be into Cheyenne later that same day. I then went to Coble and asked could I borrow the team and rig, as it was a long ways and I did not care to ride it horseback in such a cold snap. Coble quickly consented.

The weather would make a wolf shake, and I stopped in Laramie to warm my belly inside and out. It made me a little late to Cheyenne, but I was in there at the livery barn and left the horses by eleven o'clock P.M.

I took a few more drops of the medicine—it was at either the Hynds Saloon, or Tom Heany's Tiviola—and done too much talking and was later told some friends put me to bed. I only know, for sure, that next morning I had a busting head and went downtown and stood up to another bar for about an hour and commenced to feel better for it. That's where Joe LeFors found me, no matter what he says.

"Tom, come on and have another one, and then let's go up to my office. I would like to get this 'interview' business out of the way and know you would too."

By this time, midmorning, I was sure I was going to live at least another day. But I didn't want to leave the bar, as I was afraid I would fall down from not having it to lean on. This is when LeFors, damn him, says to me, "Tom, I have got a bottle of your favorite Overholt whiskey up to the office.

There is nice carpet there and you can take off your boots
and lay back in a soft chair."

"By God, Joe," I said, "you have found the recipe."

"Well, I know your brand, Tom."

"No, no, hell, it ain't the whiskey; it's the soft carpet
and shucking my boots. Christ, my feet like to kill me
when I'm standing. They've always hurt me."

So up to his office we went.

There was two easy chairs and his desk and the carpet,
and it was nice and dark and warm in there, and he did
sure enough have the bottle of Old Overholt.

Well, I pried off my number nines and said, "Ah,
Christ! that feels better" and told him to go on and do
what must be done. "I will suffer through it, for I want the
job and mean to have it."

Joe laughed and said, "I will make it easy for both of
us and not keep you too long. You will want to be on the
noon train tomorrow."

"Yes," I said, "that's right. Goddamn, but that carpet
is kind on the feet. Will you have a glass with me, marshal,
or don't you imbibe on the sabbath day?" I picked up the
bottle, but Joe LeFors wasn't drinking, and I poured half a
tumbler for Tom Horn and was ready.

For a moment before LeFors commenced, I looked
around the place we was in. It was a nice office, old wood
panel walls, a picture of Steamboat bucking off Frank
Stone, another of some homely woman I took to be Mrs.
LeFors, but it wasn't her I later learnt. Then a second door
to another office, I reckoned, but it was shut. That was all.
The door we come in was right off the hall, direct. But
compared to a saloon and standing up at a bar, it was summer pasture.

For some reason, though, my eye kept coming back to
that second door. Not even thinking to mean anything, I
hooked a thumb at it and asked of LeFors, "Where's that
lead?" I would have swore he flinched when I said it, but
the light was poor, and I had had enough to drink to where
I was blinking a lot in order to clear the blur.

"Oh," Joe said, "it's a sort of storeroom. We keep it
locked. Used to be another marshal worked up here with
me. Costs money to heat and light it."

"I could see the room was dark, was why I asked," I

told him. "There's a two-inch crack under it that you could toss a billiard ball through. You'd ought to get that door rehung, marshal. You're wasting your fire."

He laughed again and said he would see to it and then said, "Now, Tom, I wonder if you know why I've been pushing all along on this thing. You know, with you?"

"I have figured it was to get at whoever done the Willie Nickell killing. You have said right along that you need my help to nail the bastard. Ain't that it?"

"That is it precisely, Tom. Now are you clear on that? You're not drinking too much. Not drunk."

"It ain't the same question," I objected. "Damn right I'm drinking too much, but damn no I ain't drunk."

LeFors laughed again. He laughed or grinned at near everything I said; I seemed to amuse him something special. "All right, Tom; good: here is your letter of introduction to Mr. W. G. Pruitt, up in Montana." He handed me the letter and I frowned to think out another name.

It came to me and I said, "I thought our man's name was W. D. Smith. Where's this Prudjit come into it?"

"Pruitt, Tom," he answered me quietly. "You can't expect to deal with Smith; he's chief officer."

"All right." I took the letter and fumbled it into some pocket of mine, where I never found it again, and waved to LeFors. "Go ahead on. Damn, it's hot in here. Can we open that other door?"

"Afraid not, Tom. It's locked, you will remember."

"Sure, all right. But I scarcely ever sweat, and it is pouring off me like oil from a scalded shoat. Must be I've tooken on more than my usual."

"Don't take anymore; let's get this interview out of the way."

"Sure enough, Joe. Well, do you know the exact nature of the work I will have to do up there?" I squinted my eyes to ease the pounding in my head. "They ain't afraid of shooting, are they?"

"No, they're not afraid of shooting."

"Well, I shoot too much, I know. But I will protect the people I am working for. And I've never got any employer of mine in any trouble."

"Tom, they are good people up there. Just fine."

"Yes, well, I don't want to be making reports to anybody at any time. I will simply have one report to make, and that will be my final report."

"All right. Why is that, Tom?"

"This is why it is," I said, wiping the sweat off my nose and mouth. "If a man has to make reports all the while, they will catch the wisest s.o.b. on earth."

"They won't catch you, Tom. You are the best man to cover up your trail ever I saw. In the Willie Nickell killing I could never find your trail, and I pride myself on being a trailer."

My back muscles tightened. I looked at Joe LeFors. The reason he hadn't found any Tom Horn trail up on the Nickell ridge, I told him, was that there wasn't any Tom Horn trail up there to find. I said it plain and flat out, and there was no way he could not have heard me say it. And more. I told him then and there that I didn't have anything to say about the Willie Nickell matter beyond what he, LeFors already knew. Which same was that I had not killed the kid and never would. But those words of mine vanished into nowhere. They never appeared again. They were as though wrote in a different script. With ink that would fade away. Leaving only the dark print. The things that LeFors said. Or wanted said.

"Goddamnit, Joe," I heard myself growl to the marshal, "I didn't leave no trail up there. You know that."

"Sure, I know it, Tom. I was only talking about how good you cover a trail. It could be any trail."

"Not meaning on the Nickell ridge?"

"No, just anyplace."

"Well, if it's just anyplace, Joe, the only way to cover up your trail is to go in on your bare feet."

LeFors had been sitting quiet, nodding and waiting for me to answer. When I had, he nodded again.

"All right, that's damn interesting. Where did you leave your horse, Tom?"

Again I veered off sharp, holding up. I told him to quit worrying that old bone. If he wanted to talk about the Willie Nickell case, he had only to say so and we would know where we stood. But I had come up to answer questions to him for those people in Montana, and I reminded him of it. Joe laughed and reached out and put a hand to my knee and said to ease down. He was only testing

*my answers to situations any stock detective would need
to know for the Montana job, and he was using the Nickell
case only to example just any case where somebody had
been killed in range work, or so suspected. His Montana
people had just wanted him to double-check Tom Horn
for them. By him, LeFors, asking questions about the
Nickell case, which was so tough to figure out, it might be
my answers to how it was done, or could have been done,
would just help us come up with the real killer. I told Joe
I didn't like it, but I wanted that Montana work and would
play his little game with him if I had to.*

"Good," Joe LeFors said, pleased. "So just say it was
you instead of the real killer up there on the Nickell ridge
above one-mile gate. Where would you leave your animal?
It's you up there now, Tom." He paused, eyeing me sharp.
"Where did you leave your horse?"

I let down, wanting to get on with it.

"You can bet he was left a goddamn long ways off," I
said, sort of bantering it with him. I remember hazily thinking it might have been kind of fun, sparring wits with the
marshal, if only my head didn't pound so. LeFors scratched
his head, still going easy and careful.

"Hmmm, yes," he said. "Well, maybe so. But I would
be afraid to leave my horse so far away, Tom; you might
get cut off from him."

"It might be, Joe," I agreed, emptying my tumbler of
the spot left in it, "but I always depend on this gun of
mine."

"Aha, yes, the system that never fails, eh?"

"Well you know what they say of it, Joe."

He nodded but passed that one up, turning the talk
instead to a side-gully question. "Tom," he said, "I never
understood why Willie Nickell was killed. Was it because
he was one of the victims specified? Or was it a thing the
kid caused by accident? You know, like blundering up on
somebody. We're talking about the real killer now."

I wiped my face of its heavy sweat and sipped at another weak shot. I didn't feel good. I had to work like hell
to make sense. To follow Joe and answer him in a sharp way
that would guarantee me his okay for the Montana job.

"Joe," I said finally, "look at it backed off from it; I
think it was this way. Suppose our man was in the big

draw to the right of the one-mile gate. Suppose the kid
come riding up on him from the wrong way of the draw.
And suppose the kid begun to run for the house and the
fellow—that's our real killer now—he headed him off at the
gate. He must of killed the kid, I figure, to keep him from
getting up to the house and raising a commotion. That is
the way I think it went," I finished off, "but I will tell you
one thing sure: I wisht it had went otherwise, and the killer
not hit the kid and the kid got up to the house and *did*
say who it was down yonder to the gate *trying* to kill him."

"How do you mean, Tom?" LeFors said, frowning.

"I mean then there wouldn't have been no talk of Tom
Horn doing it, and no need of me going to Montana, nor
any of this. But shit. Wishing is useless as trying to graft tits
on a boar hog. They'll either slough and fall off, or, if they
take, they won't suck a drop to nursing."

LeFors let that slide by him, too, and got back to what
I'd said of our real killer. He said he had never thought of
it the way I described as possible just then. He had knowed
all along that I was bright, he added, and maybe just the
very best yet at this work.

"Tom," he said, "you had your boots on when you
run across there to cut the kid off, didn't you?"

It spooked me for a minute, then I caught his drift. I
had forgotten his little game. He wasn't really meaning me.
He was still just testing me for his Montana people.

"No," I answered him. "Had it been me, I would still
have been barefoot, the same as I described to you the first
time. It is how I work, Joe. How I go about a job of that
nature. If you want, though, marshal, I will put my boots
back on for you."

I thought a little joke wouldn't harm either him or his
Montana people, but Joe didn't catch the remark as
humorous. No, he said, he didn't want me to say the boots
were on if they weren't. But the idea of them had him going all the same. "Tom," he insisted, "you didn't run
across there barefoot."

"The hell I didn't!" I grinned, or tried to. "Or anyways
surely would have did so, had it been me. I told you,
marshal; it's my style. You ain't asking me to lie are you?"

But Joe LeFors wasn't buying any grins along in that
part of it. "Hmmm," he frowned, "well how did you get

your boots back on after cutting your feet so. Those rocks up there are like glass."

"Easy," I said, giving up on the grin a little. "If you have to go on a barefoot job, you always allow ten days extra to cover for healing and such things." I hit the grin one more lick. "But you can tell your Montana people that it all comes in the one price."

Joe just frowned, and that was the end of all the little smiles, either way. He was scowling and stubborn, and I was feeling queasier by the minute. He shook his head, trying to make it sound easy again, but it wasn't. "I still can't believe you did it that way," he said, "but you must have." Again, he shook his burr head, came again full track to where he had started it all. "I could never find your trail up there."

He was doing it again. Saying those things in a way to make them sound as though I had said them. At once, I jumped him about it, the same as the other times. And again he came back to his warm quick smiles and his pats on the arm or touchings on the knee, vowing I mistook his meanings, assuring that he might be thinking of poor Willie Nickell but that was only betwixt him and me, as fellow professionals of the range detecting business, and I was to remember it was just that the Nickell case exampled any other of its kind so perfect.

"By God, Joe," I said, when he had done, "I wisht all the same that you would quit slipping back into saying these here things to make them come out like it was me we was talking about. Where you do that, it don't sound like a game to me anymore. Hell, happen somebody was listening in the next room, they would sure figure you was taking down Tom Horn's confession."

I reckoned for a minute that Joe LeFors was going into a chest seizure. But his color come back after a bit when he seen I was still just setting there.

"It's my spleen," he said. "Doc Gaffney says it won't kill me, but there are times when it surely scares me half to death." He nodded, crispy twinkle once more lighting friendly blue eyes. "I like your humor, Tom," he said. "You've a grand sense of it." He bobbed the round bristle of his sandy hair. "Go slow on it, though. It could fool some."

Scratching back of his ear, he came around in his

chair. "Let's see," he said. "We were talking about you going barefoot on the Nickell job."

There was a beat or three of my temples pounding wild with the whiskey. I knew by then that I really didn't dare to go on playing this roundabout game of Who Killed Willie Nickell with Deputy U.S. Marshal Joe LeFors— whether barefoot or with boots on. My doubts of him began to pulse stronger, making me think of that realer friend than him, who had tried so dire to warn me to keep clear of Joe LeFors. That little fearless woman I had shut off and shamed for a blowzy hog of a blonde not fit to share the same air with Glendolene Kimmell.

"Joe," I blurted out, "you are quartering on my tracks again, and I been warned you would try it."

"Oh," he said, very quiet, "who was it warned you?"

"You likely know," I answered. "You remember the little schoolmarm?"

"Yes, Miss Kimmell."

"She was sure smooth people, wasn't she, Joe?"

"What about her, Tom?"

"She told me to look out for you, marshal. Said you were not all right. That you was trying to find out something bad about me. Like maybe hanging the Nickell kid killing on somebody the people would *want* to see swing. You want to answer that, Joe?"

LeFors lay back in his chair. He was not tensed up or seemingly shook by what I'd said. He only shrugged it aside.

"Well, Tom, you decide it," he said. "You've heard her carry on before. There was her two stories at the inquest, I recall."

There was. I had to admit it. I nodded, getting my mind back to the Montana job and my need to secure its bid of employment outside Wyoming. Whiskeyed as I was, I had not forgotten the stockmen's association and its bobtail advice: get out of town and stay there. I framed my words careful to Joe LeFors.

"Yeah, well, likely you're right, Joe. She is a good sort but don't really know nothing of this business."

"Sure, she's a woman, Tom."

"Yeah."

"What nationality is she, Tom? Some kind of chinky?"

"Sort of, Joe. She's one-quarter Jap, one-half Korean, and the other German. She talks six languages fluent."

Another little spell of quiet fell between us. Then, me not breaking it, LeFors waggled his roach-cut head.

"Tom, you must get frightful hungry laying out in the rocks like up to Nickell's place. How do you manage it?"

I slewed about in my chair. My eyes was cast down but not blind. He had said it again. He was moving in once more. From the rear. Trying to get me defending in front while he came in to cut my hocks from behind. And careful, slow, but deliberate, I accused him of it to his friendly face. It is the last of it, Joe, I told him. Don't say Nickell to me again. Or try to come behind me like that. But he was cute, oh but he was cute. He just spread his hands and said he had only said like the Nickell place, meaning similar to it. The last thing he would do to a man on whiskey, like I was, would be to muddle his words or mix him up. I had his oath on it.

"Go on, Tom," he said. "How do you manage living out like that? When you're on a kill?"

"Hard, Joe. Perilous hard. Sometimes I get so starved for grub I could kill my mother for one bite. But I never quit a job until I get my man. Tell that to Montana."

"All right, I will; what is your best gun, Tom?"

"You know that; my .30-30 Winchester."

"Do you think it carries as good as a .30-40?"

"Maybe not, but I like to get close. Closer the better. You know, Joe, if I have to shoot. Like say a man comes for me. Or fires first. Or traps me."

Joe LeFors studied me a moment, then he said it calm and ordinary as the time of day.

"How far was Willie Nickell killed?"

My nerves jumped naturally. But I wasn't going to let it pass or muddy it with more objection or let him see he had raddled me. I still wanted that ticket to Montana; I still meant to have it.

"Oh!" I laughed. "I thought I told you. About three hundred yards. Of course, you already know what I said about it. Remember? Your barkeep friend told you. It was the best shot I ever made and the dirtiest trick I ever done. Wasn't that it, Joe? I don't rightly remember saying it myself."

He didn't answer to my sarcasm of it.

"Anything else, Tom?" he said. "Did he stay anchored when you hit him from the ridge?"

"Oh, mercy me no," I said, making broad fun of his stubborn mule's pace and slow southerner's mind. "He got up and run all around like a chicken. I run out of shells and finally had to go down and bean him with a rock. Why, I thought at first he would get away, even fired at thirteen times!"

Joe LeFors just stared at me. Of a sudden I saw the blue eyes had froze over. It was like scum ice had set up between us. I was cut off and saw it too late.

"Joe, listen," I said, starting up, "this ain't right. You ain't took it straight. Back up on it. I was funning."

LeFors carried a railroad watch in his vest. I heard it ticking across the stillness. I could even hear the little pinging sounds such ticks make in dead total quiet. I had my head down, listening to the ticks. When I raised it to look at Joe LeFors and see what he was doing, he wasn't doing anything, just waiting for me. His face was friendly again, the blue eyes crinkled at the corners, warm as spring sunlight.

"Tom," he said, "you have the Montana job. Will you require any money for the trip?"

"No, Joe," I said, "I will ride the U.P. as they will give me a pass on that line. But I will have to wait until tomorrow for that. This here is Sunday, ain't it?"

"Yes, the U.P. office will be shut. Tomorrow will do fine. Let's go downstairs and get a drink."

LeFors was out from behind his desk now. He first opened the door to the hall for me, then blocked me off from it. It was like he had forgot something. And for some reason he was talking louder than his usual way. "I could always see your work clear, Tom," he said. "But I want you to tell me why you killed the kid. I mean, why you think anyone would have done it. Was it a mistake? Really?"

I wasn't going to answer that nor take him out on it. I started around him to the hallway door, talking on the way, saying anything that stumbled into my mind.

"Well, Joe," it came out, "I will tell you all about it when I come back from Montana. It is too new yet."

LeFors gripped my arm. "Wait," he said. "Have you got your money yet for the Nickell killing?"

"If I did the work, I would of got that before I did the job. I can't answer for the feller that did the shooting."

"Yes, well, the Montana people wanted to know your terms. It's business with them."

"The same here, Joe," I answered, then added one of those idiot whiskey brags of mine, out of the same bad bottle as the terrible boast to the Denver barkeep.

"Killing is my specialty, marshal. I look at it as a business proposition, and I think I have a corner on the market."

"All right," was all that Joe LeFors said. "I will tell them that."

We went down the hallway joshing and yarning on other trails, the marshal appearing happier than I could figure any good reason for him being. But I didn't auger it with him. I had my job in Montana and would tomorrow be safe away on it. That is what I had come for.

Like Joe LeFors said: it was business.

Sheriff Smalley

Next morning, Monday, January 13, 1902, I went down into the lobby of the Inter-Ocean Hotel from my room. I had not et breakfast yet when I spotted Agent Wheeler of the Union Pacific. He was over where the writing tables and leather settees was, and I went to speak to him about my pass up to Helena, Montana. I had on my good dark suit that I travel in. As was my custom, I had coat and vest unbuttoned. I kept a good Colt's revolver in my waistband, right about my stomach pit, quick to either hand.

"Morning, Mr. Wheeler, sir," I said to the U.P. man. "Mind if I share your settee?"

"Oh, hello, Horn," he said. "I hear you will want a free ride to Helena today, the noon train."

I went to answer him but never got to.

Somebody had come up behind us and now said to me, "Hello, Tom." I turned about, and it was the young sheriff Ed Smalley. He was smiling and had his hand out to shake. I took ahold of it and answered, "Hello, Eddie. How are things?"

As I said it, I went to take back my hand. He heldt it a second, and his left hand went in quick and lifted the Colt out of my waistband, slick as spit. I just couldn't believe it. Was he horsing me? I shook my head mild as buttermilk and said, "What the hell, Ed?"

"Tom," he answered me, "I have a warrant for your arrest." Now, by God, I could talk. And did.

"The hell you have!" I smoked at him. "What for?"

"Suspicion of murder in the killing of Willie Nickell."

I took that the best way that I could.

"Read it," I demanded.

He done so, and there wasn't now any question but that this was serious business. I looked about the lobby.

Sheriff Smalley was a little fellow but nervy. He saw my glance and held up one hand a little.

"No," he said. "Now, Tom you will have to come along to the jail with me. You know I don't like this."

My lobby search had shown me undersheriff Dick Proctor and Cheyenne police chief Sandy McKneal standing with their coats unbuttoned over by the street door. One was to the left, the other to my right. I was in a cross fire from them, and they would have cut me in two. Proctor, a good man, caught my eye and read its meaning. He nodded to me, as if to say, "Yes, Tom, we will do it," and I knew right then it was all over.

"All right, Eddie," I said to Smalley. "But, say, leave my gun at the desk for me, will you? They'll care for it."

"No, it must go into the safe at the jail," said the little sheriff. "It will be plenty safe there, Tom."

"Well, I am set," I said. "Let's ramble."

"I won't cuff you, Tom. Just your word will do."

"You got it."

We walked out of the Inter-Ocean together. Outside, I seen I had made the right decision about busting through them. On the walk below was a man with a Winchester short rifle. On the landing, us just passing him, was another man with an L. C. Smith 10-gauge sawed off to about fourteen inches of barrel. It was Frank Canton, a mean one.

"Morning, Frank," I nodded to him. "I will be damned if I believe you will get any geese this morning; you didn't put out your decoys right."

"You seem to have flown into them," he grated. "Keep flying."

I had slowed a bit, but I laughed and said I'd given my word to Ed Smalley and things would be quiet. I did not fail to note, however, that none of the lawmen let down. They were maybe not scairt, but sure as hell being mighty watchful. Ed Smalley read my face.

"You're dangerous game, Tom," he said. "Ease along."

We got to the jail without drawing any crowd.

Inside, Smalley had me locked up, said again that he detested doing it, and asked me if there was anything I wanted that he could do for me.

"Yes," I said, "read me that warrant again."

He done so and I asked, "Who signed it? I note you ain't said who, neither now nor over to the hotel."

"You mean the court?"

"You know who I mean. Who swore it out?"

"You will learn that from your lawyer, Tom."

I must have got pale at that stall, for Ed Smalley said, "Are you all right, Tom?" and I told him I was but that I always got a little peaked when I smelt a rat.

He looked at me, saying nothing. But he nodded in a manner to let me knew he knew the rat but couldn't say.

"You want to see anybody?" he asked me.

"Just John Coble. Ought there to be somebody else?"

"I mean the marshal, Tom."

"Yes, by God, I do want to see him. But I doubt like hell he wants to see me. Not now. I've muddied his water, sure."

"Could be," said the sheriff, "but I'll phone him."

He did so, true to his word, telling me that LeFors hadn't wanted to come over but he would "for a minute."

And that was just about the size of it, too.

LeFors walked into my cellblock and stopped out in the aisle of it, away from my cell. He just looked at me. I thought he was going to turn square about and leave.

Instead, he stood there in his rumpled tweed suit, blinking at me and rubbing his short stubble of hair.

"What's the matter?" he finally asked.

"Joe!" I blurted. "They got me in here for killing the kid!"

He acted like he didn't hear me.

"It's a shame," he said. "That Montana job was all set. I just talked to them by wire. Well, damn."

"Joe," I gripped the bars, pushing my face into them, "ain't you heard what I said? They've jailt me for killing Willie Nickell."

U.S. Deputy Marshal Joe LeFors stared right at me.

"The hell they have!" he said.

And turned around and walked out of the block, and the bars clanged behind him and I was all alone.

Lawyer Rowells

Any part, every tiniest parcel, of the trial of Tom Horn was in the papers at the time or now lays in the archives of the state of Wyoming. I will not burden anyone with repeating it. Yet I must tell of the preliminary hearing to it, whicht took place on January 24, eleven days after my arrest at the Inter-Ocean Hotel. It was there the entire black heart of the people and state of Wyoming against Tom Horn was laid bare.

Though none knowed it then, the trial was already over.

Treachery and cowardice struck in the dark of a U. S. marshal's room and stalked justice down into the courtroom of hearing officer Judge Becker. To this day I cannot see how such foulness lives in this wonderful land.

It was witness number eleven knifed me down.

First witness, at court's opening, ten A.M., was Kels

P. Nickell. Kels didn't lie any that would hurt me. He was followed by Apperson, the surveyor, backing Kels. Next was the three coroner's inquest doctors, giving the same postmortem report as before. That made five so far. Witness number six was Tom Murray, the fool coroner, who told his ninny story about finding the "butt print" of my rifle "in the rocks of the ridge." Jack Ryan and his wife next traipsed to the stand and put me on the home ranch Saturday, July 20, whicht was correct. Old Mr. John Clay, owning Swan Land & Cattle Company, then witnessed for me long and earnest. When he'd done; Judge Becker recessed for noon dinner.

First to the chair that afternoon was Vic Miller. He was number ten and told a total decent story of my visit and target shooting at the Miller place. He didn't harm me none, nor try to that I caught. In fact, the kid acted like he wanted to help me. I looked about the court, seen many of my friends there, and commenced to feeling that Mr. Coble and my famous attorneys he had hired for me (Lacey and Burke) was right; Tom Horn would get off at the hearing, never going to trial.

Then a stillness fell, and I seen witness number eleven making his way to the chair: It was Marshal Joe LeFors.

Prosecutor Walter Stoll spoke for the witness:

"Marshal LeFors shall present for the clerk to read," Stoll said, "a true copy of a conversation between himself and the defendant, Tom Horn, said exchange taking place January 12, past. Copy made by court recorder Charles Ohnhaus. Witness to same, Deputy Sheriff Leslie Snow. Both Ohnhaus and Snow are officers of this court, operating in the matter with express knowledge and permission of the prosecutor, at the direct behest of Marshal Joe LeFors."

Stoll looked around the courtroom, and the stillness closed in on me. It was smothering quiet.

"In their duty," he continued, "the officers lay flat upon a buffalo robe spread behind the locked door of the room standing vacant next the marshal's office. To facilitate their precise hearing of each word spoken by Marshal Le-Fors and defendant Horn, a two-inch cut had previously been taken from the bottom of the subject door."

Again Stoll ran his eyes over the packed room, whetting the knife of silence that now hung over me, his victim. He waited, like he was watching the blade turn.

"Recorder Ohnhaus," he went on, "employed a soft Dixon number five lead pencil for his transcribing of the exchange, a simple precaution to prevent defendant hearing the scratch or scrape of firmer instrument."

The deadly droning voice of Walter Stoll paused the third time. The prosecutor stared over at me for what seemed far too long a spell, then concluded abruptly.

"If it please the court," the little prosecutor said, "Marshal LeFors will retain a copy, the clerk shall have one, and a third be supplied His Honor."

Judge Becker only rapped his gavel. "Proceed," he said.

I crouched forward. Somehow I knew it. I had been betrayed. And betrayed beyond any sense or intended meaning of what I had told Joe LeFors in his office. I knew it as I sat there stunned. I already knew what LeFors had done to me. It was like an Apache vision seer trancing the future. I *saw* it coming.

And it came that way.

What the clerk then read to a courtroom hushed as the Willie Nickell funeral parlor was every word about the killing of little Willie that Joe LeFors had drug from me, put into my mouth, or tricked me into saying, that would sound like I had confessed the crime.

What the clerk *did not* read to that pin-still courtroom was *one* word of all the things I said to the marshal denying any knowledge of the killing and repeatedly complaining about him trying to twist what I said to make it sound like Tom Horn had done the job.

And the reason the clerk didn't read those words of my innocence was that they weren't there to read.

Joe LeFors had curried out of all I'd said only what he had wanted me to say; the rest of it was gone.

Yet the cunning devil had me boxed. I *had* said what was there that he claimed I said. I could never deny that. But, God Amighty, where was the rest of it? The parts that had me denying what he wanted me to say, the places where I flat-out declared my innocence?

They weren't there. My God, they had taken them out. Charley Ohnhaus, once my friend, how could that be?

Les Snow, you dirty bastard, you yellow coward.

And you, Joe. You, Joe LeFors. You *know* I didn't do it. And you know who *did* do it. Why have you trapped me like this, the three of you? You have to know, you all have to know, that Tom Horn didn't kill little Willie Nickell.

While my mind panicked in this desperate way, the spectators broke into a beehive of buzzing.

"Order! Order in the court!" the bailiff bawled.

"I will clear this court if order is not restored!" appended Judge Becker. "Bailiff, clear the court—!"

But the people and all the eastern reporters got quiet then, and Becker eased back on the bench and the bailiff holstered his stick. Nobody wanted to and nobody was going to leave that room, and my attorneys not yet heard from. Let alone to mention me, Tom Horn.

Well it had taken thirty minutes for the "confession" to be read, what with running interruptions of "object!" from my lawyers, all ruled down by His Honor, sustaining Walter Stoll in every ruling, not one "objection sustained" ringing down off the bench to bolster me or what now looked like my lost cause, in all the agony and drug-out rottenness of that half hour "for the people."

Lacey and Burke did their high-priced best.

They told my side of the "confession" being rigged or, in their language, "subornation of perjury." As well, when that failed, they went to "conspiracy to deprive," in this case, God forbid it might come to that, to deprive an innocent man of his life! But Prosecutor Stoll was the darling of that day, as all the days that followed. I lost my plea to disqualify the confession.

With that ruling, the reporters run for their telephones and Western Union wires. They knew, like the dumbest cowboy in the courtroom, that if that "barbered" confession stood up, Tom Horn would hang.

My trial was set for May, postponed till October, 1902.

The twenty-third of that month, the jury came in. They weren't out but a few hours. And didn't need to be. There was over half of them on that jury men I had taken to court for cow thieving! But nobody bothered to bring that fact forward. "How find you?" was all trial judge Scott said then and "Guilty, Your Honor," answered the jury foreman. And

Judge Scott read the sentence: "*You will be hanged by the neck until dead between the hours of 10:00 A.M. and 3:00 P.M. on January 9, 1903.*" The bobtailed confession had stood.

On December 31, 1902, my attorneys won a stay of execution until the Supreme Court of Wyoming could hear and determine on the case. The lawyers told me this meant I had at least six more months of life. The good news left me moody and unsure. I turnt extremely hunchy about the entire situation. Yet Johnny Coble and the others assured me it was a victory. They said the people outside were going about the streets saying, "Goddamn it, I told you so. Now the son of a bitch will get off!" I might even get a new trial out of the stay, they said, a practically certain guarantee I would go free. Cheer up, Tom. The worst is over. Six months will make it June. A glorious time to be out and riding the open grass again. It will be tough staying shut in, but what the hell? It's winter.

I thanked my people. But I knew better.

My trial had already cost the cattlemen backing me the best part of a third of a million dollars. According to the best estimate of the *Cheyenne Daily Leader,* the total would run over half a million before it was done with. God alone knew how much the state of Wyoming had so far spent. It was a great chunk of money surely.

I wasn't any attorney but could always balance a column of figures.

When a man added what I had cost the cattlemen to what I had cost the state of Wyoming, the answer was plain easy. Neither side could stand a new trial for Tom Horn. Both was near broke. Who was there left to foot the damn bill? Who could pay off everything for both sides?

The answer turned my mind dark.

It had to be me, Tom Horn.

When the year turned, I asked to see Johnny Coble.

"I want a new lawyer," I told him. "Somebody who don't owe a dime to the Wyoming Stock Growers, or a nickel to the Cattleman's Bank of Cheyenne. He will need to be a young man to fit such clothes, I know. But my *sombra* is telling me the others have backed off from us."

"You and that *sombra* of yours, Tom! Lacey has been brilliant for you. Burke, too. And all the rest."

"No, Johnny, it won't wash," I said. "Get me a young feller clean of the whole thing. And I'd better have him quick, for I am thinking some desperate things."

"Tom, for God's sake don't do anything rash!"

"How about that new man?"

"All right; I will look around. Quiet down, Tom."

"You needn't fear for my nerve," I answered. "You, nor the others."

"I know that, Tom. I only meant be careful until I can find us this new man for you. Keep your own counsel until that time."

"That is just what I am aiming to do from right here and now," I called after him. "Be careful your ownself."

He came late that afternoon to my cell. He was young, like I'd asked, and new. I'd never seen him on the street, nor in the court. He was skinny as a mustang catch colt, quick as a fox after a field mouse, but not nervous nor looking over his shoulder in any way.

"I am A. W. Rowells," he said. "Let's talk."

By "let's," he meant me; I spilled over on him like a broke-free logjam, and he just let me rip till I'd slowed down and spread out over the flats.

"All right," he said, "you've asked me and I will tell you. No, you are not wrong. It is my opinion the interests behind you cannot longer afford to defend you in face of the growing temper of the people. Things are changing in this country. The cattle companies are feeling this change. Fighting it, too, yes. But the kings are going, Tom Horn. Their empires are threatened on all sides and from the insides as well. You may quite possibly be the last knight errant of the western plains. But that won't save you."

"What will then, lawyer Rowells?"

"I am not certain, Horn. There has not been time for me to think the problem out. I have kept current with the trial, but the personal factor of the defendant Tom Horn is quite another thing altogether. I assume you asked for another attorney to put the question to him in your own terms and privately."

"Yes, that was my reason."

"Do you now feel able to trust me in that capacity?"

"What capacity do you mean?"

"That of your confidant."

"Well, lawyer Rowells, I got to trust somebody. If I had a better horse, I would saddle the son of a bitch."

He laughed. It was quick and barky but true. "Horn, we are going to do," he said. "Screw down your hull."

It was a rodeo term meaning to tighten your saddle for bronc riding, and I knew from that that I had me a western lawyer and one as good as I might find.

"All right, sir," I said. "My question is single and simple-minded, just like me. What are my legal chances from this place in the road; I mean to get off from this thing and to go free?"

"You have two chances that I see, Horn." He was immediate with it, sharp as the ring of a snapping trap. "Small, and none at all."

"Toss a coin on the two, lawyer."

"You have no chance."

"That means no legal chance. The law ain't going to turn me loose. I was right to call you in."

A. W. Rowells walked about the cell a bit, hands knotted over his backside the same way the pictures show of Abe Lincoln. Matter of fact, he resembled old Abe, but was young of course. Maybe the way Lincoln looked when he was splitting them rails. Or running for Congress and getting his butt licked, back in Illinois.

"I am going to give it to you straight, Horn," he finally decided, "and short."

He fixed me with the bright, keen eyes.

"This trial has dug far too deep into the whole business of 'rustler control' by the wealthy stockmen, both here and in Colorado," he said. "The 'people' of the two areas are simply up in arms against the big ranches and rich ranchers. Cattlemen reaching right up into the governor's office, both states, and on to the Senate of the United States are going to be brought into this thing if Tom Horn talks. Now do you understand me, Horn?"

"Some yes and some no," I answered.

"I can say it a little plainer."

"I'm a plain man, lawyer."

"Aha, and I as well," nodded A. W. Rowells. *"Both
sides want you dead.* Is that plain enough?"

I put aside the hackamore of horsehair I had kept busy
braiding the whole time we talked.

"Damn it, lawyer," I complained, "you made me drop a
loop."

A. W. Rowells barked his little laugh again.

He was a shy sort, but put a firm-quick hand to my
shoulder. "Horn," he said, "I will help you."

It doesn't make sense, but I felt better from that one
promise than all the bluster blowed up by Lacey and
Burke, et al, in their year of lawyering for me.

"You want to start that help right now?" I asked him.

"If I can."

"One last question then: Was you me, lawyer, would
you commence about now to ponder on other routes and
riding trails away from Cheyenne Jail?"

The keen eyes pounced on me. A. W. Rowells took
a long breath, thinking. Then the lean head bobbed.

"You are asking me the question only?"

"Yes. I'll find my own horse."

"Very well," said A. W. Rowells. "Here is my best
advice: find him."

Jail Break

I had to have a way to communicate with my friends
outside. It was lawyer Rowells told me how to do it. A short
time later, a young boy, a local kid, got himself arrested
for stealing a saddle. The judge give him thirty days in
Cheyenne Jail. He was the "messenger."

My plot was this:

I would write my busting-out plan on pieces of toilet
paper. Then I would scroll the paper into tiny rolls and

drop them in the kid's cell on my way past it every day at my exercise time in the cellblock aisle. Everything went smooth. The kid had my plan for my friends to get me out all complete and nobody of the jail crew wise to it. It was a beaut.

Giant powder, five sticks of it, would be got down in Colorado. By night my friends would dig it under the jail wall. It would be fused and set to blow when I gave the final sign. At that time, the friends would have put in the alley of the jail a seamless bag. In the bag would be what I would need when out: pair of winter mittens; winter cap with earguards; overcoat, with the pockets carrying extra ammunition for the six-gun that would be wrapped in a rag, no belt nor holster for it; a horse with no brand to be left hitched at a rack I would name on the last piece of toilet paper, the animal saddled and the saddlebags containing my usual cheese and rye bread, with slab of bacon; and an extra pair of my old shoes from the ranch to be in with the food. All of the friends doing any of the work around the jail to wear socks over their boots to leave no firm prints.

When the friends had all this ready for me, they were to leave a snowball in the window of Saint John's Hall across the street from the jail. The first night of the day he saw the snowball "old Tom" would light a match to his cigarette in front of the exercise aisle window at exactly 6:30 P.M. When his friends saw that match blaze, they were to re-check everything. The next night I would light a second cigarette the same place and time, and that would be it. That night the wall would blow.

January ran out, the kid's sentence with it.

He was out and still no break of my plan; in forty-eight hours I would be on that unbranded horse, riding in winter darkness, "armed and dangerous." There could be no stopping Tom Horn then. The kid had only to do his last job, deliver a letter to John Coble from me that would fuse the break. He would also turn over all toilet paper scrolls to Coble. Then he would be given his money and helped to lay low until the giant powder smoke cleared.

But the next thing I knew of my giant powder plan was when I heard it being hawked by the paper boys down on Ferguson Street. EXTRA! EXTRA! Read all about it! TOM

HORN PLANS TO BLOW UP CHEYENNE JAIL!!! And
I just stood there in the cellblock aisle staring across at the
window of Saint John's Hall where now the snowball would
never get placed.

The kid had lost his nerve. He had got to thinking he
would be found out, and he took my letter to Coble and
all my toilet paper notes of the plan up to the *Wyoming
Tribune* and traded them for a railroad ticket out of town
and twenty dollars cash.

Now I was in it over my hocks.

Sheriff Ed Smalley tightened up everything at the jail
so a cockroach couldn't have got out of the cellblock, or a
strange flea into it. Moreover, lawyer Rowells informed me
that, due to the breakout plotting, the feeling outside had
turned against me even more. We had forseen this, but it
was worse than we figured.

I had to get out now.

July fourth, I was caught with a lead pipe taped to
my leg under my pants. I meant to knock over our block
guard with it and just scramble after that. Again, on July
16, they found me with a second piece of pipe. I won't tell
yet where the pipes come from. But they made little difference, as Ed Smalley never let word of them out of the
jail. He was a very young man and under lots of heavy
pressure from the papers and the damn people.

He came into my cell one night early in August and
said to me, "Tom, for your own sake, quit this business of
breaking out. The whole town is getting ugly. People want
to rush the place. If they do, I can't hold them out. This
jail is a joke and you know it. You also know what they
will do with you, should they get in here."

"Yes, Eddie," I said, "and I likewise am familiar with
what you will do with me, if they don't."

"That's not it," he protested, in his straight, sober way.
"You still have a chance to get off by legal means or
maneuver. Each time you try a break, you damage those
chances. Now I am asking you to think it over."

"Eddie," I said, "you have treated me decent. But you
know I ain't any chance in the world to get out of this
jailhouse alive now by lawful sanction. My own lawyer, A.
W. Rowells, tells me so."

"You would do better, Tom, to heed Judge Lacey and

Mr. Burke. This Rowells seems a murky sort to me. You been nothing but trouble since he came on your case."

"Yes, he tells the truth. That's always trouble."

"Tom, what do Lacey and Burke tell you?"

"Oh, they say I will be the next governor of the sovereign state of Wyoming, Eddie. All I need do is trust them and wait."

He went away not pleased.

Two nights later he came back to tell me he was having a time with Kels Nickell running around making lynch talk. He really was getting people worked up to crack Smalley's "crowbar hotel" and take me out of it.

"Eddie, I will tell you how to handle Kels Nickell," I advised him. "You inform him, next time he starts rousering the rabble, that if he don't abate it, you will throw him in the same cell with Tom Horn."

I thought nothing of it, but the third night on his rounds Sheriff Smalley stopped at my cell and said, "Tom, your recipe was a dandy. I told Kels what you said and I thought he was going to have a blood-clot stroke. I never saw a man turn that white. He hasn't peeped since."

"He's a reason," I said, and Smalley went on.

The ninth of August, 1903, the heat was thick in the jail. It was a Sunday and outside it was quiet, save for where the carny things were setting up for the Frontier Days. They had a damn calliope organ out at the grounds I could hear from nine A.M. to midnight. But it was good to have the rodeo going. It made a fine side draw for me; I was going that day to bring off the great jailbreak, at last.

In it with me was a horse thief name of Driftwood Jim Macleod, or McCloud. I just called him Jim. He was a bad lot but had hard nerves. Or so I thought. Our plan was desperate but had a real chance. Most real, maybe, because likely—for Tom Horn—it would be the last chance.

Deputy R. A. "Dick" Proctor was six feet and seven inches tall, slow in mind, strong as a Hereford bull. And he was the nightwatch man, still on duty till ten A.M. As such, he would bring Jim's stomach pain "medicine" to our cell if it was needed before he went off duty.

It was.

Jim called him, in fearful pain, and good old Proctor

shuffled up and unlocked our door, and when he did we both of us hit it like two bronks coming out of the same chute.

Dick Proctor knocked us both down in one circling sweep of his arms. He got aholdt of McCloud and hoisted him over his head like a kid and throwed him over the second-floor railing to the first floor down below. In the time it took him to do this, I had got up and tackled Proctor from behind. God lent a hand to me. We rolled under the rail and crashed down to follow McCloud, and Jim pitched in to help with Proctor who was using me up fast. I went crazy. I got Dick by the throat and bore down to choke the life from him. I felt him slow under me and get weak. "Jim!" I yelled to McCloud. "I got him. Go and get us some guns for Christ's sake!"

Driftwood Jim staggered up to run for Smalley's office and the guns. The minute he left off holding Proctor with me, Dick heaved up under me like a volcano. He had been acting out to grow weak, and now he had me by my throat and I wasn't acting; my life was blurring out.

But again God sided me.

With a last wrench of strength I smashed Proctor's head into the stone floor of the jail. It groggied him enough that Jim McCloud and me could get his hands tied behind him with sash cord from the exercise aisle window. Next minute we were in the sheriff's office for the guns.

But damn!

The Winchesters and sawed-offs were all locked in a cabinet behind Smalley's desk. It had a safe-lock on it and no way we could bust into it. As Proctor was coming to again, McCloud found a loaded Winchester on top a file chest. He jammed it in Proctor's belly, and we told him to open the gun closet or get his innards splattered. We had to untie him to let him work the lock. I said to McCloud, "Jim, hold the rifle on him, I got to check outside."

I ran to the window and could see the jail steps to Ferguson Street. Nobody was out there except the man I hated most in all Cheyenne, Deputy Les Snow. "Jim," I called over my shoulder, "she is all clear. Nobody outside but Les Snow. He's on the steps taking the sun and also a few bows for getting Tom Horn."

I didn't hear any answer from McCloud but rather a

scuffling behind me. I whirled in time to see that Dick Proctor had got the Winchester away from McCloud. There was no move for me but to go for the deputy. I run in a crouched weave and Proctor got off two shots at me, and then I was on him and had the gun by the barrel. Jim had sense enough remaining to dive at the backs of big Dick's knees and collapse him for me. In falling, the deputy let go of the Winchester. I clubbed it and hit him a fearful blow acrost his shoulder and the side of his head. He uttered a groan and shrunk in a heap.

In that instant both me and Jim McCloud stood stock-still. There was no sound of Snow coming. Incredible luck there. He had not heard the shots fired by Proctor because of the calliope out to the rodeo grounds just then starting up to play "Meet Me in Saint Louie, Louie!"

"God, Jim," I panted. "We're going to make it!"

But I didn't know Jim McCloud.

No thought of me, he at once broke for the outside door. It was opened from the street side just as he got to it, and there stood Les Snow. More luck, but mean and rotten this time. Snow still hadn't heard nothing, but was only coming in to maybe bum a smoke off Dick Proctor, or something. Seeing McCloud, the deputy jumped out of the doorway and run along the outside of the building to escape. McCloud, the way open for him, bolted out the door and was gone.

"Jim—!" I yelled, but the yell was cut off from behind. Proctor had got up again—unbelievable!—and was on me without warning. *And he had a gun from somewhere!*

Now I knew it was me or Proctor or death for one.

My life lay out that same door the coward Driftwood Jim McCloud had just vanished through.

I have to say it once more, the Lord lent Tom Horn the strength of ten. I reckon He figured me for a man with a just cause. He could see it where those cow thieves on the hanging jury couldn't. I managed once again to get a choke-hold on the huge Dick Proctor and smother off his breath. He was turning lavendar color when I let up on him this time. I heard the automatic pistol he had pulled from some hiding place thunk onto the floor from his slack hand. This is what saved Proctor's life. Else than that, I'd have killed him sure.

Grabbing up the pistol, I jammed it in my pants top
and ran. There wasn't no other thing to do; it is a black lie
that I panicked or lost my nerve. I still saw that open door
of Cheyenne Jail. I still saw the unconscious Proctor helpless and disarmed. And I still saw me and Jim making it
away. Reason for this was that out the open jail door I could
see two things, as I got hold of the newfangled automatic
of Proctor's and rolled up onto my feet from the fight with
him. First, there wasn't yet any commotion on the street.
Ferguson was still Sunday morning empty. Second, God bless
him and forgive me for calling him a coward, Jim McCloud
hadn't forgot me!

Our plan called for us to get to the small barn back of
the jail where Sheriff Ed Smalley kept his fine saddle horse.
It was a big strapping dun, and Ed kept him saddled as a
duty horse. We was to get the horse and go on him double-
mounted just over the U.P. yards where our friends on the
outside was to have four prime horses for us to change to.
That was a relay of two apiece. And we was to split and
ride opposite directions from there.

And now yonder came old Jim around the jailhouse
corner riding the sheriff's big dun saddler hell-bent for
salvation down Ferguson toward the front of Cheyenne Jail
to pick up Tom Horn. I said something to God for the first
time in long years' memory and sprinted down the jailhouse steps and out into the street for Jim to make the old
rodeo pickup of his pal. It wasn't nothing to it as a stunt,
and we would make it clean as bright light down a new gun
barrel. All Jim needed to do was slow the big horse for
about ten yards, and Tom Horn would be up behind Jim
McCloud like a cougar on a lame calf.

I hit the middle of Ferguson and turned to my left to
be going the same way as the approaching horse and rider.
As I did, I noted out of eye-corner that people were now
running up from all directions, but no firing yet, and I knew
me and Jim would be free and riding far before ever any
crowd could get itself thinking straight.

In the last strides, I turned head over shoulder to time
my grab of the dun horse's saddle skirt going by.

What I saw was McCloud on top of me with the dun
horse flying. I hollered, "Slow, for God's sake, Jim!" but instead he cursed something at me for barring his way,

swerved the dun wide of me, dug his neels into him, and left me with heel-clods flying back into my face.

And now the people *were* clotting up, all sides of me.

I heard a shot, then several shots. Two, three bullets hit building walls near me and screamed off in wild whines. I ducked and ran for the alley back of the courthouse. At the corner of it, a big son of a bitch on a red mule tried to block me off. I snapped a shot at him, but the auto pistol only clicked, and the trigger went soft. It wasn't a misfire. It was that the damn gun was "on safe," and I didn't know how the "safe" on it worked. Winchesters and Colts don't have such flossy gadgets as safeties on them, by God, and it would be a long spell before Tom Horn ever went to anything else than a gun by Sam Colt or Oliver Winchester again in that life.

But the man on the mule saw only that I was "shooting" at him from close range, and he whipped his mule out of there. I got on down the alley, but my *sombra* was running with me now, dead even. It had finally caught up to me.

And it was saying, too late! too late!

I stretched to run faster, not listening to it; I put in my mind only the last thing it had told me before the darkness of the alley behind Cheyenne Jail. For me, my shadow-spirit was still crying, *ride out! ride out—!* and I would hear nothing else from it, then or ever.

I was hearing things from elsewhere though!

People yelling. Horses galloping. Church bells tolling like crazy all over Cheyenne. Shots firing everywhere. Ricochets screeching. Women high-pitching their yells at kids getting away from them to go "run Tom Horn."

Jesus, Christ Jesus! call me the right turn now!

The alley wasn't a blind one, I knew that. It made a T with a side street off Ferguson up ahead, and it had to be either left or right up there, for Tom Horn.

"*Sombra!*" I yelled out loud, a little dazed. "Which-away, whichaway, yonder?" I thought to hear it answer me, in Mexican, "*Izquierda!*" and I veered in full stride to cut to the left, away from Ferguson Street.

I made the turn and there in my way was a man I knew from the carnival. It was O. A. Aldrich, the fat man who ran the merry-go-round. He was the only one in the

way. Past him I could see open space, then the U.P. yards.
God, oh God! If my pals were holding steady over there,
those relay horses were two, three minutes of sprinting on
foot from where I panted toward the carny man.

"O. A.!" I cried out to him, "let me past for God's sake.
It's Tom Horn! You know I'm innocent—"

But O. A. Aldrich had a gun.

And a gun in any man's hand makes that man a different man. "Damn you, Horn!" I heard the fat man say,
and he fired right into my face. The bullet plowed a furrow
in my skin over the skull, knocking me to my knees in the
dirt and dung of the side street. I staggered up, turning
to try the other way, out toward Ferguson. I was spared
vision just long enough to see the way was clear there. Had
I gone to the right, I would be running free. The thought
twisted in me and, of a sudden, my knees began to shake
and go to water. O. A. Aldrich came up to me as I
pitched down into the dirt again. I fought back to my knees,
looking up to find that fat face in my blurring sight. All I
could see was the gun he had. It was held by the barrel and
the butt was whistling down toward my bleeding head.
The ugly sound its steel backstrap made going into the
meat of my skull was the last sound I remember. After that
it was still as the grave.

I slept peaceful as a dead calf.

Barabbas's Visitor

It was now stark clear to me that they were going to
hang me. For weeks following the big break, my regular
lawyers tried every legal delay to hold off the supreme
court ruling on our appeal. But on October 1 the high
court handed down their opinion, "verdict of the lower
court affirmed." Tom Horn *was* guilty of the murder of
Willie Nickell. His execution date was affixed at November

20, 1903. For the first time, I knew what it felt like for a man to realize he was going to die.

It shook me for thirty days.

Then, I understood that at last it was me against them all. Even the strange man A. W. Rowells was helpless to do more for Tom Horn. This was on November 1. At once, I left off the writing of desperate letters of appeal. I kept penning just enough of such notes as to keep authorities and my own defense from smelling out that I was once again—one last time—up to something.

Since the breakout, I had been denied regular visitors, only my attorneys of record and certain newspaper reporters were allowed in my cell. Even these, for the greater part, had to work outside in the block aisle, speaking twixt the bars. In fact, the sole one to make a problem over it was A. W. Rowells. He went to the high court and somehow got a writ to make Ed Smalley admit him, Rowells, to the "very cell of the prisoner, Tom Horn, for purposes of proper conduct of legal rights of the condemned." So lawyer Rowells could come in the cell and, by damn, nobody else. That narrowed my life to him.

If this gangly, homely, cow country lawyer who nobody knew nor cared about, except to get riled at, would not "aid and abet" his doomed client, I would hang.

I asked three things of him.

One: Would he carry out of the jail for me certain messages to certain people, the content of which lawyer Rowells would remain ignorant (hence innocent) of?

Two: The execution date standing, could he visit me the night of the last day before November 20—the early evening of November 19—bringing his briefcase full of innocent things that would pass jail inspection and could be left in my cell, having thus an empty case to refill for his exit with certain documentary material given him as *The Last Will & Testament of Tom Horn?*

Three: Would he arrange for a Catholic priest to visit Tom Horn without fail that same evening, *after* he, lawyer Rowells had been gone *one hour.* The priest to be told by Rowells to tell Sheriff Smalley I had requested a father of the true faith. And Rowells then to select a padre as near as could be of a size and heft to Tom Horn? (I did not care for little priests, nor fat ones.)

A. W. Rowels had three questions of his own.

A: Did I think him fool enough to enter into any such conspiracy?

B: Did I know the penalty for being accessory to the unlawful flight of a condemned murderer?

C: What time, exactly, did I want him there at my cell the early evening of November 19, the last day before they were to hang me by the neck until dead?

I just looked at him a long moment, then took his bony right hand in both of mine.

"Lawyer," I said to him, "before you come to Wyoming did you ever practice law in Galilee, or Golgotha?"

I knew my Bible from my mother beating it into me, but A. W. Rowells just looked steady at me and said, "No, why?"

"I believe you should have," I told him. "You'd have surely tried to get Him off, and likely done so."

The keen young face with the old eyes in it peered at me. There was a faint smile on it, and his barky voice went soft. "More likely," he said, "I'd have represented Barabbas. And lost the case."

He went out of my cell never looking back, and I did not know in that moment if he had said yes or no to my plea for one more chance at life.

I only knew he'd said he would be there the evening of November 19, and then one more thing:

I knew who Barabbas was.

He was a murderer.

The one that Pontius Pilate gave to the crowd the day they crucified Jesus.

God's Padre

What I tell of those closing days may seem to be bare and simple. It was by no means that. The rush and crush of lawyers and reporters and law officers all in and about Cheyenne Jail was like an asylum. It made a man think he had lost his head and that everybody on all sides of him was doing the same. It was a madhouse.

But things like all the major papers—from New York, Chicago, Kansas City, Saint Louis, Denver, everywhere that counted—having reporters in Cheyenne, well, that didn't interest me. Neither did such things as Sheriff Smalley ordering a Gatling machine gun mounted atop the jail to keep off a suspected "power break" at the last minute by "desperate friends of Horn." Not even when it was announced that those desperate friends were none other than Butch Cassidy and his Wild Bunch! What bosh. But I kept my head. It didn't even sidetrack me from my secret breakout planning to learn that Ed Smalley had got Governor Chatterton to order out the state guard and had stationed the militia boys up and down Ferguson Street. Smalley likewise had deputized local men posted at every one of the jail windows with shotguns and orders to shoot to kill. Inside the building itself, Ed Smalley told me he had up to a hundred men, changing shifts every four hours. Outside in the street, no matter the mean November weather, it was like the carnival had never left town. *That* did get into my innards, but none of the rest of it did. I was too busy with my breakout, going over and over the plan in my mind to have it all perfect on the night of the nineteenth. So the time drew down.

The day of the nineteenth, my last day that I would see a sunset on this earth—unless my wild plan worked—came on dark and cloudy, with a northwest wind.

Good.

Such a wind would blow and drift snow to fill the trackline of a horse and rider in no more than minutes of their passing. And with the clouds so low, the dark would come early, and the night to follow would be as black and blind as a bat cave. By morning of the day they were going to kill me, I would be fifty miles away and as lost to Wyoming as the icy wind that blew me home toward Arizona. No pursuit could find the way I went, no posse ever catch me. Only the Apache would know where Tom Horn had gone, where Talking Boy had flown to find sweet Nopal and little Sombra. And the Apache did not live who would

sell his brother to the *Pinda Lickoyi,* betray him to the
hated White Eyes.

Those hours of the day that I now must wait in Cheyenne Jail were passed in doing the things I had done since
they locked me in that mustering old *juzgado del norte.* I did
some of my famous horsehair braiding on a hackamore for
Johnny Coble, the work I had learned from Chikisin and
Sister Sawn, that one of the reporters called "more jewelry
than harness." I wrote at letters for last friends. I got together a little pile of personal things to go to Coble, chief of
which was the manuscript, pencil-wrote, of my life up to the
time I come to Wyoming. And it was this stack of my papers
that figured vital in the first step of my plan. It was writing
them and having them out and obvious in my cell all these
last ten months of my time that I was gambling on to cover
up what I would put in lawyer A. W. Rowells's empty handcase in place of the Coble manuscript, when Rowells left
me for the last time. This was my secret:

For the past three of those ten months of writing my
"memories," I had not been writing the Coble manuscript,
at all. I had been putting down this story that you read here
and keeping it separate and secret inside a slit in my bunk's
mattress. It was my last will and testament to the truth. The
only chance that Tom Horn would ever have to undo the
evil lies which otherwise would live forever after him.

It was the story of my Wyoming days; I had told
Rowells of it, and he had agreed that any man ought to
have the opportunity to have his side heard and testified to.
If he could, he would take it out of my cell that night and
see that it was one day printed and published. Or at the
very least placed in some safe hands where it would live on
and come to light another day and time, to speak for me.

This agreement was made the afternoon of the seventeenth of November, on Rowells's next to last visit.

At that time he also assured me he had spoken to a
Father Kennedy, of Cheyenne, and that the priest *would*
come to my cell the early night of the nineteenth.

Rowells had, too, gotten my messages to my "friends"
who had to provide my horse and supplies once I reached
the street. The lanky lawyer had, as well, brought my return
message from my friends. He had it folded on tissue inside

his big railroad watch. He had not read it, he said, any-more than he had the one I sent out with him to "the boys."

"In all of this, Horn," he told me, "I am as guilty as Judas Iscariot; except that I do not believe I am betraying the Master." He looked at me in that passing strange way of his. "I *know* you didn't kill that boy," he said. And turned away from me, called the guard, and went out of my cell, and out of the cellblock, and that was the last time he ever looked at me in that unsettling way or spoke to me in the soft, strange voice that wasn't his.

By dusk that day I was still remembering what lawyer Rowells had said and the way that he had said it. Unex-plainably it gave me a strength and certainty that all those about me in the jail could not believe. Here was a man going to die in the morning, and he didn't seem to understand it. He behaved as if tomorrow was going to be the start of his life, not the end of it.

Well, as I saw it and as it now began swiftly to work itself out, that was precisely right.

A. W. Rowells came at suppertime and was permitted with me under no guard but that of the general block—one man at the far end of the aisle by the door leading down to Sheriff Smalley's office. He left the trifling things he had brought me—special fancy shirt of mine to wear to the hang-ing, an old favored sweater, all things from John Coble out to the ranch—and we were able to get the new manuscript of fine-wrote pencil pages into his handcase without being seen. He left me then, and quickly, and the guard stopped him, and Rowells showed him a permit from Smalley to take the Coble manuscript out of the jail. The guard was the hard-nosed and hated Les Snow, and he sneered and de-manded to see the pages. A. W. Rowells only smiled in a kindly way and showed him. Snow saw the faked-up title and top pages: TOM HORN, MY LIFE AS A GOVERNMENT SCOUT & INTERPRETER in ARIZONA TERRITORY. Rowells then showed him on Smalley's permit where it stated the story did not concern Wyoming or Tom Horn's life in that area and was fit to pass out of Cheyenne Jail, remitted to Mr. John Coble, Bosler Station.

Deputy Snow scowled and threw me a snarly look up the exercise aisle but passed A. W. Rowells and the vital handcase and manuscript. My last happy thought of it was that the son of a bitch Les Snow would end up being the goat of Tom Horn smuggling his true-life Wyoming story out of Cheyenne Jail. I would have the last laugh on the bastard, after all! I would have taken it then and there, too, except that Father Kennedy was still due to come. For him, I had to keep it all quiet and peaceful about my second-floor cell. The coming of the priest and, even more, his *going*, had to flow along calm and unquestioned as his long black robes and widecrown shadowy hat. And they did.

It was just on the hour following supper with me in the exercise aisle, that I seen from its window the priest's horse and buggy coming up Ferguson from the direction of the big church. I watched him get out and just loop his lines on the dash brake handle, not even dropping a hobble weight. The old horse just drooped where she was stopped, and the bony tall form of Father Kennedy hurried up the jail steps and disappeared out of my sight.

Now everything commenced to snowball.

It all went so fast and so slick that I ever after believed the Lord had something to do with it. Even the priest's talk fell into the exact direction I would have tried to lead it.

He wanted me to pray with him.

I said I wanted to do that and had sent for him for that reason, but that I hadn't the nerve—a man like I had been—to go on my knees in the full light.

"I think we can do something there," the priest said. He went away and came back with Ed Smalley. The sheriff looked at me and listened to the priest. He then went to the wall switch and turned down the block lights. He told the guard to turn them back up when the priest left.

I thanked both God and God's priest and went on my knees with him in my cell like I had promised. He prayed so earnest and straight for me that I hated to go on with what was in my mind. But a man will do anything for his life. I prayed even a little louder while I reached under my bunk and brought out the length of old dirty sock I had saved and into which I had packed the sandy dirt from the pot of my little green plant on the cell window ledge. When the padre left off his words to cross himself before continuing, I hit him. It made only the littlest "thunk," and I saw him stiffen, quiver a trill or two, and go slack. I caught him to keep him from knocking into anything on his fall over on his face to the floor.

"Father and Son and Holy Ghost," I said, raising my voice for the guards. "Friend, Kennedy," I went on, seeing out of my eye corner that the guard was not watching. "Will you now pray with me, in my faith, sir?" And then I mumbled low something like a man would mumble saying yes and commenced to pray in *real* earnest. I used the Lord's Prayer, or the Twenty-third Psalm, and remembered it right good. Also, I stretched it out just long enough, or those old biblical fellows had wrote it so, that it covered the time I needed to get Father Kennedy's long robes off him and bundle him into my bunk, under the gray jail blanket, face to the wall. The only extra time I took was to listen to his chest just at the last.

I heard the bump of his heart, a little rough but running. "Thank thee, Lord," I said, in cellblock tones, and repeated the only three Catholic words I knew. "Name of the Father, the Son, and the Holy Ghost—Amen!"

I jammed on the padre's round, low-crown black hat, brim down over my face, collar of his winter vestment-coat high as it would turn around the Tom Horn jaws.

"Thank you, padre," I said good and loud. "I hope the Lord goes likewise with you, as you have prayed for me—"

This was it: I saw the guard turn and look our way, hearing my words to the departing priest. I stepped to cell's front, hard against the bars. Taking up the cross Father Kennedy wore belted at his middle, I rapped ever so tinkly with it on the iron of the big flat padlock fixture to my cell-door. At the same time I made a little upraised wrist motion out through the bars, as though sort of to bless the guard and beckon him too.

He came plodding right down the block, looked for Tom Horn, and seen him on the bunk turned to the wall, no doubt sobbing with the terror of his tomorrow's fate, and then he just unlocked the cell and I went out past him, head down, and making the sign of the cross over my chest as I had practiced it from watching Father Kennedy and using it now to unction the jail guard for his kindness in not crowding us at our last prayers.

There was a bad moment at the block door, when my belt sash slipped down on me because Father Kennedy had 'a much wider rump than I did. The cross damn near hit the floor, but the guard was Sully Schoopman and kindly in his ways and respectful of the holy father, being a Jew himself and careful of all religions. So he didn't see nothing nor say anything, and fifteen seconds later I was through the block door going down the stairs to the first floor. "God," I said in my mind, "stay with me."

The two tired-looking deputies at the bottom of the stair only nodded to Father Kennedy. I raised my hand to them and passed on clutching the cross. I had to raise my eyes a trace then to see the way to the outside door. That is, to pass by Ed Smalley's office, the door of which was propped wide, with full light everywhere. As I did look up, two things hit me hard. The outer door was closed and inside-barred, and four tough Cheyenne men were flanking it with shotguns. Sheriff Ed Smalley was coming almost on a trot to cut off Father Kennedy. "Father," I heard him call, "just a minute. How did, uh—"

God in heaven! was this the end of it, I thought.

I could never fool Ed Smalley, near up.

But God and my *sombra* were still in step.

Something made me put up my two hands to my face and go into a muffled sobbing of sorts, hunching my black-robed shoulders, then holding up a hand toward Smalley as it to plead, "No, please, sheriff, not now—"

And, my dear God, Ed Smalley stopped and made a motion with his own two plump hands and said, "Of course, father; I only wanted to ask about Horn. But I see you've had it hard up there. Will you be in in the morning?"

I made him a wave with the right hand to my parish hat brim, to say, yes, of course, and then I sobbed again and hurried toward that barred and heavy-guarded outer door.

The *last* door.

Again, it seemed that in the very final breath of it I would be found out. But in the instant that I got too near the door to go on without a stop and wait, Smalley's God-blessed high-pitched voice caught and passed me.

"Open up, Wade; what's the problem?"

"No problem, Ed." It was Wade Everett, a mean one and not stupid. "Just that you told us to pass nobody without you said."

"Yes, I know. Well, it has been a hell's day for all of us. Good night, father."

Again I had to bet my pile on a snuffle and another raising of the good right hand. Passing by the deputies, I hunched my black clothes higher yet and shivered, "bbbrrrrrl" as the outside cold hit me. It was that cold in fact that the parish hatbrim near buried itself in the collar of the padre's overcoat, and I couldn't see a thing for a minute and almost pitched down the stairs due to a slip on the ice and slush. I caught myself and went to the buggy where it and the old mare yet drooped in front of the hitch-rail. The damned old fool horse snorted some when she got my smell instead of Father Kennedy's. But then part of him was on his clothes and part of me on mine underneath the priest's outfit, and, well, old Dolly decided to settle down and sort it out later in the nice warm parish barn.

I swung her and the buggy out from the rail and off down Ferguson Street toward the big Catholic church. As I passed by and waved to the last of the rifle-toting National Guard troops at block's end, I heard the tower bells of some church behind me commence to chime the hour. I counted the strokes like years of my life. Each one was a beat of my heart growing stronger for the long run ahead. Eight of them I counted, and then the striking fell still. Eight o'clock of my last night on earth. Four hours yet to that last day. The day they had thought they would hang Tom Horn.

And he was free.

Tom Horn was out and going free.

For some reason the words of the old song sprang into my mind:

My foot's in the stirrup, my pony won't stand
Good-bye, Old Paint, I'm a-leaving Cheyenne—!

I laughed out loud, the tune of it soaring inside me:

Good-bye, Old Paint, I'm a-leaving Cheyenne
Good-bye, Old Paint, I'm a-leaving Cheyenne!

Great God, but the feeling of life in a man ran strong when it was let free.

I had only to haw the old parish mare down to the

U.P tracks and over them to where the boys would have Old
Pacer waiting in the lean-to shed of Earl "Shorty" Showalter's place, out south of town at the edge of the sage.
Then I *would be* free! No horse in Wyoming could catch
that big crazy bay, once off and racing.

It was in the lift of that moment that the old mare
shied and snorted, and I heard behind me from Ferguson
Street the sudden yelling of commands and the sounds in
the night, so still but heartbeats before, of angry and
frightened men running and cursing and getting to their
horses.

Going Home

I had to whip the old mare. She wanted to "gee" and
go home to the parish stable. I sawed at her mouth with the
lines to keep her straight. The whip broke, and then the left
line, and she was of a sudden running on her own. She did
get me to the yards, and over the main U.P. tracks, before
she realized her situation and broke on me. By that time, I
had jumped onto the buggy shafts and to her back and had
her by the cheek straps.

"Hee-yah, hee-yah!" I yelled at her, but she was fighting me.

By this time others in the streets of old Cheyenne were
shouting too. They were shouting to one another to know
why Father Kennedy was barebacking his old buggy mare
over the railroad tracks, south out of town in the darkening
of the young night. About this time, some of the townfolk,
beginning to show along the way with shotgun or Old Betsy
rifle to hand, were into the street ahead of me. I was having
a chancy time of it guiding the miserable mare. The last
thing I wanted was to hit somebody, or careen into some
lamp pole or paling fence trying to avoid hitting somebody.
If we wrecked that buggy with the old horse still in its

shafts, Tom Horn would be set afoot with still two miles of town settlement to get shut of. "Hee-yah, hee-yah!"

Right there, I heard the hammer of horses behind me.

They were about three blocks back, just wheeling off Ferguson Street. Looked to be five, six of them. Not soldiers. Likely hardcases from the jail volunteers. Those bastards camped by their fires all over Ferguson Street that night before the big day. Having a lark of it camping out to "stand citizen guard" over old Tom, just happen he would try anything at the last clock tick.

The "people," God bless them.

They had my track one more time. Whoever was in that posse back yonder they would, each of them, rather take care of Tom Horn with rifle or pistol ball in the back than to cart him back to Cheyenne Jail for "the law" to carry out their will, come sunrise.

Then it happened.

I was just coming to the last switch spur track to cross, when I looked back. As I swung my eyes around to the road again, a little towheaded kid and an idiot yappy mutt ran square out from behind some sided cattle cars, into my way. I couldn't do anything but haul on the mare to swerve her. It was that or hit the kid.

The buggy tipped, slewed wild, the rear wheel of it smashing into a switch pole. The shatter of the wreck and the ki-yiying of the dog, whicht had got hurt, was enough to rouse up all South Cheyenne. The kid, thank God, was all right.

I seen that at the same time he seen me.

That was when I lit on the ground, hard, where the mare throwed me in falling herself, and when I staggered up and ripped off Father Kennedy's robes so's I could run afoot, full stride. Me and the kid weren't ten foot apart, and there was a gas streetlamp at the crossing, handclose.

Well, my face had been in all the papers so many times and for so long it was better known in those parts than Teddy Roosevelt's. This little kid let out a fearful screech and lit off up toward town yowling, "Tom Horn! Tom Horn! Help, help—!" And Tom Horn, unarmed, set afoot and limping bad from the buggy wreck, ran for the only cover there was—the winter-bare brush of the creek beyond the spur siding.

The posse was past the kid now and had begun firing into everything they could see in the throw of light from the crossing lamp pole. Which did not include me. I was into the brush, still running, scarce hitting a limb or twig, as I had run through the brush of Wyaconda Creek thirty years gone. I was safe away from the tracks and the yard in five minutes and had left them no trail they could follow. As man, as boy, the tracker didn't live who could stay with Tom Horn once he was into the timber and coursing the creek draws.

Half an hour later I made Showalter's barn and was in it, its signal lantern blown out and smoking in the darkness there with me, and had found everything by its light the moment before. Saddle sack, rat cheese, rye bread, bacon, winter mittens, ammunition, an old .30-30 rifle and .45 Colt's revolver, and, praise God! in the one box stall, saddled, bridled, rigged to step up onto and go, and whickering now to smell my scent again, the great bay horse that couldn't be caught, Old Pacer!

We got out of there, into the range south. Pacer went like he could run all night and never snort. And I ran him all night. Oh, we stopped now and again, when we hit a landmark of the route I was following, or just when, out of rising spirits, I had to stop him and leap down and drag in that cold Wyoming air and stride around as long in steps as my long legs would take me. God, I was free!

On we went, following the markers on my chosen trail down into Colorado. Taking Granite Gap, the Lone Tree River road, and then the Buck Eye Cutoff, over into the Fort Collins country. We hit them all and right on the time I had figured in my mind. With day paling over east we were down off Wellington Buttes, crossing the flat toward Box Elder Creek, just north of the fort.

But the light was poor down there. A cold fog coiled in from somewhere, and it was yet not dawn enough to see easy through it. Pacer was going a little uncertain now, too, and for the first time. It was like the both of us didn't know this country, after all.

But we did, damn it.

Up ahead, acrost the creek, would be the spur of Box Elder Ridge, rising with the road to carry it over to the Fort Collins side. And at the bottom of the rise, on our side, would be Old Man Gawters's pole corral and mustanger's shanty. And in the shed of that corral, warm and full of oats and fresh as the wind, would be my relay horse, Ora Haley's famous Yellowbird. I would eat with old man Gawters and thaw my bones at his fire. Then leave Old Pacer snug and warm in the corral shed, go aboard Yellowbird, swing wide of the fort, and be gone.

The light grew a little, some of the fog thinned.

We came to the creek and to a bridge I didn't remember being there. It rung hollow to the thud of Pacer's hooves going over it. Damn. Where was the pole corral. The Gawters's cabin? The road went up ahead of us, all right, the rise was there. But this wasn't right.

Could it be I was groggy from the ride?

Or maybe me and Pacer had missed our turn somewheres?

Or that I had plain forgot, and the old man's place was on the far side of the Box Elder rise?

Yes, surely, that had to be it.

Push on, Pacer.

Get to the top yonder; up there it will come clear.

But when we came out on the top, it was not the ridge I knew, but a hill that didn't even belong in that country. I checked the tired bay, looking around. There was nothing of marker up there but the old lightening-rove stump due ahead. It was ringed with a grass that didn't grow on that range, and I got down off Pacer and said to him, "*Ho-shuh*, brother, be easy," as the Apaches gentled their wild ponies when they were spooking as Pacer was working up to do.

I didn't blame the horse; there was a mound in the grass to the left of the stump, a grave sure.

"Whoa up," I said to Pacer, louder now, and went forward. At the sound of my raised voice, there was a whine back of the stump and out from behind it limped a dog—an old farm shepherd dog—and, Christ Jesus, I knew him.

It was Shed.

Old Shed, my own dog from home.

I whirled about, wanting to go for Pacer and ride far from there. But Pacer was gone. There was no sight of him. No place even where he had bent the grass that I might see and know he *had* stood there. I ran back a few steps past where I had left him. I could see down the hill from there.

That bridge below—my God—it was Wyaconda Bridge. And that brushy stream with its trees that never knew this land —it was Wyaconda Creek.

The fog moved in, closing my view.

I turned back to old Shed. He was standing by the gnarled root stub. His ragged tail was making excited circles in the frosty air. It was clearing where he waited for me. The sun was breaking away the mists beyond him. And old Shed was barking at me, whining for me to come with him.

He turned as to lead the way, going where we had always promised to go, to the other side of Stump Hill.

I commenced to run, to stumble after him.

"Wait up, Shed," I called. "Wait for me—"

It was cold where I woke up.

I was laying on a bunk, my face to a gray stone wall. There was days marked off on the wall, months of them, by a hand I knew. And there was an Old Overholt calendar on the wall, with only one date marked on it.

It was November 20, 1903.

I shut my eyes and swung my legs to the floor. I raised my head, turning to the light. I opened my eyes and saw the morning's sun, gray pink and chill as that of Calvary, fingering through the bars of the lone, small window in that wall of gray Wyoming stone.

And it was my window:

The one to my cell in Cheyenne Jail.

• • • • •

On the last morning in Cheyenne Jail Tom Horn ate a good breakfast. He then said to the jailer, "How much time do I have?"

"Two hours," the man answered.

"Good," the prisoner replied. "A man can tell a lot in that time."

Horn then proceeded to write in his firm hand for the entire two hours remaining of his life.

It has never been agreed what it was the doomed man wrote. What subject could so compel a man about to die that he would forego all other preparation in order to finish writing down something that would "tell

a lot"? The question has baffled historians and legend
buffs for seventy years. No answer has come forth. Some
say none ever will.

But wait up, as Tom would say:

Could it be—could it *just* have been—that Tom
Horn took those precious hours to complete the strange
last segment of his testament, *I, Tom Horn?*

Did this man of the unimaginable nerves have grit
enough remaining to sit down and write out the details
of his heretofore unreported "last plan" for breaking out
of Cheyenne Jail on that eleventh-hour night of November 19th?

And then include the nightmare ending of his next
morning's awakening back in that terrible cell? That grim
cage of "gray Wyoming stone?" That horror chamber
with its single window looking out upon the "chill and
pink gray" dawn? That dawn that "fingered through
the bars" to light the gallows scaffolding that waited
just beyond for him, Tom Horn, the last knight errant
of the western cattle kings?

Who is to say?

Not the historians certainly.

They only know what they read and they will
never read this.

Nor will they ever read what follows here:

It is the scrap of paper bearing Tom Horn's writing
found in his cell following the execution. It was left on
his neatly made-up bunk, pinned there with a sliver of
wood broken from a bunkpost split. It said nothing of
his ghostly ride, nothing of the chill awakening from
that freedom dream. It did not mention the dark crime
for which he then died, did not repeat his pleas of
innocence, said no farewell to his enemies, nor to old
Wyoming.

Yet perhaps it is his true last testament.

This is all the scrap of paper said:

Is there a warrior left who remembers me? A woman remaining who will weep to know that Talking
Boy will bring his horse no more outside the jacal
of her father? A single child, a sister, an old man to
light one dark face with the candle of its smile

thinking back to him the soldiers called Tom Horn?
Yo no se, amigos. Montad en vuestros caballos.
Ride out, ride out . . .

Tom Horn
in Cheyenne Jail

Beyond the Ending

Any history of a man who actually lived will come up
short in its telling. Wherever the writer ends his story,
he will have ridden over landmarks more significant than
those he thought to include.

In the case of Tom Horn, a man who spent his life
avoiding the open, the leftover pieces multiply. The problem is again compounded when the writer must work from
an original document much damaged by fire, smoke, and
water.

Entire parts of the Starrett holograph are thus rendered
illegible. Other sections have been scribbled out by Horn.
Or confusingly annotated by him in the margins. Or simply
fail of their own content to make useful sense.

The appended errata are therefore set down in the
order of their occurrence as marginal notations. As such,
they do not follow any catalog of time, place, or importance
to the legend.

The $11 Rifle; its strange pattern in the fate of Tom Horn:
When Tom Horn met his end in Cheyenne Jail, he had
exactly $11 in his pockets and to his name—the precise
amount that storekeeper Jessup paid Tom for his rifle in the
summer of 1874 to begin his Odyssey.

Old Tag's ending: Tagidado Morales, the natural father of
Merijilda Grijole, ending his days happily, lived with Mary
Cornmeal and, it is rumored, with Tom Horn's lovely Yaqui
bride Nopal, and the infant Tomasito, down near Fronteras,

Sonora. Old Tag is said to have lived to 104, and been the only grandfather Horn's son ever knew.

Tom Horn's Indian son Sombra: Sweet Nopal named the baby "Shadow" after its white father's known inhabitation by the *sombra* or inner spirit shade. She and Mary Cornmeal called the boy Tomasito. A legend persists in Sonora that the boy grew up to be a renegade of the Sierra del Norte, a chieftain of the *monte*, with an outlaw price of fifty thousand pesos on his head. It was never collected. The story still remains to be told on Sombra Horn, the "shadow" of his famous sire.

Pajarita Morena; what happened to the Santa Fe fallen sister: A nice ending has joined the folklore, relating that Pajarita lived out long and happy days as a part of the household of Old Tag and Mary Cornmeal, down in Fronteras. A less charming but some would feel better ending is still told in Tomcat Alley; Pajarita went to Prescott and joined Miss Pet in the opening and promotion of a "house to call their own." They forced Madame La Luna into early retirement, put their money into Prescott real estate, married well, and left many prominent grandchildren in old Arizona.

"The Eye That Never Sleeps;" Tom Horn and the Pinkerton National Detective Agency: By his own grinning admission, Tom was never much of a man hunter in the traditional law enforcement sense. "Trouble was," he said, "when I would get the fellers cornered, maybe after six, eight weeks tracking and starving all over Colorado and half of Utah, like as not they was always old pals of mine and, hell, you can't take an old pal in." He detested routine detective work and in fact any work where he was not "riding free." Allan Pinkerton, famed Civil War head of U.S. intelligence and later of the detective firm bearing his name, said Horn was a first-rate man, "but inclined to disappear even better than the suspects we sent him after."

Tom Horn, mule packer in Cuba: Sources here are whatever one wants them to be. All the way from claims that Tom was a lieutenant colonel in the Rough Riders to insisting he never even got on the boat for the big fight (the yellow

fever got him at Tampa Bay). The truth seems to lie between; he did get to Cuba and himself takes credit for the
idea to throw the mules overboard into the bay at Daiquiri,
when the long-eared animals refused to debark normally.
(Teddy Roosevelt also took credit for this stroke of military
genius.) Horn was taken ill almost at once and did not see
the front or any of the fighting in the war with Spain.

Makeup of the Horn jury: The jurors were: O. V. Seeburn,
rancher, Goshen Hole; Homer Payne, cowboy, Two Bar
ranch; F. F. Sinon, foreman, White Ranch, Little Horse
Creek; H. W. Thomas, rancher, La Grange; T. R. Babbit,
rancher, La Grange; Amos Sarbaugh, foreman, Two Bar
ranch; J. E. Barnes, butcher, Cheyenne; G. W. Whiteman,
rancher, Uva; Charles Stamm, rancher, Wheatland Flats;
C. H. Tolson, porter, Cheyenne; H. W. Yoder, rancher, Goshen Hole; E. C. Metcalf, Wheatland. This is the jury Tom
said contained "several men I have arrested and seen jailed
for cattle stealing." He does not name the men but the ad-
dresses cover some of the hottest spots of Wyoming rustling
of the day.

Death weapon for Little Brother Miller: Jay Monoghan,
biographer par exaggeration of Tom Horn, says the young
Miller boy was killed by a shotgun leaning on a buggy dash-
board. The weapon slid on a bump and discharged, striking
the boy. Horn and other sources say it was a rifle being
cleaned in the Miller kitchen. It is a safe argument. Who is
going to prove it either way?

The eerie song of Tom Horn's harmonica: No modern
source mentions the mouth organ in context with Horn. But
old settlers of the Sybille and the Chugwater insist they
heard it back in the hills on those nights whose following
dawns found some new "good rustler" lying eyeballs-up and
the small rock under the head, tried by the system that
never failed. The tune, the oldtimers said, was "a eerie sort
of off-the-key rendering of _Streets of Laredo._"

Truth of the "pebble under the head" legend: Horn denied
the story consistently, pointing out that "any cheap crook
wanted to kill somebody for his own reason had only to

chunk a rock under his head and holler 'Tom Horn done it.' The last thing any professional killer would want," Horn added, "was to 'advertise' his work."

Too many queens in Brown's Hole: The woman Tom Horn calls Queen Zenobia is none other, authorities insist, than Josephine Bassett's fiery redheaded sister Anne Bassett, the later-known "rustler queen" of northwest Colorado. There is also confusion on which of the Bassett sisters was betrothed to Madison "Matt" Rash. Tom Horn (as Jim Hicks) enters it as Anne Bassett. The honorable John Burroughs agrees with him but gives Anne Bassett as both the sweetheart of Matt Rash and the legendary Queen Zenobia of the Brown's Hole basin.

Newsclippings and quotations from same, by Horn in Cheyenne Jail: Some followers of the legend do not like the idea that Tom, in his second life story (*I, Tom Horn*) enters exact quotes from press sources, as though, these detractors sniff, "he had actually cut them out and saved them for the purpose." To which charge it is only proper to sniff right back—"Right; he seemed to have done precisely that." Horn was also quite accurate in his press entries, a fact some of the detractors might employ in their own writings to substantial benefit.

The mystery of lawyer Rowells: Proof is lacking but the legend keepers insist that young attorney A. W. Rowells is that same "attorney of record for the defense, who dares not enter his name in witness," who prepared the transcript of the Tom Horn holograph found in Charley Starrett's cabin. The assumption would seem mandatory. Who else had access to Horn in Cheyenne Jail, who was also an attorney-at-law? But there is a double-back in this trail: no A. W. Rowells is to be found in either Laramie or Albany County records, and Horn trackers must then agree that Tom changed the name in his *I, Tom Horn* testament in order that "young lawyer Rowells" would be protected.

Even stranger matter and mystery; how the final "nightmare installment" of the Tom Horn testament was gotten out of Cheyenne Jail: True buffs of Horniana take two trails here.

One is that Sheriff Ed Smalley himself took this trust from his prisoner. Both men had come to respect one another, and Smalley was known to be an emotional man. However, the second method is given the more common credence; a Catholic priest did visit Tom in the last hours "as a friend from the better times," and it is this, the real-life "Father Kennedy," whom the Horn buffs believe smuggled out the bizzare "last chapter" of Tom Horn's life.

Who "truly" killed little Willie Nickell; the altered Glendolene Kimmell accusation; perjury or passion-under-oath: No corroborative evidence was ever introduced to support Miss Kimmell's sensational charge against Victor Miller. Some believed the schoolmarm's "swap of saddles," story, more did not. Perhaps the best verdict was the one ascribed to Tom Horn himself. When pressed by newsmen for his "final view" of young Miller's guilt, Horn is said to have answered, "No, the boy is all right. They'd ought to have stuck to their original 'person or persons unknowed.' That was the surest facts of it. Way it is now, they've fixed it so's it will never be found who truly killed the Willie Nickell kid."

Erratum of Horn's "no visitors after the jail break" statement: It must be assumed here that Tom meant he was allowed no visitors without full surveillance after the break. It is certain he did have visitors right up to the end, John Coble prominent among them. The romantic and kindly Iron Mountain ranchman was indeed Tom Horn's last visitor —last but for that other caller no man remembers, or bids to come in.

John Coble at the end; the incredible calm of Tom Horn; their famous brief good-bye: No man, guilty or innocent, ever faced death with the resolute courage of Tom Horn. Those who believed him then, and believe him now, contend that no human being who *was guilty* could have kept that gentle composure and surely must have broken. "I am innocent," Tom Horn said. And that was all he said, save for those famed quiet words to Coble; words that have lived on to be remembered long after the cries and curses of those who hated Tom Horn, and finally killed him:

"Keep your nerve, Johnny, for I will keep mine. You know Tom Horn."

Ad notum; a last word from the Pinkertons; Tom Horn innocent! In a letter written shortly after Tom Horn's death, Robert Pinkerton, son of the detective firm's founder, expressed regrets that the Pinkertons had not "looked more closely into the Tom Horn case," as subsequent information left the strong impression with him that "Horn might have been innocent." One is left to ponder grimly how different history could have been, *had* the Pinkertons examined more rigorously into the Tom Horn evidence. The question continues to cast its uneasy shadow on the western past. In the seventy-one years since the trial, no satisfactory answer for it has been found.

SPECIAL OFFER: If you enjoyed this book and would like to have our catalog of over 1,400 other Bantam titles, just send your name and address and 50¢ (to help defray postage and handling costs) to: Catalog Department, Bantam Books, Inc., 414 East Golf Rd., Des Plaines, Ill. 60016.

ABOUT THE AUTHOR

WILL HENRY is perhaps the West's most honored novelist. He was born and grew up in Missouri, where he attended Kansas City Junior College. Upon leaving school, he lived and worked throughout the Western states, acquiring the background of personal experience reflected later in the realism of his books. Currently residing in California, he writes for motion pictures, as well as continuing his research into frontier lore and legend, which are the basis for his unique blend of history and fiction. Ten of his novels have been purchased for motion picture production, and several have won top literary awards, including the Wrangler trophy of the National Cowboy Hall of Fame, the first Levi Strauss Golden Saddleman and five Western Writers of America Spurs.

Mr. Henry is a recognized authority of America's frontier past, particularly that relating to the American Indian of the High Plains. In fact, his novel of the last campaign of Chief Joseph of the Nez Percé, *From Where the Sun Now Stands,* was recently cited as the finest novel ever written about the American Indian. His most recent novel is *Summer of the Gun.*